# REVEALED

ALSO BY MARGARET PETERSON HADDIX

THE MISSING SERIES

*Found*

*Sent*

*Sabotaged*

*Torn*

*Caught*

*Risked*

THE SHADOW CHILDREN

*Among the Hidden*

*Among the Impostors*

*Among the Betrayed*

*Among the Barons*

*Among the Brave*

*Among the Enemy*

*Among the Free*

THE PALACE CHRONICLES

*Just Ella*

*Palace of Mirrors*

*The Girl with 500 Middle Names*

*Because of Anya*

*Say What?*

*Dexter the Tough*

*Running Out of Time*

*Full Ride*

*Game Changer*

*The Always War*

*Claim to Fame*

*Uprising*

*Double Identity*

*The House on the Gulf*

*Escape from Memory*

*Takeoffs and Landings*

*Turnabout*

*Leaving Fishers*

*Don't You Dare Read This, Mrs. Dunphrey*

MARGARET PETERSON
HADDIX

Simon & Schuster Books for Young Readers

New York London Toronto Sydney New Delhi

SIMON & SCHUSTER BOOKS FOR YOUNG READERS
An imprint of Simon & Schuster Children's Publishing Division
1230 Avenue of the Americas, New York, New York 10020

This book is a work of fiction. Any references to historical events, real people, or real places are used fictitiously. Other names, characters, places, and events are products of the author's imagination, and any resemblance to actual events or places or persons, living or dead, is entirely coincidental.



Jacket design by Dan Potash
Interior design by Drew Willis
The text for this book is set in Weiss.
Manufactured in the United States of America • 0814 FFG
2 4 6 8 10 9 7 5 3 1
Library of Congress Cataloging-in-Publication Data
Haddix, Margaret Peterson.
Revealed / Margaret Peterson Haddix.—First edition.
pages cm—(The missing ; book 7)
Summary: After returning the missing children from history to their original time periods,
thirteen-year-old Jonah must save time itself when aviator Charles Lindbergh
mysteriously appears and kidnaps Jonah's sister.
ISBN 978-1-4169-8986-8 (hardcover)
ISBN 978-1-4424-2286-5 (eBook)
[1. Time travel—Fiction. 2. Space and time—Fiction. 3. Lindbergh, Charles A. (Charles Augustus),
1902–1974—Fiction. 4. Kidnapping—Fiction. 5. Science fiction.] I. Title.
PZ7.H1164Re 2014
[Fic]—dc23
2013008368

For David

# ONE

Jonah saw the man before the man saw him.

The man—a total stranger—was standing in the Skidmore family's living room on Tuesday morning when Jonah came downstairs before school. Jonah had just gotten home from a long, secret trip the night before; as he stepped into the living room, he was lecturing himself: *Just don't say or do anything to make Mom or Dad suspicious.*

He was pretty sure that he'd fooled his parents into thinking the night before that he and his sister Katherine had just run down the street to their friend Chip's house for a few minutes. But Jonah still had to be careful. There was no way he could let his parents find out that he and Katherine—and Chip and two other kids—had actually traveled through time to the year 1918, and to the distant future, and to a few places called time hollows that were completely removed from time.

And—oh, yeah—Jonah *really* had to keep his parents from finding out that he'd come back from all that time travel with two bullet wounds in his left leg.

*You're just an ordinary kid on an ordinary day headed to ordinary seventh grade at his ordinary school,* Jonah told himself. Then he instantly corrected himself: *Well, even if none of that's true, at least you can pretend it is.*

Ordinary kids did not have secret second identities that threatened to ruin their lives. Ordinary kids had not traveled to dangerous moments in four different centuries to try to save other kids' lives. Ordinary kids had never seen all of time freeze at their school, right in the middle of seventh-grade science. Ordinary kids had not been kidnapped as babies and carried off to be adopted in a totally different time period.

Ordinary kids did not have bullet-hole scars.

But ordinary kids could see a strange man standing in their family's living room at seven a.m.—couldn't they?

*Maybe Dad's car broke down and this is some friend or neighbor who's going to drive him to work,* Jonah told himself, scrambling for explanations. *Maybe the car battery's dead, and this is the guy from AAA, here with jumper cables.*

But Jonah probably would have recognized any friend

or neighbor either of his parents would have called for a ride to work. This man standing in the living room wasn't holding jumper cables, either, and he didn't look like any tow-truck driver Jonah had ever seen.

For one thing, he was wearing a suit—kind of an old-fashioned-looking suit, actually, if Jonah let himself think about it. It was brown, with a checked pattern, and it just didn't look like it belonged in the twenty-first century.

The man was also wearing a hat.

*People wear hats like that in this time period,* Jonah told himself defensively. *Sometimes. Isn't that what people call a fedora?*

If Jonah knew the name "fedora," didn't that mean it was an ordinary thing now?

*But people now wear fedoras like a joke. Like how rappers do it,* Jonah told himself. *Sarcastically.*

This man did not look like a rapper. He looked *serious.* And determined. And—maybe a little lost?

Even though Jonah had clattered noisily down the stairs just a moment ago, the man hadn't yet turned his head to look in Jonah's direction. Instead the man seemed to be squinting down at his own hand, which was clenching the back of a chair as if he thought he needed help just to stay upright.

*That doesn't have to mean he's a time traveler who's dizzy from the trip, and who's temporarily lost his sense of hearing and sight because of timesickness,* Jonah told himself.

Before his own first trip through time, Jonah had mostly been an "act first, think later" kind of kid. But constantly facing danger in all those other centuries had changed him. So he didn't call out, *Dude! Who are you, and why are you in my living room?* He didn't rush off for one of his parents or yell to them, *Did you know there's some strange man standing in our living room?*

Instead he silently backed out of the room and off to the side, so he could keep watching the strange man just by peeking around the corner.

Unfortunately, Jonah didn't look behind him first. He smashed right into his sister Katherine as she walked by in the hall.

"Jonah! What's wrong with you?" she cried.

A few months ago if he'd run into her like that some morning before school, she would have gone into full bratty-little-sister mode—not just yelping, but threatening to tattle and ranting that he'd messed up her hair, and now all the other sixth graders were going to laugh at her, and . . .

And, really, Jonah had usually just tuned out Katherine's rants, so all he'd have heard after a while was *blah, blah, furious blah.*

But today Katherine asked "What's wrong with you?" like she was truly worried about him. Running into her, he'd knocked a strand of her blond hair down from her ponytail, and she didn't even notice.

Quickly Jonah put a finger over his lips and used his other hand to point toward the living room. Katherine raised one eyebrow and poked her head around the corner to squint curiously into the other room. But she didn't say anything else.

Jonah stretched his neck out so he could look into the living room at the same time as Katherine. And then everything happened very quickly, one surprise after another.

First the man in the old-fashioned brown suit and hat turned and stared right at Jonah and Katherine.

Next Katherine gasped and yanked her cell phone out of her pocket and, before Jonah had a moment to think about it, snapped a picture of the strange man.

And then the man vanished.

# TWO

"Who *was* that?" Katherine cried. She ran into the living room, to the exact spot beside the chair where the man had been standing. She gazed all around. "What was that about?"

Jonah ran behind her. He grabbed her arm and yanked her back. He didn't think whatever force or entity had zapped the strange man out of sight could linger to work on Katherine, too, but he wasn't taking any chances. He'd seen a lot of bizarre things during his travels through time—as far as he was concerned, anything could happen now.

"JB?" Jonah called softly. "Help?"

Jonah looked around, as if he expected someone to appear out of nowhere just as dramatically as the strange man had disappeared. JB was a time agent Jonah and

Katherine had met a few months ago, and Jonah knew JB deserved a lot of credit for making sure that he and Katherine and their friends had survived all their dangerous time travel.

Of course, in many cases JB had been the one sending them into danger, so calling for JB wasn't always the safest strategy.

Not that it mattered right now. Neither JB nor anyone else showed up.

"Didn't that guy look kind of familiar?" Katherine asked.

"Not to me," Jonah said.

"Sure he did," Katherine said. She was already fiddling with the phone, calling back the picture she'd just taken. "That dimple in his chin, that brownish-goldish hair you could just barely see under the hat . . . Jonah, he kind of looked like you!"

She held out the phone, but Jonah didn't glance at it. He let go of Katherine's arm and took a step back.

Somewhere out in the world, somewhere in time, Jonah knew, there had to be people who looked like him. Maybe the birth parents he didn't remember, maybe brothers or sisters or grandparents or aunts or uncles or cousins he knew nothing about.

But the odds against any one of those people showing

up in Jonah's living room—and then vanishing a moment later—were astronomical.

"You're crazy," he told Katherine. "He didn't look anything like me."

And even though all their travels through time together had generally made Jonah act nicer to Katherine, just as she acted nicer to him, this time his words came out growly and mean.

Katherine narrowed her eyes at him. Then she patted his arm.

"Maybe you're right," she said comfortingly. "I don't know what I was thinking. That guy was so tall—do you think he was six-three? Six-four? Anyhow, basketball-player height. And you're, like, normal height. And . . ."

*That's right—normal,* Jonah thought fiercely. *Ordinary.*

Jonah hadn't particularly noticed the strange man's height—he thought Katherine was exaggerating. But there had been something about the man that made Jonah think people probably always noticed him, even when he wasn't showing up in weird places he didn't belong and then disappearing.

Jonah forced himself to peer at the picture on the cellphone screen. He couldn't tell what was under the man's hat—a bald head? A lot more wavy, sandy-colored hair?—and that bothered him.

So did the suspicion that was creeping over him, that maybe the man did kind of look familiar.

Maybe he was someone Jonah should be able to recognize.

"Jonah! Katherine! What are you doing? You're going to be late for school!" Mom called from the kitchen. "You haven't even had breakfast yet!"

Jonah and Katherine exchanged glances.

"How can we go sit in classes all day and do nothing?" Katherine asked. "When we don't know what's going on?"

"What could we do even if we didn't go to school?" Jonah asked. "The strange man's gone now, and it's not like we could chase him. We don't know where JB is, we don't have an Elucidator to call him . . ."

Elucidators were what Jonah figured cell phones would eventually turn into. They enabled time travelers to move between various years, and let them communicate across centuries.

Between time-travel trips, Jonah generally tried to forget about all the problems Elucidators could create, too.

Katherine shrugged helplessly.

"What if Mom decides to work from home today?" Katherine asked. "What if that man comes back and she's in danger? How—"

Just then Mom stepped into the living room behind

them. Katherine froze. Jonah darted a glance toward Mom—if she'd heard anything they'd said, they would need to come up with a good cover story, pronto.

But Mom's frown just looked annoyed, not frightened.

*Oh, yeah, I guess we were whispering,* Jonah thought. All those trips through time had evidently made them more cautious, even without thinking about it.

"What's the holdup, kids?" Mom was saying, rushing toward them. "You have fifteen minutes before the bus comes. You . . ."

Mom stopped talking. Jonah realized that Katherine still had her arm out, her hand tilted just so, to let Jonah see the cell-phone screen. But Mom was close enough now that the screen was tilted just the right way for her to see too.

"Katherine, is that a picture of . . . *Charles Lindbergh* on your phone?" Mom asked curiously. "How did you make it look like he was standing in our living room? He must have died forty years ago!"

# THREE

*Okay, then,* Jonah thought. *There's proof. This does have something to do with time travel.*

He hadn't actually needed proof. From the moment he'd rounded the corner and seen a strange man towering over Dad's favorite recliner, he'd known that that man didn't belong in the twenty-first century, and that his presence was probably a bad sign.

Jonah was mostly just trying not to let himself think about the fact that he recognized the name Mom had said. Not because he was a history buff like her. Not because of any visits he'd made to the past. But because weeks ago, before his first trip through time, Jonah had seen that name, Charles Lindbergh, on a seating roster for a planeload of children stolen from time.

Jonah had been on that plane. His original name—the

identity he would have carried through life if time travelers hadn't intervened—had been on that list too. He just hadn't known what it was.

He still didn't know.

*What if I was supposed to be Charles Lindbergh?* he wondered. *Is that why Katherine thought that man looked like me?*

Only how was Jonah supposed to be Charles Lindbergh if this man who'd suddenly appeared and then disappeared from the living room was already Charles Lindbergh?

Belatedly, Jonah remembered that the name on the plane's seating roster hadn't just been Charles Lindbergh. It had been Charles Lindbergh Jr. or Charles Lindbergh III or something like that.

Jonah's knees felt so weak all of a sudden that he sank down onto the nearby chair.

Katherine glanced at him, horror spreading across her expression. Then she smoothed out her face and turned back to face Mom.

"Instagram," Katherine said calmly.

*What?* Jonah wondered. Then he realized his sister was trying to explain how she could have a picture on her phone of someone who'd died forty years ago, but who somehow magically looked like he was standing in their living room five minutes ago.

*Will Mom believe her?* Jonah thought. *Does Mom even know what Instagram is?*

Maybe Jonah needed to help out.

"Didn't you use kind of a mix of Photoshop and Instagram together?" Jonah asked faintly. He looked up at Mom. "Didn't Katherine do a good job faking everything?"

Mom tilted her head and took the phone from Katherine's hand.

"It looks so real," Mom said. "You've even got the candlesticks on the mantelpiece looking crooked, like they always do because *someone's* always jumping around in here, knocking things sideways. . . ."

She glanced accusingly at Jonah.

Accusingly was good. Accusingly meant that she didn't know there was anything truly weird and dangerous going on.

"Mom, all I did was take a picture of this room," Katherine protested. "And then I put it together with a modernized picture of, you know, Charles, um, Charles . . ."

Jonah couldn't tell if Katherine really couldn't remember the last name, or if she was trying to distract Mom from looking more closely at Jonah. Jonah could feel prickles of panicky sweat on his face; he could feel exactly how close he'd come to fainting. And how close he still was. He didn't want to be thinking, *Am I really Charles Lindbergh's son or grandson or . . . related somehow? Am I?* But he couldn't get the words out of his head.

He was just lucky Mom was focused on glaring at Katherine now.

"Katherine, *please* don't tell me this was another one of those school assignments where you spent hours making sure everything looked good, but you didn't spend five minutes actually reading about the topic you were supposed to be learning," Mom said, waving the phone at her. "It's Lindbergh. Charles Lindbergh. Do you even know what he was famous for?"

"Um . . . ," Katherine stalled.

Mom threw her hands up in exasperation.

"Jonah?" she challenged, turning back to him. "Do you know who Charles Lindbergh was?"

*My birth father?* Jonah thought. *Someone I probably would have known really, really well, if time-traveling kidnappers hadn't stolen me away?*

Now he didn't just feel sweaty and faint. He also felt like vomiting. It was a good thing he hadn't had breakfast yet.

"Mom, this wasn't *my* homework assignment," Jonah protested weakly. "I've never had to know about Charles Lindbergh."

If his original identity actually was Charles Lindbergh's

son, had he known his father really, really well back in some other time period, some other century? How old had Jonah been when the time-traveling kidnappers took him and un-aged him back to being a baby all over again—and then crash-landed while escaping from time agents, like JB, who wanted to stop them? Had Jonah had time to form a lot of memories with his original father before the kidnappers erased them all? If that man who'd stood in the Skidmore living room just ten minutes ago was actually Charles Lindbergh, had he once upon a time thrown a baseball back and forth with Jonah and told him stories about his own childhood and playfully punched him in the arm and called him "a chip off the old block"?

Those were all things that Jonah's adoptive dad—his *real* dad—had done with Jonah in this century.

"Jonah, if Katherine is learning about Charles Lindbergh this year, then you were probably supposed to learn about him last year," Mom said, frowning. "This is what I keep telling the two of you, that you're not just learning stuff so you can get graded on it and then forget everything after the test. You're eleven and thirteen years old!"

"Almost twelve," Katherine interrupted. "Remember, my birthday's just a few weeks away."

Mom barely paused to look sternly at Katherine.

"Right. So you really should know who Charles Lindbergh

is," Mom lectured. "It's like—cultural literacy! And it's interesting! Charles Lindbergh lived a fascinating life!"

This was one of Mom's favorite topics: It wasn't enough for him and Katherine to do well in school. They were also supposed to learn things "for life," so they could "appreciate the treasure of knowledge . . ."

*Yeah, right, Mom,* Jonah thought. *I really treasured finding out firsthand that they didn't have toilet paper in the year 1483. And finding out how sailors got punished in 1611—because I got put in the stocks. And watching our friend Emily almost die because medicine was so bad in 1903. And, in both 1485 and 1918, seeing how many people got killed because certain countries wanted different leaders . . .*

Now Jonah had chills, along with his sweating and light-headedness and nausea. What horrors awaited him in whatever time period Charles Lindbergh had lived in? What if there was nothing Jonah could do to avoid them?

"Jonah?" Mom said. Her voice was softer now, sounding farther away. Jonah blinked hard, trying to make her face come back into focus. She disappeared for a moment, then reappeared. Oh. It wasn't because she'd fallen into some time-travel mess herself. It was because she'd gone to the kitchen and brought back a big glass of orange juice for him, along with a slice of toast. He gulped them both down and instantly felt better.

*Note to self,* he thought. *Mom might actually be right about the whole "everybody needs a good breakfast" thing.*

"Jonah, are you getting sick?" Mom asked. She brushed her fingers against his forehead. "You don't seem to have a fever, but you were so pale a minute ago . . . and you're still clammy. Do you need to stay home from school?"

Jonah glanced up at Katherine, as if trying to ask her telepathically, *Is this our solution? Mom already thinks I'm sick—do you want to pretend you're coming down with something too? And then we can work on figuring out why Charles Lindbergh, who died forty years ago, was in our living room this morning?*

But if Jonah and Katherine did stay home "sick," then Mom would absolutely decide she needed to work from home. And what could they do with Mom hovering over them, constantly feeling their foreheads and listening for sneezes and coughs?

And how quickly would she figure out that both of them were lying?

Jonah had survived deadly dangers in four different centuries—five, actually, if he counted his own. He'd made split-second decisions that had saved other people from assassins and a speeding wildfire and a firing squad and the potential destruction of time itself. But he really didn't think he could carry off lying to his mom to get to skip school. Even for a good reason.

"I'm okay, Mom," Jonah said. "I guess I was just hungry."

Katherine glared at him. Mom glanced at the clock on the mantelpiece and sighed.

"One piece of toast is not going to hold you until lunch, Jonah. And Katherine, you haven't even had anything yet," she said. "Forget the bus—I'll see if Dad can drop you off at school on his way to work." She started toward the stairs, then stopped. "No, wait, he's got that early conference call. . . ." She sighed again. "I'll call the office and tell them I'm going to be late."

She started toward the kitchen and, Jonah guessed, the kitchen phone. But even as she walked, she was beckoning them and calling out, "Come on—start eating!"

Neither Jonah nor Katherine budged.

"*I* could have handled lying for both of us," Katherine hissed at him. It was uncanny how totally she knew what he'd been thinking.

What she'd said was also true: Katherine was a much better liar than he was.

"Sorry," Jonah mumbled.

"Now we're going to have to waste a whole day at school before we can do anything," Katherine complained. "*I* think you're just scared to find out anything else about Charles Lindbergh. In case you're, you know, his son."

At least she said this part with a little more sympathy. Jonah flushed, annoyed that Katherine knew him so well—and thought he was such a coward. Why hadn't Jonah seen Charles Lindbergh in the presence of one of his time-traveling friends who thought Jonah was some big hero? Gavin Danes, for example, the kid who had come out of that basement in 1918 with even more bullet wounds than Jonah—Gavin and Jonah had recuperated together in the same hospital room, and Gavin thought Jonah could do anything.

Only it had actually been Katherine who'd saved Gavin from dying.

Distantly Jonah could hear Mom on the phone in the kitchen, telling someone, "It's been one of those mornings." Even more distantly, Jonah could hear Dad's shower running upstairs. These were ordinary sounds from what should have been an ordinary day, but nothing felt ordinary anymore. He could feel all sorts of possible futures spreading out in front of him—all of them strange and terrifying.

And what was he supposed to do about any of it?

"If—" Katherine began, and instantly stopped. She stared past Jonah, toward the lamp.

Jonah turned in the chair and stared up . . . and up . . . and up.

Charles Lindbergh was back, standing in the exact same spot he'd been in before.

*Katherine's right. He is tall,* Jonah thought.

He scrambled out of the chair so Charles Lindbergh wouldn't tower over him quite so much. Now, looking at the man up close and straight on, Jonah realized that Lindbergh was wearing different clothes—some kind of old-fashioned flight suit, maybe, with a brown leather jacket stretched across his broad shoulders and a pair of goggles dangling around his neck.

Did he look older or younger than he had the last time? Was that something Jonah should pay attention to? Jonah couldn't tell, because Lindbergh seemed so totally in the grip of timesickness. He was blinking furiously, the same way Jonah always did when he arrived in a new time period, when he was desperate to have his vision and other senses back as quickly as possible.

"I did it!" Lindbergh murmured.

*Does he mean, "I made it back here again"?* Jonah wondered. *Why is that a bigger deal than getting here in the first place? Why does he even want to be here? Why did he disappear a moment ago?*

Jonah thought maybe these weren't the best questions to start with. But before he could say anything, he heard Mom yelling from the kitchen, her phone call evidently finished, "Jonah? Katherine? Get in here! Now!"

This was torture. If Jonah and Katherine left now, they wouldn't see what happened next with Charles Lindbergh or get a chance to ask him anything. But if they didn't leave, Mom was bound to come after them—and she'd see Lindbergh too.

Jonah inched one step closer to the kitchen, then indecisively inched back. Katherine didn't move at all.

Lindbergh cocked his head toward Mom's voice and blinked again.

"Are you Jonah and Katherine Skidmore?" he asked, pulling a small notepad and pencil from inside his jacket.

"What's it to you?" Katherine asked, as bold as ever.

Lindbergh made a small mark on the notepad.

"Confirmation of that item on my checklist," Lindbergh muttered. He turned toward Jonah. "I apologize in advance for any distress this is going to cause you."

Jonah took another step back.

And then Lindbergh reached out and grabbed Katherine by the shoulders.

"What are you doing?" Jonah asked. "Let go of my sister!"

He stepped forward again, waving his arms wildly, trying to pull Katherine back and shove Lindbergh away. But Lindbergh had too tight a grip.

"Jonah! Be careful!" Katherine cried, even as she tried to get away. "He's probably just using me to get to you!"

Lindbergh looked scornfully down at her and held on tighter.

"Such simplistic thinking," he said. "And wrong."

Lindbergh lifted Katherine, jerking her completely away from Jonah. She kept struggling, pushing away from him. But it was useless.

A split second later both Lindbergh and Katherine vanished.

# FOUR

Jonah stepped into the space that Lindbergh and Katherine had occupied only a moment before. He started swinging his arms again, as if convinced that even if he couldn't see Lindbergh and Katherine, he still might be able to grab them.

*They're just invisible,* he told himself. *Even Katherine and I managed to make that function work on the Elucidators we used. Well, most of the time. Maybe that's all this Lindbergh guy did too—he just pressed some button on an Elucidator in his pocket, and he turned them both invisible. . . .*

"Katherine?" Jonah called. "Say something. Make some noise. Please!"

No one answered. No matter how violently Jonah waved his arms around, his fingers didn't brush anything except the lamp, the chair, the candlesticks on the mantel. Things Jonah could see.

Lindbergh and Katherine were gone.

Jonah kept swinging his arms, but it was a despairing gesture now. The side of his hand connected with one of Mom's brass candlesticks, and it crashed down to the hearth below. The candle snapped in half; the brass clanged against the hearthstones like a gong ringing out someone's doom.

*Katherine's?* Jonah agonized. *And mine, when Mom sees I dented her candlestick . . . and lost her daughter?*

The clanging sounded loud enough to echo through the whole house. Strangely, Mom wasn't rushing back into the living room crying out, *What just happened? What is going on in there?*

She'd also stopped yelling about how Jonah and Katherine needed to get into the kitchen right now to eat breakfast.

This was very, very odd.

*Did that Lindbergh guy zap away Mom and Dad, too, even without touching them?* Jonah wondered. *Have I lost my entire family?*

Jonah didn't think his legs could hold him up as he thought about this awful possibility. But they didn't just hold him up—they also carried him toward the kitchen without him even having to consciously think about it.

"Mom?" he called. "Dad?"

His voice creaked and cracked and came out an octave higher than it should have. How could even his own voice betray him at a time like this?

He got to the breakfast nook area of the kitchen, where Mom had laid out sunflower place mats and perfectly spaced silverware and cereal boxes and cartons of juice and milk. The cell phone Mom had taken from Katherine was lying on the table too, as if that was supposed to be a reward for coming to breakfast. Jonah picked up the phone and slipped it into his pocket, but kept going.

"Mom?" he called again. This time his voice sank to a bass register, but he might as well have been a terrified baby wailing, *Mommy! Mommy! Mommy!*

No one was sitting in any of the kitchen chairs, not at the table and not at the desk across the room, either. No one was standing over the stove or near the refrigerator or beside the kitchen counters.

Jonah whirled around the corner and farther into the kitchen anyhow. He started waving his arms again—even though that hadn't worked in the living room, maybe it would work here. This time he hit his hand on a granite countertop. He doubled over in pain, leaning across the top of the island in the center of the kitchen. Just before he squeezed his eyes shut from the pain, he caught a glimpse of blond hair on the other side of the island, below the level of the counter.

His eyes popped back open.

"Katherine?" he cried.

It made no sense for Katherine to have disappeared from the living room in Charles Lindbergh's arms a few moments ago only to reappear here and now, crouched beside the kitchen island. But Jonah was willing to believe that that had actually happened, if it meant that Katherine was back.

If it meant he hadn't lost his entire family.

Jonah spun around the corner of the island, simultaneously crouching lower and lower himself. If Katherine had just gotten back from traveling through time while Jonah was experiencing a couple moments of panic, there was no telling what she'd suffered through; there was no telling how long she thought she'd been gone or how many lies they'd have to tell Mom and Dad to get them to believe that nothing had happened at all.

"Let me help," Jonah said, reaching out to her.

The blond hair moved. Jonah noticed that Katherine had evidently lost her ponytail rubber band during whatever trip she'd just returned from: her hair was hanging down loose now, spread across her shoulders and hiding her face. Really, the hair was all Jonah could see. But Katherine was painstakingly starting to tilt her head back to look up toward Jonah. The hair was sliding out of the way.

"Don't worry about the timesickness," Jonah said, patting Katherine's arm. "Take it slow. I'm watching out for you. You're not in any danger."

He hoped that that was true.

Katherine lifted her hand to brush the hair out of her face. Her mouth appeared. Her nose. Her eyes.

Jonah started blinking frantically, trying to make the girl crouched in front of him look like she was supposed to—to make her look like the sister he'd seen vanish only moments ago. But something was off. It was like this was some almost-Katherine, some slightly changed version that seemed familiar but not quite right.

"Katherine?" he said doubtfully, bending closer.

The girl squinted at him.

"I'm *Linda* Katherine," she said, as if correcting him. Then she moaned. "Ooohh. I feel so . . . weird. Everything's so strange."

Jonah rocked back on his heels. His feet slipped out from under him, and his tailbone slammed against the hard tile floor. He barely noticed. All he could do was stare at the girl. He knew who she was now. Not Katherine—she'd never been Katherine. This was the same person who'd been standing in the kitchen a few moments ago, when Charles Lindbergh had disappeared from the living room with Katherine clutched in his arms.

This was Jonah's mom.

Only somehow she'd turned back into a kid again.

# FIVE

"What just happened?" kid Mom groaned. "Why do I feel like . . . like . . ."

Jonah put his hand on her shoulder.

"Don't worry about it," he told her. "You're just . . . sick. Yeah, that's it. You have a very high fever, so you're imagining things."

He was proud of himself for coming up with that explanation so quickly. But kid Mom narrowed her eyes at him.

"Don't you lie to me, Jonah Skidmore," she said, and even though she still looked like Katherine—and about Katherine's age—at least now she sounded more like herself. Or like she was trying to sound like herself. She winced. "I remember now. I have a thirteen-year-old son named Jonah and an eleven-year-old daughter named Katherine. I was getting them ready for school. Why do

I feel like I should be going to school myself right now? And like . . . like maybe I should only be in seventh grade?"

*Seventh grade like me?* Jonah thought. *Not sixth, like Katherine?*

He wasn't sure what that meant. He didn't know what to say, anyway, so he didn't answer.

Kid Mom flashed him a look that seemed to be a mix of Katherine's *my brother is so annoying* expression and normal, adult Mom's *Jonah, I'm disappointed in you* stern gaze. She gave a little snort that sounded exactly like Katherine when Katherine was about to say something like, *Well, if you can't handle this, I'll take care of it myself!* Then she started to stand up.

Her clothes fell down. Her silky red sweater slipped down on her shoulder, and she had to hold on to the waistband of her black pants to keep them from sliding into a heap on the floor.

"What?" she exclaimed. "These are my tight pants!"

Jonah realized she was still wearing the same clothes she'd had on ten minutes ago when she was regular, normal, adult Mom. Now that she was roughly the same size as Katherine—give or take a few inches and pounds—the clothes seemed clownishly huge.

"Um, maybe you should go upstairs and change?" Jonah suggested. "Maybe you could borrow something from Katherine's closet?"

Kid Mom shot him another annoyed look.

"Just where *is* Katherine, exactly?" she asked suspiciously.

Jonah was saved from having to answer that because suddenly there was a burst of laughter out in the hall.

Another kid raced into the kitchen—a boy with wild, untamable-looking hair and crooked teeth and what appeared to be the beginnings of a monstrous zit on his nose. He was wearing jeans and an Ohio State T-shirt that Jonah was pretty sure had been hanging in his own closet earlier this morning.

"I am having the best dream ever!" the boy exclaimed, practically bouncing up and down. He dashed over to Jonah and threw his arm around Jonah's shoulder. "Hey, old buddy, old pal. I don't know how long this is going to last, but it's like I'm your age again. Thirteen! Whoo-hoo! What do you say we go out in the yard and throw the old pigskin around?"

Jonah was too stunned to speak.

"What's wrong—you scared I'll beat you, now that I don't have to worry about creaky knees?" the boy asked. "Or would you rather play soccer? You pick the sport—I'll take you on! Chal-lenge!"

The boy began dancing around in what Jonah guessed were supposed to be amazing soccer moves.

"Are you . . . ?" kid Mom started to ask, her tone a mix of astonishment and horror.

The boy stopped dancing and leaned in conspiratorially toward Jonah.

"I'll tell you a secret," he said. "I'm married! I'm thirteen years old, and I'm married. Isn't that crazy?" He started giggling and pointed to Mom. "And I'm married to *her*. Don't you think she's hot?"

*Oh, no,* Jonah thought, his worst suspicions confirmed. *No, no, no, no, no.*

This was the kid version of Dad.

# SIX

". . . Michael?" kid Mom finished.

Kid Dad flashed her a cheesy, slightly panicked grin and leaned back toward Jonah.

"Can you help me out here, buddy?" Dad whispered. "Can you make sure she doesn't see I've got this humongo zit on my humongo nose? Maybe you should stand in front of me. . . ."

He pushed Jonah over to the right, so Jonah blocked Mom's view of Dad's face.

"I'm not blind," Mom said sarcastically. "I already saw it. And I'm not deaf. I heard everything you said. Could you stop acting like such a fool?"

Dad cowered behind Jonah.

*What am I supposed to do now?* Jonah wondered. *Arrange marriage counseling for my thirteen-year-old parents?*

How could he keep them out of trouble while he figured out how to rescue Katherine?

Then he had another problem: The kitchen phone started ringing.

"Michael!" kid Mom called out. "Did you already have that conference call? Before we, uh . . . before whatever happened to us happened?"

Kid Dad was practically trembling behind Jonah.

"I'm supposed to call in on my cell phone at seven fifteen," Dad said. His voice squeaked. "I'm supposed to talk to China. I can't talk to China like this! What am I going to do?"

Dad's voice sounded even more unreliable and squawky than Jonah's ever had. Jonah glanced at the clock on the wall. It was twenty after seven.

The answering machine clicked on, Dad's normal adult voice asking callers to leave a message. After the click, a frantic male voice came on, begging, "Michael? Are you there? Did you oversleep? Did you forget the call with the Chinese? I'm not getting through on your cell phone. This is so not like you—"

Jonah walked over and picked up the phone.

"Mr. Wilson?" he said, because he was pretty sure this was Dad's boss. "This is Jonah Skidmore, Michael's son. My dad's been trying to call you, but something was messed up—it wouldn't even go to voice mail."

"Put him on now," Mr. Wilson ordered.

Jonah looked over at kid Dad, who was shaking his head, panic spread across his face.

"That's the problem," Jonah said. "He woke up this morning with a really bad case of laryngitis. He's been gargling with salt water, but he still can't even whisper."

"Tell him to try," Mr. Wilson growled.

Jonah held out the phone to Dad and mouthed, *Fake having laryngitis,* but Dad just backed away, shaking his head even more violently.

Jonah whispered into the phone instead, "I'm sorry, Mr. Wilson. This is a disaster . . ."

"I can't hear you," Mr. Wilson said. He sighed. "I'll let the Chinese know we have to reschedule. Stay home and try habanero peppers. That always works for me. You've got to get over this soon!"

Jonah hung up the phone. Both his parents were staring at him in astonishment.

"Everyone should be the hero of his own dreams," kid Dad complained. "But I just acted like a scaredy-cat and my own kid had to take over. This dream is really starting to suck."

Then he clapped his hand over his mouth and glanced guiltily at kid Mom.

"Oops," he said. "We aren't supposed to say words like

'suck' in front of the kids. Speaking of the kids . . . where's Katherine?"

No way was Jonah going to try to explain that one.

"Maybe your dream will get better if you go back to bed," Jonah said.

"Oh," Dad said, wrinkling his brow. "I didn't think of that."

"I'm going upstairs too, for a minute," Mom said. "I think I'll be able to deal with all this better if I'm not scared the whole time that my clothes are going to fall off."

"That's—" Dad started to say.

Kid Mom's hand shot out and covered his mouth.

"You are not saying a word about that," she said. "Not until you're a grown-up again."

Jonah barely waited until they were out of the kitchen before he had the phone back in his hand. He was pretty sure Mom planned to come right back, so he didn't have much time. There was exactly one grown-up he knew in the twenty-first century who understood about time travel—exactly one grown-up he could call who might be able to help.

*Oh, please, I* hope *she's still a grown-up,* Jonah thought, quickly dialing the number. *Like Dad's boss, not like Mom and Dad.*

Angela, the woman he was calling, had seen a plane crash-land thirteen years ago carrying baby Jonah and baby Chip and baby Gavin and thirty-three other infants who'd been stolen from history. The people kidnapping them—two men named Gary and Hodge—had intended to carry the babies on to the future, but those plans had been ruined.

So was Angela's life. She'd become obsessed with figuring out the mystery behind what she'd seen, and it had taken thirteen years before she'd gotten anything resembling an answer.

She'd also had to risk her life to help Jonah and Katherine and the other kids.

The phone rang. And rang. And rang.

"Crud!" Jonah exclaimed, hanging up.

Next he tried calling his friend Chip. Chip hadn't been on as many time-travel trips as Jonah, but in Chip's original identity—which he at least knew, and had relived part of—he'd been a king of England in the Middle Ages. Jonah could use a king helping him out, even if that king had gone back to being a seventh grader stuck in the middle of Ohio.

Talking to Chip would be a little bit complicated, since Chip was also Katherine's boyfriend. But maybe Jonah wouldn't tell him she was missing. Maybe Jonah would just ask if Chip's parents were still adults or if they were thirteen-year-olds too.

Chip's phone went straight to voice mail, meaning he

was probably already at school and he'd shut it off. *All* the kids Jonah knew would be at school now. There wasn't anyone who could help him.

"What should we do now, Kath—?" Jonah started to say automatically, because with just about every single time-travel dilemma he'd ever faced, he'd had Katherine right there beside him, helping out. In practically the only time-travel moments he'd had without Katherine, he'd had Albert Einstein's wife at his side, and she was pretty smart herself.

This time Jonah was on his own.

Jonah went back into the living room and stood in the exact spot where Lindbergh and Katherine had been the moment before they vanished. Maybe he'd get lucky and some random force would zap him to the same place they'd gone, and he'd be able to rescue Katherine that way.

Jonah could just hear what Katherine would say about this plan: *Yeah, right, Jonah. Like that's going to work.*

Jonah sank down onto the recliner and sat back in despair. Something poked against his back.

He sat up again and turned around. There, stuck in the crack between the cushions, was a little piece of paper that Jonah hadn't noticed before. Jonah pulled it out.

It was just a scrap, the bottom half of some sheet that seemed to have been torn out of a small notebook. At the top it held the words "identify Skidmore children," with a checkmark beside them.

*Charles Lindbergh was checking things off a list in a notebook!* Jonah remembered excitedly.

Had Lindbergh come back? Just to leave this bit of paper?

Jonah remembered how furiously Katherine had been flailing about in the moment before Lindbergh carried her away. In all her squirming, could she have knocked this bit of paper loose from the notebook without Lindbergh noticing? And then, was it possible that Jonah hadn't noticed it either, because he was swinging his arms around trying to find an invisible Lindbergh and Katherine—not looking for scraps of paper and other easily overlooked clues?

Jonah decided this was probably exactly what had happened.

He flattened the paper out on his knee and eager started reading the rest of it.

*Grab Skidmore girl* was the next item on the list, and it was checked off. So, too, was the next sentence: *Reset her chronophysical age to exactly thirteen years and three months.*

"What?" Jonah was so surprised he actually spoke aloud.

*Why would it matter if she's eleven or thirteen?* he wondered. *And why that exact "thirteen years and three months"?*

Something struck him: Jonah himself was exactly thirteen years and three months old.

*But Charles Lindbergh didn't even try to grab me,* Jonah reminded himself. *It wasn't like he wanted Katherine and me to be the same age.*

But now both Mom and Dad were probably thirteen years and three months too. Or close to it. Jonah hadn't asked either of them to be that precise about their current ages—and maybe they didn't even know—but Mom had talked about feeling like she should be in seventh grade. And Dad had said he was the same age as Jonah. Maybe he really was *exactly* the same.

*What's the big deal about being thirteen and three months?* Jonah asked himself. *And if Charles Lindbergh had wanted to change Mom and Dad, too, wouldn't he have put them on this checklist? Or was changing them just . . . an accident?*

Jonah saw that there was one more line written at the very bottom of the page, the only line that hadn't been checked off. But it didn't explain anything about Mom and Dad. It made Jonah forget that he needed to worry about them.

Because the last line said, *Take Skidmore girl to Gary and Hodge to seal the deal.*

# SEVEN

Jonah dropped the scrap of paper and it fluttered down to the floor.

"Nooo," he moaned.

*Why would Gary and Hodge want Katherine?* he wondered.

Gary and Hodge were kidnappers, sure, but Jonah had never heard of them trying to kidnap anyone who wasn't a famous missing kid from history. Katherine wasn't famous. She wasn't from any foreign time period. And she wasn't missing—*at least, she wasn't before today,* Jonah thought with a pang.

Gary and Hodge just wanted to make money, and lots of it. Though they claimed that they ran a charitable adoption agency, what they really did was sell famous missing kids from the past to rich families in the future, so those families could brag about who their kids were.

*Katherine's no one to them,* Jonah thought. *They would say she doesn't have any value. Except . . .*

Except Katherine had foiled or helped foil a lot of their plans. On her last trip through time, for example, she'd played a huge role in preventing Gary and Hodge from carrying off Alexei Romanov and Maria and Anastasia Romanova, part of the last royal family of Russia.

*But I've ruined their plans too,* Jonah thought. *If this is about revenge, or if they're just trying to get her out of the way so she won't mess up any more of their plans, why didn't they have Charles Lindbergh grab me at the same time as her?*

Jonah tried to think the way Gary and Hodge thought, even though he hated it.

*Is it because they still think they can make money from kidnapping me and carrying me off to the future?* he wondered. *So they need me to stay right here for now? Is that why they took her and not me?*

This still left lots of confusing details that Jonah didn't understand. What did Gary and Hodge plan to do with Katherine once they had her? What did it mean that delivering her was supposed to "seal the deal" for Charles Lindbergh? Why hadn't Gary and Hodge just kidnapped her themselves—why had they used Charles Lindbergh to do their dirty work for them? Who was Charles Lindbergh, anyway?

Jonah couldn't answer those questions, and anyhow he could hear Mom coming back down the stairs. Quickly he picked up the scrap of paper and tucked it into his pocket. He could tell by the sounds of her footsteps that Mom was practically running—Mom didn't run inside the house, did she?

*So maybe it's really Katherine, after all, magically returned?* Jonah thought hopefully.

It wasn't Katherine who rounded the corner into the living room—it was kid Mom in Katherine's clothes, which was an even more disturbing sight than kid Mom in too-big clothing. Jonah had seen pictures of both of his parents when they were kids, of course, so he should have recognized them from the very start. But Mom-as-a-teenager and Dad-as-a-teenager belonged in old, faded pictures where they wore funny-looking clothes and hairstyles from the 1980s: both of them in high-waisted pants with their shirts tucked in, Mom with her hair pulled into a ponytail that dangled down on one side of her head only . . . Jonah and Katherine used to love laughing at those pictures.

Seeing kid Mom in a pair of Katherine's running pants and a baby-blue sweatshirt that said CHEER! was just plain wrong.

Evidently Mom thought so too.

"I never realized how much of Katherine's wardrobe is

pink and/or sparkly," she said, making a face. "This was the best I could do. I feel ridiculous. You know I was a total tomboy when I was a kid, don't you?"

Jonah hadn't remembered that. But the talk of clothes made him think of something else.

*What was Katherine even wearing when she disappeared?* He wondered. He had a vague sense that it was something pink—or maybe purple?—but if this had been a normal kidnapping and he'd needed to describe her clothes for the cops, he would have been useless. Mom probably remembered, but he wasn't going to ask her. He needed to keep her from finding out that Katherine had vanished.

Jonah realized that kid Mom seemed to still be waiting for him to answer.

"Huh," he grunted, figuring Mom could interpret that however she wanted.

She bounced impatiently on the balls of her feet, which was something else that normal adult Mom would never do. Whenever Jonah or Katherine did something like that, she ordered them, "Stop fidgeting."

Jonah bit his tongue to avoid saying that to her. He needed to figure out a way to get her to go hang out upstairs with kid Dad so Jonah would be free to . . . well, do *something* to get Katherine back and restore both parents to their normal ages.

"You can't go in to work today," Jonah said. "So . . ."

"Duh," Mom said, rolling her eyes.

Real adult Mom would never have done that to Jonah. Not in a million years. Jonah was speechless.

"Sorry," Mom said instantly. She rubbed her forehead. There was something too adult about the gesture. Now she looked like a teenager playacting adult behavior. "I just feel so weird . . . like I don't know how to act. But I do have a plan!"

"Uh . . . good?" Jonah said doubtfully.

"First we need to get you and Katherine to school," Mom said.

Now, *that* sounded like Jonah's real mom. The world could be on the verge of ending, and she'd still think skipping school was a crime.

*What if Mom and Dad being teenagers again* is *a sign that the world is ending?* Jonah wondered.

He'd seen problems before that had left all of time and the whole universe teetering on the brink of collapse. Having Mom and Dad suddenly become thirty years younger was every bit as strange as the messes he'd faced then.

*But I managed to fix those earlier problems,* he reminded himself. *Well, with Katherine's help. And sometimes other people's help as well. . . .*

Jonah felt lonely all over again. If he had real, normal, adult Mom in front of him, maybe he would just break down and tell her everything and wail, *Mommy! Figure out how to get Katherine back! I can't!*

But real, normal, adult Mom had vanished. The thirteen-year-old girl standing in front of him looked like someone else he needed to protect.

"Katherine left in time to make the bus," Jonah said. Surprisingly enough, this actually wasn't a lie. Katherine *had* vanished in plenty of time to get to the bus stop. Jonah was just leaving out the fact that that wasn't where she'd gone.

Jonah could tell that kid Mom was trying to do the same narrowed-eyed searching gaze that adult Mom could always use to get Jonah to break down and admit, "I'm sorry! I'm sorry! I'll tell you the truth—the whole truth!"

But kid Mom's searching gaze had absolutely no effect on Jonah. After a moment she gave up.

Emboldened, Jonah added, "And I really do feel too sick to get to school today, after all. You'll have to call and tell them I'm going to be absent."

"I can't call the school sounding like this!" Mom protested. "They'll think I'm you pretending to be me!"

*I don't sound like a thirteen-year-old girl!* Jonah wanted to protest. But he didn't think it would help his cause.

"Pretend you have laryngitis," he suggested instead.

To his surprise Mom nodded approvingly. He followed her into the kitchen again as she dialed and then spoke quickly into the phone in a fake-hoarse voice. As soon as she hung up, he went for the next stage of getting both parents safely out of the way so he could figure out how to fix everything that had gone wrong that morning.

"You look tired," he told Mom. "Why don't you go upstairs and get some rest? I'm sure when you wake up, everything will be normal again . . ."

He'd underestimated kid Mom. Her cheeks flushed, and she shook her head stubbornly.

Who would have guessed that, as a kid, Mom was just as exasperating as Katherine?

"No, Jonah," Mom said. "I'm going to figure out what's going on here."

"How?" Jonah challenged.

"First I'm going to find out how widespread this is," she said. "I'm going to go out and knock on our neighbors' doors and see if anybody else is suddenly the wrong age."

It wasn't the worst idea Jonah had ever heard. He probably would have done the same thing, if the only problem he'd known about was his parents' messed-up ages. (How many other problems were out there right now besides the ones Jonah knew about?) Maybe if Jonah let Mom focus on the whole age thing, he could focus on getting Katherine back?

But kid Mom looked so young . . . and vulnerable . . . and unprotected.

"How about if you stay here and *I* go out knocking on doors?" Jonah suggested. "You can take it easy, and—"

"I am not going to 'take it easy'!" Mom said through gritted teeth. "I am not going to deal with something bizarre and incredible like this by sitting around playing Angry Birds on my cell phone!"

"Is that what Dad is doing?" Jonah asked weakly.

Kid Mom nodded.

"It's like *Home Alone* up there," she said.

*At least he's staying safe inside the house,* Jonah thought. He sighed.

"Maybe we should both go out knocking on the neighbors' doors," he suggested.

It would give him a chance to grill Mom about exactly who Charles Lindbergh was. And maybe after just a few houses Jonah could convince her that her plan was pointless, and maybe she would come back to the house and relax by trying on Katherine's other clothes—er, no, not if Mom had been such a tomboy. Maybe he could talk kid Mom and kid Dad into going down into the basement to play Ping-Pong. The basement would be a safe place for them, wouldn't it?

Mom was already over by the shoe caddy by the back door, grabbing her running shoes.

"Oops, these are too big too," she muttered. She pulled out a pair of Katherine's, held them beside her feet, and complained, "And these are too small. I feel like Goldilocks."

Jonah was hoping no shoes meant that Mom would have to stay inside. But before he could suggest that, she began pulling on Jonah's second-best sneakers.

They fit.

"I'm going, with or without you," Mom said.

Jonah scrambled to catch up.

By the time he had his own sneakers on his feet, Mom was already out the door. She was walking slowly, though, looking around suspiciously as she rounded the corner of the house toward the front yard.

It was a sunny November day, and nothing around them seemed to require suspiciousness. The white picket fence bordering the front of their yard stood perfectly straight; the two-story houses up and down the street were neat and well-tended; the trees and bushes and fall flowers that surrounded the houses seemed just as tidy. From what he could see around them, Jonah thought the worst danger anyone could expect here was that in a strong gust of wind the red maple in the front yard might drop a few leaves on his head.

But just last night Jonah—and Katherine and Chip and another friend, Daniella—had been kidnapped from the sidewalk between the Skidmores' house and Chip's. And only a week before that Jonah and Katherine had been zapped from the doorstep in front of Chip's house back to the year 1903. And . . .

*Stop thinking about the past,* Jonah told himself. *Figure out how to fix today's problems.*

"Um, Mom?" Jonah said, though it seemed wrong to call her that. He was almost tempted to say, *Linda?* He forged ahead anyway. "Who was Charles Lindbergh?"

Kid Mom turned and looked at him as though she had no clue why he was asking. Maybe she'd forgotten the conversation she and Jonah and Katherine had had in the living room before she'd un-aged thirty years.

"One of those old-time pilots," Mom said. "The pilot who—"

Mom broke off suddenly. Her eyes bulged slightly, as if something had taken her by surprise. She gulped, swayed dizzily back and forth—and then crumpled to the ground.

# EIGHT

"Mom!" Jonah cried.

He fell to his knees beside her, pushing back her hair and the hood of Katherine's stupid CHEER! sweatshirt.

*Check for the pulse point on her neck,* Jonah told himself, scrambling to remember what he'd learned about fainting for his First Aid badge in Boy Scouts. Healthy people didn't just collapse like that, did they? Especially not healthy thirteen-year-olds?

What if un-aging grown-ups back to being thirteen was something that could kill them?

Mom's pulse was thumping nice and strong, and her chest rose and fell in what seemed to be normal breaths. But her eyelids didn't even flutter. Jonah started to grab her shoulders to try to shake her back to consciousness. But maybe he wasn't in such great shape himself—he was trembling so much that his left hand slipped from her shoulders and slid up onto her neck.

Something metallic hit his hand.

*A necklace?* Jonah wondered.

He was pretty sure Mom hadn't been wearing a necklace.

The metal thing seemed to be embedded in Mom's neck. And it seemed to be barbed, like a dart or . . .

Jonah decided he didn't have time to analyze it further. All he needed to know was that this was some kind of projectile that had knocked Mom out. He grabbed Mom's feet and pulled her back around the corner of the house. He thought about pulling the barb out, but was afraid that could cause worse damage. Instead he flattened his back against the side of the house and peeked around toward the front.

*This is when I need Chip with all his Middle Ages training,* Jonah thought desperately. *He'd know how to figure out where that barb was shot from. He'd know how to set up a defensive battle station. He'd know how to put together scary-looking weapons from a few sticks from the ground and a handful of dead oak leaves. And he'd know how to fight off dozens of enemies. . . .*

Jonah didn't even know how far it was safe to stick his neck out, peeking around the corner of the house.

He couldn't see anything out of the ordinary—he

could barely see anything at all through the various tree limbs blocking his view. Why had his parents in their adult days thought it was such a great idea to plant a spruce tree right there at the corner? He shoved his head out a little farther—and then instantly jumped back.

"Ha-ha!" someone screamed right beside him, right at the edge of the tree. "You should have seen your face a minute ago!"

Jonah backed away even more, slamming his elbow into the side of the house. He had to get that much distance to actually see who was laughing at him: a kid. A kid who looked about thirteen; a kid with thick, glossy dark hair; a kid who was so good-looking Jonah was willing to bet all the girls at his middle school would be in love with him . . .

That is, if the kid actually was in middle school, and Jonah was pretty sure that he wasn't.

At least he wasn't *now*.

"JB?" Jonah whispered.

"He's a genius!" the kid said mockingly, and laughed again.

"You went back to being thirteen too?" Jonah asked.

This time the kid—JB—only nodded and frowned.

"Do you know how to fix it?" Jonah asked.

"Well . . . ," kid JB began.

"No," someone else said, stepping up quietly behind JB.

This was another kid—probably another thirteen-year-old, Jonah guessed. But this was a very tall, very pretty girl with dark skin.

"Angela?" Jonah said. "You're a kid now too? Are there any adults around who are still adults? What about Hadley or the other time agents—"

"We can't reach Hadley or any other time agent," kid Angela said, her face creased with worry. "Whatever changed us also zapped our Elucidator."

"We know the un-aging affected at least this immediate area," kid JB said. "We're not sure how much farther it went than that, but Angela and I were just turning in to your neighborhood—"

"—when suddenly my feet didn't reach the gas pedal anymore," kid Angela said. "Or the brake."

"I had to dive down and hit the brake for her," kid JB bragged.

"I told you, I would have gotten it myself!" kid Angela argued. "I was stretching my leg out and sliding forward . . . And then I was going to move the seat up—that was all I needed! You almost *caused* an accident, getting in my way!"

JB and Angela didn't sound like themselves. It wasn't just their kid voices—it was the fact that they were squabbling like . . . well, like Jonah and Katherine.

*It's like one of those stupid cartoons from when we were little,*

Jonah thought. *Baby Looney Tunes. Bugs Bunny should not be a baby. Tasmanian Devil should not be a baby. JB and Angela should not be teenagers.*

JB and Angela were supposed to be the adults. The ones who could take care of Jonah's problems.

Jonah looked down at kid Mom, still unconscious on the ground. She was someone else who had always taken care of Jonah. But now she had dead leaves blowing over against her body, starting to bury her.

Jonah shivered.

"So—were you two planning to shoot my mom with a tranquilizer dart even *before* you turned into teenagers?" he asked, and was surprised at how much anger his voice carried. "It *was* just a tranquilizer dart, right? What's going on?"

He was relieved to see JB nod and mumble, "Right—just a tranquilizer dart."

But then Angela admitted, "We don't know what's going on."

At least now there was a little bit of the compassion in her voice that she'd always had as an adult.

Kid JB stepped closer to Jonah, practically pushing kid Angela out of the way.

"We got a report that there was an unspecified threat against all thirty-six of the missing kids from history who were now in the twenty-first century," JB said. Jonah had come to appreciate how authoritative JB's adult voice almost always sounded; even when everything was falling apart around them, JB as an adult could usually still sound calm and confident and in control.

Kid JB sounded like this too. But that tone sounded fake coming from a kid. It made Jonah want to punch kid JB, not listen carefully and do what he said.

Jonah made himself listen anyway.

"Angela and I were hurrying to watch over you and Chip," kid JB continued.

"Yeah, well, you were too late," Jonah said bitterly. "And wrong about who was actually in danger."

The other two kids stared at him blankly.

"You're still here," JB said, practically smirking. "You look fine."

"Katherine's not," Jonah said. And somehow, having so many adults suddenly become much younger, Jonah kind of wanted to act a lot younger himself, too. What he really wanted to do was throw himself down on the grass and sob and scream and pound his fists like a toddler throwing a tantrum.

He didn't do any of that.

JB and Angela just kept squinting stupidly at him.

*They don't know,* Jonah thought numbly. *They don't know anything about what happened.*

Did that also mean that they wouldn't know how to get Katherine back?

Jonah gritted his teeth and swallowed hard. And then he forced himself to tell them everything that had happened. The other two only interrupted once, to repeat incredulously, "Charles Lindbergh? It was Charles Lindbergh in your living room?"

"That's who Mom said it was," Jonah said. "She acted totally certain."

The other two exchanged worried glances. Jonah could tell they were really hoping Mom was wrong.

"Here—see for yourself," Jonah said, remembering that he still had the cell phone in his pocket. He pulled it out, scrolled over to the photo roll, and showed the other two. "Katherine took a picture."

Angela took one glance and nodded.

"That's Charles Lindbergh all right," she said.

Digging around in his pockets reminded Jonah that he also had the scrap of paper Lindbergh had left behind. He showed that to JB and Angela too.

And then there wasn't anything else to tell.

JB was backing away from the Lindbergh paper. He smashed right into the spruce tree and didn't even seem to notice.

"This is bad," he said dazedly. "Really, really bad."

"Thanks for your expert analysis," Jonah said sarcastically. "What should we do?"

JB winced and clutched his chest. He seemed to be struggling to catch his breath.

"Had asthma as a child . . . the first time," he gasped. "I guess . . . it's back. Need . . . inhaler. Anyone have . . . ?"

Did JB think there'd be one just lying around somewhere?

Jonah racked his brain for some other solution. Hadn't they said in his first-aid training that there were treatments for asthma that didn't involve drugs?

"Do you remember any special breathing techniques you can use?" Jonah asked.

JB shook his head.

"Would it help to be around steam?" Jonah asked.

"Maybe?" JB struggled to say. "I think my mama used to . . . boil a pot of water . . ."

Jonah tugged on kid JB's arm, pulling him toward the door back into the house.

"Could you bring my mom inside too?" he hollered back at kid Angela. "I don't want to just leave her lying on the ground!"

Angela nodded, but her eyes were wide with fear and worry. She looked even more terrified than Jonah felt.

*And I thought if JB or Angela showed up, they'd solve everything,*

Jonah thought frantically. *But now JB is just someone else who needs my help. . . .*

Jonah hesitated. He stopped dragging JB toward the house just long enough to toss the cell phone back to Angela.

"After you get Mom inside, call the school," Jonah said over his shoulder. "The number's on the refrigerator door—Harris Middle. Pretend to be Chip's mom or Chip's dad's assistant or something like that—some kind of adult. Tell them there's an emergency at home and Chip needs to get out of school *now*."

If the adults weren't going to be any help—for that matter, if they weren't even adults anymore—then Jonah needed another kid around he could count on.

And since Chip had lived part of his life during the Middle Ages, maybe he knew how someone could survive an asthma attack without an inhaler.

Or maybe everyone with asthma back then just died?

Jonah didn't bother watching to make sure that Angela understood what he was talking about. He pulled JB, still wheezing, through the back door of the house and then into the downstairs bathroom. He turned the shower on, full strength.

"Maybe if you just try to relax?" Jonah said. "And lean your head in?"

The steam began to rise, fogging up the mirror and the shower door.

"K-Katherine," JB stammered.

"Don't worry about her right now," Jonah said. "Don't think about anything but breathing."

*Because I'm worrying enough for both of us,* Jonah thought. *I'm trying to save your life and keep Mom and Dad safe too—and meanwhile no one's going after Katherine; none of us know what to do. . . .*

Someone knocked at the bathroom door. Jonah opened it just a crack, trying not to let the steam out.

He was glad to see Angela pressing her face close. If it had been kid Dad, Jonah would have had no idea what to tell him.

But Angela's face was taut with distress.

"We can't get Chip," she said.

"Why not?" Jonah demanded. "Couldn't you convince the school that you were an adult?"

"That's not the problem," kid Angela said. "It's because . . ."

She paused, as if trying to steady herself enough to keep speaking.

"What?" Jonah exploded.

Angela gazed sadly back at him.

"Because," she whispered. "He's vanished too."

# NINE

The steam swirled around Jonah's head. For a moment his brain felt just as foggy, but he reminded himself that Katherine and Mom and Dad and JB and Angela—and now Chip as well?—needed him to stay sharp.

*Focus,* Jonah told himself. *Try to think . . .*

"Did Charles Lindbergh snatch Chip, too?" Jonah asked. "Did anyone see it happen? Why—"

Kid Angela winced.

"The school office says Chip hasn't been there all day," she said. "So I went over to Chip's house and snooped around. . . . His parents look like they've turned back into thirteen-year-olds too. Not very pleasant thirteen-year-olds, actually. But because Mr. Winston was smoking and had the living-room window open to let the smoke out—and because he and his wife were screaming at each other—I heard exactly what happened."

"Which was . . . ?" Jonah prompted.

"Chip had been standing by the front door, ready to go to school," Angela said. She'd slowed down the pace of her voice, as if she was dreading describing what happened next. "One minute he was there; the next minute . . . he wasn't."

"Maybe he *did* go out the door," Jonah said. "Maybe he just didn't go to school."

A few months ago, when Chip had been angry about finding out that he was adopted, Jonah could have imagined Chip skipping school just to get back at his parents. But after traveling back to the Middle Ages—and sort of temporarily growing up—Chip wasn't like that anymore. This morning he should have been trying just as hard as Jonah and Katherine to act like everything was normal.

"Jonah, Chip's mother saw him disappear," Angela said. "That's what his mom and dad are fighting about—Chip's dad says she has to be lying. So she just keeps telling the story over and over again, in her whiny voice. . . . Sorry. Editorial comment there. But I *really* don't like Chip's parents."

"Nobody does," Jonah muttered.

He felt numb.

*Chip can't help?* he marveled. *And now I need to figure out a way to rescue him, too? All by myself?*

He realized that Angela had actually helped a lot. He shouldn't think she was useless just because she was only thirteen. Didn't Jonah hate it when people assumed that about him?

"We need to check on everyone else, then," Jonah said. "The other missing kids, I mean, to see if they're okay. Gavin and Daniella and . . . and Andrea . . ."

Jonah choked up and couldn't say another name after Andrea's. She was another missing child he and Katherine had helped back in the 1600s, when everything about history had been horribly confused. There was a time when he'd hoped she'd become his girlfriend, but she'd given him the "just friends" speech. Or the "we can't be anything except friends right now, because time travel has left me too messed up" speech, which was even worse.

Something slammed into Jonah from the back. It was JB, still wheezing a little, but able to talk better now.

"No," kid JB said, his imperious tone back. "There's no time for checking on anyone else. First things first. If Chip's been taken, we've got to get you to safety. So nothing happens to you."

JB was pushing Jonah forward, trying to hustle him out the door. Jonah shoved him back. JB was actually a little smaller and shorter than Jonah right now—the force of Jonah's elbow knocked the other boy against the back wall.

"What about the others?" Jonah asked. "What about their safety?"

"They already have time agents assigned to them, taking care of them," JB growled.

"Yeah, because you and Angela did such a great job protecting Chip," Jonah grumbled.

*And Katherine,* Jonah thought, though maybe it wasn't fair to blame JB and Angela for her disappearance. Katherine wasn't a missing kid from history and wasn't supposed to have been in danger.

While Jonah was thinking all that, JB shoved off from the wall, pulling a towel with him.

"Get down!" kid JB ordered. "Hide!"

He tackled Jonah with the towel, covering his head and knocking him down to the floor halfway out into the hall.

Jonah heard footsteps nearby. He peeked out from the towel.

"What are you all doing?" kid Dad asked, standing over them. "Playing tackle football inside the house? Or capture the flag? Can I play too?"

Real, normal, adult Dad would never in a million years ask that. He'd be lecturing Jonah about how much it would cost to replace the towel racks or the wall tiles if Jonah broke them with his roughhousing.

"Actually, Dad . . . ," Jonah began, trying to think of a good explanation.

JB didn't wait for words. He lifted his hand. Jonah heard a zinging noise, and a second later kid Dad slumped to the floor.

"You had to knock him out too?" Jonah protested.

"Didn't have to, but it saves time," JB explained. "We've got to get you out of here *now*."

Jonah curled his fingers around the edge of the hallway rug, holding on tight.

JB sighed, a little bit of a wheeze left in the sound.

"Your parents will be fine," he said. "We'll leave them here, and those tranquilizer darts will keep them knocked out until we can fix everything. . . . They'll be safe. After all of this is over, they'll wake up their normal ages and not remember much more than a weird dream."

Jonah wanted to believe him. But kid JB—or adult JB either, for that matter—hadn't realized that Katherine was in danger. How could Jonah leave his parents behind when he didn't know what was going on? When he couldn't be 100 percent sure that they would be safe?

"You can keep them tranquilized," Jonah said through gritted teeth. "But if you're taking me to safety, you're bringing my parents, too."

JB sighed again.

"It's not—" he began.

Angela stepped in front of him.

"I'll go get the car from in front of Chip's," she interrupted. "Won't take me a minute. Why don't you two start carrying Jonah's parents toward the garage? We'll take them out that way—less chance of being seen."

"We can't protect everyone!" kid JB fumed. "We don't have time to worry about people who aren't actually in danger!"

"These are his parents," Angela said simply as she turned to go.

Jonah was glad that Angela, at least, was on his side. He picked up kid Dad—the boy was scrawnier than he looked, and Jonah had no trouble lifting him by the armpits and dragging him across the floor. Real, normal, adult Dad was six inches taller than Jonah and kind of heavyset; it was frightening to have Jonah's father seem so lightweight and frail.

*Fragile,* Jonah thought. *Easily hurt.*

It was a huge relief that JB picked up Jonah's mom—he seemed to be going along with Angela's plan without any more arguments. Jonah had such a lump in his throat he couldn't have said anything else.

Angela already had the car in the driveway when Jonah hit the garage door opener.

"You run out and crouch down in the backseat," JB told him. "I'll get your parents in beside you and then we'll throw a blanket over all three of you to keep you hidden."

"But I need to shut the garage door before we leave—" Jonah began to argue.

"I'll handle that!" JB ordered. "You stay out of sight!"

There was such tension in his voice that Jonah obeyed.

*Who does JB really think would be watching?* Jonah wondered. *Gary and Hodge? This Charles Lindbergh character?*

The entire street looked deserted, and as far as Jonah could tell, the blinds were still drawn in the front windows of all the houses around them. But Jonah knew from his past experiences with time travel that there were ways for people to watch him without being anywhere nearby—without even being in the same century, actually. In one of his first encounters with time travelers, he'd learned that it wasn't even safe to write down certain things that a time traveler might see at some moment in the future.

*Charles Lindbergh—he's the past,* Jonah reminded himself. *Mom said he was an old-timey pilot. . . .*

This didn't make Jonah feel any better.

In no time at all Jonah was huddled in the backseat of Angela's car, with the unconscious kid versions of both of his parents beside him. JB tossed a quilt from the hall closet over the top of all three of them.

Jonah reached over and fastened seat belts around both his parents. It didn't seem like enough protection, not after he'd watched Katherine disappear right before his eyes barely an hour ago. Because he was under the quilt anyhow, and no one could see him, he reached out and held on to Mom's right hand and Dad's left hand.

*There,* Jonah thought. *If anyone or anything zaps them to some other place or time, we all go together.*

But would that make it more or less likely that he would be able to rescue Katherine?

# TEN

From the way the car lurched around corners, squealing tires at every turn, Jonah could tell that Angela was more concerned about driving fast than anything else. He poked his face out from the quilt a little so he could tell her, "You may have forgotten what it's like to be thirteen, but if the cops stop you for speeding, they're not going to believe you're who your driver's license says you are. They'll think you stole your mom's car *and* her license."

"We'll slow down once we're out of the afflicted area!" JB yelled back to him. "Now—stay hidden!"

*Afflicted area?* Jonah thought. He guessed JB meant the area where adults had un-aged into teenagers. But "afflicted" made it sound even more horrifying than that.

He grasped his parents' hands with only one of his own, and used his other hand to pull the quilt back up in front of his face. But he left himself a small peephole beside the window, no bigger than his eye. This was enough that he could see they were still in Jonah's neighborhood, on the main street that led out of the subdivision.

There wasn't another car in sight. For that matter there wasn't another person in sight.

Jonah suddenly realized how odd that was.

*Where are the grown-ups driving to work?* he wondered. *Where are the dog walkers? Where are the moms pushing their babies and toddlers in jogging strollers?*

Had they *all* turned back into thirteen-year-olds? Were they all so stunned and terrified by the change that they could only cower indoors? (Or argue, in the case of Chip's parents?) Was Jonah's mom the only one brave enough to step outside to try to figure out what was going on?

*And look what happened to her,* Jonah thought grimly.

Kid JB reached over the back of the seat.

"I said stay down!" he screamed at Jonah, shoving Jonah's head lower. "It's for your own good!"

"You can come out when you're safe!" Angela yelled back at him. "We promise!"

It was too unnerving to try to look out, anyhow. Jonah did notice that after a few more turns Angela slowed down to a pace more suited for a staid old lady driving to church on a Sunday morning.

*Does that mean that the adults who became thirteen-year-olds were all within a mile or two of my house?* Jonah wondered.

Was Jonah's school close enough to be affected? He tried to imagine his teachers as thirteen-year-olds; he tried to imagine the principal and the custodians and the cafeteria ladies as teenagers too. In another mood the whole scenario would have struck him as hilarious. But he had too much else to worry about to laugh right now.

*Katherine . . . Charles Lindbergh . . . Am I Charles Lindbergh's son?*

He thought about hissing to JB and getting him to answer some of Jonah's questions as Angela drove. But Jonah could hear bits and pieces of an argument going on in the front seat, and it sounded like JB was way too busy yelling at Angela about the quickest and safest way to get wherever they were going.

"We'll have to take the back way in—" JB was demanding.

"No. I told you," Angela argued back. "When I went back, a lot of those trees were gone. Right up to the front entrance. It looked like there'd been a storm, and—"

"A storm, right," JB said, and Jonah could tell even without seeing him that the other boy was rolling his eyes.

"Are we sure this place is still safe?" Angela asked. "What if our enemies just want us to think that it's safe?"

"Do we have any other choice?" JB asked.

"Hadley will—" Angela began.

"If Hadley or any of the other time agents could get to us, don't you think they'd already be here?" JB asked.

Jonah's stomach lurched. Maybe he'd be better off not listening to the other two? What if by insisting on bringing his parents, he was leading them into danger rather than keeping them away from it?

*Just like I put Katherine in danger by letting her help me and Chip way back at the beginning,* Jonah thought. *Before we knew our identities had anything to do with time travel . . . I shouldn't have ever let Katherine in on any of our secrets.*

He was being silly: The way Katherine was, once she'd known there was some mystery connected to Jonah and Chip, there was no way Jonah could have kept her out of his business. He'd never been good at bossing her around, even when she was a really little girl.

And anyhow, if Jonah hadn't had Katherine alongside him on all their time-travel trips, would any of the missing kids from history they'd helped still be alive? Would Chip and Alex? Would Andrea and Brendan and Antonio? Would Dalton and Emily? Would Daniella and Gavin and Maria and Leonid?

*How can I know that any of them actually are still alive right now?* Jonah thought, remembering that Chip had vanished that morning.

Angela's driving changed again, from old-lady staid and sedate to reckless-teenager wild and crazy. She also seemed to have left all pavement behind, and Jonah jolted up and down and side to side. Kid Mom and kid Dad, still unconscious, flopped around like rag dolls, held in place only by their seat belts and Jonah's hand. Branches lashed the side of the car; what seemed to be boulders beneath the tires made the whole car tilt dangerously.

*Angela's car doesn't look like the type with four-wheel drive,* Jonah thought. *Do Angela and JB have a plan for what to do if we get stuck?*

Bouncing up and down, Jonah risked another peek around the edge of the quilt. All he could see were trees and sky.

"Stay hidden!" JB screamed from the front seat. "We're almost there—stay out of sight!"

*Is this what it would feel like to be kidnapped?* Jonah wondered. *Is this what it felt like when I really was kidnapped?*

Jonah reminded himself that JB and Angela were actually trying to rescue him. He pulled the quilt back over his face.

The car kept bouncing and bouncing and bouncing before it finally slowed down, before it finally came to a stop. Jonah felt scrambled.

"I'll shut the door and put in the code!" JB hollered. "Stay put!"

Jonah heard the car door scraping open, JB running away, and then something grinding or being ground. It was a familiar noise that teased at Jonah's memory; it made him feel tense and worried and frightened even without quite remembering when or where he'd heard it before.

Jonah heard the footsteps running back toward the car.

"We did it!" JB shrieked, his voice soaring a full octave. "We're safe!"

Jonah took that as his cue to uncover his entire face. In the dim light around them, he could see rock on all sides of the car. Rock, and rows of benches shoved off to the side . . .

*Familiar rock,* Jonah thought. *Familiar benches.*

He'd been here before—twice. Once right before his trip to the 1400s, and once right after it.

"What?" he screamed. "Why'd you bring me to Gary and Hodge's cave?"

# ELEVEN

Jonah let go of his parents' hands and grabbed the handle of the car door. Weeks ago, the first time Jonah had been in this cave, he'd pretended he had claustrophobia. Then, when the walls seemed to be closing in on him, he'd started wondering if he really did have that problem.

The sensation hit him even harder this time. The rock walls seemed to be moving closer, closer, closer . . .

Jonah jerked the car door open and took off sprinting toward the keypad he knew was nestled in the rock on one of the walls. If he got to it in time, he could open the rock door again. He could see the open sky again; he could drag himself and his unconscious parents back out into the fresh air. . . .

JB tried to tackle him, but Jonah kept going, even with JB's arms around his neck.

"Angela!" JB screamed.

Angela slammed against Jonah. All three of them toppled to the ground.

A second later Angela was sitting up and scooting away even as she brushed dirt off her blue jeans.

"Do *not* make me do that again," she said sternly, and she sounded so much like her regular self—her true, regular *adult* self—that Jonah felt the fight and the panic go out of him. This was Angela and JB taking care of him, even in their kid forms. These were his friends.

JB shoved away from Jonah too.

"You're right—this *was* Gary and Hodge's cave," JB said. "But we time agents took it away from them. When we sent them to time prison. Remember?"

There was something about JB being the same age as Jonah that made Jonah want to be surly to the other boy. Even if he was a friend.

"And then Gary and Hodge escaped from time prison, and you don't know where they are now. *Remember?*" Jonah said in his snarkiest voice. "How do you know they're not hiding out in the back of this cave? How do you know they didn't want us to come right here? How do you know it's not a trap?"

He suddenly realized that those were the very questions JB and Angela had been arguing about in the car.

"There are sensors on the door," JB said. "They showed the cave was empty."

"Oh, and if Gary and Hodge can hide from your entire time agency, don't you think they could tamper with a few little sensors?" Jonah asked.

Angela pushed Jonah and JB farther apart. She held up her hand like a traffic cop. Or a referee.

"Peace, you two," she said. "Truce, all right?" She stared down at her own hand. "You made me break a nail tackling you. I am not sacrificing my entire manicure to keep you two from beating each other up. Why don't we focus on finding out what we want to know?"

"Exactly," JB said, as if he'd been the one acting like an adult all along.

Jonah bit his tongue to keep from arguing.

"Right now I'm the biggest and the toughest-looking of the three of us," Angela said. "So I'll search the whole cave to make sure there aren't any surprises lurking in the shadows."

Jonah realized she was right: As an adult, Angela had probably been about six feet tall. As a thirteen-year-old she wasn't much shorter. For the first time, Jonah noticed that changing ages hadn't created any clothing problems for her, like they had for Mom. Angela had rolled up the legs of her jeans an inch or so, but other than that her adult clothes seemed to fit her fine. She must have been one of those kids who'd gotten her growth spurt early.

It wasn't like kid JB, who had his belt tightened past its last notch and his pants rolled up three or four times. The baggy pants made him look ridiculously scarecrowlike—Jonah felt a little bad that he hadn't offered JB some of his own clothes to change into.

Not that they would have been small enough either.

And not that there had really been time for that.

"This cave is still a functioning time hollow, right?" Jonah asked JB as Angela went off on her search. This was kind of Jonah's peace offering, giving the other boy a chance to act all know-it-all like he seemed to want to.

"Right," JB said. "So we can find out what's going on, and we can fix things. We can take all the time we need. And then when we open the door and go back to the twenty-first century, it will be like not a single moment passed since we left. Because no time ever passes in a time hollow."

Jonah knew that was how time hollows worked. He'd known that since his very first experience with a time hollow—in this very cave, in fact. But he refrained from telling JB to shut up.

"But how are we going to fix anything—or even see what's going on—without a working Elucidator?" Jonah asked.

JB flashed him a disgusted look and stood up.

"There are monitors here in the cave," he said. "I wouldn't have brought us to a place where we had no way of getting information. The monitors are supposed to work with an Elucidator, but I'm sure I can jury-rig something."

*Of course you're sure,* Jonah thought but didn't say.

He stood up and followed JB over into a dark section at the back of the cave. The last time Jonah had been in this area, he'd been worried about getting Tasered. This time JB hit some sort of switch on the wall that Jonah hadn't noticed. Instantly the entire wall lit up with what appeared to be an array of TV screens.

Or maybe broken TV screens? None of the screens actually showed a recognizable image. They were all full of fuzzy, jumpy pixels, like the TV at home when someone hit the wrong button on the remote and the cable cut out.

"That's what I was afraid of," JB muttered. "This is going to take a while."

"But that doesn't matter, since time never moves in a time hollow," Angela said, coming up behind them. She made a mocking salute. "Reporting back for duty, sir! I've checked out the entire cave, and there's nobody here but us chickens. What's the next assignment?"

Jonah tried not to gape at her. Normal, adult Angela was one of the coolest people he knew. How could she be so goofy as a thirteen-year-old?

JB didn't seem to be paying much attention.

"There's not anything you or Jonah can do until I get these monitors working," he muttered, his head bent over a keyboard of sorts that had appeared in the stone wall. "It's not like either of you would know enough to help me without taking about eight years' worth of advanced training. . . ."

*Of course not,* Jonah thought.

Angela just shrugged.

"Okay, then," she said.

Jonah didn't want to just stand there. He wandered back toward the huge open part of the cave, where kid Angela had left the car parked haphazardly. Both of Jonah's parents were still unconscious and slumped awkwardly in the backseat. Jonah opened the doors to give them some fresh air. He reached in and tried to straighten them up a little, so they wouldn't be sore when they woke up.

*Though I guess that wouldn't happen in a time hollow,* he reminded himself. *You never get hungry, you never get thirsty, you never have to go to the bathroom . . . I guess you couldn't get a crick in your neck, either.*

At least it made him feel better to make them look more comfortable.

"Did you totally freak out when you first saw your parents looking like teenagers?" Angela asked. "I know when I was thirteen . . . I mean, when I was thirteen the first time around . . . I would have had a spaz-fit."

"They were more freaked out than I was," Jonah said. "I've already seen so many strange things with time travel, and I was already so worried about Katherine . . ."

Angela reached over and patted him on the back, which was exactly what she would have done as a grown-up.

"We'll find her," she said. "You'll see. Katherine will be fine. And anyhow, you know nothing bad could be happening to her right now, since time isn't moving outside the time hollow. We'll find out where she is, and then we'll go rescue her, and for her it won't be like any time passed at all."

*But what if she's in a time hollow somewhere too?* Jonah wondered. *What if it feels to her like she's enduring hundreds of years of torture?*

He decided not to share that thought with Angela. He gulped and made himself ask a different question.

"Am I related to Charles Lindbergh?" he asked. "Is that my original identity in time—Charles Lindbergh's son?"

Somehow it was easier to ask Angela this than it would have been to ask JB.

Kid Angela's eyes widened.

"Gosh, Jonah, I don't know," she said. "JB and Hadley and the other time agents—there's a lot they won't tell me. They say they have to keep me as 'untainted' by time travel as possible. It's really annoying."

"Katherine thought I kind of looked like Charles Lindbergh," Jonah mumbled.

Angela began studying Jonah's face, looking at him straight on, then from the left, then from the right.

"I don't know," she said. "You do have that chin-dimple thing like him, and your hair's light like his, but . . . I don't know."

Jonah resisted the urge to put his hands over his face and hide. It occurred to him that he could just walk back over to JB and ask him.

Jonah didn't do that.

*Katherine,* he told himself. *Just think about Katherine.*

"You recognized Lindbergh's picture—what else do you know about him?" Jonah asked. "Can you think of any reason he'd want to kidnap Katherine? Or what deal he would be trying to 'seal' with Gary and Hodge by taking her to them?"

Angela frowned.

"Jonah, you know, things get messed up with time travel," she said. "What Lindbergh wants might be totally different from in original history, if Gary and Hodge got to him somehow."

"But he came out of history! He was in my living room!

He stole my sister!" Jonah shouted at her. He was surprised at how little control he had over his voice.

On the other side of the cave JB glanced up, then quickly looked back at the blur of monitors around him.

*Yeah, ignore me and just keep working,* Jonah thought bitterly, even though he knew he was being ridiculous. He *wanted* JB to keep working. That was the only way to find out anything about Katherine, the only way to have any prayer of rescuing her.

Angela tilted her head sympathetically.

"Here. Pull up a seat," she said, sliding back into the car. She sat behind the steering wheel and pointed to the passenger-side front seat for Jonah. "I'll tell you everything I know about Charles Lindbergh."

Jonah walked to the other side of the car and sat down.

"Lindbergh was a pilot," he prompted.

"Yep," Angela said. "And when I was—well, about thirteen, the first time around—I really wanted to be a pilot. I read up on all the famous pilots. Bessie Coleman was my favorite, but—"

"Who?" Jonah asked.

Angela gave him the same kind of disappointed glance Jonah's mom had given him when he hadn't known who Charles Lindbergh was.

"The first African-American female pilot," Angela said.

"Okay, I know she's not well-known now, but she was *something*! When she couldn't get anyone to give her flying lessons in the United States because she was a black woman, she went to Paris. And that was in 1921!"

"Um, okay, I'm sure she was great," Jonah said. "But she's not the one who stole my sister this morning."

"Oh, right," Angela said sheepishly. "About Charles Lindbergh . . . In like 1926 or 1927, something like that, he flew across the Atlantic Ocean. New York to Paris. He did it all by himself, and it took him something like thirty-three hours—he stayed awake the whole time. He was the first one to fly that route. People had tried it before, but they always died."

Jonah knew he was supposed to be impressed. But he just couldn't care, when Katherine was missing.

"Do you know about Lindbergh's son?" Angela asked. "It was like, I don't know, five or six years after Lindbergh's famous flight. His son was kidnapped."

"I know, I know," Jonah said glumly. "By Gary and Hodge. Just like all the other missing children from history."

Angela wrinkled up her nose as if she was trying hard to remember something.

"It's funny," she said. "My memory of this is so fuzzy. And . . . it seems to be getting fuzzier the more I think about it. But Lindbergh's baby was kidnapped in real, original time too. Even before Gary and Hodge got involved. The kidnapper was executed, but—did they ever find the baby's body? Or did they find a body that they thought was the Lindbergh baby, but . . ."

Her voice trailed off.

"It was a baby *boy*, right?" Jonah asked. "Not a baby girl, where Charles Lindbergh might think that if he kidnapped Katherine . . ."

He was working on a theory: What if Gary and Hodge had told Charles Lindbergh that Katherine was really his child? What if that was the reason Lindbergh had snatched her?

It didn't make sense. And anyhow Angela was shaking her head.

"The Lindbergh baby who got kidnapped was definitely a boy," she said. "No doubt about it."

Jonah slumped in his seat. He knew he should be thinking of other questions to ask about Charles Lindbergh, but none of it seemed to matter.

"I hadn't thought about all those historic pilots in years," kid Angela said. "Did I ever tell you—I started working at the airport in the first place because I thought that was how I'd eventually get to be a pilot? I was too poor to pay for flying lessons, and I didn't want to go into the military to learn. I used to *idolize* Charles Lindbergh. Well, before I found out some of the bad things about him."

"You mean, like the fact that he went more than forty years into the future to kidnap Katherine?" Jonah muttered.

Before Angela had a chance to answer, JB let out a whoop from across the room.

"It's up!" he screamed. "I got the monitors to work! Come see!"

Jonah hurled himself out of the car and raced toward the wall full of monitors. He had a head start, but Angela passed him after three steps.

Even as he approached the wall, Jonah could tell that JB had set the monitors to cycle through the same moment in time in several different locations. On one screen there was Chip, standing in the foyer of his house, right by the front door. And then, a second later, he vanished.

On the next screen there was a dark-haired girl—*hey, isn't that Ming Reynolds?* Jonah thought.

She was another missing child from history, but Jonah hadn't seen her since the last time he'd been in this cave. On the screen Ming was sitting at a table dropping blueberries into a bowl of yogurt.

And then a moment later, Ming vanished, just like Chip. The table and the bowl and the yogurt and blueberries were still there, but not Ming.

All across the monitors, kids were vanishing.

There was Brendan . . . and now he was gone.

Emily . . . gone.

Antonio . . . gone.

Gavin . . . gone.

Daniella . . . gone.

Andrea . . . gone.

*Andrea!* Jonah felt like screaming. *Andrea!*

In front of him, several yards back from the wall full of monitors, Angela stopped short.

"Who's left?" she asked, her voice breaking with anguish. "Of all the missing children from history . . . how many *didn't* disappear today?"

JB turned around.

"Just one," he said, his eyes burning. "Only Jonah."

# TWELVE

Jonah fell down. Angela instantly dived on top of him.

"Don't you disappear now too!" she screeched. "We won't let you! JB—help!"

Jonah lifted his head from the rock floor pressed against his cheek. Forget being a pilot or physicist or airport worker—what Angela really had a talent for was football. He didn't know any other thirteen-year-old who was this good at tackling people.

"I just tripped," he muttered. "I just . . ."

He didn't want to admit that his knees had crumpled beneath him at the thought of being the last missing child left, the only one stolen from history who hadn't been stolen once again from the twenty-first century.

*Andrea,* he thought. *Andrea, Chip, Alex, Brendan, Antonio, Dalton, Emily, Gavin, Daniella. And Ming, and . . .*

He and the other missing kids were from different places and different centuries, and in the beginning the only connection they'd had was that Gary and Hodge had kidnapped all of them and put them on the same airplane. And then abandoned all of them when they were being chased by time agents.

But that was a lot to have in common. It was almost like they were his family now too. Today Jonah hadn't just lost his sister and the adult versions of his parents—he'd also lost all the kids who were most like him.

"Why?" Jonah asked. "Where did they all go? Who took them?"

JB shrugged helplessly. Jonah shoved Angela aside and stood back up.

"I don't see Charles Lindbergh in any of those scenes," Jonah said, peering at one screen after another. JB had apparently set them on a loop, so the disappearances kept replaying. It made things that much worse, to watch thirty-five kids vanish again and again and again. "Why did he show up in our living room to grab Katherine, but everyone else just vanished?"

"Because Katherine's not a missing kid from history?" Angela said. But she didn't sound sure even of that.

"I am, though," Jonah said, his voice shaking. "Why didn't I disappear along with everyone else?"

"Maybe because Charles Lindbergh was already there in your house kidnapping Katherine at about the same time?" JB suggested. "Like, his presence jammed the frequencies somehow?"

*Losing my sister protected me?* Jonah thought.

It wasn't a bargain he would have made, if he'd had the choice. Maybe three months ago, when Katherine was annoying him constantly, but . . .

*No, not even then,* Jonah thought.

"Wait a minute," Angela said. She was still sitting on the ground, but squinting up at the wall full of screens. "*Was* Katherine kidnapped at the exact same time that everyone else vanished?"

"These are low-tech monitors," JB said apologetically. "I can't get exact timing without hooking them to an Elucidator that actually works."

"Can you show us Katherine being taken away?" Jonah asked.

"Sure," JB said.

He typed something into the keyboard on the wall, and one of the monitors shut down in the midst of its endless loop of missing children vanishing over and over again. Instead Jonah watched himself and Katherine gaping at the tall man who'd suddenly appeared in their living room; he saw Lindbergh checking items off his list; he saw Lindbergh grab Katherine and vanish.

Jonah gulped.

"Replay it," he told JB, because he'd forgotten to watch for the one detail he'd wanted to see.

"Are you sure?" Angela said. "You kind of look like you might faint or something."

"I'm sure!" Jonah insisted.

This time Jonah kept looking back and forth between Lindbergh and the clock on the mantelpiece behind the man. He gritted his teeth and watched until the exact moment that Lindbergh and Katherine disappeared.

"There!" Jonah said. "Lindbergh and Katherine disappeared a few minutes before seven. It's right there on the clock behind them."

"Do your parents keep that clock set to atomic-clock precision?" kid JB asked. "Can you be sure that that's the exact right time?"

"Oh—no," Jonah admitted.

How was he supposed to remember things like atomic-clock precision when his head was spinning and his knees were weak and he kept thinking, *How can I save Katherine? How can I make my parents normal again? Why was I the only missing kid left behind?*

He wasn't letting his brain think, *Am I the son of that man I've watched kidnap my sister three times now?*

"Can't we at least look and see if Chip's mom turned into a thirteen-year-old before or after Chip vanished?" Angela suggested.

"Oh, good idea," JB said. "Let me see."

He began fiddling with the keyboard on the wall again. Jonah fixed his attention on the monitor showing Chip there and gone, there and gone, there and gone . . . The screen just kept showing the same scene again and again and again. Chip's mom was nowhere in sight.

"Sorry," JB said, stepping back from the keyboard. "She was standing too far away. Without an Elucidator, I can't . . ."

"Do anything," Jonah finished for him. He kicked the rock wall.

"But you can see every single one of the missing kids," Angela said, sounding confused. "Why does that still work?"

JB squirmed uncomfortably in place, shifting from foot to foot.

"These monitors were preset to . . . um . . . er . . . ," he began.

"Spy on us, right?" Jonah said bitterly. "Was it all set up by Gary and Hodge when they were using this cave, or was that a change you time agents put in place?"

"Gary and Hodge started it," JB said defensively.

Jonah couldn't understand why he felt so upset. He'd known all along that time travelers—both his friends and his enemies—were able to watch his actions practically whenever they wanted.

Seeing these monitors just made it real.

"So why can't we still see where all these kids went next?" Angela asked. "The monitors are connected to watching every moment of their lives, right?"

"Only in this portion of the twenty-first century," JB said apologetically. "These monitors can't follow them if their time paths are interrupted."

On one of his early time-travel trips, Jonah had gotten a sort of vaccine that enabled him to understand and speak other languages in other time periods. He wished he'd also gotten some sort of mind implant that would allow him to translate the garbled terminology time travelers used.

"You mean this proves that they were all taken out of the twenty-first century," Jonah said, trying to figure out the translation on his own. "They didn't just turn invisible; they weren't just zapped to some other place—they were taken to another time. And Katherine was too."

JB started to nod; then he stopped himself and tilted his head thoughtfully.

"Well, we don't actually know for sure about Katherine," he said. "The monitor only shows Katherine vanishing because she was standing next to you at the time—it's gauged to your actions, not hers. If we wanted to, we could actually continue showing what you did after Katherine disappeared."

"That's okay," Jonah said quickly. He didn't want JB and Angela to see how desperately he'd waved his arms around, searching for Katherine; how despairingly he'd run into the kitchen calling for his parents.

"I guess there's no way to watch Charles Lindbergh right before or right after this moment either," Angela said. "I wish we could just see him talking to Gary and Hodge before showing up at the Skidmores' house . . ."

"Oh," kid JB said, jerking his body oddly, as if he'd just thought of something that surprised him. "We can actually watch Lindbergh from these monitors. Some of his earlier life, anyway."

Angela looked as puzzled as Jonah felt.

"Why him and not Katherine?" she asked.

JB squinted hard. He seemed to be struggling to remember something, maybe something that he would have expected to know easily.

"Um . . . because he's connected to one of the missing kids from history?" kid JB said, and it was strange how doubtful his voice sounded.

Angela turned her head toward Jonah as if she was

waiting for him to speak next. Jonah didn't say anything. Angela sighed.

"Is it Jonah?" she asked. "Is Jonah related to Charles Lindbergh?"

Jonah gulped in a deep breath and held it. He could barely force himself to look at JB to see if he would nod his head yes or shake his head no.

JB did neither of those things. He scrunched up his face even harder, like a kid in school who'd encountered a virtually impossible question on a test.

"I—I don't know," he said, sounding stunned.

"You are such a liar!" Jonah exploded. He balled up his fists and took a step closer to JB. "I asked you about my original identity days ago—well, before we went back to 1918. I asked you again when I was healing from the bullet wounds. You sure acted like you knew then! Like you knew but you weren't going to tell me!"

"I did know then!" JB insisted, cowering before Jonah. "But—it's gone now. I've forgotten!"

# THIRTEEN

Jonah took a step back. He didn't want to believe JB. He would have preferred to keep looming over the smaller boy—maybe even punch him a time or two—until JB screamed, *All right! All right! I was lying! I'll tell you everything! You're really . . .*

But Jonah did believe JB. The boy looked so baffled, so anguished—he had to be telling the truth.

"You're forgetting things too?" Angela said softly.

"Nothing else as important as this," JB assured her. "But it's like there's a war going on inside my head. I keep wanting to think in German."

"German?" Jonah repeated incredulously.

Then he understood. A long time ago—in a different century, a different life—JB had been somebody else. During all the unraveling of identities with the missing children, JB had discovered that he himself had once had a different identity in a different time as well: He'd been the troubled second son of Albert and Mileva Einstein. To save him from the ravages of a mental illness that wasn't curable in the twentieth century, Mileva Einstein had secretly sent him on to the future.

"So . . . you're forgetting your life as JB and remembering your life as Tete Einstein?" Jonah asked, trying to figure everything out.

"Kind of, but not exactly," JB said. "It's more like . . . everything's frayed and patched and jumbled together. The wires keep getting crossed, and I'm having trouble telling the memories apart. What I told you about my mother boiling a pan of water for steam for me to breathe in? I'm pretty sure that that was Mileva Einstein, not my adoptive mom."

"Yeah," Angela said as if she'd just thought of something. "Didn't you tell me once that doctors can cure asthma by your time period in the future?"

"Probably," JB said. His face twisted again. "But—I don't remember."

*Katherine's been kidnapped, all the other missing kids besides me have disappeared, Mom and Dad are teenagers and knocked out, JB and Angela are teenagers who are losing their memories—what could go wrong next?* Jonah wondered.

He decided he probably shouldn't ask that question. He turned to Angela.

"Do *you* have some secret second identity you're starting to remember now too?" he asked.

Angela laughed, and at least that was a reassuring sound.

"I've never been anybody but myself," she said. "And I guess this proves it. I'm not remembering any other childhood but my own. It's just . . . some of my memories are getting vague and, well, *questionable.* I think that'd be the word for it. It's like I'm losing certainty."

JB frowned, as if concentrating hard.

"I remember . . . this is why the original time rescuers found they couldn't go back in time and snatch endangered adults and un-age them back to being adoptable babies," he said. "The adult brain is too established. Kids' brains are still malleable and adaptable. Your brain can handle the changes. If someone tried to turn me back into a baby again, my mind would be . . . mush."

Jonah cast an anxious glance over his shoulder toward the car where both of his parents sat, totally unaware.

"But you only went back to thirteen, not all the way to babyhood," he said pleadingly. "Your mind *mostly* still works right. When you and Angela and Mom and Dad are turned back into adults again—you'll be fine then, won't you?"

JB shrugged hopelessly.

"It's not something that's been tested," he said. "There are some experiments you just can't do."

Jonah gulped.

"Maybe we should try to make sure you spend as little time as possible as a thirteen-year-old?" he asked. "Maybe we should . . . fix everything as fast as we can?"

"Be my guest," JB said, gesturing helplessly at the wall full of monitors, the images of Jonah's sister and friend vanishing again and again and again.

Jonah watched Charles Lindbergh grab Katherine for the umpteenth time.

*Whether he's my biological father or not, that's not what matters right now,* Jonah thought.

"You said we should be able to watch some of Charles Lindbergh's life, because he's connected to *someone* who's a missing child in history," Jonah said to JB. "Right? Maybe we can't see where Lindbergh took Katherine, but can't we do what Angela suggested, and try to find him talking to Gary and Hodge beforehand? Making plans to kidnap her?"

JB gave Jonah another puzzled squint.

"I guess . . . we could try," he said.

Jonah pulled out the cell phone again and called up the picture Katherine had taken of Lindbergh.

"How old do you think he looks here?" Jonah asked. "Let's check his life right before he's this age."

Angela peered down at the picture.

"Late twenties?" she guessed. "Early thirties? He was twenty-five when he flew to Paris. I do remember that."

"We'll start with that, then, and work forward," JB said.

He began typing on the wall keyboard again. Jonah noticed that he stopped every few moments to rub his hand across his forehead. Had JB been doing that all along? Or were his memory problems getting worse?

*Nothing's supposed to get worse in a time hollow,* Jonah reminded himself. *Nothing's supposed to change at all.*

Then he stopped watching JB because Angela gasped beside him.

"That's Lindbergh's plane," she said in an amazed-sounding voice. "The *Spirit of St. Louis.* The real thing, not the one from the Jimmy Stewart movie."

Jonah looked up at one of the monitors, where a small silver airplane seemed suspended over a vast spread of water. There was no land in sight.

"Zoom in," Angela suggested.

JB rubbed his forehead again and typed in some kind of code.

The airplane took up a larger and larger portion of the monitor's screen. And then something odd happened.

Jonah's head began spinning. The lights of the time hollow seemed to blink out, and Jonah felt like he was falling. Down, down, down . . .

He felt like he was going to fall into the ocean below the small silver airplane, which was crazy, because he was still in the time hollow—wasn't he?

Everything spun around him, and Jonah felt the same sped-up sensation he always felt traveling through time, right before landing. Jonah broke through a cloud, and something silver glinted beside him in the moonlight. He threw his arms out without even thinking about it, and his fingers brushed something metal. He grabbed on tightly.

"Do I see spirits? I'm hallucinating. . . . Stay awake!" a voice said, just above Jonah's head.

Jonah looked up, toward his own hands, which were clutched onto the rim of a window. An airplane window.

And through that window Charles Lindbergh was looking down toward Jonah.

# FOURTEEN

*I'm back in Charles Lindbergh's time,* Jonah thought dazedly. *I'm with him, flying across the Atlantic.*

"What? What's happening?" Lindbergh said, turning frantically away from the window.

The action sent up a burst of light. Jonah could no longer see Lindbergh himself, but a glowing, ghostlike version of him who still had his head hung out the window, staring down toward Jonah and the water below.

*His tracer,* Jonah thought, his heart sinking. *I've just changed time.*

Jonah *hated* tracers, the ghostly representations of what would have happened in original time if no time travelers had intervened. Only time travelers could see them, and they were almost always a sign of trouble. On Jonah's previous trips through time they had caused him no end of anguish and worry.

Although he'd also discovered during his time in the 1600s that *not* seeing tracers when you were supposed to could be a very bad sign too.

"Are we slowing down?" Lindbergh was muttering above him. "Could there be more drag all of a sudden? And more on the right than the left . . ."

*Um, yeah,* Jonah thought. *Because I'm hanging on to the right-side window.*

The soft glow of Lindbergh's tracer gave a little more light to see by than just the moon and the stars. Jonah turned his head right and left, hoping to see someplace he could move to that wouldn't create worse problems.

*Like maybe a seat in first class?* he told himself.

He was being ridiculous. Lindbergh's plane was tiny, almost toylike. The window Jonah was clinging to didn't even have glass in it. He couldn't actually see into the cockpit, but he could tell there would only be room in there for one seat: Lindbergh's. It was like Lindbergh was flying over the entire Atlantic Ocean in a slightly modified tin can.

*No,* Jonah thought, suddenly figuring out what he had his face pressed against on the side of the plane. *Most of this plane isn't even metal. It's cloth.*

"Psst, Jonah," someone hissed at him. "Do you think you could climb over to the other side?"

Jonah looked down toward the voice and almost had a heart attack.

There, clinging to a support under the wing, were kid JB and kid Angela.

All three of them had come back to Lindbergh's time. All three of them were on the right side of the plane.

"Not . . . sure . . . how . . . long . . . can hold . . . on," Angela whispered.

Jonah realized he couldn't actually feel his fingers. If it was just the numbness of timesickness, that would wear off in a moment or two. But with his face turned away from the plane, now he could tell exactly how biting and cold the wind was. His face was going numb now too.

"I'll see . . . what I can do," Jonah hissed back to the other two. Though maybe it didn't come out like that, since his tongue felt numb and clumsy and useless too.

With great effort he started pulling his body up toward the window.

*No different from doing a chin-up in phys ed class,* he told himself.

That was a lie. Everyone thought Mr. Grunnion, the phys ed teacher, was mean, but he had never once made Jonah or any of the other kids do a chin-up while dangling thousands of feet above the ocean, in the freezing air, while the metal rim of an airplane's window cut into his fingers.

*Oh, great. Now's the perfect time to start feeling my hands again,* Jonah thought.

It was almost unbelievable, but Jonah's biceps really were pulling his head and the rest of his body up. He inched higher and higher. He had some vague notion that he could lift his whole torso above the level of his hands, and then bring a foot up to stand on the window ledge. And then maybe he could flip himself over onto the top of the wing. . . .

Jonah's knee hit something hard. He looked down.

*Oh, stupid me,* he thought, squinting down into the darkness. *There's another support there I could just stand on.*

He brought his foot up onto the metal beam, which—Jonah squinted—also seemed to stretch up to the wing, to hold it in place.

*This is a lot easier than chin-ups,* Jonah thought, cautiously starting to stand up. The wing was right above the plane's window—he didn't want to bang his head.

Jonah edged up high enough that his face drew even with the bottom of the window ledge. Now he could see into the fuselage. By the light of Lindbergh's glowing tracer, Jonah could see the crude, primitive instrument panel, the piles of maps, the pilot's seat—*Is that wicker?* Jonah thought. *It's just made out of wicker? Lindbergh's flying across the ocean on patio furniture?*

It was a moment before Jonah figured out where Lindbergh himself was, because he was only partly separated from his tracer, and Jonah had to look *through* the tracer to see him. The real Lindbergh had his body turned toward the interior portion of the plane right behind the window. There was some sort of shelf there, and Lindbergh was pulling down a clear rectangular piece of glass or plastic or something like it.

*Did they even have plastic back in the 1920s?* Jonah wondered.

Lindbergh turned, moving the rectangular whatever-it-was toward the window on the other side of the plane. The rectangle seemed to be almost exactly the same size and shape as the window.

*Oh, it's like he's putting the glass back in that window,* Jonah thought. *That's a really high-tech way to roll up a window, Charlie!*

That window pane slid into place. Then Lindbergh picked up another rectangular piece and turned toward the window whose edge Jonah was clinging to.

"Oh, no—don't!" Jonah said without thinking, because he suddenly saw how Lindbergh closing the window would leave Jonah nothing to hold on to.

Lindbergh froze.

"Who said that?" he asked.

Before Jonah could say or do anything, Lindbergh

reached into his jacket and whipped out a flashlight. He shone it directly into Jonah's face.

"Aaaahhh!" Jonah and Lindbergh both screamed at the same time.

Jonah's numb fingers slipped off the window rim. He fell backward. Fortunately, his right knee caught around the support bar beneath him. Now he was dangling upside down over the ocean.

On the other support bar, kid JB and kid Angela screamed out, "Jonah, be careful!" and "Are you all right?"

Above them all, Lindbergh thrust his head out the window again. He swept the flashlight back and forth in the darkness. The light landed on kid JB and kid Angela, who froze in terror.

"Who are you?" Lindbergh screamed. "How is this even possible?"

He jerked back from the window, hitting something inside the plane so hard that even Jonah heard the thud.

And then, barely an instant later, the plane began to plummet toward the water.

# FIFTEEN

"No!" Jonah and JB and Angela all screamed together. Maybe inside the plane Lindbergh was screaming too.

The wind whistled through Jonah's hair. He was falling fast. It was too dark below him to see how close the water was, and anyhow it hurt to keep his eyes open against the rushing wind. But Jonah had a thousand images in his head from movies and video games about what was going to happen next:

*We crash, maybe the engine explodes, everyone dies . . .*

The wind was so loud he could barely hear Angela on the other support above him, praying or screaming or crying, "Please! Save us! Get us back to the time hollow!"

And then Jonah stopped falling. He stopped moving at all. He just lay still, struggling to understand why none of what he'd imagined had come true.

*Maybe this is what being dead is like . . . except wouldn't I remember the crash and the explosion?*

He forced himself to open his eyes, and there was no brutal, cold wind to blind him anymore. He still had to blink two or three times to make sense of what he saw around him: not water and sky. Rock.

He really was back in the time hollow.

Someone groaned beside him—kid JB.

"That shouldn't have worked," he muttered. "There was no reason we should have been able to come back here. . . ."

"I have a better question: How'd we end up back in Charles Lindbergh's time in the first place?" Angela said from the other side of Jonah.

JB sat up.

"Yeah . . . about that . . . I should have remembered," he said, grimacing.

"Remembered what?" Angela demanded, wincing as she propped herself up on one arm. "To bring a parachute or two before jumping onto Lindbergh's plane?"

"And maybe a blow-up raft?" Jonah asked, sitting up as well.

"No . . . ," JB said. "I should have remembered to double-check the code, since the one to *watch* a certain time is very similar to the one for actually going there. . . ."

He gingerly stood up and walked over to the wall, where he started flashing back through screenfuls of information.

"That's weird," he said. "I did do it right."

"Well, okay, whatever," Jonah said. "If those monitors can send us back in time without an Elucidator, let's go back to this morning and stop Charles Lindbergh from kidnapping Katherine! And everyone else from disappearing!"

He jumped up, ready for this next mission. For some reason JB and Angela didn't look so excited.

"We can't, remember?" JB said, frowning. "All three of us already lived through that time period. You can't go back to the same time and relive it a second time. You can only go to new times—moments you haven't been to before."

"Oh, right," Jonah said. He'd known that. It was just easy to forget.

"Okay, okay," Angela said, waving her hand in a way that seemed to forgive Jonah for being so stupid. "We don't know exactly how the monitor malfunctioned to send us back to 1927. Was it the same malfunction that brought us back here?"

Kid JB looked more puzzled than ever.

"It couldn't have," he said. "A low-tech monitor like this wouldn't have that range."

"Your Elucidator didn't suddenly start working again, did it?" Jonah asked.

JB pulled a small electronic device out of his pocket and held it up to his mouth, like someone giving voice commands to an iPhone.

"Show screen," he said. "Show recent actions. Show power reading. Show anything you've got!"

He lowered his hand.

"It's still broken," he said.

"Didn't seem like it back in 1927," Angela said. "I screamed out, 'Get us back to the time hollow!' and, like, one second later, here we were."

"It was like a miracle," Jonah said. "I thought we were dead, for sure."

JB jerked his head up to look directly at Jonah.

"Dead—that's it!" he said.

"Oh yeah, that would have been it for all of us," Angela said.

"No, no—it was because you were in fear for your life," JB said. He began hitting his head. "Oh, I am an idiot!"

Angela and Jonah watched him cautiously.

"Uh, do you want to tell us your evidence for that, and see if we agree?" Angela asked.

"The Elucidator is *voice* activated!" JB said. "This one is set only to my voice, which is standard agency operating procedure in a situation like we had this morning. But when I went back to being a thirteen-year-old again, my voice changed. The Elucidator didn't recognize it anymore!"

"So when Lindbergh's plane was falling toward the ocean and you were screaming like a little girl, *then* the Elucidator knew who you were?" Angela asked.

Jonah couldn't help himself: He laughed.

JB just shook his head.

"No," he said. "Then the Elucidator recognized *your* voice, Angela. Standard operating procedure is also that, and I quote: "'When a time agent is in the field accompanied by a time rookie, even if the time agent must keep his/her Elucidator set at extreme security, the setting must also allow for the time rookie to request assistance in the event of potentially fatal consequences. . . .'"

"So I'm just a time rookie to you guys?" Angela asked. "And you people really haven't figured out some other way in the future to say 'his/her' without actually saying 'his/her'?"

*So JB can still remember complicated time regulations, but he really can't remember my original identity?* Jonah wondered. "How about you translate that into regular English?" he asked.

Kid JB nodded, some of his normal confidence returning.

"In almost every case, this Elucidator will only respond to my voice—my normal adult voice," he said, peering hopefully down at the Elucidator in his hand, even as he strained to make his voice sound deeper. Evidently the Elucidator wasn't convinced, because kid JB shrugged and put it back into his pocket. "But because Angela was the time rookie in my care, when we really were in a life-threatening situation, the Elucidator took orders from her instead."

Angela seemed to be thinking hard about that one.

"So, hey," Jonah said. "I'll threaten to kill Angela, and she'll wish for an Elucidator all her own to save her, and then we'll have a way to solve all our problems."

JB shook his head.

"You can't manipulate it that easily," he said. "The Elucidator knows you wouldn't really kill Angela. It has to be a 'true, credible threat.'"

Jonah thought he was quoting again.

Angela's eyes got wide.

"So we really were about to crash into the ocean," she said. "And Charles Lindbergh—what happened to him after we were saved?"

JB put his hands against his face in dismay and darted his eyes toward Jonah.

*Is he watching me to see if I'll just suddenly stop existing?* Jonah wondered. *Because if Charles Lindbergh was my biological father, and we changed time to make him crash into the ocean before I was even born—then* would *I still exist?*

Jonah crossed his arms and clutched his own biceps. He *felt* normal. His biceps weren't exactly bulging and muscular, but that wasn't any different than usual.

"I don't know what happened to Charles Lindbergh next," JB said in a panicky voice. "I don't know if he survived, or . . ."

"Let's look!" Angela said, pointing to the wall full of monitors.

Jonah realized that the screen that had contained the view of the *Spirit of St. Louis* now held nothing but random dark-and-light pixels, even as the rest of the monitors kept showing endless loops of his friends and his sister vanishing.

"Angela, we can't," kid JB said, his face twisted with worry again. "I don't trust these monitors. No matter how carefully I set the coding, we could end up dangling from that little plane again."

"So? I'll just scream for help and the Elucidator will rescue us again," kid Angela said.

"And then, even if Charles Lindbergh survived his last encounter with us, this time we really could end up killing him?" kid JB asked.

Jonah could see why this might not be a good idea.

"Then let's go to some other time in Lindbergh's life after that, to see if he's there or not," kid Angela argued. "We have to find out! What about—what about when he lands in Paris? It was kind of like a stampede; everyone was so eager to get close to Lindbergh. So that would be life-threatening too. People *were* in danger of dying. So that way I'd scream and we'd get back here right away."

*Angela's using "It's life-threatening!" as an argument for doing this?* Jonah marveled.

She would never have done that as an adult.

JB wasn't disagreeing. He had his head tilted sideways, considering.

"In the early days of time travel, Lindbergh landing in Paris was one of the moments in history that a lot of people wanted to go visit," kid JB said. "They loved the excitement, the sense of triumph—it was one of those moments of pure joy. . . ."

"Okay, that's even better," Jonah said. "So why don't we just go meet up with one of those time travelers? We could hitchhike back home with them. Or ask to borrow their Elucidator."

"Exactly what I was thinking," kid JB said. He started punching codes into the keyboard on the wall. "Except I wasn't going to ask. Anybody ready to play Grand Theft Elucidator?"

# SIXTEEN

Jonah stood with the other two in front of the wall full of monitors. They'd taken a short break because JB had suddenly realized that they couldn't appear in 1920s Paris in twenty-first-century blue jeans and T-shirts. Until they got a working Elucidator, they wouldn't have the protection of invisibility.

Fortunately, it turned out that there was a small stash of what JB called "emergency costumes" at the back of the cave. Now Jonah and kid JB were both wearing light pullover sweaters; a weird kind of pants that ended at their knees; and stiff, uncomfortable brown shoes. Angela had on what she called a "flapper" dress. It just looked baggy and shapeless to Jonah.

"Ready?" JB said, stepping toward the keyboard in the wall. "I can't do projections ahead of time, and I can't target our landing position very precisely, so we may have to react quickly when we arrive."

"We know," Jonah said impatiently. "You've already said that ten times."

Had becoming thirteen again turned JB into an even bigger worrywart than he had been as an adult?

Or was he repeating himself because he couldn't remember what he'd said before?

"Oh, right," JB said sheepishly, in a way that made it *seem* like he knew what he was saying.

He started typing in the code. Jonah felt his muscles tighten up. This was like standing on the sidelines of a soccer game, on the verge of being sent in to play. Except in a soccer game Jonah only worried about messing up and letting the other team get the ball. This time he was worried about ruining all of history and making time collapse and not being able to rescue Katherine or fix his parents.

Oh yeah—and dying. He was worried about dying, too.

JB stepped back from the wall. The monitor that had sent them into the past to cling to Lindbergh's plane was coming back to life again.

*Oh no,* Jonah suddenly thought. *Did JB or Angela think about what would happen if the monitor sends us back in a way that has us on the plane again? What if us being there makes Lindbergh crash into a crowd of thousands of people?*

There wasn't time to ask. As soon as the scene on the monitor came into focus—showing hordes of people packed together near an array of bright lights—Jonah's head began spinning and he felt himself falling.

"Tried to aim for . . . back of crowd," JB mumbled beside him. Or maybe it was above or below him. Jonah's sense of direction had vanished.

It seemed like only a moment later that Jonah felt solid earth beneath him.

*Timesickness . . . shouldn't be as bad this time,* he told himself. *Since I was already in the 1920s before . . .*

His senses of sight and hearing were coming in and out, but he could feel someone pulling on his sweater.

"Get up! Not enough room . . . to lie on ground!" kid JB was commanding him.

Jonah wasn't sure his legs would work—especially now that being out of the time cave had reawakened the pain from hitting his knee on Lindbergh's plane over the Atlantic, and his older wounds from being shot back in 1918. But it wasn't just JB tugging on him. Dozens of hands were yanking him upright.

"Such a shame! People fainting with the excitement!" someone yelled near his ear.

"And the waiting!" someone else screamed back.

The crowd surged around him, filling in the space

Jonah had taken up when he'd been flat on the ground. Jonah felt dizzy enough that he thought he might faint for real. But even if he did, he didn't think he could actually fall to the ground—he was packed in too tightly along with the rest of the crowd.

*Someone said "waiting"—does that mean Lindbergh's not here yet?* Jonah wondered.

Had the monitor sent them back a little too early? Or was Lindbergh never going to arrive because Jonah, JB, and Angela had made him crash into the ocean?

Jonah blinked a few times to get his eyes to work right, and he pounded his hand against the side of his head in hopes that that would make his ears work better. He made himself think about what language the people around him were speaking—was it French? Were they definitely in France? Having the ability to understand all languages in all time periods sometimes made it hard for Jonah to remember that he wasn't just constantly hearing English.

On his third blink Jonah's eyes cleared up completely, and he instantly wished they hadn't.

Now he could see that beside him, kid JB and kid Angela were gazing around with looks of absolute dismay on their faces.

And streaming past all of them were hordes of tracers.

It was like a stampede of ghosts, the wispy versions

of thousands of Parisians flowing through and past Jonah, and through and past every single one of the real people standing around him. The ghostly tracers all looked triumphant and overjoyed—maybe like fans storming a football field after their team had just won a national championship.

The real Parisians standing around Jonah looked hopeful and expectant but maybe also a little worried.

*And the real people and the tracers are different because . . . ,* Jonah thought.

He rose up on his tiptoes and looked in the direction all the tracers were running: Yes, there was a small tracer plane descending toward the ground, appearing out of the night sky.

But it was only a tracer. No actual plane was anywhere in sight.

*Because Charles Lindbergh was supposed to be in sight now,* Jonah thought. *He's supposed to be landing, and all the Parisians who have been waiting for him are supposed to be storming the runway, and . . . and . . . he's supposed to have survived!*

Jonah turned his head toward kid JB, ready to say, *Is this our fault? Did we kill Charles Lindbergh?*

But just then a cheer went up. It was like everyone in the crowd was speaking with a single voice, everyone screaming together, "There he is!"

Jonah looked up and saw a *real* plane overhead. It truly was the plane Charles Lindbergh had piloted across the Atlantic. He'd made it to Paris—even with the little distraction of three time travelers surprising him in the midst of his trip.

But Jonah had no time to say or do anything, not even to cry, "There he is!" along with everyone else. Because instantly the crowd was pressing against him even tighter. The people behind him were rushing forward, and the people in front of him had nowhere to go because of all the people in front of them.

"Hold on! Just wait a minute!" Jonah tried to scream at the people behind them.

But maybe he accidently yelled in English rather than French—or maybe they couldn't hear him—because the people from behind just kept pressing forward.

Jonah still wasn't sure that his legs were working very well yet, but it almost didn't seem to matter. The pressure of the crowd carried him along.

"Jonah! JB! We've got to stay together!" kid Angela screamed.

Jonah reached out his arm and grabbed for Angela's hand or arm or *something*. He caught her by the sleeve and the material ripped away in his hands. But then Angela wrapped her hand around his wrist, and he was able to wrap his hand around hers. He couldn't actually see the rest of her because of the crowd, but he was *so* glad she had darker skin than the other people around them. At least he knew he was holding on to the right person.

Jonah reached out his other hand and somehow managed to grab on to kid JB's arm.

"Get us out of here!" Angela was screaming. "Get us out of here!"

Nothing changed. The crowd just kept surging around them.

*So . . . the Elucidator doesn't really believe our lives are in danger?* Jonah wondered.

Maybe this should have made him feel better, but it didn't.

Still a little numb from the timesickness, Jonah let himself be carried forward with the rest of the crowd. Back in 1600 he'd had a moment of almost drowning, and this was the same sensation: He couldn't control which way the crowd carried him any more than he could have controlled the storm-tossed waves off Roanoke Island.

"Try . . . looking . . . around . . . ," JB said, which was ridiculous, because Jonah wasn't even sure he could control the direction his head was pointed. He caught glimpses of the sky, the ground, the elbow of the man in front of him, someone's cap lying on the ground . . .

The next time Jonah got his head turned toward the place where he'd seen Lindbergh's plane before, it was much lower in the sky, and Jonah could actually read the words "Spirit of St. Louis" on the side. Lindbergh was leaning out the window and yelling. Jonah couldn't tell what he was saying, but the pilot didn't look happy at the sight of all the people welcoming him to Paris. He waved his arm, and it wasn't a *Hey! Good to see you! Glad to be here!* type of wave. It looked more like he was trying to tell the crowd, *Get out of the way!*

*Oh, um . . . are there so many people down here that there's nowhere for Lindbergh to land?* Jonah wondered.

Lindbergh's plane came closer and closer.

*Does he maybe not even have enough fuel left that he could go somewhere else to land?* Jonah thought.

Some in the crowd apparently understood what Lindbergh's wave meant—or maybe they heard what he'd yelled—because they began scurrying off to the side, out of the direct range of the plane. But they just collided with others in the crowd who didn't understand, who just wanted to keep running toward Lindbergh to be the first to give him a hero's welcome.

And then maybe even those people understood, because the area around Jonah seemed to empty out. Jonah tugged JB and Angela closer and yelled to both of them, "We've got to run to the side! Out of the way!"

They both squinted at Jonah like they couldn't quite hear him, or couldn't quite understand—or maybe couldn't quite get their bodies to do what they wanted either. Maybe, without the crowd carrying them, they couldn't even walk well, let alone run. Angela half turned toward Jonah. And then Jonah could tell that she was looking past him; her eyes got bigger, and she put her hand over her mouth like she was too terrified to scream.

Jonah whirled around as best he could to see what she was looking at.

There, directly behind him—only inches away and speeding closer—was the whirring propeller of Lindbergh's plane.

# SEVENTEEN

*So this is how I'm going to die,* Jonah thought.

Beside him Angela screamed, "Get us out of here! Take us back to the cave!"

Jonah squeezed his eyes together because he didn't want to see the propeller hitting him or JB or Angela. He felt a floating sensation.

When he opened his eyes again, he really was back in the time cave.

"That . . . was too close," he moaned.

"And for all that, we didn't get an Elucidator," JB groaned beside him.

Angela sat up woozily.

"That propeller wasn't really that nearby, was it?" she asked.

"Oh yeah," Jonah said, sitting up as well. "Timesickness

messes up your sense of distance. So the propeller just seemed like it was seconds away from hitting us."

"No, it really was that close," JB said grimly. "I'd say that we had less than a second left."

Jonah shivered even though he knew it wasn't technically possible to feel cold in a time hollow.

"So now do we have to worry about changing time, because thousands of Parisians saw three kids vanish into thin air the minute Lindbergh landed?" Angela asked.

How could she have been less than a second away from death and shift so quickly into worrying about the effect of her actions on time?

"My guess is that there will be all sorts of fantastical stories floating around about that moment," kid JB said. "But no one will actually believe them. There were fantastical stories about that moment anyway. I think we're safe."

"I saw an entire airplane vanish into thin air, and nobody believed me," Angela muttered.

Jonah knew she was talking about the airplane that had carried Jonah and the other missing children from the past to their modern-day lives.

Kid JB sat up and scooted over so he had the rock wall of the cave holding him up. He rubbed his temples, his face contorted as though he had a killer headache.

"So, okay, that didn't work," Jonah said. "I guess we

didn't make anything worse, and at least now we know we didn't actually murder Charles Lindbergh. But what should we do next? We've got to get Katherine back!"

JB kept rubbing his temples. Angela frowned.

"Is there some other moment in Charles Lindbergh's life we could go to?" she asked. "Someplace we know we could get an Elucidator, but we'd have a little bit more time before I'd have to scream, 'Get us back to the time cave!'?"

JB pulled his hands back from his forehead as if just that simple motion was a huge challenge. Jonah could tell that the other boy was gritting his teeth.

"I should be able to remember more about Lindbergh," JB moaned. "But . . ."

"But what?" Jonah asked.

JB winced.

"There's only one other moment I can think of that might work," kid JB said.

"That's better than none!" Angela said. Jonah could tell that she was trying very, very hard to sound hopeful.

"There's got to be some other way," JB said, shaking his head as though he was fighting with himself over what to do. He squinted toward the rock wall across from him. "Maybe if . . . no, that won't work. Or . . . no, if the time agency hasn't come for us yet, there's no way we can expect them to help. Or . . . no, not that either."

A long moment passed, with kid JB just staring at the wall.

Jonah racked his brain, but he knew so little about Charles Lindbergh that he didn't expect to think of anything. He couldn't think of any other solution that wasn't connected to Lindbergh either.

*Because he's the one who stole Katherine,* he thought stubbornly. *Because we don't just need to find a working Elucidator—we also need to see Lindbergh with Gary and Hodge, to find out what "deal" Lindbergh was supposed to seal by carrying off Katherine.*

"If you know of even one thing that will work, then that's what we need to do," Jonah told JB. "Let's stop wasting time and just do it!"

JB turned his head slowly toward Jonah. Jonah remembered how, when he'd first seen JB as a thirteen-year-old, Jonah had thought that all the girls in middle school would be in love with the other boy. But maybe that wouldn't be the case now. JB's hair was a total mess, and his shirt was ripped and hanging from his arms in shreds. He also looked a little . . . wild-eyed.

Angela's hair was just as messed up, and one of her sleeves was ripped, probably where Jonah himself had torn it. But her face at least still looked normal.

"The problem is . . . ," JB began slowly, "the only time I can think of to go to is when Lindbergh's son was kidnapped."

Jonah gulped, but tried to hide it.

"So?" he asked, trying to put on an air of bravado. He could tell by the other two kids' faces that they could see right through it.

"So, if you are Lindbergh's son—and that *seems* right; *maybe* you are—you wouldn't be able to live through that time period again," JB said.

"But with his tracer . . . ," Angela began. She stopped, then froze as if she'd just thought of something horrible. She brought her hand up toward her mouth. "Ohhh . . ."

"I'm not talking about when Gary and Hodge kidnapped Lindbergh's son, leaving behind a tracer that Jonah could join with, if that's who he is," JB said. "I'm talking about the kidnapping in original time. When I can't remember what happened next."

Jonah wanted to say *So?* again. Because if they were talking about going to a time where Lindbergh's son was still present, that wasn't Jonah's problem. He wouldn't end up there.

Angela was still grimacing.

"So the monitor might suck the two of us back into the past but leave Jonah right here?" she asked JB. "Because he can't be duplicated in time?"

JB nodded. He seemed to be struggling to keep his gaze on Jonah's face. Jonah thought that he could still see the real JB in that gaze—regardless of his age, regardless of his memory problems, regardless of that whole other life he'd lived as Tete Einstein. JB was still trying to do his best for Jonah.

"But . . . but . . . ," Jonah began. No matter how scared he was, he couldn't let the other two chicken out because of worrying about him. "This is a time hollow. You'd vanish and then, to me, no time at all would pass before you'd be back! With an Elucidator! And then we could find Katherine, and—you've got to do it!"

JB turned and looked at Angela. She shrugged and nodded.

"I think he's right," she said quietly.

JB made a rueful face and stood up.

"And anyhow, I've got my parents to keep me company!" Jonah said, trying to make a joke. He looked toward the car, where Mom and Dad still sat, totally unconscious.

JB took a deep breath and walked unsteadily toward the keyboard in the wall. He typed something quickly, and then stood back to watch the monitor's screen.

The screen was dark and empty.

*No, not empty,* Jonah thought, starting to make out shapes in the darkness. *It's just showing nighttime. And this night looks cloudy and moonless.*

He could see a ladder leaning against the side of a house—a kidnapper's ladder, maybe?

Instinctively Jonah reached out to hold on to JB and Angela.

They were already gone.

# EIGHTEEN

Jonah reeled away from the monitor.

"What?" he cried. "I *am* Charles Lindbergh's son?"

Somehow he'd never quite believed it. But maybe any other identity besides Jonah Skidmore would have seemed wrong to him. At various times Katherine had suggested that maybe he was really John Hudson from 1611 or Alexei Romanov from 1918, and those possibilities had quickly been disproved—maybe Jonah was just used to *not* knowing his original identity.

"I'm Charles Lindbergh Jr., or the third, or whatever it said on that list," Jonah said out loud. Not knowing about the "junior" or "third" part made it seem even more preposterous for him to claim that identity.

Jonah looked around quickly, expecting kid JB and kid Angela to be back right away. He didn't want them to think he was losing it, talking to himself.

They weren't back yet.

Jonah waited a moment, or what would have been a moment if time could actually pass in a time hollow.

Kid JB and kid Angela still didn't come back.

"Um, was there maybe something JB forgot about traveling back and forth to a time hollow?" Jonah said aloud. "Is there something I'm forgetting?"

His words echoed a little off the rock ceiling of the cave. But JB didn't come back to answer him. Neither did Angela.

"Okay, maybe it's just taking you two a little longer than you expected to find an Elucidator, and your lives haven't been in danger to let Angela's voice zap you back," Jonah said, even though he knew that wasn't how time hollows worked. JB and Angela could spend decades in the past, in Lindbergh's lifetime, and still come back to the time hollow without Jonah perceiving that any time had passed.

"Guys?" Jonah said, which was truly ridiculous, because it wasn't like he thought the other two had come back and were just hiding from him.

He didn't want to, but he forced himself to look back at the monitor screen before him.

He could see two shapes now at the bottom of the ladder—the kidnappers? His old enemies Gary and Hodge?

*Was Lindbergh's son—I mean, me—was I kidnapped twice? First by whoever kidnapped me in original time, then by Gary and Hodge?*

he wondered. *Or was that how Gary and Hodge messed up time, by kidnapping me before the original kidnapper had a chance to?*

Jonah peered closer at the shapes beneath the ladder. They were standing up now: one tall person, one not so tall, maybe even kid-size. . . .

*Oh,* Jonah realized. *It's JB and Angela.*

The taller person—kid Angela—seemed to be looking around frantically, whipping her head back and forth.

"Let's get out of here!" Jonah heard her hiss. "Before they think *we're* the kidnappers!"

Had one part of his kidnapping already happened? Had Jonah missed seeing it?

*But if Gary and Hodge already kidnapped me, why wouldn't I have been zapped back there with Angela and JB?* Jonah wondered. *Is there something I'm missing?*

Jonah suspected that he was missing lots of things that he needed to pay attention to. Maybe JB would explain something to Angela that would help?

Kid JB's reply was a pained, "Unnhhh . . ."

*Okay, that's not helpful,* Jonah thought.

Angela seemed to be thinking the same thing, because she muttered, "We don't have time for this. Climb on my back."

Was JB hurt somehow? Or stricken by a much worse case of timesickness than Angela?

*But why would that be?* Jonah wondered.

Jonah couldn't tell if JB was helping at all as Angela lifted him up and started carrying him piggyback. She seemed desperate to get away from the ladder.

Both of Jonah's friends disappeared into the shadows at the edge of the screen.

"Follow them! I want to see where they're going!" he yelled at the screen, as if he had any control over it.

The scene in front of him shifted, but it didn't follow JB and Angela. Instead the viewpoint zoomed upward, focusing on a window above the ladder.

Jonah couldn't have said how much time passed before he heard a woman cry from beyond the window, "The baby! Where's the baby?"

*So I have already been kidnapped,* Jonah thought despairingly. *By someone, anyway.*

He backed away from the monitor and stumbled over to the car where his parents—his *real* parents, his twenty-first century adoptive parents—still sat, still knocked out. They were still thirteen-year-olds, of course. Even unconscious, kid Dad had a goofy look on his face, and kid Mom wore the fierce, determined expression that made her look like Katherine.

"You're still my real mom and dad," Jonah told them in a choked voice. "No matter what."

But what had adopting Jonah ever done for them?

It was the reason their real, actual biological daughter, Katherine, had been exposed to danger again and again and again, in one century after another. It had to be the reason behind Katherine being kidnapped. And adopting Jonah had been the first step toward how Mom and Dad were now: zapped back to being teenagers and tranquilized and left behind in a time hollow.

If JB and Angela didn't come back, it was quite possible that Mom and Dad would be stuck this way forever.

"You should have adopted some normal kid from your own time period," Jonah told Mom and Dad. Since they couldn't actually hear him, he could say anything he wanted. "You would have been better off."

In his sleep, kid Dad made a fist, and almost without thinking Jonah tapped his own fist against his dad's.

*Ohhh*, Jonah thought in agony. *Dad was even the one who taught me how to do fist bumps. He and Mom have done so much for me.*

"I promise," Jonah said, his voice cracking, "I will do everything I can to get Katherine back. I will do everything I can to get you two back to normal—to get our family back . . ."

But there was only one thing Jonah could think to do that might help: He had to go back to watch the scenes of his original family in despair over losing him.

He gritted his teeth and went back to the monitor.

He wasn't sure how much time he'd missed watching, but the scene on the monitor had shifted. Now he was watching a large group of people in what seemed to be a child's nursery. Several policemen bent over an empty crib, examining large safety pins in a blanket on the mattress. Two women stood in the doorway, one hiding her face in her hands and sobbing, the other looking numb and stunned and shell-shocked. It took Jonah a moment to realize that this woman was crying too. Her tears streamed down her face so silently that she didn't even seem to be aware of them. The loud-sobbing woman was wearing some kind of an old-fashioned nurse's uniform; the silent crier wore an expensive-looking dress.

*Is that Charles Lindbergh's wife?* Jonah wondered. *The kidnapped baby's mother? My birth mother?*

She looked so anguished it was impossible not to feel sorry for her. But Jonah felt no burst of recognition, no sense of deeper connection.

Across the room Charles Lindbergh was standing next to the window and addressing another cluster of uniformed policemen. The viewpoint zoomed close enough that Jonah could read the words on their badges: NEW JERSEY STATE POLICE.

"This is where I found the ransom note," Lindbergh was telling the officers.

Jonah jerked back.

*Ransom note?* he thought. *Gary and Hodge wouldn't have asked for ransom.*

That meant that, regardless of Gary and Hodge's involvement, the original kidnapper had already been there.

The beginning of what could have been a hysterical laugh gurgled in the back of Jonah's throat.

*Lucky me, getting kidnapped twice! I must be the only famous missing kid from history that so many people wanted that badly,* he thought. *How much ransom money did the original kidnapper think he—she? They?—could get for me?*

This time the monitor actually seemed to know what he wanted to see: The viewpoint zoomed in closer to where Lindbergh was holding out a piece of paper with messy, scrawled handwriting and an odd pattern of circles and holes at the bottom. Jonah could read the note about as well as if he'd been holding the note himself. It was something about having fifty thousand dollars "redy" in precise amounts of five-, ten-, and twenty-dollar bills. Then it said:

After 2-4 days
we will inform you were to deliver
the mony.
We warn you for making

*anyding public or for notify the Police*
*The child is in gut care.*
*Indication for all letters are*
*Singnature*
*and three hohls.*

*Okay, so I was kidnapped by someone who couldn't spell,* Jonah thought. *And—concerned about my intestines? What does "gut care" mean?*

"I deduce that the kidnapper was a German speaker," one of the policemen said. "The pattern of spelling mistakes—'gut care' would mean 'good care,' right?"

The man looked at Lindbergh like he was expecting the famous man to look immensely impressed.

"I don't know German," Lindbergh said coldly.

"That pattern of circles and holes at the bottom," another policeman said. "Does he mean that that will be the sign on all ransom notes, so you know that it's come from the actual kidnapper?"

Jonah was no expert, but these didn't seem like very talented cops.

*Why aren't you dusting for fingerprints?* he wondered. *Why aren't you all wearing gloves and being very careful not to disturb anything in the crime scene? Why aren't you looking between the window and the crib for loose hairs that might belong to the kidnapper?*

Surely they had fingerprinting back in the early twentieth century. Even if they didn't have ways to test hairs for DNA matches, surely they'd at least be able to look for hair color and length.

Wouldn't they?

Jonah heard shouting from outside the open window. One of the policemen leaned out and seemed to be listening. Jonah could tell that the man wouldn't have done this in original time: A tracer version of the man still stood there, peering at Charles Lindbergh.

*Did Gary and Hodge change something to cause that shouting and the policeman leaning out the window?* Jonah wondered. *Or was it JB and Angela?*

Jonah couldn't hear what was being said down below, but he could make out the reply from the policeman in the window: "Bring him in!"

The policeman turned and spoke quietly to Charles Lindbergh.

"My men have found . . . well, we're not sure right now if it's a suspect or a witness," he said. "It is your choice whether you stay for the interrogation, but you might want the ladies to remove themselves in case anything unpleasant is revealed."

Lindbergh turned, creating another tracer, another change from original time.

"Betty?" he said, looking at the woman in the nurse's

uniform, whose sobbing had diminished slightly. "Could you take Anne back to her bedroom?"

Lindbergh crossed the room, separating entirely from his tracer. He hugged the woman Jonah thought must be his wife.

"Anne, we'll find him," he said. "I'm certain of it. Kidnappers don't leave ransom notes unless they intend to keep their victims alive."

Lindbergh's wife—Jonah's birth mother?—seemed too numb to respond, but she let the other woman lead her away.

*And if Katherine were here with me now, she'd be furious at how the women are shoved away, as if they're too fragile to hear anything unpleasant,* Jonah thought.

Thinking about Katherine, Jonah wondered if maybe he himself was too fragile to be exposed to anything else unpleasant.

He forced himself to keep his eyes trained on the screen anyhow.

The room was aglow with tracer lights now: the tracer versions of both women still lingering in the doorway, the tracer versions of Lindbergh and the police officers still hunched over the crib or the ransom note, even as the real versions of all the men turned expectantly toward the door. Jonah could hear dozens of feet tramping up the stairs. A policeman burst into the room, ahead of the rest of the crowd.

"The young man we found will only speak in German," he said breathlessly. "None of us know German—is there anyone here who can translate?"

"*German*, just as I suspected," said the policeman who'd tried to interpret the ransom note. He sounded quite proud of himself.

Before anyone had a chance to claim any German translation skills, the rest of the pack of policemen from down below reached the room.

At the center of the pack, manhandled by the burliest of all the cops, stood kid JB.

"Noooo," Jonah moaned.

Kid JB looked even wilder than ever, his hair in total disarray, his clothing still torn from the mob scene in Paris. He *was* screaming something in German, the same phrases over and over again.

Lindbergh and all the police officers were staring at him blankly, clearly not understanding.

Thanks to the translation vaccine Jonah had gotten before one of his trips to the 1400s, Jonah could understand perfectly.

He just didn't understand why kid JB was screaming it.

Because what kid JB was saying was, "The child is dead! He's dead, I tell you! I saw him fall myself!"

# NINETEEN

Jonah had to clutch the rock wall beside him, just to hold himself up.

*JB, I'm right here,* he thought. *I didn't die!*

Did kid JB think he was telling the truth? Or was this some kind of elaborate lie—a way to force the time agency to come back and rescue him and Angela before they did any more damage to time? Was this JB's way of trying to get help for Jonah and Katherine and their parents in the twenty-first century?

Why *wasn't* the time agency intervening to stop him?

Jonah just couldn't see cautious JB trying something so radical and extreme. And mean. Even as a thirteen-year-old he wouldn't be that reckless. Would he?

And where was kid Angela? What had happened to her?

On the screen Lindbergh seemed to be responding to the strain in JB's voice, even if the man didn't understand the words.

"Get a translator," Lindbergh snapped, with the tone of someone who was used to being obeyed.

A man in civilian clothing was hustled into the room, and his face went pale when he heard what JB was saying. The man appealed to the policeman who seemed to be most in charge.

"Perhaps I could translate just for you, and then you can decide what to share with Colonel Lindbergh?" the translator asked.

"I want to know everything going on in this investigation!" Lindbergh commanded. "This is my *son* we're talking about!"

*And that's why he's trying to protect you,* Jonah thought.

The translator was a skinny guy, and probably seven or eight inches shorter than Charles Lindbergh. But Jonah thought the man was incredibly brave. He looked at Lindbergh, looked at the head policeman, and then said flat out, "He says he saw your son fall. He says your son is dead."

Lindbergh froze. So did every cop in the room.

"Did he do it?" Lindbergh asked in the iciest voice Jonah had ever heard. "Am I facing my son's killer?"

Jonah stared at JB.

*You understand English!* Jonah wanted to scream at him. *You know how to speak it! Don't you know speaking German just makes you look guilty? Don't you know you've got to get out of this?*

JB didn't even seem to have heard what Lindbergh said. The boy was rolling his head around as if he was the one in anguish.

The translator repeated Lindbergh's question for kid JB in German.

"Didn't you see the broken rung on the ladder? Didn't you all figure out what happened? How the kidnapper slipped and dropped the baby?" JB asked. Jonah had to remind himself that the answer was still in German; that was why neither Lindbergh nor any of the policemen reacted.

Before the translator had a chance to explain to the others, JB began clutching his own head, tearing at his own hair.

"It's my fault he's dead," JB said. "I never thought it would work this way."

The translator told Lindbergh this part of what JB had said.

Instantly Lindbergh lunged across the room, aiming for JB. He had his fists up, ready to pummel JB.

Jonah couldn't watch. He slid off to the side and slipped down into a crouch.

*Why would JB say that?* He wondered. *How could he not know I'm still alive, still back here in the time cave? Isn't that what he warned me about?*

Jonah leaned back against the hard rock wall and tried to figure everything out.

*JB can't just be acting,* Jonah thought. *He really seems to believe he saw Charles Lindbergh's son die. Saw* me *die.*

What would make him think that?

*Maybe JB thought he really did see me go back in time with him and Angela?* Jonah thought. *Maybe he thought I rejoined my own tracer when the original kidnapper was carrying me down the ladder?*

Jonah could kind of see how this might have happened. It'd been dark. Maybe Gary and Hodge had snatched Jonah out of time so quickly that JB really did believe he'd fallen from the ladder and been killed. Maybe the original kidnapper had reacted as though that was really what happened.

*But if I vanished from my original time period because of Gary and Hodge kidnapping me from the other kidnapper, what's keeping me from ending up back there right now? Why isn't the monitor sending me back like it did JB and Angela?*

There had been a moment during his time travel through the 1600s that Jonah still hated thinking about. One of JB's former employees had forced time itself to unravel by making it possible for two copies of the same person to appear at the exact same moment. It broke all the rules; it practically destroyed all of time. Was something like that happening now?

*Only maybe I vanished twice, rather than appearing twice?* Jonah wondered.

He didn't understand. He had to go back to watching the scene on the monitor.

Lindbergh was practically beating up kid JB, and the police were standing back and watching. It went on and on—until finally one of the policemen pulled Lindbergh away from him.

"We'll need to have a trial," he said apologetically. He was apologizing to Lindbergh, not JB. "The world will have to see that we do things fairly here in America."

"This man killed my son!" Lindbergh raged.

"This is what I deserve!" JB said, still in German. His battered face was starting to swell; one of his sleeves hung in tatters from his arm.

*JB, what are you talking about?* Jonah wondered. *What's wrong with you?*

"What's the murderer's name, anyway?" one of the policemen asked the translator. "We'll want to get the news out instantly that we've found our man. We'll need his address, too."

The translator asked JB the same thing all over again in German.

JB kept his head down, as if in shame.

"I am Tete Einstein," he said. "I live in Zurich, Switzerland. I'm the son of Albert Einstein."

The translator told the others what JB had said.

"Albert Einstein's that scientist in Germany with the crazy ideas," the translator said, suddenly looking queasy. "How could this be his son?"

"Is it possible we're dealing with an escapee from an insane asylum?" one of the policemen asked. "Is it possible he had nothing to do with the kidnapping—he just wandered onto the grounds with the rest of the curious public and made up a story to get into the house?"

"But why would he *confess* to killing the son of America's greatest hero?" one of the other officers asked. "Right to Colonel Lindbergh's face?"

"Is that confession proof that he's guilty—or just proof that he's totally nuts?" another officer asked quietly.

Jonah had other questions.

"What are you thinking?" he yelled at kid JB's image on the screen. "Why would you tell them *that* identity?"

It was almost worse than JB admitting that he was a time traveler from the future. Why hadn't JB just come up with a convincing lie?

*Is it because he's back in the twentieth century for the third—no, fourth—time around?* Jonah thought, horrified. *Did going back again and again trigger something? What if he really has forgotten that he ever became anyone besides Tete Einstein?*

Why else would he tell the police he was Einstein's son?

Jonah forced himself to calm down and think about dates. In another time hollow, in what seemed like an entirely different lifetime, he'd been able to watch virtually every moment of the lives of Albert and Mileva Einstein and their family. It wasn't actually a different lifetime: Tete Einstein had been born in 1910. Mileva Einstein had secretly sent him into the future when he was a teenager, so that would have been sometime in the 1920s.

*It would have had to have been the early 1920s,* Jonah thought. *Before Lindbergh's flight, or else JB wouldn't have been able to go back to that time period with Angela and me. He would have been the one left behind in the time cave here, and Angela and I would have been doomed because we wouldn't have had an Elucidator with us to save us.*

Jonah shivered, even though it wasn't possible to feel cold in a time hollow. He went back to concentrating on dates. He caught a glimpse on the screen of a notebook one of the policemen was using, with a date written clearly at the top: March 1, 1932.

*So JB—as Tete Einstein—was supposed to be twenty-two in 1932,* Jonah thought. *Not thirteen.*

How messed up could time get from JB returning to part of his original time period as a teenager instead of the young adult he was supposed to be? And then—how could he have told policemen who he was? What if they took him seriously and tried to double-check? Jonah wondered if it wouldn't be the best thing in the world if everyone just thought kid JB was crazy. Especially if JB started trying to explain his strange age with time travel.

Then Jonah remembered the mental institutions he'd seen Tete Einstein in during the original time he'd watched of the Einsteins' lives.

He really hoped the mental institutions in America were better than the mental institutions in Switzerland in the first half of the twentieth century. But he kind of doubted it.

*Angela, where are you?* Jonah wondered. *Please tell me you're off somewhere finding an Elucidator so you can rescue JB and come back for me. Or come back for me so we can rescue JB together.*

Jonah looked around the cave. No Angela. She wasn't showing up anywhere on the monitor screen, either.

He remembered how the two women had been hustled out of the room.

*Katherine would be standing here telling me, "Duh, Jonah, women weren't allowed to do much of anything back in the early twentieth century,"* Jonah thought. *That was why Angela was making such a big deal about that one woman finding a way to become a pilot when she was both female and black. Cut Angela some slack—she's probably having a terrible time finding any way to get help!*

Thinking about the black female pilot Angela had told him about also made Jonah notice: Every single face he'd seen in the Lindbergh house was white. Every single police officer was male.

*Well, if anyone can succeed as a black female in the 1930s, it's Angela,* Jonah thought loyally.

She still didn't show up back in the cave.

Jonah went back over to the car where his parents still slept.

"What am I going to do?" he asked them.

Nobody could actually hear him, so he let himself say what he really wanted to say.

"Mommy? Daddy?" he whimpered. "What am I going to do?"

# TWENTY

Jonah thought about trying to figure out how to open the door of the time cave and go back to the twenty-first century. But that would just set time in motion again. His parents would wake up, and he didn't know what he could tell them or how he would keep them out of trouble.

Weeks ago Jonah would have rushed to do this anyway. It would have been *action*. It would have been *something* to do.

But how could Jonah open the door and let in all sorts of unknown dangers, when he might still learn more in the safety of the time cave? Even if he did end up having to open the time cave, shouldn't he know everything he could before he did it?

Jonah winced and grimaced and ground his teeth and tried to think of some other plan.

And then he walked back to the monitor and went back to watching the Lindberghs agonizing over their missing son.

He saw kid JB led offscreen, and everyone else rejoining their tracers, time closing over the hole JB had made in it—had JB done that on purpose? Or just because he really was as confused and mentally ill as the original Tete Einstein?

Jonah couldn't tell. He didn't see anything else of JB, and he never heard anyone else mention him again. Evidently once the police decided he was crazy, they lost interest in him.

Jonah didn't see any sign of Angela, either, even though he watched for her devotedly. He was constantly scanning shadows and hiding places.

*I'll just wait until I see Gary and Hodge show up,* he thought. *No matter when they kidnapped me,* I know *they eventually met with Charles Lindbergh. Because they were the reason he came to kidnap Katherine.* I have *to hear what they told him.*

But in the meantime all Jonah could see was Charles and Anne Lindbergh despairing and hoping and despairing again, and desperately trying anything they could think of to get their son back.

It was so hard for Jonah to watch, because that was exactly how he felt about getting Katherine back.

Days passed on the monitor screen. A week. Two weeks. A month.

Lindbergh was dealing with 1930s gangsters now, tough-talking criminals who promised him they could find out who the kidnapper was; they could find the boy for him. Lindbergh made it known that he was perfectly willing to pay the ransom—he'd do anything to get his son back safely. Lindbergh worked with a go-between who followed a trail of clues to a meeting in a cemetery. Lindbergh was everywhere in the investigation, actually telling the police what to do.

*That's how I would want to be,* Jonah thought. *That's what I really want to be doing, searching for Katherine.*

Anne Lindbergh could do nothing. Jonah heard her and Charles talking about how she was pregnant with their second child, and so she needed to rest and take it easy. But not having anything to do just made the ordeal worse for her. She cried and wrote letters and journal entries about how helpless she felt. The letters and journal entries were heartbreaking in how hard she was trying to hold on to hope.

*And . . . that's more what I'm like,* Jonah thought. *She can't do anything but hope and write. I can't do anything but hope and watch.*

Sometimes Jonah had to take a break from what was happening on the screen. He figured out how to pause it.

At first all he could think of to do instead was go visit his sleeping parents. But then he started playing around with the other monitor screens as well, the ones showing the other missing children from history and their stories.

*Oh—stupid me!* he thought one morning—or afternoon—or, really, who knew what time of day it was? *If the monitors zap people back to any time period they haven't visited already, why don't I find someone's time to go back to that's at least quasi-safe, and I'll glom onto the Elucidator of whoever returned them to history? If it's JB as an adult, he'll understand! He'll help me!*

Jonah thought hard about this theory and eventually picked Ming Reynolds. Except for the people Jonah himself had been involved in returning to and then rescuing from their original time, Ming was the only one whose original identity Jonah knew anything about: She was a minor Chinese princess from some time period thousands of years ago.

*I definitely* wasn't *in that time period originally,* Jonah told himself excitedly.

He set up the monitor to watch her original life. Tingles of excitement spread through him as he watched the first scene start.

*Are those . . . water buffaloes she's standing beside?* he wondered.

He saw Gary and Hodge steal her away; he saw

JB—the real JB! The adult!—carry her back, letting her second cousin get one glimpse of her beside the water buffaloes. And then he saw JB yank her back out of time as the water buffaloes began stampeding.

Jonah's heart pounded and he started breathing hard, like he thought he'd need to run away from the water buffaloes any instant.

But the rock of the time cave stayed firmly beneath him. The water buffaloes stayed only on the screen.

*So . . . is it only the monitor screen connected to the Lindberghs that can pull people back in time?* Jonah wondered.

He became a little reckless, calling up the original time periods for every single one of the other thirty-five missing children from history. He saw fires, floods, plagues, more stampedes. Also: secret stabbings and secret shootings and, once, a secret beheading by guillotine in the middle of the night. He rewatched the stories where he knew the ending because he'd been present: the 1485 battle where Chip and Alex were supposed to have perished; the 1903 plague that was supposed to have killed Emily; the 1918 squad of assassins that had meant to kill Daniella and Gavin. He saved the 1600s for last, because that was when JB's former employee, Second, had nearly ruined all of time. Even in those cases Jonah watched Andrea, Brendan, Antonio, and Dalton escape all over again, free and clear.

None of those viewings sucked Jonah back into another time. He didn't expect it from the scenes he'd already witnessed in person, but he was surprised that the moments he was seeing for the very first time didn't pull him back. And he was surprised that starting a familiar scene a second too early or lingering in it a second too long didn't change anything either.

*At least I'm seeing everything about how Gary and Hodge operated, kidnapping children,* Jonah thought. *At least I'm seeing all the creative ways JB managed to safely return and rescue those kids, even when Katherine and I weren't involved.*

It wasn't until he had watched the very last kid's story that Jonah realized something big:

Of the thirty-six missing kids who had been on the time-crashed plane at the beginning of Jonah's modern life, all but one of them had already been safely returned to and then rescued from their original time period.

Jonah was the only one left.

# TWENTY-ONE

*What does that mean?* Jonah wondered. *Why didn't JB ever tell me I'm the only one who hasn't resolved his earlier life? When did all the rest of the kids have a chance to go back in time—was it before or after I was in 1918? Was it when Gavin and I were recovering from our bullet wounds?*

Jonah didn't have answers to any of his questions.

He went back to watching the Lindberghs' desperate lives.

He wasn't the only one: There were crowds outside their home, journalists from all over the world breathlessly covering every new lead.

On April 1, 1932, a month after the kidnapping, the Lindberghs received their tenth ransom note. This one told them to have their money ready the very next night.

Jonah watched Charles Lindbergh climb into a car

with fifty thousand dollars in a wooden box. Another car followed with an additional twenty thousand—the ransom demands had gone up.

The man who was acting as go-between for the Lindberghs, Dr. John Condon, began following a clue hunt through the Bronx: Go to a flower shop on Tremont Avenue and look for the next instructions under a rock. Walk to the intersection at the edge of St. Raymond's Cemetery.

Lindbergh stayed a few hundred feet away from Condon, watching.

"Ay, Doctor," a voice called to Condon from the cemetery.

Condon froze, halfway across the street. Then Jonah saw him start running toward the cemetery. He was a heavy man—he didn't seem capable of running fast. Jonah saw a second man waiting for him in the shadows.

*My kidnapper?* Jonah wondered. *Is it really him or just someone trying to steal the Lindberghs' money?*

It had to be that Jonah-as-the-Lindbergh-baby was still *somewhere* in the world in April 1932. If Gary and Hodge—or anyone else—had pulled him out of time by this date, then the monitor would suck him into the past, just as it had kid JB and kid Angela.

Wouldn't it?

Jonah missed some of what the shadowy man in the cemetery was saying to John Condon. Condon gave him the box containing the fifty thousand dollars, and the shadowy man gave him an envelope that he said contained an exact description of where the Lindbergh child could be found.

"Give me your word that you'll wait six hours before opening the directions," the shadowy man said.

"I will," Condon said, nodding with great sincerity.

Condon took the directions back to Charles Lindbergh, who was waiting in the car. Jonah couldn't believe they made no effort to follow the man in the cemetery.

The camera—or whatever was giving Jonah the ability to watch the entire scene—let the man from the cemetery disappear back into the shadows as well.

*Why doesn't the monitor give some view of where the baby is—where I really am?* Jonah wondered.

All the other monitors had shown what actually happened to the missing kids themselves. Was this monitor different because Jonah hadn't been returned to his native time yet? Or was it just because Jonah had asked JB to show Charles Lindbergh so they could see him meet with Gary and Hodge?

Keeping one eye on the screen, Jonah went back to the keyboard. But he couldn't figure out how to change the scene.

On the screen Lindbergh and Condon were driving away. They were discussing whether or not they really should wait six hours before looking at the directions for where to find the baby.

"I gave my word, but you didn't give yours," Condon argued. This sounded like the way kids at school would reason. Jonah had to do a double take to make sure that Condon hadn't been suddenly turned into a thirteen-year-old too.

*But Condon and Lindbergh are dealing with a stolen baby,* Jonah thought. *How can they wait? How can they not rush to look for the child—for me!—as quickly as they can?*

Jonah saw Lindbergh pull his car back over to the curb and rip open the envelope. The short letter inside said:

> *The boy is on Boad Nelly. It is a small Boad 28 feet long. Two person are on the Boad. The are innosent. you will find the Boad between Horseneck Beach and gay Head near Elizabeth Island.*

"He's on a boat near Martha's Vineyard!" Lindbergh explained. "It's by where Anne and I had our honeymoon!"

Then Jonah watched as Lindbergh flew three other men over the water near the Elizabeth Islands. Every time they spotted a boat that might fit the description of *Nelly,* Lindbergh swooped down low and close. Coast Guard cutters spread across the water as well, searching, searching, searching . . .

Jonah held his breath.

*Will they find me? Or will they find where I'm supposed to be? What will happen then?* he wondered.

Jonah lost track of how much time Lindbergh and the others spent searching. But he saw Lindbergh in a dark car at night after a long day of searching—had it been the second full day of searching? The third?

Lindbergh was dropping off his fellow searchers in New York before he himself drove on to his home in New Jersey. It seemed at first that Lindbergh was not going to say a word. But then Lindbergh looked the others directly in the face.

"We were double-crossed," he said. "The kidnappers never meant to tell us where to find the boy."

Everyone stopped looking at the Elizabeth Islands.

Jonah slumped against the rock wall of the cave.

*How do Charles and Anne Lindbergh survive this?* he wondered. *Do they survive? Do they dare to keep holding on to hope?*

He didn't want to think about how the Lindberghs had hundreds and thousands of people helping them look for their son: the entire New Jersey state police, the Coast Guard, every single person who read a newspaper or listened to a radio report. And they *still* couldn't find the boy.

As far as Jonah knew, he and kid JB and kid Angela were the only ones looking for Katherine. And what had any of them accomplished?

*This is the best thing I can do for Katherine,* Jonah told himself. *When I see Lindbergh meeting with Gary and Hodge, then I'll know how to help.*

Painful as it was, Jonah went back to watching the Lindberghs.

Another man had shown up, claiming to have a connection to a gang of kidnappers. Charles Lindbergh went sailing with that man to meet the gang near Cape May, New Jersey.

"And you trust this man?" Jonah yelled, as if Lindbergh could actually hear him. "You really think he's going to lead you to your son?"

But what else could Lindbergh do?

Lindbergh and the other man sailed and sailed and sailed, going around in circles for hours on end. Even Jonah was starting to feel dizzy.

Then suddenly the scene shifted. Two men Jonah had never seen before were sitting in the cab of a truck, moving along a small, muddy road.

"Who *are* these people?" Jonah muttered. "What happened to the Lindberghs?"

While Jonah watched, the man on the passenger side squirmed in his seat.

"Would you mind pulling over?" the man asked. "I'm not going to make it to the next town."

*Does he mean he has to pee?* Jonah wondered. *Didn't his parents ever tell him he should always go before he goes?*

Jonah snorted, mostly with disgust at himself for making such a lame joke. But after days of watching the tense, worried Lindberghs and the tense, worried cops, it was almost peaceful to watch people whose biggest concern seemed to be finding a place to pee.

The truck stopped; the man tramped far out into the woods. Jonah guessed he was trying to find a place he wouldn't be seen from the road—not that there appeared to be any other traffic nearby.

Jonah could see only the man's back. The man seemed to freeze in place. Had time stopped? Had the monitor malfunctioned? No, now the man was turning back around, shouting back to his friend still in the truck.

"Uh, Orville?" the man said, and now his voice was tense and worried too. "I think this is a dead body. It's a . . . it's a baby."

The camera zoomed close, seeming to accompany the

second man—Orville?—as he rushed to his friend's side. Now both men stood over a small body lying facedown in the dirt. The first man picked up a stick to shove away a layer of dead leaves, revealing a cluster of golden curls.

"It's got to be the Lindbergh baby, don't you think?" the first man said.

Watching, Jonah felt his knees give way. He sank down to the rock floor.

"I'm dead?" he mumbled. "I'm dead?"

How could that be?

# TWENTY-TWO

*A fake corpse,* Jonah told himself. *Duh. Use your brain.*

He knew that his friends Gavin and Daniella—and their sister Maria and a family friend, Leonid—had been able to escape from 1918 only because fake remains were left behind in their place. Their fake skeletons were realistic enough to fool twentieth-century science and twenty-first-century science. By the time science would become advanced enough to detect the forgery, it wouldn't matter if everyone knew that those four kids had survived.

*So how is this any different?* Jonah wondered.

It felt different.

*Just because that's the fake version of your dead body they're poking at?* Jonah told himself. *Just because you know now that that was supposed to happen to you in original time?*

It was impossible to get an upset stomach in a time hollow, but Jonah started retching anyway.

*Stop it,* Jonah told himself. *None of this really did happen to you. You were rescued. You were saved. You're still alive. Even in 1932 you're still alive.*

Didn't he have proof of this? If Jonah-as-the-Lindbergh-baby really had vanished from 1932, wouldn't Jonah himself instantly be zapped back to that moment?

Jonah knew that was how things worked. And he was still in the time cave. He was still able to watch 1932 on the monitor without being sucked into it.

Jonah went back over to his sleeping kid parents in the car.

"I'm still alive," he told them. "Maybe JB or Angela managed to fake my body, and they just couldn't get the word to me that everything's okay. Maybe I won't ever have to go back to my past. Maybe they're just quietly in the background taking care of everything, and any minute now they'll show up here, with everything fixed. And with Katherine. Maybe they'll have rescued Katherine already, and I won't have to. And then they'll make you two the right age again, and everything will be fine."

In their sleep, kid Dad still looked goofy and kid Mom still looked fierce. Jonah reached in and gave both of them hugs. They were both so small now. Diminished. But they were still his parents.

"You know I think I'm lying, don't you?" he asked them.

"You know I don't really believe that any of this is going to be easy?"

Kid Mom's fierce expression seemed to be saying, *If you don't believe it's going to be easy, why are you over here talking to us instead of doing everything you can to get Katherine back and rescue JB and Angela and fix time and us? Why aren't you doing what you know you should?*

Kid Dad's expression seemed to say, *I love you, Jonah. I know you'll do your very best.*

How could it hurt so much just to look at his own parents?

Jonah went back to watching the Lindberghs on the monitor—watching his other parents—and this hurt too. Anne and Charles had both been told now that their child's dead body had been found. They'd been told that their little boy had been dead since the very first night. For seventy-two days they'd been searching and hoping, and every government agency available in 1932 had been searching and hoping, and the whole time the child had been dead.

*That's a fake dead body they're talking about,* Jonah thought hollowly. *It's not really me. And there's no connection with Katherine—her kidnapping is not the same situation. She's still alive. Somewhere in time. Somewhere I'm going to be able to find her.*

But Jonah saw how completely the hope died in Anne

Lindbergh's face—how completely it died even as she maintained, "I never really thought he was still alive. From that first night I knew he was dead."

Charles Lindbergh set his jaw and said very little. He didn't cry, not even when he went to identify the body. Jonah didn't know how he could stand it. Even knowing the body was fake, Jonah was still horrified to see how much a body could decompose in seventy-two days of lying in the dirt. Which was worse—the parts of the fake corpse that were gone, or the parts that were still recognizable, like the golden curls?

Jonah had to turn away when Charles Lindbergh began examining the fake corpse's face. It was still possible to see the dimple in the chin. Without thinking, Jonah lifted his hand and fingered his own chin—fingered his own dimple.

*What I see on the screen isn't real,* Jonah told himself. *That corpse isn't real, isn't real, isn't real, isn't real . . .*

It didn't matter. Jonah still had to walk away.

"You understand, don't you?" he asked his parents. "You wouldn't be able to look either, would you? You wouldn't be as cold and heartless as Charles Lindbergh."

Even kid Mom's fierce expression looked less fierce now. How could she look so lost and afraid when she wasn't even awake?

Jonah was almost certain the corpse he'd seen on the screen wasn't real, but the people he loved really were that fragile. Even the strongest, most determined people he'd met or seen or heard about in history were still just flesh and blood, bones and skin.

*And this is why people believe in God, isn't it?* Jonah wondered. *Because we can tell there's something bigger out there that we're part of. Because we can tell that there's something more to all of us, and more to all of our lives.*

And then it felt like Jonah was talking to God, not to his parents: *Please help me figure out what to do. Please help this all work out.*

He went back to watching the monitor.

Somehow he'd missed a huge chunk of time. It was summer now on the screen, maybe even August. Charles Lindbergh was climbing back into an airplane, flying high over the water again. Jonah caught a glimpse of one of Lindbergh's maps, which seemed to match the coastline he was leaving behind—Lindbergh was flying out over the Atlantic Ocean once again. When he was far past the last sight of land, he pulled the window back so the wind flowed directly onto his face. He lifted a small urn toward the open window and uncorked it. And then he shook fine dark powder out into the wind.

*Ashes,* Jonah thought. *They had the fake body cremated.*

*Lindbergh thinks he's spreading his son's ashes over the ocean.*

Lindbergh held his head out the window, watching until every last ash disappeared into the waves below.

And then Lindbergh began to howl.

"Nooooo," he wailed, the sound so painful and intense that Jonah actually put his hands over his ears. He could still hear Lindbergh anyway.

"This was supposed to bring me peace?" Lindbergh screamed. "This doesn't bring me peace! I refuse to accept it!"

He pulled out one of the maps and flipped it over and began to write, the paper braced against his own knee.

The camera angle spun, as if Jonah himself were whirling around the cockpit, spinning into position over the paper Lindbergh was writing on. Now Jonah could see what the man was writing. He could see what his original father was writing:

*I will not accept it. I cannot. I will find a way to turn time back around.*

*I will get my son back.*

*I will make it so we never lost him.*

# TWENTY-THREE

*Time travel,* Jonah thought numbly. *He's talking about time travel.*

Wasn't that what Lindbergh meant?

*But he's in 1932,* Jonah reminded himself.

As far as Jonah could tell, they didn't even have computers yet in 1932. Jonah had seen video games that were more sophisticated than the airplane Lindbergh was flying right now. No—even when Jonah's *father* was a kid, there'd been video games that were more sophisticated that Lindbergh's airplane.

*It's not like Charles Lindbergh is going to invent time travel right then and there,* Jonah told himself scornfully.

On the screen Lindbergh was swooping and rolling his plane, as if his refusal to make peace with his son's death had unleashed an odd, frantic playfulness.

*He's not going to succeed,* Jonah thought. He felt small and mean. How could Jonah be so cruel as to *want* Lindbergh to fail?

*Because if he succeeds, that ruins my life,* Jonah thought.

Lindbergh had turned back toward shore again, flying the same route he'd been over before, only in the opposite direction. The playfulness was gone; his flying seemed methodical and precise.

When he landed, Lindbergh waved away the others at the airfield who were ready to help him.

"I just want to sit in my plane for a while and be alone," he called to them. "Keep the press away, all right? Don't let any reporters near."

For a long time Lindbergh just sat in the plane, staring out the window at nothing. Then he ripped a fresh sheet of paper out of his flight logbook and began to write. It wasn't until Lindbergh finished and placed the letter on his pilot's seat that Jonah saw what Lindbergh had written:

*To Whom It May Concern:*

*I have a mechanical mind. I understand engines and gears, how one gear turns another. The gear of my fame turned the gear of my son's kidnapping. And then that turned the gear of my son's death.*

*How do you un-turn a gear? How do you roll back time? How do you bring the dead back to life?*

*I have been changing my focus in recent years, from exploring the air to exploring the inner workings of life. I thought finding the secrets of immortality would be man's ultimate achievement—perhaps my ultimate achievement.*

*I aimed too low. Or, rather, I have reason now to see where even that lofty goal will never be enough. Surely someday man will learn how to undo time, how to rewind and repair his worst mistakes. When he does, how will this ultimate tool be used?*

*And how can I lure the possessor of that marvel back to my time to assist me? Why would he want to?*

*This is my answer. I address you, the time traveler of the future: You can look and see what I have accomplished thus far in my life. You can see my determination, my single-mindedness. You can see what I want, and how hard I am willing to work for you, what willingness I would bring to helping you in almost any way. For myself. For my wife. For my son.*

*You have my bounden word: I would make it completely worth your while to come to me. To hire me.*

*All I want in exchange is my son back.*

*Sincerely,*
*Charles Lindbergh*

Lindbergh left this letter on his seat barely long enough for Jonah to finish reading it. And then Lindbergh picked up the letter, lit it on fire, and stomped it down into ash on the ground.

*He understands things about time travel that I took ages to figure out,* Jonah realized. *He understands that there is no reason to leave the letter in place for a long time. As long as it exists at one point in time, a curious traveler from another time will be able to see it.*

And Jonah guessed that by destroying the note, Lindbergh was making sure that nothing would leak to any newspaper or radio reporter about how he had gone crazy with grief and was writing letters to nonexistent time travelers, asking for help.

*But he* is *acting crazy with grief, isn't he?* Jonah wondered. *How could he think that any time traveler would want anything from him?*

Sure, Charles Lindbergh had proved himself brave enough to fly across the Atlantic Ocean all by himself in essentially a tin can covered in cloth. But what could he do for any time traveler? Time travelers had Elucidators. They had all the marvels of the future. They didn't need Charles Lindbergh.

Lindbergh was looking around the runways stretching ahead of him. The airfield seemed deserted now. Other planes had been flying in and out earlier, but they were all either abandoned or aloft now. It was getting late in the day. Lindbergh began strolling toward the airfield office, a small space off to the side of a cavernous hangar. Jonah could see two shadows in the windows of the office. Lindbergh evidently saw them too: He picked up his pace.

*Did he have some appointment to meet friends there?* Jonah wondered. *Who is it?*

"Strangers," Lindbergh whispered to himself. "And I know I would have seen anybody the guard let in through the gate. . . ."

Lindbergh was beaming. He looked more hopeful than he'd looked even on the most optimistic day of searching for his son. Jonah had never seen Lindbergh look this happy to see anyone.

Lindbergh reached the door of the office and yanked it open. He stood in the doorway, his tall frame and broad shoulders blocking Jonah's view of the people inside. And then Lindbergh stepped across the threshold and to the side. In the moment before the door slammed behind him, Jonah saw just enough to understand.

Jonah had not been the only one who'd seen Charles Lindbergh's letter. The letter had worked exactly the way Lindbergh had wanted it to: It had indeed summoned time travelers to 1932.

For Jonah himself recognized the two men sitting in the dusty airfield office, ready to meet with Charles Lindbergh.

The two men were Jonah's enemies Gary and Hodge.

# TWENTY-FOUR

"Don't trust them!" Jonah yelled, even though of course Charles Lindbergh couldn't hear him. "They're liars and cheats, and—and kidnappers! They're kidnappers, your worst enemies! They kidnapped your son, or they will, or—well, I don't know how the timing works, but you can't trust Gary and Hodge!"

Jonah was surprised at how much he wanted to keep yelling.

*You should be relieved,* he told himself. *You've been waiting for ages for Gary and Hodge to show up. Finally! Now you have your chance to see what deal they offered Lindbergh, how they got him to kidnap Katherine.*

But how could Lindbergh kidnap any other parents' child, after what he'd been through himself?

Jonah forced himself to shut his mouth. He forced

himself to keep watching Lindbergh and Gary and Hodge on the screen.

And . . . he watched as the door finished its swinging arc, coming to a stop firmly against the wooden frame of the doorway.

*Okay, readjust the camera angle,* Jonah thought. In the hours and hours and days and days Jonah had already watched, the camera had almost always jumped automatically to the best viewpoint. But now, in the one moment Jonah wanted to watch the most, the camera seemed stuck, trained on nothing but the closed door.

*What are they saying?* Jonah wondered. *Can I hear even if I can't see?*

Jonah pushed his ear close to the screen, as if he were right there beside the real door and putting his ear against the wood were possible.

He still couldn't hear anything.

*What? Why not? Who's controlling this?* he wondered.

What if it was Gary and Hodge?

The door stayed firmly shut, shutting Jonah out.

Jonah kicked the rock wall beneath the monitor's screen. This didn't help: It only jammed his toe.

"This isn't fair!" Jonah yelled.

He thought about how JB hadn't really seemed to understand how the monitors worked; how even JB hadn't known that this particular monitor would be capable of plunging viewers back into the past.

*JB was having memory problems,* Jonah reminded himself. *He couldn't even remember my original identity.*

But what if there was a different reason that JB hadn't understood the monitors? What if they'd been sabotaged from the very start?

What if the only reason kid JB hadn't been more concerned about that was because he already had so many problems of his own?

*Why would Gary and Hodge want me to see some of the scenes with Charles Lindbergh but not others?* Jonah wondered.

Just then the camera angle finally changed. It was almost like the camera zoomed through the door—Jonah had seen that effect in movies. He wasn't going to worry about how it had happened from a technical sense. He just stared hard at Gary and Hodge and Lindbergh, and tried to figure out what he'd missed.

"Yes," Lindbergh was saying as he nodded his head eagerly.

*Oh, thanks a lot!* Jonah thought. *All I get to see is Lindbergh agreeing to help Gary and Hodge, but I don't know their exact deal!*

"We thought as much," Hodge said. His voice and his smile were so full of smugness that Jonah clenched his fists.

*It's not possible to punch him—you'd just destroy the monitor,* Jonah reminded himself.

"Yeah," Gary said, smirking. "What he said."

Was it Jonah's imagination, or did Gary look slightly less muscular than the last time Jonah had seen him? Did he and Hodge both have more lines in their faces, more gray in their hair?

Jonah had last seen Gary and Hodge in 1918, but Jonah knew he shouldn't expect the two men to look fourteen years older in 1932. For them, it could be five seconds later—or fifty years.

*They don't look fifty years older but . . . maybe a decade or two?* Jonah guessed. *How much trouble have they stirred up since the last time I saw them?*

How much had happened that Jonah didn't know about?

Gary and Hodge were leaning back in their chairs—they looked relaxed and comfortable and completely at ease. But Lindbergh was hunched over a table, writing something down.

"This is my checklist," Lindbergh said, holding up a small notebook that Jonah recognized. It was the same one Jonah had seen Lindbergh holding in the Skidmores' living room, right before Lindbergh grabbed Katherine and vanished.

"Did I leave anything out?" Lindbergh asked Gary and Hodge.

Jonah peered eagerly toward the screen. The camera quickly focused on four lines at the bottom of the page:

*Identify Skidmore children.*
*Grab Skidmore girl.*
*Reset her chronophysical age to exactly thirteen years and three months.*
*Take Skidmore girl to Gary and Hodge to seal the deal.*

"What about the rest of the checklist?" Jonah shouted at the screen in frustration. "I already know all that!"

The camera angle didn't change.

"Good so far," Hodge said. "What did you write on the back?"

*On the back?* Jonah thought.

Had he looked on the back of the sheet of paper he'd picked up in his own living room? Jonah started rifling through his own pockets; then he remembered that he'd changed clothes before going back to the 1920s. He'd left the scrap of Lindbergh's checklist in his twenty-first-century blue jeans. Jonah kept his eyes on the monitor and scooped up his untidy bundle of clothes. Without looking, he began searching through his jeans pockets.

On the screen Lindbergh flipped the paper over, showing the back of it to Gary and Hodge.

The camera stayed focused on the bottom half of the back of the page—the blank bottom half of the back of the page. Jonah had no idea what was written at the top of the back of the page.

"Are you trying to drive me crazy?" he yelled at the screen.

Simultaneously he found the scrap of paper in his own pocket. The back of the scrap he'd managed to carry away was equally empty.

*But is it important to know that there's more on his checklist after he takes Katherine to Gary and Hodge?* Jonah wondered.

He dropped the note and his clothes and went back to focusing intensely on the monitor.

"Very good," Hodge was saying as he nodded approvingly at the portion of the list Jonah couldn't see. "You carry through your part of the deal, we'll carry through ours."

Lindbergh tucked the notebook and a stubby pencil into the jacket of his flight suit.

*Oh, that flight suit,* Jonah suddenly realized. *That's the exact same one Lindbergh was wearing when he kidnapped Katherine.*

But wasn't Lindbergh supposed to appear in the Skidmores' living room first dressed in a 1930s suit and fedora?

"Give me the navigational device and I'll take my leave," Lindbergh was saying to Gary and Hodge. He shook hands with both men, and Hodge handed him a rectangular black device—an old-fashioned camera, maybe?

"The Elucidator," Hodge said, sounding almost as formal as if he were making an introduction. "Remember, when you get to the twenty-first century, it will take on a different appearance, to match the technology of that time. But it will still be able to follow your commands. The commands we have agreed upon, anyway."

Jonah half expected Lindbergh to ask for operating instructions, but he simply tucked the Elucidator inside his jacket, alongside his notebook.

"I should like to leave as soon as possible," Lindbergh said.

Gary looked at his watch.

"This timing works," he said.

Lindbergh nodded, took a step forward—and vanished.

Jonah didn't even have time to blink before Lindbergh was back, firmly placing his shoe in the exact spot he'd been stepping toward.

His hair was more windswept than before, and he was glancing around frantically. But the main difference—the main proof that Jonah could see that Lindbergh had actually been away—was that now Lindbergh carried some sort of bundle in his arms.

And the bundle was crying.

# TWENTY-FIVE

*Lindbergh traveled through time and succeeded in getting his baby back?* Jonah thought numbly. *He got me back—even though I'm still right here in the time cave?*

Jonah was confused. Deeply confused, actually.

*But . . . Lindbergh kidnapped Katherine, not me,* Jonah thought. *Unless . . . he kidnapped Katherine and did everything Gary and Hodge wanted, and took Katherine to them in some other time period. And then after that he went off into my future and grabbed me and took me back to the 1930s? And I haven't seen him grab me yet, but I'm seeing the results of him grabbing me?*

Jonah shook his head, not sure he understood even yet.

The odd thing was, for a moment it seemed as if Gary and Hodge were confused too. Both of them were staring at the crying, squirming bundle in Lindbergh's arms. Gary sprang up from his chair and exclaimed, "What? But that's not—"

Hodge put a warning hand on Gary's arm.

"Tell us . . . about your adventures," Hodge practically purred to Lindbergh. "Did you have any trouble adjusting to the plane?"

*Plane? What plane is he talking about?* Jonah wondered.

Lindbergh turned his head toward Hodge's voice. Jonah was willing to bet that Lindbergh was slightly time-sick, and his vision hadn't swung into focus yet.

Hodge reached his hand up toward Lindbergh's jacket.

"Or perhaps you are weary from your trip and would prefer to let the Elucidator reveal everything about your travels?" Hodge asked. His voice arced higher, competing with the crying baby, who was getting louder and louder.

Lindbergh shoved Hodge's hand away, a gesture that was just shy of being rude.

"It's . . . more fun to tell everything myself," Lindbergh murmured, shielding the baby in his arms from Hodge. He turned slightly, almost as if he was trying to keep the baby's face hidden. "Just . . . give me a minute. Just . . . let me soothe the baby first."

*However the time travel worked out, if that's really the baby version of me in Lindbergh's arms, I've got incredible lung power,* Jonah marveled.

"My colleague and I have extensive experience keeping children quiet," Hodge said, and Jonah wondered if Lindbergh heard the menace in those words.

*Because you're kidnappers!* Jonah wanted to yell. *That's where you got all your experience!*

Hodge was reaching for the baby in a sneaky way—a way that would almost force a fight over the baby if Lindbergh didn't let go.

Lindbergh clutched the baby tighter to his chest.

"I think I could be excused for not wishing to let the child out of my sight," Lindbergh growled.

"Oh, all we're asking is that you share the sight," Hodge said smoothly. "And—don't you think the child will be happier without being so tightly bundled?"

He feinted to the right, then stepped quickly to the left, knocking the blankets the opposite direction from where Lindbergh seemed to expect. Three layers of blankets peeled back from the baby's face, revealing it clearly.

Jonah had seen his own baby pictures, of course. When he and Katherine were little, Grandma Skidmore had been big into scrapbooking, and so she'd given them all sorts of albums full of their own photos. There was one in particular that Katherine had called "The Book of Us," which she'd demanded that Mom or Dad "read" every night at bedtime for a solid year. Jonah probably hadn't looked at that album since he was five, but it didn't matter. Those pictures were engraved in his memory and probably always would be. He could close his eyes and see himself at four months, at six months, at nine months, at a year . . . He'd had thick hair and long eyelashes and, even back then, a distinct dimple in his chin. And when he was four or five, he'd thought it was funny that in his baby pictures he had so much hair and Katherine, in hers, had none.

Katherine as a baby had been as bald as a cue ball.

So was the baby that Lindbergh held in his arms on the screen back in 1932.

*So—for some reason Lindbergh shaved his kid's head when he stole him back?* Jonah wondered. *He shaved my head?*

Jonah was being ridiculous.

If Jonah had his own baby pictures memorized, he knew the ones of Katherine just as well. She'd barely even started to grow hair until she was six months old, and her eyes were little and squinty, and her nose was often wrinkled up as if she wasn't quite sure she trusted the world yet. And, even though he was never ever allowed to say this when he was four or five years old, she'd actually been a rather ugly baby.

The baby Charles Lindbergh held was absolutely, positively not the infant version of Jonah.

Instead that baby was absolutely, positively, definitely, without question his sister Katherine.

*Duh, duh, duh,* Jonah thought, disgusted with his own stupidity. *You saw right on Lindbergh's checklist that he was supposed to bring Katherine to Gary and Hodge. You know time travelers can play around with age. Why didn't you figure out right away that Lindbergh was holding baby Katherine, not baby you?*

Jonah knew why he hadn't figured that out—why he hadn't wanted to figure it out. As long as he'd thought that Lindbergh had carried off Katherine exactly as she'd been back in her regular time in the twenty-first century, he'd been able to believe that she had a decent chance of rescuing herself. (Maybe he'd even been half counting on her coming and rescuing *him*?) Though he'd never quite admit it to her face, Katherine was smart and brave and resourceful—a true hero, or heroine, whatever. If anyone could escape on her own from a time-traveling kidnapper from another century, it'd be her.

But that was Katherine as her real self, a feisty almost-twelve-year-old.

Katherine as an infant would be like any other baby: helpless. Totally dependent.

Absolutely incapable of rescuing herself or anyone else.

Jonah was so busy being horrified that it took him a moment to realize that Gary and Hodge seemed equally outraged by the sight of baby Katherine.

"I thought you understood our directions!" Hodge was bellowing at Lindbergh. "This is *not* where we told you to bring that baby!"

"What else did you mess up?" Gary growled, towering threateningly over Lindbergh.

"Put the baby down before you start fighting!" Jonah screamed, even though no one could hear him. "Don't let Katherine get hurt!"

But no one started throwing punches. Lindbergh just stood there, tall and confident and peering defiantly back at Gary and Hodge.

"I have been dealing with mobsters and gangsters and the criminal element since March," Lindbergh said quietly. "I paid ransom money for a child who'd been dead for weeks. I followed tips and leads and promises of certain help that turned out to be absolutely worthless. I have met many, many untrustworthy men. Why should I trust you? I have seen proof now that you've harnessed the power to travel through time. But I have not seen any proof that you can bring my child back and deliver him to me. I think you can understand why I'd like that proof before I finish the rest of the checklist."

*Whoa, dude,* Jonah thought, so stunned by the force of Lindbergh's words that he actually took a step back from the monitor. Jonah wished that just once, in any of his dealings with Gary and Hodge, he'd been able to muster up even a fraction of that quiet authority.

On the screen Gary and Hodge were gazing frantically

back and forth between each other and Lindbergh and baby Katherine.

"If that baby's presence in this time period ruins—" Gary began.

"No, no, it's what happened at the point of contact that we need to worry about," Hodge interrupted. "We had that calibrated down to the nanosecond." He held his hand out to Lindbergh. "Give me your Elucidator so I can check."

"I'm sure you have navigational devices of your own that you can consult," Lindbergh said calmly. "Did you not tell me that you could spy on me anywhere, anytime?"

Defeated, Gary and Hodge both looked down at their watches.

*Oh, those are their Elucidators,* Jonah realized.

Both men were silent for a long moment.

"I'm sure you'll see that after I changed the girl's age, I traveled back twelve years and eleven months in time, just as you told me to," Lindbergh said. "The girl—what did you call it? She un-aged? Un-grew? Anyhow, I watched her change on the trip through time until she returned to being a baby."

*He made Katherine thirteen years and three months old and then went back twelve years and eleven months to turn her back into a . . . four-month-old baby?* Jonah thought confusedly. *Why? Why those exact numbers? My current age and . . .*

Jonah had to force himself to finish the thought.

*. . . and the age I was when I crash-landed on that airplane with all the other missing children from history.*

So had Gary and Hodge wanted Lindbergh to meet them with Katherine on the airplane, maybe?

Was that why they'd asked if Lindbergh had had trouble adjusting to the plane?

Wouldn't they know whether Lindbergh had met them or not?

Jonah shook his head, starting to get lost in confusion again.

"I don't understand why you didn't just tell me to make the child four months old from the very start, rather than using the time travel to change her age," Lindbergh was saying with a shrug. "Since you told me ages don't *have* to change with time travel. And I saw the proof of that, bringing myself and this child through the better part of a century."

"The un-aging works best if it's done in conjunction with time travel," Hodge muttered. "One second taken away in chronological age as a person travels a second back in time . . . until he or she reaches the right age . . . The body likes that. There's less chance of permanent brain damage, especially when we're erasing such a large portion of someone's life."

*So there is a chance of permanent damage for Mom and Dad and JB and Angela?* Jonah agonized. *Their un-aging wasn't done naturally!*

"And we were making sure all your Elucidator commands would be simple, so you could handle them," Gary growled. "You were supposed to follow our orders exactly!"

Lindbergh didn't even flinch.

"Have you satisfied yourself that I did land at the meeting point you asked me to?" Lindbergh asked. "And then I instantly left to come here. And I'll go back and finish the job as soon as you provide me proof of my son."

Gary dug his elbow into Hodge's side.

"Boss—the time," he muttered. "We're cutting it close."

Hodge snapped a lid over the face of his Elucidator watch.

"We'll provide your proof, all right," he said, his usual arrogant tone returning. "My colleague and I will only need you to wait here for a few minutes. And then we'll be back."

"Now," Gary said, peering intently down at his watch.

He grabbed on to Hodge's arm. And then both men vanished.

Lindbergh looked around, his eyes wide.

"Phenomenal," he muttered.

In his arms baby Katherine had been reduced to only

whimpering. Lindbergh glanced down at her, frowned, and put her down on the table beside him.

"Don't treat my sister like that!" Jonah yelled, as uselessly as ever. "Don't you know babies can roll off tables?"

Lindbergh did keep one hand on Katherine's arm to hold her in place. But he didn't say anything comforting to her like Jonah's parents would have—he didn't say, *There, there,* or *You'll be all right.* Now that Gary and Hodge were out of sight, he seemed to regard Katherine as little more than an annoying doll.

He acted much more concerned with reaching his free hand into his jacket and pulling out the camera Elucidator Gary and Hodge had given him before he'd kidnapped and un-aged Katherine.

"And would it be possible for me to see where they're rushing off to?" Lindbergh muttered, turning the controls. He eased down into a chair beside the table and squinted at the back of the camera. "Is there anything else I can find out that they don't know I can find out?"

*Anything* else? Jonah thought. *What does that mean? Did Lindbergh already find out things Gary and Hodge don't know he knows?*

Jonah leaned close, hoping he could catch a glimpse of whatever Lindbergh was studying so intently.

At first Jonah thought he'd lost his balance, or maybe

just his sense of equilibrium. Because it seemed like he kept getting closer. No—he was falling. It was just like when he'd fallen into the monitor and ended up dangling over the Atlantic Ocean, or when he'd fallen into the monitor and ended up almost cut by the propeller of Lindbergh's plane.

Now, finally, after watching months of time on the monitor, Jonah was going back to 1932.

# TWENTY-SIX

*Why now?* Jonah wondered, as he whirled dizzily toward the past. *Why not five minutes earlier in what was happening in 1932—or five or six months earlier? Why didn't I get zapped back into the same time as JB and Angela?*

Even spinning and dizzy, Jonah could figure out the answer: It must not have been until that moment that Jonah in his original life had disappeared from 1932. Because he hadn't been able to go back to 1932 as long as there was already another version of him there.

But now, evidently, his original self had vanished from 1932.

*Because that's when I was kidnapped—again?* Jonah wondered. *This time by Gary and Hodge, when they took me out of time and planned to take me to the future to be adopted?*

It seemed like odd timing. Pointless, even.

A darker possibility occurred to him.

*Or maybe because that's when I was . . . killed?* Jonah had to inch up on the word to allow himself to think it. There were lots of reasons he didn't like this idea. He seized on the most practical ones.

*But if that's what happened, why was the fake corpse put in place to be discovered way back in May? And how could I be alive now if I already died in 1932? Unless . . . I'm supposed to die in that moment in 1932* after *I was alive in the twenty-first century?*

Jonah landed. He was still confused, and dizzy and timesick as well.

*Listen!* he told himself frantically. *Blink fast, so you can see again as soon as possible.*

Sounds wavered in and out; he could see nothing but a dirty linoleum floor, so close that his eyelashes fluttered against it each time he blinked.

*Turn your head!* Jonah ordered himself.

It seemed to take forever for his neck muscles to obey the command. Now he could make out pairs of shoes beside him.

Were those *six* shoes? Were three people standing beside him?

Jonah decided to focus on his hearing again.

". . . we told you we'd bring back your son," a voice was saying.

*Hodge?* Jonah thought. *Hodge is back? Does that mean Gary is too?*

"My son is incapable of doing anything but lying on the floor?" Lindbergh asked incredulously.

Jonah felt strong arms grab him by the back of the stupid pullover sweater he'd been wearing from the 1920s. The arms—Gary's, evidently—lifted him to a standing position.

"He's just coming from a more distant time than Gary or me," Hodge said apologetically. "Some people are more affected by timesickness than others."

Jonah found himself directly face to face with Charles Lindbergh for the first time since he'd seen the man in the Skidmores' living room. For the first time since Lindbergh had kidnapped Katherine.

*Don't punch him in the gut,* Jonah told himself. *Don't kick him in the shins. Remember—he's your father. He's been searching for you for ages. And . . . maybe you need to get him on your side so he'll help you save Katherine from Gary and Hodge?*

Jonah sneaked one glance toward baby Katherine to see if Lindbergh was still holding on to her—he was. Then Jonah tried to get his facial muscles to pull up the sides of his mouth into a smile.

"H-hi," he said weakly. Lindbergh looked away, back toward Gary and Hodge.

"Is this boy feeble-minded?" he demanded.

"Just give me a moment to get over the timesickness!" Jonah snapped.

He sneaked his gaze toward baby Katherine again. Maybe there was no hope of Lindbergh helping them? Maybe Jonah should just kick Gary away and snatch Katherine from the table and take off running?

*Maybe after I really do get over the timesickness,* Jonah thought weakly.

"Let me get a good look at the boy," Lindbergh said, shoving away Gary's hands from Jonah's shoulders.

Jonah must have looked every bit as weak as he felt—neither Gary nor Hodge seemed worried about the notion of Jonah possibly running away. They just stood back and let Lindbergh walk all around Jonah, studying him.

Jonah felt a little bit like a prize dog. He wouldn't have been surprised if Lindbergh had pulled back his lips and studied his teeth and gums.

"This is just that boy from that other time," Lindbergh said, sounding disappointed. "Jonah Skidmore. You just put him in different clothes. How gullible do you think I am? Don't you know how many hoaxes I've already seen connected to my son?"

*What if he also remembers seeing me holding on to his plane over the Atlantic?* Jonah wondered. *What if he thinks I was trying to make him crash?*

Lindbergh had such a flat expression on his face that Jonah decided that was impossible. Lindbergh had probably decided he'd just imagined seeing a face in that one quick pass of the flashlight beam.

Hodge waved away Lindbergh's questions.

"Could we really have expected you to pluck the child *we* wanted from the future, if you'd known that the son you'd been searching for was standing right there beside the girl?" Hodge said.

"Do you think we're stupid?" Gary asked, sounding insulted.

"But . . . you said . . . that girl's future was in danger," Lindbergh said, narrowing his eyes at Gary and Hodge. "That was the only reason I agreed to take her, to get her away from the danger. Are you saying you left my son in danger that was just as bad? While you were playing games with me? And if you could bring back my son from the future, why couldn't you bring back this girl on your own?"

He took his hand off baby Katherine's arm long enough to point accusingly at her.

*Now?* Jonah wondered. *Do I grab Katherine now?*

His legs still felt like rubber. The throbbing from his old bullet wounds seemed to have come back faster than his strength—at the moment he suspected that even crawling was still a bit beyond him. Maybe he should wait.

"Calm down," Hodge said, patting Lindbergh on the shoulder.

Lindbergh jerked away—Jonah took it as a good sign that Lindbergh didn't want Hodge touching him.

"It's always hard for time natives to understand the intricacies of time travel," Hodge said in a soothing voice. "The future you saw—shall we call it Skidmore time?—that wasn't where we'd planned to stash your son. But we had to dispose of our enemies before we could safely retrieve him. Bringing Katherine Skidmore to safety was also part of our mission, and we couldn't do that ourselves because our enemies were watching for us. They didn't know to look for you. And we *could* bring back Jonah—I mean Charlie—on our own, because he has a connection to this time period. It's like he has a homing device in him. Linked to you and your wife. We just had to activate it, now that it's safe."

Jonah opened his mouth, wanting to correct all the lies Hodge had told. Or, they weren't even lies, exactly—Gary and Hodge did have enemies, and the entire time agency JB worked for had been watching for the kidnappers to show up in the time period where all the missing children were living. And Gary and Hodge—or *someone*—had certainly done something to keep the other time agents from helping JB protect Jonah and the other kids.

It was just that Hodge's version made it sound like he and Gary were the good guys.

Jonah winced and shut his mouth and decided to wait until he was sure he could trust his voice.

Lindbergh kept looking Jonah up and down.

"I would have thought I'd have certainty," Lindbergh said. "I thought I'd know at one glance, 'This is my boy.'"

"Would you like us to un-age him back to being the same age your son was when he disappeared?" Gary asked, pointing his wrist toward Jonah. His watch Elucidator glistened. "We can do it right here. Then you'll see—"

"—that that could cause permanent brain damage?" Lindbergh challenged. *"No."*

"Then I'll carry him through time and bring him back again," Gary said, starting to grab for Jonah's shoulders once more.

Lindbergh shoved Gary's hands away.

"And what else might you do in that moment you're away?" Lindbergh asked bluntly.

He narrowed his eyes at Jonah.

"His hair is so much darker than it used to be," Lindbergh muttered. "And not as curly."

"Your wife's a brunette!" Hodge protested. "And her hair's straight!"

"How old are you, boy?" Lindbergh asked, addressing Jonah directly for the very first time.

"Th-thirteen," Jonah said, his voice shaking.

Were his knees stable yet? Would he have any chance at all if he grabbed Katherine and ran away now?

Lindbergh nodded thoughtfully.

"I believe I was six feet tall by the time I was thirteen," he said. "I thought my son would be taller, more like me."

"Your wife's what—barely five feet?" Hodge asked scornfully. "Look, you've seen the boy now. That's all you asked. Go finish the tasks you promised you'd do for us, and then you'll see. You will have your son, and he *will* be the right age then. And if something's not right . . . how are you any worse off than you were before we made our deal? You're getting to see time travel, sir! That's something no other gentleman of your era will ever experience!"

Lindbergh was nodding slowly, as if he were about to give in.

"Now that I think about it, maybe there is a way to know for sure," he said. "To see if this is really my son or not."

*Make it something lengthy—stall!* Jonah thought. *Give my legs a little more time to be ready to run!*

Lindbergh reached into his flight jacket. For a moment Jonah wondered if Lindbergh was going to pull out his notebook again and make Jonah take some sort of drawing test. Did Lindbergh think his son would automatically know how to draw an airplane engine or something like that?

But when Lindbergh pulled his hand back out, he wasn't holding the notebook. He was holding the camera Elucidator.

And he reached out and placed it directly in Jonah's hands.

# TWENTY-SEVEN

Jonah's muscles were out of practice after months of sitting in the time cave doing nothing but watching the monitor. And he could still feel the aftereffects of timesickness along with his bullet wounds throbbing. But maybe he'd inherited Lindbergh's laser-fast pilot's instincts, even if he hadn't gotten the height or the exact hair color.

Jonah's right hand instantly closed around the Elucidator. With his left arm he scooped up baby Katherine from the table beside Lindbergh. Jonah held her at his side, like a football. And then, before anybody else had a chance to react, he danced past Gary and Hodge and out the door of the airport office.

"What'd you do that for?" Gary screamed behind him.

"I had to see if he thinks like a Lindbergh," Lindbergh said calmly.

*Oh, no pressure,* Jonah thought.

Then he wiped that from his mind, because he didn't care if he thought like a Lindbergh or not. All he cared about was getting Katherine to safety and himself to safety and finding kid JB and kid Angela and rescuing them and fixing their ages and Mom and Dad's ages, and of course fixing Katherine's age too. And then hunting down and rescuing the other missing kids from history who'd vanished from the twenty-first century, and . . .

*One thing at a time, maybe?* Jonah thought.

He spun around the corner of the building, because the only other choice seemed to be running flat out across the empty airfield, in plain sight.

*But maybe Gary and Hodge would expect me to hide around the corner of the building?* Jonah thought, even as he crouched down low, running past a window.

In his arms baby Katherine started to make fussing noises again.

"Shh, shh," Jonah hissed. "I'm saving you! Don't give us away!"

She screwed up her face like she was ready to let out a full-blown wail. Jonah didn't exactly remember what Katherine had been like as a tiny baby the first time around, but probably she wasn't that different from the Katherine she'd been after that: When she was upset, there wasn't much you could do to shut her up.

Jonah peered down at the camera Elucidator Lindbergh had put in his hands.

"Get us out of here!" he demanded in a hushed, frantic tone. "Take us back to the time cave!"

Words lit up the back part of the camera: I CAN'T. BECAUSE OF THE WAY I'VE BEEN PROGRAMMED, I CAN OFFER YOU ONLY A LIMITED NUMBER OF DESTINATIONS. WOULD YOU LIKE TO MAKE ANOTHER SELECTION?

"Somewhere safe!" Jonah said impatiently, barely remembering to keep his voice down. "Somewhere it won't matter if Katherine's loud!"

THAT IS NOT A SPECIFIC ENOUGH INSTRUCTION, the back of the camera flashed at him, and even the typeface seemed to be scolding him. WOULD YOU LIKE TO SEE YOUR CHOICES?

"Yes!" Jonah hissed.

Tiny type began to scroll across the camera back. Jonah could hear footsteps coming around the corner behind him. He didn't have time to read anything right now.

"I can change where I'm going while I'm traveling through time, can't I?" Jonah asked the Elucidator.

OF COURSE, appeared on the camera back.

"Then aim Katherine and me toward the farthest place on that list!" Jonah demanded.

The stucco building beside him and the dusky airfield beyond instantly disappeared. The sound of the running feet behind him instantly stopped. Now he and Katherine were floating through Outer Time.

They'd gotten away.

"I didn't do too badly, did I?" Jonah bragged to baby Katherine. "And I didn't even have you trying to tell me what to do!"

He looked down at her tiny form. He was holding her upside down now, and palming her head like a basketball. It was probably a good thing there wasn't exactly gravity in Outer Time, or else he would have dropped her. It was also amazing that she hadn't started screaming yet, because that couldn't be a comfortable position.

Jonah shifted her weight in his arms, clutching her more securely. Now he could see his sister's face more clearly: She was wide-eyed and awed-looking, turning her head to peer around at the darkness and scattered lights of Outer Time. It was like this was the first time she'd ever seen such a thing—well, maybe it was, technically. Maybe after Lindbergh had un-aged her, he'd kept her so tightly wrapped in blankets that she couldn't see anything.

A tiny wrinkle appeared between Katherine's eyebrows, as if it had just occurred to her baby brain that Outer Time might be as terrifying as it was amazing.

"Hey, hey, don't worry," Jonah said quickly, jiggling her a little to keep her happy. "We'll be fine. We're just going to—"

He remembered he didn't have the slightest clue where they were going.

Baby Katherine was peering up at him now, her expression just as astonished and clueless as when she'd been staring at Outer Time. It was unnerving to have her looking at him like she didn't recognize him. It was unnerving to be holding her, and to have her be such a little baby.

It was unnerving that she couldn't even talk.

"Okay," Jonah said. "First order of business. Elucidator, as we're traveling through time, let Katherine age back up to her right age. Eleven and . . . let's see . . . eleven years, eleven months and fourteen days. That's it. Then—"

AGING HUMANS TO THAT CHRONOLOGICAL MARKER IS NOT A TASK I CAN ACCOMPLISH, the Elucidator camera glowed up at him. And then, as if to make sure Jonah understood, it flashed the words, NO CAN DO.

*Oh no,* Jonah thought, little prickles of panicky sweat breaking out on his forehead.

On his trip to 1918 he and Katherine and their friends had had to use a severely limited Elucidator set up to manipulate them into doing only what Gary and Hodge wanted.

Of course Gary and Hodge wouldn't have handed

Charles Lindbergh an Elucidator that unlocked all the possibilities of time travel for him. Of course they wouldn't have let him have that much power.

Of course they wouldn't have trusted him.

Hadn't the Elucidator already told him it was programmed to be limited?

"Okay, okay," Jonah said, trying to calm himself down. "I *know* this Elucidator was used before to turn people thirteen years and three months old. So make Katherine that age again."

She would make a big deal about being the exact same age as Jonah, and it'd be really annoying. But he could put up with that while she helped him fix everything else, couldn't he?

But the Elucidator was still flashing objections: THAT FUNCTION HAS BEEN DISABLED NOW AS WELL.

"What?" Jonah said. "But you just *did* that. You made her thirteen this morning!"

Well, this morning in a different century. But Jonah thought the Elucidator would know what he meant.

AND THEN AFTER THE AGE CHANGE IN THE TWENTY-FIRST CENTURY, CHARLES LINDBERGH RESET MY FUNCTIONS SO I COULD NO LONGER DO THAT, the Elucidator explained.

*Charles Lindbergh figured out how to tamper with the Elucidator's settings?* Jonah thought with begrudging respect.

In his own time travels Jonah had barely managed to get Elucidators to do what they were set to do when they were supposed to obey him.

*But maybe on this Elucidator I would have the Lindbergh skill?* Jonah wondered.

He started to bend down to peer more closely at the Elucidator. But that motion made him more aware of everything flowing past him: Time. Space. Choices. Changing the Elucidator could take ages, and he probably didn't have much more than a few more moments to play around with.

He glanced at baby Katherine once more: She was blowing spit bubbles.

"Okay, last try," Jonah told the Elucidator. "What age *can* you make Katherine?"

FOUR MONTHS OLD, the Elucidator glowed back at him. THAT WOULD BE A SUBTRACTION OF TWENTY MINUTES AND EIGHT SECONDS. WOULD YOU LIKE ME TO MAKE THE CHANGE?

"Don't bother," Jonah muttered.

He resisted the urge to bang his hand against his head—or smash the Elucidator over his knee.

*Focus,* he reminded himself.

He could feel Outer Time rushing past him and Katherine. They seemed to be speeding up.

"Tell me where we're going," Jonah commanded the Elucidator. "And then tell me my other choices."

THIS IS WHERE YOU'RE HEADED, the Elucidator flashed at him. It showed a very precise time and date and location. But it was somewhere Jonah had already been: his family's living room at 6:57 that morning. As far as Jonah could tell, it was probably the very moment that Katherine had vanished.

"Are you kidding?" Jonah complained. "I already lived through that moment! If I went back, it'd create a paradox! It'd unravel time! It's not even physically possible for you to send me there, is it?"

The Elucidator flashed a lengthy answer at him, which seemed to be explaining all the theories of time. It was like scrolling through all the legal fine print for accepting a software upgrade on a computer. Jonah didn't know anybody who ever read all that.

*Well, except my dad—my adoptive dad,* Jonah thought nervously. *But even he would say this is an emergency, and it's okay to cut corners now.*

Jonah caught sight of the name Second Chance—his other enemy besides Gary and Hodge—and that was all he needed to see.

"Never mind," he told the Elucidator. "Just tell me the other times and places you can take me. And make sure you don't list any moment in time where Katherine and I have already been."

THEN YOU HAVE TWO CHOICES, the Elucidator flashed at him. YOU CAN GO BACK TO 1932, BUT ONLY AT THAT NEW JERSEY AIRFIELD WITHIN A LIMITED TIME RANGE.

*Where Gary and Hodge would just finish the task of recapturing me?* Jonah thought. *No, thanks.*

"Or?" he challenged, glancing anxiously toward the lights of the future speeding toward him, faster and faster.

OR YOU CAN GO TO THE SCENE OF THE TIME CRASH, the Elucidator began.

"You mean, *my* time crash?" Jonah asked. "Thirteen years ago, at that airport, when the planeload of babies appeared out of nowhere? You know I can't go there! I was on that plane!"

I CAN LAND YOU THERE UP TO THIRTY MINUTES BEFORE THE TIME CRASH, the Elucidator flashed back at him. Jonah didn't know how the Elucidator could convey exasperation with just flashing lights, but it really did seem annoyed with him. YOU WEREN'T PRESENT IN THAT TIME THIRTY MINUTES BEFORE THE TIME CRASH. AND NEITHER WAS KATHERINE.

*Why would I want to go there?* Jonah wanted to shout at the Elucidator.

But with time speeding past him faster and faster, maybe his brain sped up a little too. An idea jumped into his mind. Maybe there *was* a good reason for him to go to the scene of the time crash a half an hour before it happened.

"Okay! Okay!" he screamed at the Elucidator. The winds of Outer Time ripped the words from his mouth, and baby Katherine started wailing at the brutality of the forces pounding against her tiny frame. Jonah clutched her even tighter and struggled to say what he had to say.

"Take! Us! Then!" he bellowed into the Elucidator. "Take us to thirty minutes before the time crash!"

# TWENTY-EIGHT

They landed on the runway.

"Ha-ha," Jonah muttered. "Very funny."

He seemed to be flat on his back, with baby Katherine lying on his chest and the Elucidator clutched in his right hand. The Elucidator felt smaller—oh, it was a digital camera now, not a boxy 1930s type. Jonah blinked up at the blurry runway lights instead. The timesickness seemed to be having an odd effect on him, making the lights seem to stream closer and closer with each moment that passed.

*Closer?* he thought groggily.

He squinted, trying to bring the lights into focus against the twilight sky. Then he bolted upright.

*Oh, crap! Those lights really are getting closer! They're on an airplane!*

The motion and panic made Jonah dizzier than ever,

but he managed to clutch Katherine to his chest and scramble across the concrete.

*Hmm . . . maybe it's better if I don't crawl parallel to the runway lines?* Jonah wondered.

He rolled off the cement into frozen mud, just as a huge jet zoomed past him.

"Is there some requirement that you had to put me down in a life-threatening situation?" he shouted at the Elucidator.

YOU SAID TO LAND AT THE SITE OF THE TIME CRASH, the Elucidator flashed back at him. THIS IS THE SITE.

Jonah looked back at the runway, empty now that the jet had zipped on by.

*So that's where we all landed,* he thought numbly. *Me and the other thirty-five kids. Thirteen years ago. Er, no—where we're going to land. In thirty minutes. Or maybe just twenty-five or twenty-six now?*

He looked down at the Elucidator.

"Can you start a countdown to when the time crash is supposed to happen?" he asked. "So I know how much time I have left?"

He almost expected the Elucidator to refuse, but red numerals glowed at the top of the camera frame: 24.

*I've already wasted six minutes just landing and getting off the runway?* Jonah thought in dismay.

He struggled back up to his feet, wrapping his arms more tightly around baby Katherine. She whimpered slightly.

"Sorry, kid. We've got to hurry," Jonah muttered to her.

Standing upright, Jonah felt horribly exposed by the runway lights—for now that the jet was out of the way, he could see the actual lights lining the runway.

*It's probably a felony or something for people who don't work at the airport to walk around on the runways,* Jonah thought. *I'm probably just asking to be busted by security.*

Jonah glanced wistfully at a ditch to the side of the runway—should he crouch down there, and maybe commando-crawl toward the terminal?

*No time for that,* Jonah told himself.

Just then the red 4 on the Elucidator's countdown clock blinked out and was replaced by a 3. He had twenty-three minutes left.

"Here goes nothing," Jonah muttered to baby Katherine.

He held her tight against his chest and took off running blindly toward the brighter lights of the terminal off in the distance. He was close enough to see the Jetways dangling from the side of the building like so many caterpillars; near the scattered planes parked beside the terminal he could see baggage handlers driving carts labeled SKYTRAILS AIR.

*SkyTrails Air—that's the airline Angela worked for thirteen years ago!* he thought excitedly.

No—that was the airline Angela worked for now. Today. Right at this moment. He was in the time he still thought of as thirteen years ago. He was at the airport on the one and only day Angela worked for SkyTrails.

And Angela was the person he needed to see and talk to sometime within the next twenty-three minutes.

*It's probably not a good idea to ask one of the baggage handlers if they know where I can find her,* Jonah told himself.

He was close enough now that if any of the baggage handlers looked his way, they'd see him. And then they'd probably yell and set off alarms—and make it impossible for him to get in to see Angela.

Jonah stopped running and crouched down beside the front wheel of a small SkyTrails jet parked near the terminal.

A baggage handler parked a cart full of suitcases next to the jet.

*Okay, run over behind that next,* Jonah told himself. *And then . . .*

And then there was a long stretch of open concrete between him and the airport terminal.

*Can't be helped,* Jonah thought. He clutched baby Katherine to his chest and took off running again.

There was an open door in the shadows under one of the Jetways. Jonah was already stepping through it before it occurred to him that he would probably be entering baggage-handler territory: a place of conveyor belts loaded with suitcases and big burly men who were so used to throwing around fifty-pound bags that they'd probably think nothing of pummeling Jonah.

Jonah struggled to come up with a decent excuse: *How about, 'My baby sister was crying so much they made us get off the plane, right in the middle of the runway'? No, that doesn't sound plausible. . . .*

Then he blinked and realized the doorway just led into an empty stairwell.

*Wouldn't that be a huge security violation, having an open door like that?* he thought uneasily. *Should I be suspicious, that maybe this is a little too . . . easy?*

The Elucidator showed that he had only twenty-two minutes left. He didn't have time to be suspicious.

"Gaa," baby Katherine said, waving her arms as though she approved of getting inside, away from the cold. The stairwell even had a heater roaring loudly at the bottom of the stairs.

"Oh, right, I guess you are just wearing . . . ," Jonah began, looking closely at Katherine's clothing for the first time. She was wrapped in a pink-and-purple-striped blanket over some sort of white cotton nightie or . . .

No. She was wrapped in the pink-and-purple-striped sweater she'd put on that morning as a sixth grader getting ready for school. It just looked like a blanket because it was so much larger than her body now that she was a four-month-old baby. And the white cotton "nightie" below was a strategically knotted version of the T-shirt she'd been wearing this morning too.

"So, um, no diaper?" Jonah muttered, patting Katherine's rear.

That was yet another reason he needed to hurry.

He crept up the stairs and was relieved to find them empty all the way up to the next level. He came to a closed door and opened it just enough to see out into the long crowded hallway of passenger waiting areas. Nobody was looking his way, so he stepped out. He started to let the door shut behind him, but at the last minute he grabbed the handle.

*Don't forget your escape route,* he told himself.

He saw a crumpled-up gum wrapper on the floor and slid it back between the door and the door frame to keep the door from latching completely.

*Brilliant,* he told himself.

He so wished Katherine were her correct age right now, so she could admire his genius.

*But she'd probably just tell me I should be focusing on what's next,* he thought.

He did need to be focusing on what was next.

*Blend in so nobody kicks you out before you find Angela,* he told himself.

He stepped out onto the broad carpeted area where people were walking from the security checkpoint to their gates, or from just-landed planes toward the baggage-claim escalator. He wasn't sure how much he could blend in when he was wearing 1920s knickers and a nerdy-looking pullover sweater—and carrying a baby wrapped in a teenager's clothes—but he tried to plaster a cheerful look on his face that said, *Hey! I belong here!*

For all his experience with time travel, Jonah was surprised at how odd it felt to be just thirteen years away from his regular time period. The colors seemed too bright somehow. The Christmas decorations hanging from the ceiling looked too big. The carpet he was walking on looked too new—probably because it was supposed to be another eight years before he'd remember seeing it, from that time his family flew to Florida when Jonah was in second grade. A man in a business suit walked past telling another guy, "Hey, did you see my new cell phone? Newest model Sprint has!"—and he was holding out a flip phone, of all things.

Honestly, there were even people walking around with what looked like portable CD players instead of iPods.

Jonah was turned around looking at someone wearing prehistoric-looking headphones rather than earbuds, when he bumped into an airline worker in a navy blue uniform.

"Watch where you're going!" she snapped.

Before Jonah had a chance to apologize, she stepped around him, leaving a ghostly tracer version of herself to walk straight through him.

*Of course she left a tracer, moving away from me,* Jonah thought. *Well, just wait another twenty minutes or so, lady. When the planeload of babies lands, this airport is going to be overrun with tracers!*

And then something struck Jonah with such force that he stopped in his tracks.

In his first thirteen years of life, he had never once seen a tracer. And he *should* have. Anyone who traveled through time could see tracers, and Jonah had made his first trip through time when he was only four months old. His entire childhood had been a time-travel disruption. Practically every move he'd ever made should have set off a flurry of tracers.

*Maybe it didn't because I was so young the first time I traveled through time?* he thought. *Maybe there's some kind of age limit—time travelers can see tracers only after their first time trip that they're aware of?*

But baby Katherine, in Jonah's arms, was definitely peering directly at the stream of tracers Jonah had just created in the middle of the airport hallway, as everyone had to step around him. Her eyes were wide and scared, and she gave a little gulp every time one of the ghostly figures brushed past her. She reached out as if trying to stop the tracer of a SkyTrails pilot that seemed to walk right through her and Jonah. *She* could see tracers, and she was just a baby.

*And anyway, after Alex, Chip, Katherine, and I came back from the 1400s, we definitely should have been able to see tracers in our own time period then,* Jonah told himself. *Why didn't we? Why didn't we ask JB why we didn't see tracers in the twenty-first century?*

They'd just had too many other things to think about. And Jonah, at least, had really not wanted to think too much about all the weird and scary aspects of time travel.

This was definitely weird and scary.

*In 1611 when the tracers vanished, it was because time was unraveling, because our enemy Second Chance was ripping time apart. . . . Second Chance isn't here now! Second Chance wasn't involved in the time crash that stranded me and the other babies on the plane!*

At least not as far as Jonah knew.

The Elucidator in Jonah's hand flashed a glowing red numeral up toward Jonah: 15.

He had just fifteen minutes left. He didn't have time to

worry about tracers or unraveling time or Second Chance or anything else except finding Angela.

*Think, think . . . did she ever tell us what gate she was working at that night?* Jonah asked himself.

He couldn't remember. But he looked around frantically, thinking it might help to at least see which gates were nearby: 2A, 2B . . .

Something about 2B jogged his memory. It was right beside the door he'd sneaked through only moments ago, but also . . .

*Didn't Angela say the planeload of babies pulled up to 2B?* Jonah wondered. *And didn't she say she could see it from the gate she was standing at?*

Jonah pushed his way through the crowd to the other side of the aisle. There was gate 3. Two women were standing in front of clunky-looking old computer terminals at gate 3. One was the surly-looking lady who'd snapped at Jonah, commanding him to watch where he was going.

The other one was Angela.

# TWENTY-NINE

Jonah resisted the urge to run over to Angela and give her a big hug. He resisted screaming out, *Angela! I thought I'd never see you again! It's been months!*

*She doesn't know who you are,* Jonah reminded himself. *As far as she knows, she's never met you before in her life.*

And this Angela, the Angela of thirteen years ago, truly *hadn't* ever met Jonah. Their first meeting was still supposed to be fifteen minutes away, and Jonah wouldn't remember it.

But Angela would. Angela would stubbornly remember every single detail—even the ones she was supposed to forget. And that would ruin her life.

"Sorry," Jonah muttered.

What if Jonah's current plan made Angela's life even worse? What if it backfired?

Angela looked up from her computer just then, and Jonah almost gasped. Angela looked so young. She'd at least graduated from high school before taking the job with SkyTrails, hadn't she? In a weird way, she almost looked younger on her first day on the job at SkyTrails than she had the last time Jonah had seen her as an un-aged-to-being-thirteen-again kid with JB and Jonah in the time cave.

*It's because she looks so naïve and trusting,* Jonah told himself. She doesn't look suspicious at all.

Jonah had never seen Angela not looking either suspicious or worried. Or both. That was what witnessing the time crash had done to her.

But here she was, pre–time crash: her dark skin glowing, her smile so eager to please, her navy blue uniform a little too crisply ironed. She wasn't yet a woman who'd defy the FBI; she was just a girl who thought working at the airport would be a good way to become a pilot.

Maybe, as JB had said once, she really was supposed to marry a plumber and have five kids.

Jonah squeezed baby Katherine a little too tightly, and she whined in response.

"I don't have any other choice, do I, Kath?" Jonah asked her.

Katherine waved her hand in a clumsy motion that sideswiped Jonah's ear.

*Okay, don't expect help from a four-month-old,* Jonah told himself.

He wished Katherine really could help him. He wished someone else could make this decision. He wished he had more time to think. But while he'd been standing there watching Angela, the timer on the Elucidator had clicked down to fourteen minutes left.

He sighed.

"We need to find some paper really fast," he told Katherine.

The baby waved her arms vaguely. Jonah knew she really wasn't capable of helping, but her gesture did make him notice the row of trash cans in front of gate 5.

"You're right. That's probably our best option right now," he muttered to baby Katherine.

At least thirteen years ago was recent enough that some of the trash cans were paper-only recycling, so Jonah didn't have to paw through ketchup-covered food wrappers. He found a mostly empty sheet of paper where someone had printed out an e-mail that just said, *Okay, that's fine.* He ripped off the top part of the page, and asked an older woman wearing a Christmas sweater if he could borrow a pen.

"Do you want me to hold your baby for you while you write?" the woman asked.

"No, that's okay," Jonah said quickly.

She was probably just being nice, but how could Jonah be sure?

It was hard to hold Katherine and the Elucidator in one hand and brace the paper against the side of the trash can while he wrote.

*And I need to make sure that I don't make any mistakes in what I write. . . .*

The Elucidator countdown said 13 now. Jonah pressed the pen against the paper and began:

*Dear Angela,*

*You don't know me yet, and I can't explain much because that could mess up everything.*

Was even telling her that much enough to mess up everything? Jonah reminded himself he didn't have time for second-guessing. He kept writing.

*You're going to see some strange stuff tonight that you won't understand for a long time. But I promise you, you will eventually. When you do, it's very important that you carry your own Elucidator the morning of*

Jonah had to think very hard to remember the date of the morning that Charles Lindbergh had kidnapped

Katherine; and Angela, JB, Mom, and Dad had all turned into thirteen-year-olds. But he wrote it down. And then he finished up:

*Don't tell me or JB anything about your Elucidator that morning. Just have it with you. Also, when you see me again, don't say anything about getting this letter. But then, when you go back to 1932, meet me at the airfield where Charles Lindbergh flies on the afternoon of August 15. Hide out of sight until you see me run out of the office. And then, as soon as you can get me away from Gary and Hodge, we can go rescue JB.*

He signed it *Sincerely, Jonah Skidmore,* and went back and reread the whole thing.

It sounded crazy.

Angela would just throw it away. Or maybe she'd turn it over to the FBI when they showed up later tonight, and that would make a whole lot of problems for Jonah's parents.

Jonah ripped off the bottom part of the letter, where he'd written his name. Then he ripped that part into shreds and tossed it back into the recycling.

"Changing your mind about whether you're in love

with some girl or not?" the Christmas-sweater woman asked with way too much interest.

"No, just made a mistake," Jonah said, trying not to sound as panicked as he felt.

"Unnhh," baby Katherine groaned, waving her arms at the Elucidator.

It said Jonah had eight minutes left.

Jonah folded the letter in half and tucked in the ends. Normal-age Katherine would definitely have been useful now—wasn't she always writing secret notes to her friends back when she was in elementary school? And then folding them perfectly? Jonah wished he had tape or an official-looking envelope or *something* that didn't look like it'd been chewed by a dog or a baby. But this was the best he could do. He wrote on the outside of the tucked-together letter: *Do not open for another twelve years and eleven months.*

"Thanks a lot," he said, handing the woman back her pen.

"No problem," the woman said.

Jonah could feel her watching him as he walked toward gate 3, where Angela was standing. But it couldn't be helped. He didn't have time to distract her by walking in the opposite direction and then coming back when she'd stopped watching. He didn't have time to review his plans. He didn't have time to think. He barely had time to speak to Angela.

Just as Jonah approached her desk, a large man elbowed his way in front of Jonah.

"Where's the New York flight?" the man screamed at Angela. "Which gate?"

"Umm . . . ," Angela said uncertainly. She peered helplessly down at her computer. "Give me a minute to check. . . ."

She seemed paralyzed just trying to figure out what to type into the computer to find out.

"*I'll* help you," the woman beside Angela told the man, even as she glared at Angela. Jonah was glad for Angela's sake that she had her head bent down and didn't catch the full force of the glare.

*Who says looks can't kill?* Jonah thought.

He hitched baby Katherine a little higher up, so she wouldn't be in danger of sliding out of his grasp if she squirmed a little.

Angela wasn't bobbing her head back up to look toward Jonah. Maybe she had caught more of the other woman's glare than Jonah had thought.

"Hi," Jonah said, trying to sound friendly and cheerful and like someone Angela should be happy to see.

Angela looked up and seemed to be trying very hard to smile and look professional.

"Yes?" she said fearfully.

Jonah could see how the corners of her smile trembled.

"I just had something to give you," Jonah said, sliding the folded-up letter across the desk. "It's for later. Nothing you have to worry about now."

Angela glanced nervously toward the other woman, who was still talking to the New York man.

"Okay," Angela said hesitantly. "Thanks."

She made no move to pick up Jonah's letter. Did she think she would have to ask the other woman what to do with bizarre letters she received from bizarrely dressed kids holding bizarrely dressed babies?

"Put it someplace safe—your pocket or your purse or someplace like that," Jonah said. "It's really important. Don't forget."

"All right," Angela said, and at least she did move the letter off the ledge and down closer to her computer.

"You'll understand all this later on," Jonah said, and something changed in Angela's smile: It started looking more suspicious. More like what Jonah had seen on Angela's face the first time he'd met her.

*Oh, no,* Jonah thought. *I'm making it sound like the letter's a bomb threat and I'm a terrorist or something like that.*

"That's all," Jonah said, doing his best to sound like a good kid. Or maybe a stupid one—maybe it would help if he didn't sound bright enough to build a bomb? "Well, me and my sister, we have a plane to catch now. Bye!"

And then it was the hardest thing in the world to make himself walk away from Angela without another word.

But surely that was what he had to do to make everything else work right?

Jonah glanced back over his shoulder once to make sure Angela wasn't picking up the phone to call security. Fortunately for him—but not her—she was already distracted: The other woman seemed to be screaming at her for not helping the New York man the instant he asked.

Jonah wanted to go back and defend Angela. He wanted to go back and double-check: *Do you understand that this letter is important—but not dangerous? Do you promise that you won't read it for another twelve years and eleven months?* He wanted lots of things. But if he was going to get safely away before the time-crashed plane arrived—with the baby version of himself on board, ruining time—he needed to zoom back to 1932, where, hopefully, Angela would be waiting with a better Elucidator that could save them both.

It didn't seem like a very good idea to just disappear from the middle of the airport, right in front of dozens of people.

Hiding in a stall in the bathroom might work, but it looked like the nearest bathroom was several gates away, and it might be just as crowded as the hallway.

Jonah was glad that he'd thought to prop the door open back out to the stairwell at gate 2B.

"I'm going to tell you about this when you're eleven again," he muttered to the baby version of Katherine. "And you're really going to be impressed."

Jonah tried to look like he was sauntering casually through the crowd over to the door beside the deserted gate 2B. First he leaned on the wall by the door, glancing back to make sure that Angela wasn't watching him.

No, she was still being yelled at.

There weren't any security guards in sight, and none of the passengers flocking through the hall seemed to be looking in Jonah's direction.

Jonah jerked open the door to the stairwell and slipped through. After the bright lights of the main part of the terminal, his eyes didn't have time to adjust—as far as he could tell, he was just stepping into darkness.

The door eased shut behind him. Jonah took one step to the side, thinking that it'd be good to be out of the way if anyone followed him through the door.

*Not that it matters, since I'm just going back to 1932, where, if I'm lucky, kid Angela will be waiting with an Elucidator,* he thought. *A real, full-strength Elucidator, not one that only gives me three choices of places to go.*

The limited Elucidator in his hand said he still had five

minutes left on the countdown. Should he risk taking at least a few of those minutes to plan what he should do in 1932?

Jonah wavered on what to do. And then that didn't matter either. Before Jonah even finished his step to the side, two pairs of hands grabbed him and Katherine.

# THIRTY

"Right on time," a voice growled in Jonah's ear.

*Hodge,* Jonah thought, trying to squirm away. *And* . . .

Jonah felt baby Katherine and the Elucidator being ripped from his hands by an overwhelming force. There was no way for Jonah to fight against it.

*So Gary's here too,* Jonah thought.

"Take me back to 1932!" Jonah screamed, just in case he could still manage to get a voice command to the Elucidator. "Or to my own time! I mean, thirteen years from now! And—bring Katherine, too!"

Hodge laughed.

"A little confused, are we, about where you want to go?" he taunted. "And about what your own time is?"

"The Elucidator should have known what I meant," Jonah muttered.

His eyes were starting to adjust. He could tell that Gary was putting baby Katherinc down on the floor. She immediately began to cry.

"Hey!" Jonah complained. "Be careful with my sister! That floor's dirty! Pick her up again—or let me hold her!"

Gary snorted.

"She's not your problem anymore," he said, leaning over the baby. Was he putting something in her mouth? Katherine instantly stopped crying.

"What'd you do to her? You didn't hurt her, did you?" Jonah asked, squirming frantically.

Hodge tightened his grip on Jonah and slid his hand over Jonah's mouth.

"It was just a sedative," he muttered. "Easiest way to travel with babies. If you don't calm down, we'll have to knock you out too."

"Yeah," Gary echoed, twisting Jonah's arm behind his back.

In a practiced move so smooth Jonah almost missed it, the two men had switched off, so now it was just Gary holding on to Jonah, Gary whose hand covered Jonah's mouth.

*Should I try to scream anyway?* Jonah wondered.

As if he knew exactly what Jonah was thinking, Gary held up a hypodermic needle.

"You make a sound louder than a whisper, this is going into your arm," he hissed in Jonah's ear.

"It's from the future," Hodge added threateningly. "Sedatives in the future work instantly. That is if it's really a sedative, and not something worse."

Jonah flinched, and evidently that was enough to make Gary and Hodge think he believed them. Gary's grip on Jonah's face eased up a little, going from a "could cause permanent disfigurement" level down to merely "very painful." Hodge backed away ever so slightly.

*They wouldn't really hurt me,* Jonah told himself. *I'm still valuable to them. Because I'm Charles Lindbergh's son.*

But he decided it wouldn't be such a bad thing to pretend he was too terrified to scream or struggle anymore. At least until he figured out what they were planning to do.

"Three minutes," Hodge said, stepping over Katherine so he could peer out a window toward the runway.

"You mean until the plane full of babies gets here?" Jonah asked, though it was a challenge trying to talk with Gary's massive hand clenched over the bottom part of his face. "Shouldn't we leave now so none of us are, um, duplicated in time? So all three of us don't ruin time just by standing here?"

Jonah really didn't want to go anywhere with Gary and

Hodge. But he couldn't help remembering how messed up 1611 had been when his other enemy, Second Chance, had forced there to be multiple copies of people in the same time period.

Hodge laughed.

"You thought Gary and I were on that plane during the crash landing?" he sneered. "Don't you think we have more of a sense of self-preservation than that?"

Jonah squinted uncomprehendingly at him.

"Oh man, we *bailed,*" Gary said, digging his elbow into Jonah's side in a way that might have been intended as friendly. "We had fifty time agents chasing us, they had their sights trained on the plane—that's what time parachutes are made for!"

Jonah had always assumed that Gary and Hodge had sneaked away only *after* the plane was on the ground. Had anybody ever told him that? Or had he just thought it because he couldn't imagine Gary and Hodge abandoning the thirty-six babies in midair? He knew Gary and Hodge weren't exactly nice people, but . . . how could anybody do that?

"So you were just going to let me and the other thirty-five babies die?" Jonah asked. He forgot that he was trying to sound terrified, but it didn't matter. His voice couldn't have been shakier.

"Oh, we were sure the autopilot would land *somewhere* safely," Hodge said.

"Well, pretty sure, anyway," Gary added.

"And we knew the time agents would be too afraid of injuring time to just shoot you all down," Hodge continued.

"And we did come back for all those babies who are going to make us billionaires many times over," Gary finished. "So—no harm, no foul."

Jonah could feel Gary shrugging. A more confident kid than Jonah might have taken that moment to jerk away from Gary, scoop up baby Katherine from the floor, dive back through the door into the open space of the airport terminal, and scream, "Help! Kidnappers!" loud enough for everyone to hear. But Jonah didn't actually think he could do any of that. And he was stuck trying to make sense of Gary's words.

*Gary and Hodge came back to try to kidnap us all again at the adoption conference, when they took us into the time cave,* Jonah thought. *But the men I'm with now are the same Gary and Hodge I saw in 1932. They're older than they were in the time cave, so they have to know that they didn't get any of us then. We didn't make them billionaires after that. They just ended up in time prison.*

But then they'd escaped.

*And so . . . does Gary mean that now they're coming back* again *to capture us? Right now?*

"Two minutes," Hodge said.

"You can't fly that plane back out of here when it lands," Jonah said, frantic enough to try to squirm away from Gary's hand on his mouth. Enough to talk, anyway. "You'll just get us all killed! The time agents will shoot you down, or—or—"

"You thought we were going to risk our *own* lives on this rescue mission?" Gary said, sounding amused enough by Jonah's theory that he loosened his grip on Jonah's face even more.

"Let's just say we've found someone we trust to help us," Hodge said. "And in a few minutes, the time agents are all going to be too distracted to worry about one little plane or the babies on it."

Jonah heard a thump down below at the bottom of the stairwell.

"He's here," Gary said.

*Who?* Jonah wondered, even as another part of his brain was calculating, *Is the timer down to a minute and a half now?* Are *they planning to get me out of here before the time runs out entirely?*

Hodge glanced at something in his hand—Jonah realized that it was the camera Elucidator he himself had been holding only a few moments ago. So Gary and Hodge had passed that between them too, when they'd traded off who was holding on to Jonah.

That meant Jonah didn't have any hope of worming the Elucidator away from Gary and quickly switching times before Gary understood what had happened.

He *really* didn't have any hope of lunging at Hodge and grabbing the Elucidator from him, and then also grabbing baby Katherine from the floor before Gary or Hodge stopped him. And there was no way Jonah was leaving Katherine behind.

"We'll give him a moment to get over the timesickness, and then I'll bring him through," Hodge said.

Who were they talking about?

Hodge picked up baby Katherine and began climbing down the stairs.

"Kath—where—?" Jonah started to protest, but Gary pressed his hand harder than ever against Jonah's face.

"Believe me, your sister is going to be better off this way," Gary growled in Jonah's ear. "Don't mess up our plan."

"I don't know your plan!" Jonah protested, his words muffled by Gary's hand. "I don't know what's going on!"

"I thought you would have figured it out by now," Gary muttered. "Do I really have to spell everything out? You're the bait, of course. You're the reason our new pilot is willing to fly our planeload of babies to the future for us. Because he thinks that will save you."

Jonah stared blankly at Gary.

*JB?* Jonah wondered. *Would JB betray everything he believes in and everything he's worked for as a time agent to save me?*

Jonah didn't think so. He thought JB had his limits—and anyway, as far as Jonah knew, JB was still stuck in 1932. There were plenty of other people who cared about Jonah: his parents, Katherine, Angela, several of the other missing children from history. But Jonah didn't think any of them were in any position to help him. His parents were knocked out, Katherine was knocked out *and* just a baby at the moment . . .

Gary shook Jonah impatiently.

"Who would want to save you who's already a pilot?" he hinted.

And then Jonah understood. Gary was talking about Charles Lindbergh. Gary and Hodge were using Jonah as bait, to get Lindbergh to fly the planeload of babies to the future for them. Gary and Hodge would get their billions from baby selling after all.

And Charles Lindbergh would get his toddler back.

He would get Jonah, un-aged and time-traveled back to 1932.

# THIRTY-ONE

"But I'm already on that plane!" Jonah protested, squirming against Gary's grip. "Why wouldn't Lindbergh just pick me up from my seat on that plane and go back to 1932 and leave everyone else behind?"

Jonah was partly just thinking aloud, in shock. But there was also a part of his brain already calculating, *If I can get Gary to doubt their plan, maybe he'll make some mistake that will stop everything—that really will save me. And Katherine. And all the other kids on the plane.*

Gary just looked bored. He didn't even bother to flex his muscles to hold on tighter.

"You aren't going to be on the plane this time around," he said. "Let's just say your moment in history isn't over yet."

*Because I never went back to my original time and fixed the problems of the past,* Jonah thought numbly. *All the other kids did. They're taken care of. Taking them out of the past doesn't cause any problems with history anymore. Everything that Katherine and I did, everything JB and the other time agents did—it's just going to end up helping Gary and Hodge!*

Jonah was trying to get his brain to move along to another dilemma—should he be trying to figure out what Gary and Hodge had done with the baby version of himself back in the 1930s, if they *hadn't* put him on the plane? But then he heard footsteps on the stairs, coming toward them. Gary pinched Jonah's arm. Or maybe it was the warning poke of a needle.

"We're going to show you to Lindbergh so he trusts us," Gary whispered. "So he'll believe that when he gets back from the future, you'll be waiting for him in 1932. But if you say or do anything that messes up our plans, I'll have this needle in your arm so fast you won't know what hit you. And then—pow." He made a motion with his hand that was probably supposed to look like a person fainting. Or dying. "Don't expect me to care what happens to you then."

Jonah couldn't think of a plan that would be worth the risk of Gary knocking him out or killing him. He couldn't think of a plan at all.

Hodge and Lindbergh appeared at the top of the steps.

Jonah wasn't too surprised to see that Lindbergh was now wearing a more modern uniform, identical to the navy blue ones he'd seen pilots wearing out in the terminal only moments ago. Lindbergh was even carrying the same kind of black roller bag that those pilots had carried.

Gary took his hand off Jonah's mouth, but he kept a tight grip around Jonah's shoulders. And Jonah could feel the prod of the needle—now behind his back, the tip just touching the skin through his pullover sweater.

"As you see, your son did think like a Lindbergh—he figured out to come here to meet you," Hodge was saying. "He just didn't realize that we had complete tracking capacity on that Elucidator. Or that you still have a noble duty to carry out before the two of you can be reunited for good."

"Dad," Jonah said, and that sounded completely wrong. He started over again. "I mean, Father . . ."

What was he supposed to say? What could he say that would prevent him from spending the rest of his life as some stranger everyone thought of as Charles Lindbergh's son? What could he say that would prevent Chip and Andrea and all the other missing kids Jonah was friends with from spending their entire lives growing up in the future? What could he say that would rescue Katherine, JB, Angela, and Jonah's twenty-first century parents?

"Can't I give my father a good-bye hug?" Jonah

appealed to Gary and Hodge, because at least that would buy him a few more seconds to think about what to say. And—oh yeah—it would also give him a chance to whisper something privately to Lindbergh.

But Hodge must have figured that out too.

"Now, now, Jonah, you with your modern sensibilities!" he scolded. "You should know that the Lindberghs weren't hugging types." Now he looked toward Charles Lindbergh. "Colonel, didn't your wife leave instructions for the nanny to avoid hugging and coddling your child too much, so he wouldn't be spoiled?"

"She did," Lindbergh said, and he seemed to be speaking through clenched teeth. "I believe that was the standard policy."

But in that one moment Gary and Hodge were both looking at Lindbergh. Lindbergh was still gazing toward Jonah, so Jonah took a risk: He decided to mouth a message to Lindbergh.

*Don't trust them,* Jonah said, moving his lips with great precision but not making a sound. And then, because there was a very good chance that the next time Jonah saw Charles Lindbergh, Jonah would have no memory of the person he'd been for the past thirteen years, Jonah added just as emphatically, just as silently, *I'm not your son. I'm Jonah Skidmore.*

Lindbergh's expression didn't change, but Jonah wasn't sure if that was because he was trying to be careful around Gary and Hodge, or because he hadn't understood what Jonah was saying. Or maybe he hadn't even noticed Jonah's lips moving. That was possible too.

"The plane is just pulling up to the gate now," Hodge said. "Colonel Lindbergh, it's a shame we don't have time to show you around the entire airport, to see the state of aviation nearly a century after you started flying. Maybe another time? Or maybe you'll be more interested in the aviation in *my* time period, in the future?"

Still carrying baby Katherine, he shoved open the door out into the main part of the terminal. Lindbergh followed close behind.

Gary held Jonah back from the door as it slammed shut.

"*Is* the plane here now?" Jonah hissed at Gary.

Jonah strained toward the stairwell window Hodge had been looking out earlier, and Gary let him pull both of them in that direction. Jonah pressed his face against the glass.

Most of his view was blocked by the Jetway extending out from gate 2B. But Jonah could see that a small plane was just rolling up on the other side of that Jetway. The plane looked like it was going too fast; then it jerked to a stop that seemed almost impossibly sudden.

*That's what Angela remembered seeing,* Jonah thought. *That's exactly what she described, when she told Chip and Katherine and me about the plane. She's probably watching this right now from over at gate* 3.

Jonah had more of a front-row view: He could see the seats inside the plane—the back few rows, anyway. They were odd contraptions that seemed to hold the tiny babies inside completely immobile no matter how much the plane jerked. Jonah blinked—no, now they were just regular airplane seats, each holding the kind of baby seat he remembered from old home movies of him and Katherine.

*Everything changed that fast?* he marveled.

"Did Hodge just—" he began, even though he couldn't see any sign of Hodge or Lindbergh through the plane's windows.

"We had the plane set to do that automatically," Gary said. "And the time agency thought we weren't careful enough about protecting time. Who are the true time heroes now?"

He snorted as if that question really amused him. But he kept his grip on Jonah as strong as ever.

"The FBI's going to get involved," Jonah said, because he could fight back against Gary with words, even if he had no hope of breaking away physically. "This whole airport's going to be a time disaster area. After Angela steps on that plane and sees the babies, there's going to be thirteen years of Damaged Time. No time traveler's going to be able to get in or out."

It occurred to him to wonder if Gary and Hodge were dead certain about the exact moment that Damaged Time began. *Was* it when Angela stepped onto the plane? Or when she and everyone else started pulling babies out into the airport? Or when the babies all went to new homes, changing thirty-six families' lives?

*Or will it just be thirty-five families' lives, if I'm not on that plane?* Jonah wondered. He winced at the thought.

"Oh no, Damaged Time," Gary mocked, taking his left hand off Jonah just long enough to put it up to his face in a gesture of mock terror. "For thirteen years!"

"I'm serious," Jonah insisted, trying to stay focused on arguing with Gary. "When does it start? How much time do we have before you and Hodge and Katherine and I have to get out of here?"

Gary started laughing.

"You're really still worried about that?" he asked. "Don't you see? If Lindbergh takes that planeload of babies off to the future, there *is* no Damaged Time. There's no damage. We've fixed everything!"

Gary's smirk was too much. Jonah turned his face to the side.

*I should have figured that out,* Jonah thought. *Katherine would have, in nothing flat. She would have been screaming at Gary, "But what about the babies' families here? What about the lives they had for thirteen years?"*

Jonah couldn't scream that at Gary. He didn't think he could squeeze any words past the lump that had formed in his throat. And anyhow, now the plane was starting to jerk back from the Jetway.

*Angela will never step onto that plane,* Jonah realized, a bubble of panic starting in his chest. *Nobody at this airport will see those babies. Angela will probably start doubting she ever saw that plane. She'll think it was just a reflection in the glass, just a trick of the eye. She won't quit her job and spend thirteen years researching physics, trying to understand time travel. She'll . . . she'll throw away the note I gave her.*

"Please," Jonah whispered to Gary. "We were already so close to fixing everything. I was the only missing kid from history who hadn't gone back in time already. Well—I guess I have gone back now. And I guess maybe there's no way to keep me from having to live in the 1930s. But . . . for the other kids, for their families—can't you just let them stay here?"

Gary started laughing even more.

"Do you know how much money I'd have to give up?" he asked.

"But—for thirty-five families' happiness," Jonah began. "All those parents who desperately wanted a kid . . . remember Andrea? Remember how her parents are going to die when she's twelve years old? Don't they deserve twelve years of happiness with Andrea before they die?"

Gary kept laughing.

"I can't believe that goody-goody JB lied to you for so long," he said. "I can't believe you fell for it."

"What are you talking about?" Jonah asked, even as he saw the plane pulling farther back from the Jetway. Most of the plane windows were in shadow now, so Jonah couldn't get one last glimpse of his friends as babies. But he could see into the cockpit as the plane went past. Charles Lindbergh sat in the pilot's seat, his face lit by the glow of the instrument panel.

Gary's laughter was horrible in Jonah's ears.

"It was *never* possible for time to survive with you or any of the other babies from that plane living in this time period," Gary said.

"We had thirteen years here!" Jonah countered. "Once we fixed the past, everything was going to be great!"

Gary shook his head and rolled his eyes and laughed even harder.

And then Jonah couldn't argue anymore, because he could see the plane getting into position on the runway.

Evidently Gary and Hodge had gotten lucky with their timing, or they'd planned the plane's departure better than its arrival. Either way, there were no other planes in front of Lindbergh's waiting to take off; there were no other planes landing. The runway ahead of Lindbergh's plane was open and clear.

The plane zoomed forward, picking up speed. Jonah could see only its lights now, and they were a blur. Going, going . . .

"Andrea," Jonah whispered. "Chip . . ."

There were other names he wanted to say, but they didn't matter now. The plane was gone. It rose from the runway—and vanished into thin air.

# THIRTY-TWO

"Yahoo!" Gary screamed.

He let go of Jonah and began pumping his fists in the air. He spun around, practically howling with glee.

*He thinks I'm too upset to do anything,* Jonah told himself. *But while he's celebrating, maybe I could just sneak away?*

Jonah eased away from the window and inched toward the door. Gary made no move to stop him. Jonah sneaked his hand toward the door handle and quietly turned it.

*I'll go find Angela and tell her everything. Maybe the two of us together can figure out what to do,* he thought. *No, I'll look for one of those time agents who were chasing the plane before. . . . No, first of all, I have to get Katherine back from Hodge. And the Elucidator, too. Or . . .*

The door was moving outward faster than Jonah was pushing it. He turned to face the doorway head-on—and smashed directly into Hodge.

Jonah sprang back, because he didn't want to hurt the baby Hodge still carried in his arms. He was actually quite relieved to see that Hodge was still carrying Katherine around. Hodge had even wrapped her in an additional blanket, probably taken from the plane. Jonah couldn't see her face or head because of the way Hodge was carrying her, but it looked like she was contentedly sleeping against his chest.

*Grab her without waking her up and making her scream,* Jonah revised his instructions to himself. *Grab the Elucidator. And then . . .*

Was there anyone out there in the airport who could actually help him? Or would Jonah do better trying to escape from Gary and Hodge once they went back to 1932? Or would Jonah already be a toddler again by the time he landed, so he wouldn't be able to do anything even then?

Gary slapped his hand against Hodge's in a dramatic high five.

"We did it!" he crowed.

Should Jonah worry about the fact that neither one of them seemed the least bit concerned about grabbing Jonah again? Even though Jonah was still standing right beside the door?

Was there anything else he should be worrying about?

"How can you be so excited when Lindbergh's flying off in a plane that time agents are watching and wanting to attack?" Jonah asked, even though it made both Gary and Hodge look toward him. They still didn't try to grab him. "What if they shoot the whole plane down?"

"We've got nothing to fear from time agents," Hodge said, beaming at Jonah. "Never again."

"But—" Jonah began.

"Should we just go ahead and tell him everything?" Gary asked. "It'd be . . . like a kindness, to make him understand what just happened."

"*You* want to be kind?" Hodge asked incredulously.

Gary broke out with a grin that was even wider than Hodge's.

"No, not actually," he admitted. "I want to gloat. I want to rub it in how thoroughly we won and his side lost."

Hodge high-fived him again.

"Not a bad idea," he said.

"Shouldn't we be leaving for 1932?" Jonah asked. "So we can meet up with Charles Lindbergh there?"

He really meant, *So I don't have to listen to the two of you gloat. So we can get on with this—and my side really can win. So I can see for sure if Angela is there waiting for me with an Elucidator, and deal with everything if she isn't.*

Maybe Jonah would have to spend some amount of

time as Charles Lindbergh's son. But surely JB and Angela would rescue him eventually, somehow.

*Even if Charles Lindbergh's son is really who I'm supposed to be? Even if there's no other way to save time?* Jonah's treacherous mind threw at him.

He decided not to think about that.

"So, all right, here's the first secret we're going to tell you," Gary said, leaning his face close to Jonah's in his exuberance. "Are you ready? We're not going to take you back to 1932 to meet up with Charles Lindbergh. You're never going to see him again."

Jonah did a double take.

"What? But you promised him—" Jonah began.

"We aren't the type of people who keep their promises," Hodge said with fake solemnity. "Didn't you ever notice that about us?"

Well, yes, Jonah had. Gary and Hodge had told awful lies to Jonah's friend Gavin, to convince him to pull Jonah, Chip, Katherine, and another friend, Daniella, back to 1918.

Jonah felt a little pang just thinking about his friends, who were now on their way to the future with Charles Lindbergh because Gary and Hodge had tricked him, too.

Jonah must have let some of his emotion show through on his face, because Gary said, "Ah, you can't tell me you actually wanted to go back and live out your life as that man's son! He wouldn't even hug you, remember?"

Jonah grimaced.

"You know I don't, but—what happens when Lindbergh gets back to 1932 and I'm not there?" Jonah asked. "What if he takes revenge by talking a lot about time travel? What if he uses the Elucidator you gave him again and again and again? Or—the plane?"

"Kid, you are not very good at thinking like a criminal," Hodge said, shaking his head. "Or like a liar."

Jonah just looked at him.

"Charles Lindbergh's never going to make it back to 1932," Gary said. He slapped his knee as if he'd told a good joke. "Once he drops off all the kids we want him to take to the future, he's not ever going to be able to return."

"Genius," Hodge said. With the hand that wasn't holding Katherine, he kissed his fingers to his lips like someone complimenting an excellent meal.

"Who could have thought of such a thing?" Gary asked. "Oh, that's right—us!"

He strutted around the cramped stairwell yet again.

"But—won't that ruin 1932 if Charles Lindbergh never goes back?" Jonah asked.

Hodge shrugged.

"It doesn't matter now," he said. "We're going to be

crazy-rich. Who cares if we mess up 1932? Maybe it will even help us!"

Jonah's jaw dropped. The problem with dealing with liars like Gary and Hodge was that it was so hard to tell if anything they said was true.

He could believe that they cared about the money more than anything else.

"But . . . if it was such a big deal for me not to mess up 1932—such a big deal that you aren't sending me to the future and making a lot of money from me—then wouldn't it matter even more to have Charles Lindbergh vanish?" Jonah said. "I was just a little kid. He was famous! Nobody would have known anything about me if I hadn't been his son!"

Both Gary and Hodge started howling with laughter. The baby Hodge held against his chest startled at the noise, punching at the blanket as if Katherine objected to their mockery.

"He—actually—believed—our—lies!" Gary gurgled, the words coming out between bursts of merriment. "It . . . wasn't just . . . because I had the needle at his back. JB . . . must have told the same lie!"

"What are you talking about?" Jonah said. He didn't understand, but he felt prickles of panic along his hairline anyhow. It was like his body knew that he needed to prepare for shocking news.

"Jonah, Jonah, Jonah," Hodge said, shaking his head slowly and condescendingly yet again. "Can't you figure it out? Why do you think we'd let you stand here in this stairwell while all the children of any value zoom on toward our glorious, wealthy future? You aren't Charles Lindbergh's son. You weren't born to be anybody important at all. You're nobody!"

# THIRTY-THREE

Jonah stumbled backward, slamming against the wall.

"Nobody?" he repeated numbly. "But—but—I'm a famous missing kid from history! That's why I was on that plane. The first time, I mean. That's why you kidnapped me!"

It wasn't that he'd wanted to be Charles Lindbergh's son. It wasn't that he'd ever wanted to claim any identity besides Jonah Skidmore. But he'd had months—and centuries—of getting used to the notion that he'd started out life as someone incredible, someone worth kidnapping. Maybe even worth kidnapping again and again.

It felt like a punch in the gut to hear Hodge say he wasn't important.

Hodge was smirking.

"No, we kidnapped you because we could pass you off as Lindbergh's son," he said, shrugging. "It was too hard to get in to kidnap the boy himself. You look enough like him to fool his own father, and you were born the same year—your parents dropped you off at an orphanage in 1932 because they didn't want you anymore, and we just picked you up before the orphanage opened its doors. You were going to die of malnutrition a few days later, so nobody cared."

*Nobody cared?* Jonah thought. *I was supposed to die as a toddler and nobody was going to care?*

There was an echo to those thoughts, immediate answers: *In this time period, Mom and Dad would have cared. Katherine would have cared.*

He had such an ache in his throat now, because if Gary and Hodge really had won, then Mom and Dad would never get the chance to care about Jonah. If Gary and Hodge were telling the truth and Jonah wasn't in the planeload of babies this time around—and the planeload of babies had just flown on to the future, anyway—then Jonah's parents would never even meet him. And Jonah would just . . . well, what would happen to him now? If Gary and Hodge weren't going to take him back to 1932, what were they planning to do with him?

*And Katherine?* Jonah wondered, because it was a little too terrifying to think about himself. *What are they going to do with Katherine?*

Gary and Hodge had given such specific instructions to Lindbergh, to have him age her up and then turn her back into a baby. It had definitely not been random. What could they still be planning?

Hadn't they already ruined enough lives?

Jonah reached out and touched Katherine's blanket-covered back, because even if she wasn't the right age—even if he was scared to death about what might happen to either of them—it was still comforting to have her close by.

Hodge jerked the baby away from him. Jonah's fingers barely brushed the blanket. He couldn't even feel the ribbing of the pink-and-purple sweater that must still be wrapped about Katherine, beneath the blanket.

"You don't look like you're quite ready for the next revelation," Hodge said. "Pace yourself, kid."

"I don't care who I am," Jonah said, trying for a defiant tone. What he really wanted to say was, *I don't care about being anyone except Jonah Skidmore.* But he wasn't sure he could get those words past the lump in his throat. He tried a different approach, snarling, "Everything you're doing can still be undone. There's still time."

Gary looked down at his watch Elucidator.

"Actually, we're running out of time," he said. "Maybe we should wrap this up, boss. Just in case."

Hodge laughed merrily.

"No worries," he told Gary. "Don't you want to savor this next part?"

"I'd rather savor the riches waiting for me in the future," Gary said, a giant smirk breaking over his face.

"JB and the rest of the time agency—they're never going to let you collect all that money in the future," Jonah said, turning his head side to side so he could address both men at once. "Maybe they'll go easy on you if you turn yourself in. Maybe if you get Lindbergh to bring back all those babies on the plane right now, then—"

"You're right," Hodge said to Gary. "The boy has become tiresome. Let's go."

"Don't forget," Gary said, pointing to the baby cradled against Hodge's chest.

Jonah lunged at Hodge, ready to rip baby Katherine out of his grasp. Because it suddenly seemed like the two men were planning to just head off into the future, leaving Jonah behind. Alone. He still didn't understand what was going on—or why they weren't worried about the time agents—but there was no way he was letting them get away with baby Katherine without him.

Hodge didn't react the way Jonah expected. The man didn't jerk the baby to the side out of Jonah's reach. He didn't command his Elucidator to take him and the baby away.

Instead Hodge dropped the baby into Jonah's arms.

In his surprise Jonah almost let the baby slip on down to the floor.

"Katherine!" he cried, grabbing for the edge of the blanket, or for an arm or a leg he could get a firm grip on. He finally stopped the baby's downward motion with one hand clenched around the baby's right ankle and the other hand around her left wrist. The blanket snaked its way down to the floor.

And then what Jonah saw almost made him drop the baby all over again.

Because there wasn't a purple-and-pink-striped sweater under the blanket. There was a patched, threadbare sleeper, covering the scrawny form of a baby that Jonah recognized from old photos. But it wasn't baby Katherine he was holding in his arms. It wasn't even a baby girl.

It was the baby version of Jonah himself.

# THIRTY-FOUR

"What? No!" Jonah moaned.

This was a time violation—a time abomination. Every second that ticked by with Jonah as a thirteen-year-old and Jonah as a baby occupying the same time period threatened to make all of time collapse forever. It wasn't even possible for both of them to occupy the same time period—unless someone was deliberately trying to ruin time.

"How could you?" Jonah snarled at Gary and Hodge.

Jonah was still holding on to the baby by one wrist and one ankle, and just those two points of contact seemed to make Jonah guilty too. He eased the baby version of himself down to the floor and let go. He stepped as far to the other side of the stairwell as he could. But Hodge was blocking the door and Gary was blocking the stairs down—Jonah couldn't get more than three feet away.

Gary and Hodge burst out laughing once again as Jonah pressed himself tightly against the wall.

"Finally the boy understands without us having to explain everything," Hodge said to Gary.

"Yes, you do!" Jonah insisted. "But—explain after you undo this! Fix time before it collapses! Stop this! What's wrong with the two of you?"

The two men just kept laughing. Jonah pointed a trembling finger at the baby on the floor.

"Send one of us away!" Jonah insisted. "Before time splits!"

He reached blindly for Hodge, as if there were any hope that Jonah could fix time himself by snatching the watch Elucidator from the man's wrist or the camera Elucidator from his pocket or wherever he'd stashed it. Hodge easily shoved Jonah away. Jonah landed on the floor right beside his baby self.

"I guess he doesn't understand," Gary mocked. "Jonah, we did this on purpose! Splitting time is exactly what we wanted to happen!"

"This is your destiny! Your contribution to history!" Hodge said, waving his hands dramatically.

Jonah couldn't let himself think about how much he was destroying, just by his very existence. His doubled existence.

"Then where's Katherine?" he asked, shifting worries, because the entire fate of the universe and time itself was too overwhelming to think about. "What did you do with her?"

He craned his neck, as if he'd be able to see past Hodge and out the door.

Hodge's smirk looked even more self-satisfied than ever.

"Ah, but that was the pure genius of our plan," Hodge said. "We still get to benefit from selling thirty-six famous endangered children from history in the future. She replaced you on the plane!"

Jonah's tortured brain tried to make sense of this. Hodge had walked out of the stairwell carrying baby Katherine wrapped in a purple-and-pink sweater. He'd guided Lindbergh onto the plane, the plane had taken off, and Hodge had returned carrying another baby wrapped in an ordinary baby blanket.

*But Gary and Hodge said I wasn't on the plane this time,* Jonah thought.

No. They'd said he wasn't going to be on the plane to the future with Lindbergh. They hadn't said that he hadn't been on the plane from the past. They'd split hairs answering him, just like they were trying to split time.

"But—but . . . Katherine's not from history!" Jonah protested.

"The early twenty-first century *is* history, to us in the future," Gary sneered. "Stupid!"

He kicked Jonah in the side, as if trying to make the insult hurt worse. Jonah guessed he should be grateful that Gary hadn't kicked the baby.

"But Katherine's not famous! Or endangered!" Jonah persisted.

Hodge crouched beside him, almost as if he were trying to show some sympathy.

"Sure she is," he said. "Because of you, in both cases."

Jonah could do nothing but stare blankly at him.

"Thanks to all her time travel with you, Katherine was solely or partly responsible for rescuing a dozen other endangered kids from history," Hodge said. "She *is* famous in our time period for that. Most experts will argue that she played a much bigger role in saving kids and time than you ever did. But that will partly be because people are going to resent how you ended up."

Dimly Jonah realized that Hodge was trying to get him to be jealous of Katherine.

"Wait a minute," Jonah stopped him. "What do you mean, how I ended up?"

"This," Hodge said, waving his hand to indicate Jonah sprawled on the floor right beside the baby version of himself. "The way you claimed JB's rogue assistant, Second

Chance, as your role model, and tried to destroy all of time forever by going back to the night of the time crash—and staying even after the baby version of yourself appeared. The way you *would* have destroyed all of time, if Gary and I hadn't exiled you and this entire time period into a dead-end split."

"Dead-end split" sounded like time-travel gobbledygook once again, but Jonah could make enough sense of it that it gave him chills.

"I'm not trying to destroy anything!" Jonah protested. "You're making this happen!"

Hodge shook his head with fake sadness.

"That's not how history is going to record this moment," he said.

"But time travelers will see the truth!" Jonah said. "The time agency will come back and stop you! JB and Hadley—they'll be here any minute!"

"So why aren't they here already?" Gary taunted.

Jonah couldn't answer that question.

"This time period is already shutting down," Hodge said. "The first thing that goes is time travel *into* a period. Gary and me, *we'll* still be able to get *out* for a little while longer."

*But not me?* Jonah wondered.

He decided this wasn't a good question to ask out loud.

"And then, eventually, your whole branch of time—kablooey," Gary said, throwing his hands up in the air, acting out an explosion. "Total destruction. Game over."

"And then there won't be any future for you to make your billions in!" Jonah protested. "You're destroying time for nothing!"

Hodge shook his head.

"This one really is a slow-brain," he said. "I pity anyone who ever tried to educate him."

Gary kicked Jonah again.

"Time's splitting, remember?" Gary asked. "Thanks to you and baby you? We get our future, all right. Free and clear and trouble free."

"*Our* future won't have time agents," Hodge clarified. "You might say we modeled it exactly on what's best for us."

"But, but—" Jonah sputtered.

"You should be thanking us for at least saving your sister," Hodge said mockingly. "Because if we'd left her here, she would have died with everyone else."

"That's if this time period even exists long enough for her to be born," Gary added.

*A year from now,* Jonah thought frantically. *Katherine's not supposed to be born for another year.*

He was getting confused—if time didn't last long

enough for Katherine to be born, how could he have eleven years of memories with her? How could he have just carried her baby self from 1932 to now, before Gary and Hodge snatched her away?

He decided he didn't have time to worry about any of that right now.

"This time period won't last anywhere close to a year," Hodge said, glancing at his watch. "I'd be surprised if there are more than a couple days left."

"Maybe even just a couple hours," Gary agreed.

Were they just trying to psych Jonah out? Make him give up?

"You can't do this," Jonah said desperately. "You can't. It's not fair. It's not right."

Hodge leaned in close, almost as if he and Jonah were best buddies.

"We don't actually have much choice," Hodge said. "Once that plane crash-landed in this time period, this time was doomed. It's always been doomed. You lived through thirteen years of it being doomed."

"I tried telling the boy that," Gary interrupted. "I don't think he understood that, either."

Jonah remembered what Gary had said: *It was never possible for time to survive with you or any of the other babies from that plane living in this time period.*

"Didn't you ever wonder why you never saw tracers, growing up?" Hodge asked.

*Not until twenty minutes ago,* Jonah thought numbly.

He didn't want the missing tracers to be important. But he knew they were. The only other time he'd seen tracers vanish completely from a time period was when Second Chance messed up everything in the 1600s.

When he was making time split.

*Why didn't JB or any of the other time agents notice this problem?* Jonah wondered. *Or—did they know, and they just didn't want to upset us kids by telling us the truth?*

"All the time agency's frantic efforts—all *your* frantic efforts—those were like rearranging the deck chairs on the *Titanic,*" Hodge said. "Though they did enable us to set up a backup safety plan. A second future to be gloriously wealthy in . . ."

"So what are we waiting for?" Gary asked.

"Nothing," Hodge said. "Nothing else."

"Good-bye, Jonah," Gary said.

Were they leaving? Now?

Jonah lunged once again for Hodge, who was squatting down so close, right in front of him. If Jonah just grabbed Hodge and held on, then Jonah would go with them. It didn't even matter where they were going. Jonah had to get out of this time period. How much time had passed with him and his baby self here together? Was it little enough that Jonah could still rescue his time period and thwart Gary and Hodge?

Jonah slammed hard into concrete. He'd fallen straight through the space where Hodge had been crouched.

Gary and Hodge were already gone.

# THIRTY-FIVE

Jonah just lay sprawled on the concrete for a long moment. He could practically feel the bruises starting to form on his elbows and knees. And maybe on the side of his face as well.

*But what does it matter if all of time's about to end?* he asked himself.

No. Not all of time. Just *his* time, where he'd spent almost his entire life.

*My adopted time. Which I'm now ruining just as much as I ruined my adopted family,* Jonah thought.

It felt like he deserved the pain shooting through his body.

*Shake it off,* Jonah told himself. *Play through the pain.*

He felt like he was quoting somebody—oh yeah, his soccer coach thirteen years from now.

*So stop lying here,* Jonah told himself. *Stop feeling sorry for yourself. Get up and—*

And what? What could Jonah possibly do to stop Gary and Hodge's plan? He didn't have an Elucidator. He couldn't get out of this time period or do anything to fix it. He couldn't contact any time agents, and even if he could, they couldn't get in to help him. He did know plenty of people in this time period—but none of them would recognize him as a thirteen-year-old. His own *parents* wouldn't recognize him.

*And now they never will,* Jonah thought, blinking hard. *They'll never have a chance to be my parents.*

Maybe Gary and Hodge were lying about that? Maybe they were lying about everything?

Jonah looked over at the baby version of himself, who seemed to be sleeping entirely too peacefully for an infant who'd been dropped and dangled by his wrist and ankle only moments ago.

*Sedated,* Jonah thought dully. *Just like Gary and Hodge said they always do with babies. That part of their story checks out.*

In his sleep the baby twisted his face, as if concentrating hard on some dream. That one action made him look exactly like the hundreds of pictures Jonah's parents had taken the day he'd arrived.

There was no question that this really was the infant version of Jonah.

*What about an identical twin?* Jonah thought stubbornly. *A clone? Gary and Hodge could have faked everything, and—*

Gary and Hodge were lazy. There was no reason they would have bothered faking a clone and then telling Jonah such a long story about splitting time if none of it was true.

And anyhow, why weren't time agents right this minute rescuing Jonah, if Gary and Hodge had been lying about Jonah's doubled presence splitting time?

And why would Gary and Hodge have just left Jonah behind, unattended, if there was anything he could do to stop or undo their plan?

Jonah slumped helplessly against the cold concrete beneath him. Beside him, the baby version of himself opened his tiny mouth in a jaw-splitting yawn.

Mom and Dad had taken plenty of pictures of him doing that, too, on their first day with him. Jonah had looked at the pictures so much that he apparently had every single one of them still memorized; he'd heard Mom and Dad's story of his arrival so many times that he had the words ingrained in his mind: *We thought it would be years and years and years before we'd get a baby, and then that call came out of the blue the week before Christmas, and they said we could have him right away, and he was so cute, with his big eyes and his dimples and all that brown hair . . .*

Jonah could even remember the negotiations Mom

and Dad had had over the wording of the story—Jonah would have called his hair blond when he was little, but Katherine as a toddler had always insisted everyone call it brown because it was darker than her own. And she got her way because Jonah didn't care.

Now none of that would happen—not the pictures, not the story, not Katherine's stubbornness in claiming Jonah as her brother by laying down the law about how everyone described him.

*Katherine and I won't even be brother and sister anymore in any branch of time,* Jonah thought, with an ache that had nothing to do with the pain in his knees and elbow.

Would Mom and Dad even get to be parents at all, with this branch of time probably ending even before Katherine was born?

"They really were great parents," Jonah whispered to the baby version of himself. "I mean, are. Will be. *Should* be . . ."

In his sleep the baby startled at the sound of Jonah's voice, throwing his arms out, and then gradually letting them relax.

Jonah had also seen himself do that exact motion in the hours of home video Mom and Dad had filmed during their early days of having baby Jonah. In the video Mom and Dad laughed and cuddled their new baby and said sappy things like, "This is the happiest moment of our lives. I can't imagine being any happier than we are right now."

*Never. Going. To. Happen. Now,* Jonah told himself, trying to shut down the memories and all the sappy emotions they encouraged.

But if this time period was going to end in a matter of minutes or hours or days, what did it matter if he went out acting tough or sobbing like a little baby? If there wasn't anything Jonah could do to stop Gary and Hodge from splitting time, why did it matter what he did?

*Because . . . isn't there still* something *I could do?* Jonah wondered. *Something God would want me to do, something . . . right?*

He guessed he could be as stubborn as Katherine. He didn't like to give up either.

*Katherine . . .*

He really did need to pull himself together. If he did have only a matter of minutes or hours or days left, he didn't want to spend the whole time driving himself crazy being sad.

*Katherine's going to be okay in the future,* he told himself. *The other missing kids too. They'll be fine. And me—well, at least I got thirteen good years. I wasn't Charles Lindbergh's famous son, but at least I didn't die of malnutrition as a toddler. I got life with Mom and Dad and Katherine.*

It was useless trying to talk himself into being cheerful about being trapped and having his life end. He rolled over and kicked the wall.

"Gary and Hodge weren't supposed to win!" he snarled.

That felt good, even though it made his toes ache from the impact with the wall. Shoes from the 1920s weren't as cushioning as the ones he was used to. It just felt good to do *something*, rather than lying around moaning and groaning. Jonah stood up so he could kick the wall with more force.

"Time wasn't supposed to split!"

Another kick.

"I shouldn't be stuck in this time period!" Kick. "I'm not supposed to be in this time period at all!"

Well, technically, he guessed, if he were born the same time as the Lindbergh baby, maybe he was supposed to be in this time period—as an old man. Maybe that was why he'd never felt out of place in the twenty-first century, the way Chip said he always had.

But maybe that out-of-place feeling for Chip was more because Chip got lousy parents who were mean to him, while Jonah's did nothing but tell him how wonderful he was and how grateful they were to have him and Katherine. Even though everything Jonah knew in this time period had started out with an accident—Gary and Hodge randomly crashing the planeload of babies—it had all seemed so right, his entire childhood. JB could get theological or philosophical or whatever you called it about time travel and fate and destiny and God's plan, and before, all that talk had always just made Jonah's head hurt. He didn't understand it. But there were some things that made perfect sense to him.

"No matter what, my parents were *supposed* to be my parents!" he yelled, kicking the wall again. This contradicted what he'd said a moment ago about not belonging in this time period, but he didn't care. Ranting about his parents felt so good that he began pounding his fists against the wall too. He was like a little kid, kicking and screaming and throwing a tantrum.

"This is wrong! This is so wrong! Why is everything so messed up? Why can't I fix anything? Why do I have to die this way? Why can't I even say good-bye to my parents? Why can't they even get one stinking moment of being parents?"

Someone else was screaming with him. No—it was the baby crying. Jonah had been screaming and kicking and pounding his fists so loudly that he'd awakened the sedated baby.

Jonah turned around and awkwardly picked up the baby version of himself.

"Sorry, kid, I'm no good with babies," Jonah mumbled.

The baby hit at Jonah with his fists. In another mood Jonah would have found it funny that his baby self was reacting the same way as his thirteen-year-old self. But in this moment having a baby hit him just made him madder.

"Hey, kid, it's not my fault you're stuck with me," Jonah grumbled. "It's not my fault we're ruining time together. It's not my fault you don't already have Mom taking care of you right this—"

He stopped, jolted. It was true: Jonah hadn't caused any of this baby's problems. Jonah hadn't done anything wrong, but he'd failed anyway. He'd ended up trapped and outsmarted and alone. He couldn't think of anything he could do now to stop Gary and Hodge or undo their time split.

But there was still one thing he could fix, one thing he could do before he died and everything he'd ever known ended. One thing that would be perfect and right and good, even as everything else went wrong.

He could deliver the baby version of himself to Mom and Dad.

# THIRTY-SIX

Jonah moved instantly, smashing his shoulder against the door and stepping back into the main part of the airport. How much time did he have—minutes? Hours? Days? Hours and days were good; minutes would mean he had to move fast.

The baby was startled enough by the sudden motion that he stopped crying—or maybe he just liked the warmth and lights of the airport terminal. The door snapped shut behind Jonah, making him jump.

*Doesn't matter that I didn't prop it open,* he told himself. *It's not like I'm coming back.*

Jonah quickly jerked his head around, barely seeing the bright lights and the crowd and the Christmas ornaments. He wasn't looking for Angela this time—what could she do to help him?

*It's not like I could ask her to drive me to Mom and Dad's,* he thought. *It's not like she'd say, "Of course I can, kid-I-don't-even-know-who's-acting-strange! Of course I'll take you anywhere you want to go!"*

It wasn't like any of the other people he saw walking by would do that either.

*So . . . do I get help from the adoption agency? Do I ask to borrow someone's cell phone and call and . . .*

And say what? "This baby has to be delivered immediately to the Skidmores because . . ."

Jonah couldn't think of any excuse that didn't sound insane. And anyhow, he knew from his aunt Joan and uncle Brad adopting his cousin Mia that everything with adoption agencies took forever. Months had passed between the time they'd first announced, "We're getting a baby!" and the moment when Mia had actually arrived.

*I'm pretty sure that's how adoption usually works,* Jonah thought. *Mom and Dad just got me fast because the FBI wanted the babies from the plane taken care of quickly.*

The FBI wasn't involved this time around, and if Jonah only had minutes or hours or days, there wasn't time for getting the adoption agency's help.

*You've got feet,* Jonah told himself. *Use them. Mom and Dad don't live* that *far from the airport.*

He rushed out of the secure section of the airport

terminal, following other people down through the baggage claim and out the exit doors toward the darkness beyond.

It was freezing outside.

*So? You've dealt with cold this bad before,* Jonah reminded himself. *You're in middle school! Middle schoolers never wear coats!*

But Jonah was holding on to a baby covered in only a thin sleeper and a flimsy blanket. And Jonah remembered from his Boy Scout first-aid training that babies were much more likely to die from hypothermia than anyone else.

"Are you in the taxi-stand line or not?" someone asked behind him.

*Taxi?* Jonah thought. *What a great idea!*

But before Jonah had a chance to answer the person behind him, a second voice chimed in snottily, "You know the minimum fare from the airport to anywhere is thirty dollars. Do you have thirty dollars with you, little boy?"

Jonah could have whirled around and protested, *I'm not a little boy!* But first he checked his pockets.

Nothing. He had no money with him at all.

"Sorry," he muttered to the surly people behind him.

He stepped back toward the terminal.

*I am going to have to call the adoption agency,* he thought. *Or ask someone for help or money, or . . .*

He'd had this image in his head of taking the baby

version of himself directly to Mom and Dad's house, and getting to see the three of them happy together in the home he'd known his entire life. But maybe all he could do was call Mom and Dad?

He tried to imagine what he could say to Mom and Dad to lure them to the airport: *I've got a baby to give you. But you have to come and get it in person.*

Mom and Dad had always told Jonah and Katherine about how badly they'd wanted kids before Jonah and Katherine arrived. Those were the eager, desperate people Mom and Dad were right now. But they were just eager and desperate, not crazy. They wouldn't believe that a kid-sounding voice calling out of the blue on a Wednesday evening would be able to legally give them the baby they'd always wanted.

The baby squirmed in Jonah's arms, and Jonah felt like squirming just as impatiently. Why did every idea he'd had since stepping out of the stairwell seem stupid? Couldn't he do even this one thing before everything ended?

Jonah glanced around frantically. People weren't just lining up to get taxis. They were climbing onto buses and vans under signs that said, PARKING LOT SHUTTLE, RENTAL CAR SHUTTLE, and HOTEL SHUTTLE.

*Maybe I could stow away in one of those shuttles, and then . . .*

Getting to the airport parking lot or a rental car lot

wouldn't do him any good. But a hotel—there were hotels all over the city. Jonah didn't have to get himself and the baby right to his parents' doorstep; he just had to get close.

He rushed up to a shedlike structure under the hotel sign. On the outside of the shed there was a list of hotels that ran shuttles.

*Airport Hilton, Airport Marriott, Renaissance Hotel Downtown, Holiday Inn Express of Liston . . .*

Jonah's parents lived in Liston. And Jonah knew where the Holiday Inn Express was—he'd been to birthday parties there when he was younger and the big trend was to book a hotel so everyone could swim in the hotel pool.

The Holiday Inn Express was still probably three or four miles away from his parents' house.

"Can we make it?" Jonah whispered to the baby version of himself.

The baby was already shivering. Its face looked oddly pale in the fluorescent light beaming from the shuttle signs.

Jonah turned and sprinted back into the airport. He ran over to an information desk.

"Is there a lost and found here somewhere?" he asked the elderly man sitting at the desk. "I dropped my baby brother's coat, and it's so cold outside . . . maybe someone turned it in?"

"We can look together," the man said, standing up. Jonah could almost hear the man's bones creaking.

The man seemed to move at the pace of about a centimeter an hour. Jonah could barely stand not to race ahead of him.

"My parents are waiting," Jonah said. "Could you just tell me where the lost and found is, and I'll look myself?"

*And grab whatever looks warm?* he thought to himself.

Probably the man could tell Jonah was thinking that, because the man shook his head. Slowly.

"Against . . . protocol," he said, speaking as slowly as he walked. "I'm not allowed to give the key to anyone else. Because what if you didn't bring it back?"

Jonah might not have brought it back. Not now, not when everything was about to end.

They finally reached a nondescript door, and the man took forever putting the key in, unlocking the door, and turning on the lights.

"On that table," the man said, gesturing toward a pile of mittens and gloves and scarves and even an odd coat or two.

There wasn't a single item that looked the slightest bit babyish.

Jonah took a deep breath, trying to come up with a convincing lie.

*Maybe, "My parents don't believe in buying baby clothes? And they're penny-pinchers. So they bought Junior a coat he could wear until he's twenty or it falls apart, whichever comes first"?* Jonah thought.

Was that really the best he could come up with?

Before Jonah could say anything, the man let out a deep sigh.

"Look," he said. "Everything on that side of the table has been here for ages. We're scheduled to donate all of it to a homeless shelter tomorrow. So just take whatever you think will keep your brother warm until you get home. Then have your mom or dad donate it themselves."

"Thank you!" Jonah cried. "Thank you!"

It was strange how much Jonah felt like crying right now.

*Because this must show that this was meant to be,* he thought. *My parents are supposed to get me. They are. They are. They are.*

Jonah grabbed the nearest coat and took off running.

# THIRTY-SEVEN

Jonah's luck held: The Holiday Inn Express shuttle was just pulling up to the curb as he sprinted toward the stop. He crowded up close to a couple with two little kids between them, so the shuttle driver would think Jonah and the baby were just the oldest and youngest brothers in the family.

Nobody said anything to him as he stepped onto the shuttle.

*This is working, this is working . . .* , Jonah told himself excitedly.

As long as he focused on delivering the baby to Mom and Dad, he wouldn't have to think about how he'd failed at everything else.

Jonah settled into a dark seat at the back of the shuttle bus. That wouldn't seem strange to anyone, would it? Couldn't he just act like a surly teenager who resented getting stuck taking care of his baby brother?

*If people only knew,* Jonah thought.

As the shuttle bus pulled away from the curb and out into traffic, Jonah stared back at the airport. Jonah hadn't exactly spent huge portions of his childhood hanging out at the airport, so he didn't have much to go on. But everything he could see looked calm and unremarkable: people walked in and out of the terminal at a normal pace; there were no screaming sirens and flashing lights, no emergency vehicles—or cars labeled FBI—speeding onto the scene.

It was strange how much the ordinary scene around Jonah made his heart ache.

*This was supposed to be an incredible night,* Jonah told himself. *This was supposed to be a moment the FBI would still be puzzling over thirteen years from now.*

But now this stream of time wouldn't even exist thirteen years from now; everything connecting Jonah to this time period would collapse and vanish.

In the other stream of time, Jonah guessed—the one that would be allowed to continue and flourish and lead to Gary and Hodge becoming incredibly wealthy by selling Jonah's sister and friends in the future—Jonah would just be an anonymous little boy who died of malnutrition in the 1930s.

Jonah looked down at the baby sleeping against his chest, huddled under the oversize coat Jonah had grabbed from the lost and found and wrapped around both of them.

"I'm doing the best I can for you," Jonah whispered to the baby—whispered to himself. "If I could change anything else, I promise you, I would."

The shuttle bus pulled onto the highway, then onto the Liston exit.

Jonah found he couldn't look out the window anymore. His brain still ticked off the sights he would be seeing at every stoplight: *the church where I would have had Cub Scout meetings, the Dairy Queen where my baseball team in third grade would have held its end-of-season party, the park where Mom would have taken Katherine and me when we were little kids . . .*

The shuttle turned and stopped, and the motor sputtered into silence. They were at the hotel. Jonah got out behind everyone else.

*Should I walk into the hotel and keep pretending I'm with that other family?* he wondered. *Just so nobody gets suspicious?*

What did it matter if anyone suspected anything now? What was the shuttle driver going to do—threaten to take him back to the airport?

Jonah wrapped the oversized lost-and-found coat more securely around himself and the baby, and took off running into the darkness.

Everything looked strange around him. Wasn't there supposed to be a Walgreens on the corner of Main and Pine?

*No, because they didn't build that until I was in kindergarten,* Jonah reminded himself. *Remember how I always made Mom and Dad drive past so I could see the bulldozers?*

The entire Woodland Falls subdivision was missing too. The house at the corner of Archer Springs was yellow when it should have been brown. An auto parts store stood in front of the Kroger where there should have been an insurance office.

*I guess thirteen years is a long time,* Jonah thought. *Time enough for lots of things to change.*

Time enough for lots of things to be undone if you went back thirteen years in time.

Jonah tried to make himself focus solely on running. He turned onto Harley Street, which had no sidewalks, and he had to run on the uneven ground alongside the road. The jostling made the baby moan.

*Yeah, I agree, kid,* Jonah thought. *But we're almost there, and time hasn't run out on us yet. . . .*

His house was in the fourth subdivision along Harley. First came Forest Glen, then Summer Vista, then River Gable . . . Jonah's feet pounded faster and faster. He turned in to his own neighborhood, sped around the corner toward his own house—and stopped.

Even his own house looked unfamiliar. The picket fence out front was missing.

*Duh,* Jonah told himself. *Mom and Dad put that up when you and Katherine were little—remember? When the neighbors got a big dog?*

The trees and bushes were too small, too—*duh again,* Jonah scolded himself. *Everything would be thirteen years smaller, right?*

But it was enough to make Jonah wonder: What if other, more important things had changed too? What if Jonah was wrong about how everything worked, and Mom and Dad didn't even live here now?

A shadow moved across the front window, which was oddly unprotected by any curtains or blinds. Jonah stepped a little closer so his view wasn't blocked by the tree in the front yard. Now he could see into the well-lit house, even though he was pretty sure he was still far enough away that no one looking out would see him in the dark yard.

*Oh,* Jonah realized. *Mom and Dad are painting the living room. That's why the curtains are down.*

Dimly he remembered that in some versions of the "night that we got Jonah" story there was a mention of Mom and Dad being in the middle of a painting project. Even more dimly he could sort of remember Katherine—and maybe Jonah, as well—complaining that that detail wasn't important enough to talk about. Who cared about paint on walls? Who cared that much about anything that had happened before Mom and Dad became parents, before Jonah and Katherine had arrived on the scene?

But now Jonah watched the steady way Mom ran her paintbrush up and down in the corners while Dad used the roller behind her.

*They were a good team, even before they were parents,* Jonah thought, blinking hard. *I was really lucky, getting them.*

Jonah recognized the paisley bandanna tied around Mom's hair, the dark T-shirt Dad was wearing—those were details from Jonah's earliest baby pictures. Jonah definitely had the right moment for giving them the baby in his arms.

*But how do I do it?* he wondered.

He thought about putting the baby on the doorstep and ringing the doorbell and running away. But that was too much like the ding-dong-ditch pranks that all the boys in the neighborhood had started doing in sixth grade—had it been sixth grade? Just last year?

*You don't ding-dong-ditch and leave a baby behind,* Jonah thought.

Leaving a baby behind made it—what? Child abandonment? Child cruelty?

Whatever it was called, it'd be something Mom and Dad would be horrified by. Something that would make them look at him differently the rest of his life.

And even if the rest of his life with them was only a matter of minutes or hours or days, he didn't want to ruin it.

*So I ring the doorbell and hand them the baby directly and tell them a story that makes them think I'm just someone from the adoption agency?*

Jonah did not look like a grown-up. Even if he hadn't been wearing a ridiculously large coat and a nerdy-looking sweater and goofy knickers, there was no way he could pass himself off as an adoption agency employee.

*So . . . do I have to tell them the truth?*

Just as Jonah thought that, he heard a car pulling up behind him. He turned around to see a window gliding down in a dark car.

And then a woman's voice called out to him: "Are you the boy who's bringing the baby for the Skidmores to adopt?"

# THIRTY-EIGHT

"Y-yes?" Jonah said, squinting toward the car. "I mean, yes. Absolutely. This is the Skidmores' baby."

He took a few steps closer to the car and lifted the infant sleeping in his arms. But his mind was racing: *Besides Gary and Hodge, who knows I'm here in this time period? Who would know that I'm not only in this time period but standing in front of my own house? Time agents? Wouldn't a time agent just say, "Jonah, let's get you out of here! Let's fix this mess!"*

The woman in the car opened her door and stepped out. She was shorter than Jonah and middle-aged lumpy, but maybe she just looked that way because she was wearing a bulky coat. She stuck out her hand.

"Eva Ronkowski from the Hope for Children adoption agency," she said, introducing herself.

*Didn't Dad say the social worker who helped them get me was named Eva?* Jonah thought, stunned. *And didn't she work for the Hope for Children agency?*

But how would she have known that Jonah was here, now, with the baby? Why would she think the baby for the Skidmores would be delivered by a teenage boy standing in the middle of their yard?

Automatically Jonah put out his own hand and shook Eva's.

"I'm Jonah Sk—" He barely managed to stop himself from saying his last name. "Just call me Jonah."

The woman regarded him solemnly.

"It's okay—I understand that you probably feel strange about this whole business," she said. "Please don't be mad at your older sister. It's a very difficult decision, putting a child up for adoption. This is one of the most unorthodox ways I've ever handled it, but your sister was most insistent yesterday when she came in to sign all the paperwork. She must trust you a lot, that she wants you to be the one who sees where the baby goes. And the Skidmores were willing to go with the idea of an open adoption, so if she changes her mind, and she wants to make arrangements to meet with them herself at some point in the future, then . . ."

The woman was still talking, but Jonah blanked out from listening.

*Sister? Yesterday? Paperwork? Open adoption?*

None of it made any sense.

"Could I get a look at the little fellow?" Eva asked.

Numbly Jonah shrugged back one side of the coat. The sleeping baby stiffened at the cold air rushing in.

"It's too cold for him," Jonah explained.

"Of course," Eva said, nodding as if she was proud of Jonah for noticing that. "I can see that you're a good uncle. It's probably hard for you, too, to give him up."

Jonah didn't know what to say to that. Eva filled in the silence.

"Perhaps we should get the baby inside as quickly as possible?" she suggested.

Did she mean that she and Jonah together were supposed to ring the doorbell and walk inside? Is that what Jonah's supposed "older sister" had told Eva yesterday that he'd want to do?

*Is this "older sister" on my side?* Jonah wondered. *Or Gary and Hodge's? Why would Gary and Hodge make these arrangements for a time after they'd already won? Why would they care what happened when this time period is about to collapse anyhow?*

While Jonah was pondering all this, Eva had started easing the baby from his arms.

Jonah let her.

"Your sister said you might not want to wait for me to come back out of the house," Eva said. "But if you do, I would be happy to give you a ride home afterward."

"No thanks," Jonah said, shocked into answering.

He was afraid she'd ask for a reason, and in the stunned state he was in, he might accidentally tell the truth: *Because I don't have a home anymore. This is the only home I've ever known. Where else could I go?*

Eva just nodded as if she understood.

"That's fine," she said. "I know this is an emotional time. Tell your sister to call me if she needs to talk. Or—you can do the same."

She started to walk toward the house; then she turned back around.

"Oh, I almost forgot," she said. "When your sister was in my office yesterday, she left this behind. Could you give it back to her?"

Eva skillfully shifted the baby to one side so she could hold him with just one arm. With her other hand she reached into a purse hanging from her shoulder. She pulled out some kind of electronic device and pressed it into Jonah's hands—an old-style BlackBerry, maybe? Had BlackBerrys been around thirteen years ago?

Jonah turned the object over in his hands. It wasn't a BlackBerry; it was one of those old-fashioned handheld games, from before people had everything on their phones. This game said CONNECT 4 at the top.

Then the letters in "Connect 4" rearranged and changed, and Jonah finally understood. The social worker hadn't just handed him a game.

She'd handed him an Elucidator.

# THIRTY-NINE

Jonah resisted the urge to pump his fist in the air and scream out, *Whoo-hoo! I'm saved!* He barely remembered to keep his expression solemn and sober for Eva's sake.

"Uh, thanks," Jonah said. "My, uh, sister will be happy to get this back."

He quickly tucked the Elucidator Connect 4 game into his pocket before Eva could see that the words on its face now read, WHERE DO YOU WANT TO GO?

*I have choices now,* Jonah thought. *I'm not helpless anymore. I can go back to 1932 and fix this mess. I can find Angela and JB; I can help them; I can rescue Katherine and the others; I can make my parents the right age again. . . .*

His brain spun with all the things he needed to do.

But Eva was still standing in front of him, holding the baby and watching Jonah.

"Thanks for helping your sister so well," Eva said. "At a time like this, she needs people around her who will be sympathetic and understanding, and—"

There was no way Jonah was going to stand there listening for advice about dealing with a fictional sister with a fictional problem. Not when he had a real sister to find, and lots of other real problems he needed to solve.

"I know all that," he said. "Shouldn't you get the baby inside before he catches cold?"

"Oh, right," Eva said. "Do you want to give him a hug or kiss good-bye?"

*No,* Jonah thought.

But he dipped his head toward the baby, ruffled the baby's hair, and muttered, "Stay cool, dude."

The words running through his head were more detailed: *Don't worry. I'm going to make everything okay for you—and me, too. I'm going to make it so this time period doesn't end, so you can grow up into me, so our lives—I mean, my life—can go on and on and on. . . .*

But evidently he'd already met Eva's low standards for a teenage boy's emotional good-bye. She nodded, patted Jonah's shoulder, and turned up the front walk.

Jonah stepped back into the shadows. Every cell in his body seemed to be screaming, *Go now! Hurry! Get back to 1932 and fix everything!* But Jonah waited. He crouched down beside Eva's car and watched as she rang the doorbell. The door opened. As far as Jonah could tell, Eva didn't even say a word at first—she just placed the baby in Mom's arms.

Mom and Dad looked confused at first, then tentatively hopeful, as if they were both thinking, *Could this possibly be true? Is this real?* Then overwhelming joy broke over both of their faces. Watching them come to understand that they finally had a baby of their own was like watching a sunrise. It was like looking *at* the sun—too intense for Jonah's eyes.

*I'll make it so this really is an entirely good moment in your lives,* he promised them in his head. *I'll make it so this isn't the beginning of the end, so I don't ruin your lives or anybody else's. . . .*

He bent down close to the Elucidator in his coat pocket and murmured, "Now. Take me back to August 15, 1932."

And then everything around him vanished.

# FORTY

Jonah was already floating through time when he thought to add a slight modification. He took the Elucidator out of his pocket and told it, "Make me arrive right after Lindbergh and Gary and Hodge left."

*Finally I'm learning how to talk to Elucidators so they don't constantly put me into even more danger,* he thought.

But as he floated through darkness, the Elucidator flashed up at him, LINDBERGH AND GARY AND HODGE DIDN'T LEAVE TOGETHER.

"Then get me there a minute after the last of them left," Jonah said. "Sheesh, do I have to spell out everything?"

YES, the Elucidator flashed back.

Jonah wished he had someone else traveling through time with him, so they could make fun of the Elucidator together. It would have even been comforting to have baby Katherine back, to hold on to.

*Soon,* Jonah told himself. *After I meet up with Angela and JB, after we track down Lindbergh's plane in the future, after time agents arrest Gary and Hodge—then we'll get Katherine back.*

Though he'd want Katherine turned back into an eleven-year-old again as quickly as possible. And he wanted all his friends back from the future; he wanted time fixed so all of them could just go home.

An uncomfortable thought flitted through his mind about how Gary and Hodge had said his life in the twenty-first century had always been doomed. According to them, that was true for all the other missing children from history too.

*Gary and Hodge could have been lying,* Jonah thought. *They're liars and kidnappers, and they cheat, and even they admit that they don't keep their promises. . . .*

But some of the other information they'd told Jonah seemed to be true. They were right about him never seeing tracers in the twenty-first century. And as Jonah had thought before, why would they bother lying when they already thought they'd defeated Jonah?

*Habit,* Jonah told himself. *Just like they said I wasn't any good at thinking like a criminal, they're not any good at not thinking like criminals and liars and cheats. . . .*

But Jonah didn't feel like pumping his fist in the air and screaming anymore.

*What if Angela's not there when I get to 1932?* he wondered.

*What if she didn't ever read the note I gave her at the airport?*

A new, dreadful thought hit Jonah: Why would Angela have read and obeyed the note? How could she have? Sure, time had split, but in both new versions of time Gary and Hodge had changed everything, and in each new version the planeload of babies had vanished from the airport almost immediately after it arrived. In the version that was going to collapse and die, Jonah's parents were left with him as a baby, but none of the other missing children's adoptive parents even knew that their children existed. In the version that led to Gary and Hodge's glorious wealthy future, none of the endangered children from history would have any connection to the twenty-first century. In both cases, the FBI would never get involved; even if Angela got a glimpse of the time-crashed plane, she wouldn't have thought anything of it. She would have blinked, and it would have been gone.

Speeding through time, Jonah clutched his Elucidator more tightly, as if to reassure himself it was there. His mind reeled, sorting through what was possible—and what wasn't.

*Is everything I thought wrong?* he wondered.

Without fully experiencing the weirdness and mystery of the time-crashed plane, Angela would have had no reason to hang on to a confusing scribbled note an oddly dressed kid had handed her on her first day at a new job.

And anyhow, if Angela never got more than a quick, easily forgotten glance at the time-crashed plane, she also never would have met any time agents thirteen years later; she never would have helped Jonah and Katherine and their friends in the time cave; she never would have known anything about Elucidators or time travel. She certainly never would have traveled through time herself.

Based on what Jonah knew, was there any way that Angela would be waiting on the airfield in 1932?

*No,* he thought miserably. *None.*

He spun through the emptiness of Outer Time, too stunned to keep himself from flipping over and over. He let the outside forces take control of his body.

*But I have an Elucidator!* he reminded himself. *I can find Angela myself. And JB, too. I can go anywhere in time! I can ask the Elucidator anything I want to know! I have control now!*

But could he trust the Elucidator in his hand?

He'd been vaguely thinking that Angela and JB—and probably other time agents as well—had arranged for Eva the social worker to meet him in front of his parents' house, take the baby version of himself on in to his parents, and give him an Elucidator. He'd kind of thought he deserved some credit himself for Eva appearing—because the note he gave Angela had to be the tipoff that his teenage version would be in that time period and needed an Elucidator.

It wasn't exactly a leap for anyone who knew him very well to think that, after giving the note to Angela at the airport, he'd also make a stop at his parents' house.

*But how would JB and Angela know that I'd be carrying the baby version of myself?* Jonah wondered. *How would anybody know that but Gary and Hodge? And if my note to Angela went straight into the garbage . . . who did provide this Elucidator for me? If, in the new versions of time, Angela never gets to travel to any other time periods, how much else has changed about my past and what I thought I knew?*

Jonah was tying his own brain into knots. Then he hit the point in his time-travel trip where everything sped up, and it felt like his entire body was being torn apart. He couldn't think at all.

He landed. The mind-blurring, sense-dulling numbness of timesickness hit him harder than usual.

*Because I just traveled not just from the future, but from a branch of time that's about to collapse?* Jonah wondered. *Or just because I'm terrified of what I'm going to find out when I open my eyes?*

He opened his eyes anyway. With great effort he got them to focus on a face bent down close to his. With even more effort he tried to make sense of the sound roaring around him.

It was screaming.

A moment passed before he could recognize the face, before he could pick out distinct words in the screaming.

The words were "Jonah! You made it back!"

And the face was Angela's.

Jonah sat up quickly and cried, "Angela! What are you doing here?"

# FORTY-ONE

Angela gave him a shove, knocking him back against the side of the airfield office building. She was still kid Angela, Jonah noticed, which meant that she shoved *hard*.

"I thought you'd be happy to see me!" she complained. "I did what your note told me to do! Where's the gratitude? Don't you know how awful it is to be a black female in the 1930s? Don't you know what all I've done for you? I was expecting excitement and hugs—not that it's really safe for a black girl to be seen in public being hugged by a white boy in 1932, but—"

She stopped.

"Jonah, you're as white as a ghost. What's wrong?" she asked.

Jonah moaned, and slumped back against the wall of the airfield office.

"I don't understand anything," he said.

Quickly he told her what had happened to him since the time cave, and what he'd figured out on his trip back to 1932. By the time he was finished, Angela was squinting in confusion too.

"But . . . of course I've traveled through time," she said. "Of course I saw all the babies on the plane and talked to the FBI agents. Of course time agents were the ones who arranged for you to get that Elucidator—"

"Then why aren't time agents here now, helping us out?" Jonah asked.

Angela didn't seem to have an answer to that.

Jonah saw Angela glance around the deserted airfield. She seemed to be looking for enemies who might materialize from anywhere, rather than friendly, helpful time agents.

"Are you afraid Gary and Hodge might come back?" Jonah asked.

Angela bit her lip.

"Right now I'm afraid of everything," she said. "You're right. None of this makes sense, so I don't know what we're supposed to do. What if we make a bigger mess of things?"

"Let's find JB first," Jonah suggested. "He can help us. And then—"

Angela started to say something, but a shout off in the

distance made her stop. She put a warning hand on Jonah's arm, and her other hand over his mouth. A moment later she pushed him down toward the ground and crouched beside him.

The shouting in the distance grew louder.

"I think they've seen us," she whispered.

"Um, Gary and Hodge?" Jonah asked, his voice squeaking. He was still too weak with timesickness to be any good at running away. And where would they run to? Where could they be safe?

"No, it's the newspaper reporters who follow Charles Lindbergh around," Angela whispered back. "There's some sort of security guard over at the gate keeping them out of the airfield, but they still shout questions at anyone they see."

Now Jonah's timesick ears could make out words in the shouting: "Is it true Colonel Lindbergh just took his first flight since his child's body was discovered three months ago?" "Where did he go?" "Did he have a good flight?" "Could you get him to come over to the fence to make some comments for my newspaper? We've always been on his side—*my* paper hasn't printed any of those disgusting rumors . . ."

"Maybe they'll shut up if we go into the office," Angela said, making a face. "But first I have to warn you—"

"What?" Jonah asked. She looked so serious Jonah's mind went back to all his worst fears. Were Gary and Hodge back in the airfield office? Had somebody died? Were he and Angela somehow trapped in 1932 forever?

"JB's in the office," Angela said.

Jonah did a double take.

"But—that's great!" Jonah said. "So we don't have to worry about finding him. He can tell us how to do everything else—get Katherine back, get the other kids back, fix my parents . . ."

Angela was grimly shaking her head.

"It's going to be hard for you even to look at him," she warned.

Jonah remembered that in the last glimpse he'd had of JB in this time period, JB had been standing in the kidnapped Lindbergh child's room, and the police had just decided that he was too crazy to be a suspect. Had they put him in prison anyway? Or had they put him in some sort of mental institution? Even with an Elucidator, had Angela had trouble getting him out of the institution?

*Twentieth-century mental institutions—not the greatest places to hang out,* Jonah remembered. He'd seen the types of places where the original Tete Einstein had been confined before his mother had figured out a way to save him and send him to the future and let him grow up as JB.

The shouting from over at the fence intensified.

"Could Colonel Lindbergh comment about what it was like to find out that the whole time he was looking for his child, the baby was dead and lying in a shallow grave not even five miles away?" "What safety precautions will the Lindberghs take to make sure that their second child won't be kidnapped too?" "When is the second child due?" "Could Colonel Lindbergh make a comment about his family's emotions regarding the second child?"

Angela tugged on Jonah's arm.

"Come on," she said. "We've got to get away from that."

Still crouching down low, they crept around to the door of the airfield office and stepped inside. Now Jonah could barely hear the shouting from outside.

But JB was sprawled in a chair right in front of him, just inside the door, and Jonah could see exactly what Angela had meant about it being hard to look at him.

JB was still a thirteen-year-old boy. But his eyes were vacant and glazed over now, and even though they seemed to be staring straight back at Jonah, they showed no gleam of recognition.

JB was also drooling.

"It's like JB's vanished from inside his own body," Angela said, choking up. "I think the un-aging and the time changes made his schizophrenia come back, kind of like his asthma. I've been afraid to leave 1932 to get medicine for him, because I wasn't sure I could get back in to meet you. And the medicine they had in 1932 to treat schizophrenia . . . I've been afraid to give that to him too."

"Wait—you mean, you've stayed in 1932 this whole time?" Jonah asked. "Since—since you arrived in March, the night of the Lindbergh baby kidnapping?"

Angela nodded.

"The first thing I saw was the baby already dead on the ground under the ladder—I think JB saw even more. We both went a little crazy, because we thought that was you," she said. "We thought we'd failed at everything that mattered."

Jonah thought about how that must have looked to Angela and JB.

"I'm not the Lindbergh baby," Jonah said. "I already told you."

Angela lifted her hands in a helpless gesture.

"Yeah, well, I knew that as soon as I thought to consult the Elucidator I'd secretly smuggled into 1932 with me without telling JB," she said. "The one I'd been afraid to use *until* we got to 1932 because I thought it'd mess everything up."

*Is that true?* Jonah wondered, thinking about the narrow escapes he and JB and Angela had had, clinging to the

*Spirit of St. Louis* over the Atlantic Ocean and almost being struck by the plane's propeller in Paris. *Or was it not possible for Angela to use the Elucidator on those time-travel trips because it would have been too much of a paradox—since I went on those time-travel trips before I gave Angela the note at the airport telling her to carry an Elucidator with her almost thirteen years later?*

Jonah's head was starting to hurt again, and he didn't think it was just from timesickness.

"JB was so grief-stricken at the thought that he'd caused your death that I guess it broke his last connection to being JB, not Tete Einstein," Angela continued. "Though I didn't realize it at the time. I didn't go to help him right away because I thought he could handle everything better than me anyway."

Jonah remembered JB's crazy screams about the child already being dead and everything being his fault.

*Because he thought I'd been zapped back in time with him and Angela,* Jonah realized. *He thought that Gary and Hodge had kidnapped me before that moment, and that bringing me back had led to my death. So of course he blamed himself.*

It was a relief to at least figure out this much of the time-travel details that Jonah hadn't understood from the very start.

"I saw on the monitor what JB told Charles Lindbergh and the police," Jonah said. "But the monitor didn't let me see what happened to JB after he left that room."

Angela pulled a necklace out from inside her dress. It had an oversize locket dangling from it. Jonah guessed that it probably wasn't actually a locket.

"Having this Elucidator with me meant that I could turn myself and JB invisible and get him out of police custody," Angela said. "And then we could find food for ourselves even without any money. . . . I'm not even sure either one of us would still be alive without this Elucidator. So thank you for telling me to bring it."

Jonah shrugged off the thanks.

"Weren't you afraid it would mess up time too much to have JB show up as a suspect and then disappear?" he asked.

"No," Angela said. "There were all sorts of crazy tips coming in and suspects and allegations—pretty much everything about that crime and the investigation was insane, so it didn't change anything."

This was a relief too.

Jonah turned so he didn't have to keep looking at the vacant-eyed JB.

"But you couldn't just tell the Elucidator, 'Make JB sane again'?" Jonah asked. "You couldn't tell it, 'Stop Gary and Hodge from kidnapping Jonah'? Or 'Fix everything that's messed up right now'?"

"Jonah, you of all people know that nothing with an

Elucidator is that simple," Angela said, rolling her eyes. "I have asked it, practically every hour, 'Let me talk to Hadley Correo or some other time agent from the future.' And it always tells me, 'Not possible at this juncture.' It's as frustrating as the Magic Eight Ball I had when I was a kid."

Belatedly Jonah remembered that he was still clutching an Elucidator in his own hand. He looked down at it—it wasn't a handheld Connect 4 game anymore. It was a giant marble, like the cat's-eye shooter he could remember his grandfather showing him, back when Jonah was little. Grandpa had always claimed that marbles were a thrilling game, but he'd never managed to convince Jonah.

*This is almost as bad as the fifteenth century, when the Elucidator showed up as a rock,* Jonah thought.

Still, he noticed that this marble glowed with the words DO YOU HAVE ANOTHER QUESTION?

"What if my Elucidator gives a different answer?" Jonah asked Angela. He bent down close to the marble Elucidator and asked it, "Could you let me talk to Hadley Correo or some other time agent? Or maybe JB from some point in the future when he's perfectly sane?"

NOT YET, the Elucidator flashed.

Jonah lowered his hand in disgust.

"Well, at least it's a slightly different answer," Angela said, shrugging helplessly.

Somebody knocked at the door just then.

"Make all three of us invisible!" Angela hissed into her locket Elucidator.

"And both Elucidators!" Jonah added, because he could see that the marble and the locket weren't fading away instantly.

The door opened, revealing a man in overalls.

"Colonel Lindbergh, I just wanted to warn you that—" the man began.

Before he could even finish his sentence, a horde of men shoved him out of the way and trampled into the office.

"Colonel Lindbergh, I just have a few questions!" "I've asked and asked and asked for an exclusive interview." "I know this flight you just took was supposed to be of 'no particular significance,' but we just got a news tip that . . ."

Jonah was relieved that it was only the newspaper reporters, not Gary and Hodge. And then his relief turned to horror, because the pack of reporters was just moments away from slamming into the invisible JB. Jonah and Angela, by themselves, could have climbed out a window or pressed tightly into a corner, out of the way. But JB was apparently incapable of moving.

Jonah leaned over his marble Elucidator and whispered the best command he could think of in a pinch: "Take all three of us back to the time cave with Mom and Dad! Now!"

# FORTY-TWO

"What if we can't ever get back into 1932?" Angela screamed at Jonah, even as the three of them floated through Outer Time. "What if it turns out that there's still something there that we need to fix?"

"Oh, no, you're right!" Jonah groaned. "Let's find out! Elucidator, take us back to—"

Angela clapped her hand over Jonah's mouth. Why was she constantly shutting him up? This was almost as bad as hanging out with Katherine.

"Since we're on our way to the time cave anyway, why don't we hole up there for a little while and think through things?" Angela asked. "And *then* we can go back to 1932 if we have to, once we know what we're doing?" Angela asked.

*Oh yeah,* Jonah thought sheepishly. *Not such a bad idea.*

He nodded, and Angela took her hand off his mouth.

Katherine probably would have left him muzzled a bit longer. Was it crazy that Jonah missed all the annoying things about Katherine as much as her good traits?

"You think we really can figure everything out, right?" Jonah asked Angela. He glanced nervously at JB, who bobbed silently along through Outer Time. "You think there is something we can do to cure JB and get Katherine and the other kids back and make you and JB and my parents the right ages again and—"

"Could you maybe not list *everything* we need to take care of?" Angela moaned. "Can't we just start with one thing at a time?"

They landed back in the time cave, and everything looked just as it had before Jonah had been sucked into 1932 in the first place. He went over to crouch beside his sleeping parents in the car. He found there was nothing he could say to them, so he just threw his arms around their shoulders.

They were still thirteen-year-olds. Hugging them was nothing like hugging his real, actual, adult parents.

Or maybe the problem was just that they didn't hug back.

"Good news," Angela said softly from behind him. "I just asked my Elucidator if it would be possible for us to go back to 1932, and it said yes."

"Okay!" Jonah said enthusiastically, lifting the Elucidator in his hand. "Let's—"

This time Angela only pushed his arm down, rather than muzzling him again.

"After we figure out what to do, remember?" she asked.

"Right," Jonah said.

"We can be leisurely," Angela reminded him. "We can think and think endlessly, and still go back to 1932 only a split second after we left. Or—to anywhere else we might need to go."

It sounded like torture to Jonah, to think that hard and that long without doing anything. He'd used up his patience for that kind of thing watching months and months of time pass in 1932 on the monitor, before he got sucked back there. But he didn't complain to Angela. Instead he suggested, "Can we make sure JB is comfortable first? Or—see if traveling through time cured him?"

"JB?" Angela said doubtfully.

JB lay on a heap on the ground staring at the ceiling of the cave. He didn't answer.

As if they'd both been thinking the same thought, Jonah and Angela together hoisted JB into the front seat of the car, so he was right in front of Jonah's kid parents.

"It's like he's in a coma or something," Jonah complained.

"I think the technical term would be more like

'catatonic,'" Angela said. "But I'm sure somewhere in the future, once we get him back to the future, he can be cured."

She didn't sound sure.

Jonah went over and sat down on the ground with his back against the rock wall.

"Elucidator, can you show me exactly what happened when Gary and Hodge made time split?" Jonah asked, looking down at the object in his hand. It wasn't a marble anymore; now it looked more like a cell phone with a perfectly clear screen.

But the only thing the screen showed was Jonah standing with Gary in the stairwell at the airport. An airplane landed in the darkness outside the window before them.

"I just lived through all that!" Jonah complained. "I mean, give me the broader view. The big picture!"

Now the scene Jonah saw was an image of planet Earth. From space.

"Ergh!" Jonah growled in exasperation. He so wanted to throw the Elucidator down to the ground and smash it into a million pieces.

"Look," Angela said, sitting down beside him and holding out her own Elucidator, which had turned into an ID-style rectangle of plastic on a lanyard. But it, too, had a screen on its face.

"I asked it to let me draw a graph, because my mind keeps tripping over what could and couldn't have happened in each stream of time," Angela explained.

"You're miles ahead of what I've managed to get my Elucidator to do," Jonah admitted.

He studied Angela's drawing, which looked like a tree with only two branches. But she zoomed in on the drawing, showing him more details. At the point where the branch split, Angela had written, *Moment when both 13-year-old Jonah and baby Jonah were in same time.*

Then on the first branch she'd written, *Only baby Jonah taken off plane at airport. Plane and all other babies taken on to future by Charles Lindbergh. 13-y.o. Jonah delivers baby Jonah to parents; Gary and Hodge say this time stream will collapse soon.*

On the second branch she'd written, *Path to glorious future for Gary and Hodge. Not sure exactly what happens with airplane and babies, but they don't disrupt anything about the 21st century. And there are no time agents.*

Jonah looked back up and saw Angela frown.

"This is what I don't understand," she said. "Doesn't there have to be *some* version of time where you and the other babies on the plane stay in place after the time crash, and grow up to be thirteen years old in the twenty-first century? Doesn't there have to be some version where I saw the babies and got suspicious and studied physics and then met JB and found out about time travel? Doesn't *some* time stream have to lead to this moment right now, where you and I are together in a time cave and JB's crazy and your parents are both thirteen years old?"

"Ummm . . . ," Jonah said, because what she was saying made sense to him. He racked his brain, trying to remember everything he'd ever learned about time travel. Even the theories he barely understood. "Maybe Gary and Hodge just haven't released the ripple of changes from the time split? Maybe this and everything else we remember since the time crash is about to be . . . erased?"

"But wouldn't that be too big of a paradox?" Angela asked. "Wouldn't that also erase you showing up at the scene of the time crash and making time split?"

She was making Jonah's head ache more than ever. He dipped toward Angela's Elucidator.

"Do Angela and I have the right explanations?" Jonah asked it. "Does the graph she just drew show exactly how the time split worked?"

NO, the Elucidator flashed at him.

"Could you fix my drawing so it shows how things really turned out?" Angela chimed in.

NO, the Elucidator flashed again.

Now Jonah wanted to throw that Elucidator on the ground too. And stomp on it.

"Why not?" he demanded.

EVERYTHING IS STILL IN FLUX, the Elucidator flashed. OUTCOMES AREN'T DETERMINED YET. A LOT DEPENDS ON WHAT THE TWO OF YOU DECIDE TO DO NEXT.

That was good, wasn't it?

"What should we do?" Jonah asked eagerly, leaning closer to the Elucidator. "To help JB, I mean, and to rescue Katherine and the others, and to make everyone the right age and—oh yeah—to save time once and for all?"

THAT'S NOT FOR ME TO SAY, scrolled across the Elucidator's screen.

"What can you say?" Angela asked.

HELLO unfurled across the screen.

Jonah slammed back against the rock wall.

"Maybe *both* these Elucidators secretly came from Gary and Hodge," he muttered. "Or some worse enemy—Second Chance, maybe?"

Now it was his own Elucidator that flashed up at him.

NO, it said. GARY AND HODGE DID RIG THE MONITORS IN THIS TIME CAVE SO YOU WOULD FALL IN TO 1932 WHEN THEY WANTED YOU TO. BUT ANGELA'S ELUCIDATOR AND YOURS BOTH CAME FROM HADLEY CORREO. SEE FOR YOURSELF.

The Elucidator seemed to want to prove its point: It began rolling a scene of Angela—grown-up, time-travel-experienced Angela—standing in a kitchen holding out a piece of paper to the time agent Hadley Correo. Hadley looked just like Jonah remembered, with a grizzled beard and twinkling eyes that seemed to lose a bit of their twinkle as he stared at the paper. Jonah suddenly realized that the paper was the note he himself had given Angela at the airport. But the note was much more tattered that it had been the last time Jonah had seen it. Apparently Angela had folded and unfolded and looked at it many times over the past thirteen years.

Jonah guessed she hadn't exactly waited twelve years and eleven months to open it.

"That was just last night," Angela said huskily, looking over Jonah's shoulder. She cleared her throat. "I mean, the last night I spent in the twenty-first century. Since you told me to keep everything secret from you and JB, I was afraid to tell anyone about the note. But I had to tell *some-one* in order to get an Elucidator. And I chose Hadley."

"So Hadley gave you an Elucidator right away, and then he went back thirteen years to leave one with Eva the social worker so I would have one too?" Jonah asked.

"He told me about that part," Angela said, nodding. "But I don't know how he knew to do everything else with the social worker and the baby. . . ."

ISN'T IT OBVIOUS? Jonah's Elucidator flashed up at them.

The Elucidator shifted to other scenes: Hadley

watching a monitor showing Jonah getting the baby version of himself from Hodge. Hadley going back thirteen years in time and hiring an actress to pretend to be a teenage mother who'd decided adoption was the best option. Hadley giving the actress an innocent-looking Connect 4 game to leave behind in the social worker's office.

"How did he keep all that secret?" Angela asked. "Didn't anyone else at the time agency see what he'd done?"

NO, the Elucidator flashed. THEY WERE MORE FOCUSED ON EXAMINING EVERYTHING AFTER THE TIME-CRASHED PLANE LANDED. AND THEY DIDN'T SEE THE TIME STREAM WITH LINDBERGH TAKING THE PLANE ON TO THE FUTURE BECAUSE THEY DIDN'T KNOW TO LOOK FOR IT. THEY DIDN'T KNOW ABOUT THE TIME SPLIT.

"How do you miss something like that?" Jonah asked incredulously.

MILLIONS OF YEARS OF TIME TO EXAMINE, the Elucidator flashed. AN INFINITY OF VARIABLES TO CONSIDER. EVEN I CAN'T THINK OF EVERYTHING.

*Not comforting,* Jonah thought. *Not actually very helpful at all.*

How could he have two Elucidators within reach and still feel so much like he was flying blind?

"I don't get it," Angela admitted. "If Hadley knew Gary and Hodge were going to split time, why didn't he warn us? Why didn't he warn the time agency—or even just JB? Why didn't he stop them before it happened?"

HE THOUGHT THIS METHOD OF MINIMAL INTERFERENCE WAS BEST, the Elucidator told them.

The Elucidator on the lanyard around Angela's neck began flashing a solid red light, as if trying to get everyone's attention.

"What?" Jonah asked it.

NO, that Elucidator flashed. HE THOUGHT THIS WAS THE ONLY CHOICE THAT MIGHT WORK.

*Great,* Jonah thought. *So now the Elucidators don't even agree?*

"So you mean Hadley thought everything depended on us from here on out?" Angela asked, her voice quavering. "On Jonah and me?"

YES. The flashing light was a little overwhelming. Jonah realized that it was because both Elucidators were saying the same thing. ON THE TWO OF YOU. AND CHARLES LINDBERGH.

"Lindbergh?" Jonah repeated incredulously. "But he already flew Katherine and the other babies on to the future. Gary and Hodge made it so he couldn't come back! His part's over!"

Once again the two Elucidators flashed back the same message:

IS IT?

# FORTY-THREE

Jonah pounded his fists against his forehead. He put his Elucidator down on the ground and got up and walked around, pacing between two rock walls.

"I hate Elucidators!" he snarled. "It isn't fair! This is like—riddles! Can't they ever give a straight answer?"

There was a burst of light again from both Elucidators—Jonah wasn't close enough to read either screen, and he still knew the answer they were giving was NO.

Angela held her Elucidator up and read from the screen, "It says time is too complicated for simple answers. So is life in general."

Jonah made a disgusted growl. His pacing took him back close to Angela and the Elucidators. He crouched down and asked the Elucidators, "What can we do from here? What can Charles Lindbergh do?"

Both Elucidators flashed back the reply: INFINITE POSSIBILITIES.

"Well, show us some of them," Jonah asked. "Start with Lindbergh's."

He figured that would be less frightening.

Both screens flashed with a quick succession of scenes. Lindbergh was climbing a mountain; he was flying a plane that looked much more high-tech than anything Jonah had ever seen; he was giving a speech; he was hugging a child; he was dropping bombs on an old-fashioned-looking building. In some of the scenes he was middle-aged or older; in others he was just a baby or a child.

"Wait—there's some possibilities ahead of Charles Lindbergh where he's a baby again?" Angela asked. "Or a little kid?"

The Elucidator screens flashed together: YES.

Jonah collapsed from his crouching position. He hit the ground, and he picked up his Elucidator again.

"Is that how Gary and Hodge plan to keep him in the future?" Jonah asked, feeling proud that he was finally starting to figure *something* out. "They're going to un-age him back to being a baby on his trip to the future? Why try selling Charles Lindbergh's kid, when you can sell the baby version of Charles Lindbergh himself!"

YOU HAVE PERFECTLY ENCAPSULATED ONE PORTION OF GARY

AND HODGE'S VIEWPOINT, the Elucidator flashed back at him.

It was almost like having a teacher write *Good job!* on a test. Maybe he didn't hate Elucidators so much, after all.

"But I thought adults couldn't be un-aged back to being infants through time travel," Angela said. "It was dangerous even making some of us teenagers again. Look at what happened to JB!"

Jonah glanced toward the car containing his sleeping parents and JB.

*Please let it be possible to cure JB,* he thought. *Please let my parents be okay when they come out of this too.*

ADULT-TO-INFANCY UN-AGING IS PROHIBITED BY ALL TIME-AGENCY RULES, Jonah's Elucidator flashed up at him. He was pretty sure Angela's was saying the same thing. BUT AS YOU KNOW, GARY AND HODGE HAVE VERY LITTLE REGARD FOR TIME-AGENCY RULES. THEY FIGURE EVEN A 30 PERCENT CHANCE THAT LINDBERGH WILL ARRIVE UNDAMAGED IS A 30 PERCENT CHANCE THAT THEY WILL MAKE HUGE PROFITS.

"But that means it's a seventy percent chance that—" Angela began numbly.

THAT CHARLES LINDBERGH WOULD LIVE OUT HIS LIFE IN THE FUTURE WITH BRAIN DAMAGE AND/OR PHYSICAL IMPAIRMENT, the Elucidator said. OR HE MIGHT JUST DIE. YES.

For a moment neither Jonah nor Angela said anything. Then Jonah exploded angrily, "And Gary and Hodge don't care! They don't care whose life they ruin, or how much of time they destroy! As long as they get rich!"

AGAIN, YOU SHOW A KEEN GRASP OF THEIR REASONING, the Elucidator acknowledged.

Jonah snorted, furious with Gary and Hodge, and exasperated that the Elucidator could stay so calm about it.

Angela was acting perfectly calm as well. She squinted thoughtfully at her own Elucidator.

"But they could have gotten even richer if they'd taken baby Jonah on to the future and passed him off as Lindbergh's son," she said. "To make time split, they only needed the two versions of Jonah in the same time for a few moments, right?"

YES, both Elucidators flashed.

"So why didn't they still have the baby Jonah go on to the future on the plane with everyone else?" Angela asked.

"Because they put Katherine in my seat," Jonah growled.

He was surprised that his Elucidator flashed an additional explanation at him.

AND THEY THOUGHT LEAVING THAT BABY WITH YOU WOULD BE ENOUGH TO MAKE YOU FEEL TOTALLY DEFEATED, it said. THEY THOUGHT YOU WOULD GIVE UP. BUT YOU DIDN'T.

*Proving Gary and Hodge were wrong,* Jonah thought. He was proud of that. It was something to hold on to, no matter how frustrated and stymied he felt right now.

"And I guess they could no longer pass Jonah off as Lindbergh's son if they had Lindbergh himself right there, available for DNA testing, to compare," Angela said.

"Hey, I could have been just as much of a 'famous missing kid of history' as Katherine," Jonah protested. "Since she got her fame through saving the other kids with time travel—I did that too!"

Angela shrugged.

"Then they really were all about making you feel defeated," she said. She grinned mischievously, a look that she couldn't have carried off as a grown-up. "I didn't think the baby version of you was *that* terrifying when I saw it!"

"But you never saw—" Jonah began. Then he realized what she meant. "Oh, right. You mean you saw the baby me in the version of time where you stepped onto the plane and everyone carried the babies off. And we all got adopted right afterward."

"The version of time that we aren't sure exists anymore, because of the time split," Angela reminded him, wrinkling up her face in confusion. "Except it has to, or we wouldn't be here."

Something tickled in Jonah's brain.

"The last time I saw time split," he began slowly, "it was different. In 1611, the new versions of Henry Hudson and the other sailors went in one direction, into the time period Second Chance created. The other versions of all those people rejoined their tracers and pretty much went back to time the way it originally happened."

Angela's jaw dropped and her eyes got big.

"So how come both versions of you ended up on the same side of the time split?" she whispered.

# FORTY-FOUR

Jonah gaped back at Angela. Was this what was missing from the graph Angela had drawn? Or was the difference something bigger?

"Then . . . then . . . maybe there wasn't even a time split at all!" Jonah cried. "Maybe there's some sort of technicality we don't know about. . . . Elucidator! Was there actually a time split or not?"

He looked down, eager for confirmation of the new ideas starting to grow in his mind. But the Elucidator in his hand flashed up, THERE WAS A TIME SPLIT. IT JUST DIDN'T WORK THE WAY ANGELA DREW IT.

"Then how did it work?" Jonah demanded.

BADLY, the Elucidator answered.

Another exasperating answer.

"Could you explain a little bit more than that?"

Angela asked, sounding as annoyed as Jonah felt.

SURE, the Elucidator flashed up. But it didn't give the explanation Jonah expected. YOU HAVE TO UNDERSTAND NOT JUST GARY AND HODGE'S MOTIVES, BUT THEIR MODUS OPERANDI scrolled across the screen.

What in the world was a *modus operandi*?

Jonah didn't bother stopping the Elucidator to ask. It was continuing to explain.

GARY AND HODGE ARE CARELESS AND RECKLESS AND LAZY, the Elucidator flashed. MOST OF THEIR PLANS CONTAIN FATAL FLAWS. BUT IT'S HARD TO TELL THEIR MISTAKES FROM INTENTIONAL LIES AND MISDIRECTION. SOMETIMES THEIR OWN INEPTNESS BECOMES SOMETHING OF A TALENT. IT PROVIDES THEM PROTECTION FROM THE TIME AGENCY, BECAUSE THE TIME AGENCY FINDS THEM COMPLETELY UNPREDICTABLE.

"Well, that was as clear as mud," Jonah complained.

Was it at least a good sign that the Elucidator was acting like there still was a time agency?

*Or is that something else that will disappear after Gary and Hodge release the ripple from all their changes?* Jonah wondered.

"How about giving some concrete examples?" Angela asked. She seemed to have a lot more patience with the Elucidator than Jonah did. "Something connected to Jonah, maybe?"

SURE, the Elucidator said. WHEN GARY AND HODGE WERE

TRYING TO PASS JONAH OFF AS CHARLES LINDBERGH'S SON, THEY LISTED HIM ON THE AIRPLANE ROSTER AS CHARLES LINDBERGH III.

"So?" Jonah asked.

THE BABY WAS THE SECOND CHARLES AUGUSTUS LINDBERGH IN THE FAMILY, NOT THE THIRD. SO HE WAS ONLY A JUNIOR. HIS GRANDFATHER'S MIDDLE NAME WAS JUST AUGUST—A SUBTLE BUT SIGNIFICANT DIFFERENCE, the Elucidator explained.

"Who cares?" Jonah asked in disgust. He rolled his eyes.

BECAUSE OF THAT ONE MISTAKE, THE TIME AGENCY WAS ALWAYS AFRAID THAT THEY WERE MISTAKEN THEMSELVES ABOUT JONAH'S ORIGINAL IDENTITY, the Elucidator flashed. JB IN PARTICULAR WONDERED IF YOU ACTUALLY CAME FROM ANOTHER DIMENSION—MAYBE THE ONE THAT SECOND CHANCE CREATED—WHERE THE NAMES WERE JUST SLIGHTLY DIFFERENT, AND MAYBE THE FIRST FLIGHT TO PARIS CAME A GENERATION LATER.

*So that's why JB was always so cagey about discussing my identity?* Jonah wondered. *Just because of a name?*

"Couldn't they have done DNA tests?" Angela asked.

THE DNA COULD HAVE BEEN DIFFERENT IN A DIFFERENT DIMENSION TOO, the Elucidator flashed. AND DNA TESTS WOULD HAVE SHOWED THAT JONAH IS DISTANTLY RELATED TO THE ACTUAL CHARLES LINDBERGH.

"I am?" Jonah said, surprised.

EVERY HUMAN IS RELATED TO EVERY OTHER HUMAN IN ONE WAY OR ANOTHER, the Elucidator replied.

"You might as well say, 'Tricked you! Psych!'" Jonah complained. "I thought maybe you were going to tell me that Gary and Hodge lied about me dying in an orphanage in original time."

SORRY. THAT PART IS TRUE, the Elucidator flashed back.

Angela tilted her head, looking back and forth from her Elucidator to Jonah's.

"Wait," she said. "You just told us who Jonah really is, and you told me back at the Lindberghs' house. But no Elucidator ever let JB or any of the other time agents know the truth for sure? Why not?"

THE TIME STREAM WAS STILL MUDDIED, Jonah saw on his own Elucidator's screen. TOO MUCH WAS STILL IN FLUX.

"But it's not now?" Jonah asked excitedly.

NOT ABOUT YOUR IDENTITY, the Elucidator replied.

Strangely, this did make Jonah feel good. He remembered how, way back at the beginning of the whole time-travel mess, Katherine had told him off for asking questions about his past and upsetting their parents. She'd said every middle-school kid wondered who they were supposed to be. Jonah imagined teasing Katherine: *Even an Elucidator admits that nothing about my identity is still in flux! I am who I am! And you're still wondering about yourself, right? What does that make you?*

Would Jonah ever see Katherine again to tease her? Or even just to talk to her?

He shook his head, trying to clear his brain.

"What else did Gary and Hodge mess up, connected to me?" Jonah asked.

THIS IS INDIRECTLY CONNECTED TO YOU, BECAUSE OF WHO THEY CLAIMED YOU WERE, the Elucidator began.

And then it showed a series of scenes of Gary and Hodge trying to kidnap the actual Lindbergh baby. This would have been like watching funny outtakes from a movie if every scene hadn't ended with a baby dead on the ground. Once Hodge dropped the baby from the ladder himself. Once Gary wavered in and out of the scene—there, not there, there, not there—as he tried to lift the baby from the crib. Each time he picked the baby up, he immediately dropped him.

PORTIONS OF THIS TIME PERIOD WERE CLOSED OFF TO TIME TRAVELERS, the Elucidator explained. THAT'S WHY HE DISAPPEARS.

"Is it because time travelers had made that Damaged Time?" Angela asked. "Because so many people had gone there, curious about what happened to the baby?"

NO, BECAUSE JAPAN HAD JUST INVADED CHINA IN THE RUN-UP TO WORLD WAR II, AND LOTS OF TIME TRAVELERS WERE WATCHING THAT, the Elucidator flashed back.

Jonah decided not to admit that he'd never known Japan invaded China.

FINALLY GARY AND HODGE JUST GAVE UP AND KIDNAPPED YOU INSTEAD, SEVERAL MONTHS LATER, the Elucidator told him and Angela.

"Because nobody cared about me disappearing," Jonah said, and the words came out sounding more bitter than he would have expected.

Oops. Maybe some things about his identity still were "in flux," as the Elucidator put it.

But something new struck him.

"But if nobody cared, then how was there anything connected to my kidnapping that needed to be fixed in time?" Jonah asked.

THERE WASN'T, the Elucidator flashed back. THE ONLY ISSUE THE TIME AGENCY HAD WITH YOU WAS THAT THEY WORRIED ABOUT YOU BEING FROM ANOTHER DIMENSION. WHICH YOU'RE NOT.

Jonah felt as if the Elucidator had just lifted some huge burden from his back. He wouldn't have to go back in time to live out some dangerous life as some other kid. He was free.

*Well, except for needing to stay in this time cave thinking and thinking and thinking until we figure out everything about the time split,* he thought. *And except for worrying about rescuing Katherine and the other kids and curing JB and making everyone the right age again. And having the Elucidator say that everything depends on me and Angela.*

He'd left someone out. The Elucidator hadn't just said that everything depended on Angela and Jonah. They'd said it depended on Charles Lindbergh, too.

*Why?* Jonah wondered.

Jonah remembered that he'd never actually seen what Gary and Hodge had told Charles Lindbergh to do.

"Even if you can't tell us what happens with Charles Lindbergh next, can you at least tell us how Gary and Hodge *want* things to go?" Jonah asked his Elucidator.

YES, the Elucidator said.

It began showing another scene, though this one held the words "NOT ACTUAL EVENTS—DEMONSTRATION PURPOSES ONLY" stamped across the screen.

Behind those words Charles Lindbergh took off from the airport back home in the airplane with thirty-six babies in the passenger seats—baby Katherine, plus all the original babies on the plane except Jonah. Lindbergh landed the plane a split second later in a place so brightly lit that Jonah could make out only one detail in the glare: Gary and Hodge were standing on the runway waiting for him. Lindbergh stepped out and greeted them. Jonah was stunned to see that it was still the adult Lindbergh, tall and slightly stooped.

"Didn't you just say that Lindbergh was going to be

un-aged to a baby on his trip through time?" Jonah interrupted.

THIS IS ONLY THE FIRST STEP OF THE PLAN, the Elucidator replied. JUST WAIT.

Jonah didn't understand this, but he kept watching.

There was a sped-up sequence where Gary and Hodge had employees pull each and every baby off the plane. Then Lindbergh got back into the plane.

"Where's he going now?" Jonah asked.

"My Elucidator says it's to a time hollow nearby," Angela said, holding hers sideways so Jonah could see it too.

PERSONALLY, I THOUGHT YOU COULD FIGURE THAT OUT FOR YOURSELF, ONCE YOU SAW IT, Jonah's Elucidator flashed.

In the background Lindbergh was landing the plane again, though Jonah wasn't sure it could be called "landing" when the plane suddenly just appeared in an enclosed space. A crowd seemed to be waiting on the ground beside the plane. In the cockpit Lindbergh took a deep breath, as if steeling himself for what came next. A voice came out of the speaker in the cockpit: "Remember, these are enemy combatants. They want to destroy time forever, and make it so that you never see your son again. They will be hostile. You must knock each and every one of them out, and then load them onto the plane to be taken to time prison."

Lindbergh unbuckled his seat belt and picked up a small object from the seat beside him. Jonah guessed that it could be anything from a Taser to a ray gun. Lindbergh took another deep breath, then stood up, walked out of the cockpit, and opened the door of the plane.

Lindbergh started shooting his weapon even before the door was fully open.

Beside Jonah, Angela gasped.

"He's just tranquilizing them or something," Jonah muttered, without lifting his gaze from the screen. "The voice said he was just supposed to knock them out. Not kill them."

"L-l-look," Angela stammered. "Look who he's shooting."

Jonah squinted, watching bodies fall. And then he recognized the bodies. Everyone looked to be thirteen years old; everybody was a person Jonah knew: Chip. Emily. Ming. Brendan. Antonio . . .

Andrea.

Charles Lindbergh was shooting all the other missing children of history.

# FORTY-FIVE

"Stop!" Jonah screamed at the Elucidator screen. "Stop shooting!"

"He can't hear you!" Angela screamed back at him.

On the screen all the bodies had fallen. Lindbergh began methodically carrying each and every body onto the plane. He strapped them into the futuristic seats, and double-checked dials on the sides of each seat that said UN-AGE TO FOUR TO SIX MONTHS OLD.

"He's taking them to the future as babies too?" Jonah asked incredulously. "A different future, I guess, since Gary and Hodge already got a first set of them all as babies?"

"They're not dead," Angela whispered beside him. "They're not. I can see them still breathing. There's still time to save them . . ."

Jonah watched Lindbergh finish strapping in the last

teenager, Dalton, whom Jonah himself had saved from having to live through the end of his life as Henry Hudson's son. There was still one seat left empty.

*Oh,* Jonah thought. *The seat I would have been in originally. And then Katherine sat in it the second time around. . . .*

Lindbergh went back into the cockpit and took off. The camera's view stayed trained on his face, which seemed to be smoothing out, growing younger. . . . At what point would he realize he himself was turning back into a baby?

Jonah was pretty sure it would be too late for Lindbergh to do anything about it.

"So, both times, Gary and Hodge get thirty-six babies to sell," Jonah muttered.

"What's that going to do to time?" Angela asked in a horrified voice. "Especially if this set of babies goes to the same place Lindbergh took the other group?"

Jonah was too shocked to answer her. He guessed both Elucidators were ignoring her question too, since his Elucidator just kept showing Lindbergh in the cockpit, getting younger and younger and younger.

Then Angela clutched Jonah's arm.

"The Elucidator changed my drawing," she whispered, sounding stunned. "To show what will happen if everything goes the way Gary and Hodge want."

Jonah looked at the Elucidator she was holding up.

The drawing still looked like a tree, but the split between the trunk and the branches started with a point labeled, AUGUST 15, 1932. DIFFERENCE IN FAKE "CHARLES LINDBERGH JR." PUT ON PLANE THAT WILL TIME-CRASH DECADES LATER. ALSO, CHARLES LINDBERGH DISAPPEARS FROM HISTORY.

"So there's a version of time where I'm never even on the plane?" Jonah marveled. "And that plus Lindbergh's disappearance is enough of a disturbance that it's possible for time to split decades later?"

It was hard to tell what happened right after 1932, since the section of the drawing for that time period was covered with heavy black lines and the words "unsettled time." But no branch totally broke away from the trunk until a point farther up marked TIME-CRASH OF PLANELOAD OF BABIES. After that, the branches split dramatically, into not two but three new branches. Two were basically the same as the ones Angela had drawn earlier: one with the time-crashed plane flying on without making any impact on the late twentieth or early twenty-first centuries; the other with only one baby coming off the plane.

*Me,* Jonah thought. *Only baby me. That's the version of time I just saw. The one that was about to collapse.*

Quickly he turned his attention to the third branch. This one showed time as Jonah remembered it, with all the babies—including Jonah—staying and growing up to be thirteen-year-olds in the twenty-first century.

"This is good!" Jonah cried. "There is a stream of time that works the way we want it to!"

Silently Angela pointed to words at the top of the branch: LINDBERGH TAKES KATHERINE SKIDMORE OUT OF TIME, DISTURBING TIME ENOUGH THAT GARY AND HODGE CAN ALSO REMOTELY ZAP ALL THE MISSING CHILDREN BESIDES JONAH INTO A SECRET TIME HOLLOW OF THEIR CHOOSING. THIS STREAM OF TIME COLLAPSES SOON AFTER BECAUSE OF THE EXTREME DIFFERENCE OF LOSING THIRTY-SEVEN KIDS WHO'D BEEN THERE FOR UP TO THIRTEEN YEARS.

"Thirty-*seven* kids?" Jonah read numbly.

"Because of you, Jonah," Angela said. "Gary and Hodge wanted you out of this branch of time before it collapsed too."

*They were actually being nice to me?* Jonah wondered.

Then he decided they must have had other reasons.

"But only because they want me in that other branch when *it* collapses," Jonah muttered.

GARY AND HODGE TOOK A PARTICULAR DISLIKE TO YOU, Jonah's own Elucidator explained, and somehow its glow seemed apologetic. THEY BLAME YOU FOR GETTING THEM SENT TO TIME PRISON.

*Well—yeah!* Jonah thought. *I did do that!*

"Did you notice this?" Angela asked, pointing to the

middle branch of the time split, which showed Gary and Hodge getting their glorious, wealthy future. It was the only branch that wasn't broken off at the end.

Instead it split again.

At that split the screen read, IMPACT OF HAVING THIRTY-FIVE DUPLICATED KIDS IN THE SAME TIME CAUSES TIME SPLIT SO EXTREME THAT IT ERASES THE POSSIBILITY OF TIME TRAVEL EVER AGAIN.

# FORTY-SIX

"What's *that* mean?" Jonah moaned. "All of time ends, after all?"

He looked down, not sure he actually wanted to know the answer. But that just meant that he was looking directly at his own Elucidator.

NO, it said. TIME WOULD CONTINUE WITHOUT A PROBLEM, EXACTLY AS GARY AND HODGE WANT IT. BUT IT'S LIKE ENDLESS DAMAGED TIME. THE TIME AGENCY CEASES TO EXIST, BECAUSE THERE'S NO TIME TRAVEL ANYMORE. GARY AND HODGE AREN'T IN TROUBLE, BECAUSE IN THIS VERSION OF TIME THEY NEVER ILLEGALLY CRASHED A PLANELOAD OF BABIES INTO THE WRONG TIME. ALL THEIR BABY-SMUGGLING LOOKS PERFECTLY LEGIT. AND PEOPLE WILL BE PARTICULARLY PROTECTIVE OF THESE ENDANGERED BABIES FROM HISTORY, BECAUSE THEY'RE THE LAST ONES ABLE TO ESCAPE. IN EACH OF THE TWO BRANCHES REMAINING, GARY AND

HODGE HAVE THIRTY-SIX VERY, VERY VALUABLE BABIES TO SELL.

The Elucidator seemed to be hesitating; then it added, AND THEY'RE CONSIDERED HEROES FOR SAVING THOSE KIDS.

"No!" Jonah yelled, shaking his head ferociously. "NO!"

Angela just sat there as if she was too stunned to move.

"And us?" she whispered. "What happens to us? And JB and Hadley and Jonah's parents and—and everyone who isn't in those time streams?"

She pointed to the branches where Gary and Hodge triumphed.

PEOPLE END WHEN THEIR TIME STREAMS END, her Elucidator flashed back. PEOPLE IN TIME HOLLOWS LIKE THIS ARE STUCK THERE FOREVER.

Jonah thought about what it would be like to stay in a time hollow forever. There'd be nothing to do, and no reason to do anything, because nothing ever changed. It was bad enough to stay in a place like this temporarily—but *forever*?

"You said we could get back to 1932," Jonah wailed. "You promised!"

YOU STILL CAN, the Elucidator said, and now its glow seemed soothing. NOT EVERYTHING THAT GARY AND HODGE PLANNED HAS HAPPENED. YET.

Jonah looked around frantically.

"We've got to stop Charles Lindbergh," he said. "Send us back now. Send us to—"

"Don't!" Angela yelled, yanking the Elucidator out of Jonah's hand. "We need a plan first, remember? *How* are we going to stop Charles Lindbergh?"

Jonah would have been willing to make it up as he floated through time.

"I'll tell Charles Lindbergh I'm not really his son," Jonah said. "Then he'll have no reason to do what Gary and Hodge told him to do."

"Didn't you already try to tell him that?" Angela asked.

Jonah remembered his silent mouthing of the words in the stairwell at the airport.

"I bet he didn't hear me," Jonah said.

"All those early pilots were really good at lip-reading," Angela said. "Because it was so loud in their cockpits. I bet he could tell what you were saying."

Jonah frowned, not wanting to admit that she was probably right.

"Then we'll prove it to him," Jonah said. "We'll prove I'm not his son, and I'll prove that Gary and Hodge have no way of giving him back his real son—they couldn't even manage to kidnap the boy. . . ."

Jonah expected Angela to object to this as well, but she didn't.

"I think if we *could* prove those two things, it would stop him," she said. "But how can we possibly prove anything?

And when can we get to him without Gary and Hodge stopping us? What can we do to make him trust us?"

Jonah looked down at his Elucidator, which Angela was still holding a safe distance away from him. But Jonah could see it still showing Lindbergh in the cockpit of the plane, growing younger and younger and younger.

Jonah pointed toward the Elucidator screen.

"Lindbergh's a pilot," Jonah said. "Don't you think he'd trust us more if we went flying with him?"

Angela looked back and forth between her own Elucidator and Jonah's.

"Can either of you Elucidators get us on that plane?" she asked. "Early enough that it's still possible to fix everything?"

NO, both Elucidators flashed. NOT BOTH OF YOU.

Jonah had been talking to Elucidators enough now that he knew to ask another question: "What about just one of us?"

It seemed to take a long time for the Elucidators to consider this question. Jonah wasn't sure how many millions of variables they were sorting through. Maybe it really was an infinity of possibilities, and he and Angela were sitting there waiting for the Elucidators to think about each and every one.

But then, in unison, the Elucidators flashed the same answer: YES. THERE IS A POSSIBILITY.

"All right!" Jonah screamed, thrusting his arm in the air.

"But with just one of us getting on that plane?" Angela asked cautiously.

YES, the Elucidators flashed again. And then there was a pause that almost seemed apologetic, because the next words showed up:

IT HAS TO BE JONAH ALONE.

# FORTY-SEVEN

To Jonah's way of thinking, it took forever for him and Angela and the Elucidators to work out all the details of his trip.

First Angela seemed to want the Elucidators to explain every single reason she couldn't go with Jonah. It boiled down to one problem: The only safe, open time for anyone to sneak onto the plane was while it was parked at the airport, right after the time crash, right after the time split, right before Lindbergh flew it out of time again. And Angela was already present in all versions of time that resulted from the time split. Throwing another version of her into the mix would make everything too unstable, create another time stream, and, as Jonah's Elucidator calculated, CREATE A 99.99999 PERCENT CHANCE OF DESTROYING TIME FOREVER.

Then it flashed with what had to be faked innocence, YOU DON'T WANT THAT, DO YOU?

"But Jonah's present in that time period too!" Angela protested, sounding almost exactly like Katherine always did when she didn't get her way.

"Not in every version," Jonah reminded her. "Remember the one where Lindbergh flies the plane on to the future without there being a baby removed first—because I was never on it?"

Part of Jonah wanted to do a victory dance, to rub it in to Angela that he got to go and fix everything, and Angela would be stuck waiting in a time hollow.

Another part of him wished fervently that it was the other way around.

Angela was still talking to her Elucidator, asking for suggestions about what Jonah could tell Lindbergh to get him to defy Gary and Hodge's plans before it was too late.

Jonah was having trouble listening very well. He kept glancing over toward the kid versions of Mom, Dad, and JB in the car.

*If I fail,* he thought, *all time travel ends. I won't be able to come back for them. And all of them will be stuck in this time cave with Angela forever. Mom and Dad will be stuck here sleeping forever. JB will be crazy forever.*

And Angela would, for all intents and purposes, be alone forever.

The planning went on and on. Finally, Angela looked

up at Jonah and said, "Is there anything else you can think of to ask?"

"No," Jonah said quickly. Angela looked at him doubtfully, and he added, "I'll have the Elucidator with me. I can ask it anything I want, as I go along."

Jonah expected her to scold him for wanting to do just seat-of-the-pants planning. Instead she nodded.

"That makes sense," she said sadly. She seemed to be trying to smile. "I think you're ready, then."

Jonah took a deep breath.

"No," he said. "I'm not. I want to say good-bye to Mom and Dad first. In case I fail and I never see them again."

"Well, go ahead," Angela said, gesturing toward the car.

"No," Jonah said. "I want to say good-bye where they can hear me. We need to open the time hollow and go back to the twenty-first century so we can wake them up. And *then* I'll say good-bye."

"Jonah—" Angela began. And then she stopped, reconsidering. "You want them to know the truth either way, don't you? And are you giving me a choice, too? In case things don't work . . . you're giving me the option of living out the rest of my life in real time. Even if time collapses."

"Don't you think that's better than being trapped in a time hollow with three people who aren't even awake?" Jonah said.

Angela seemed to be studying his face intently. Then she gave a quick bob of her head, up and down.

"You're really a nice kid, you know that?" she said.

"No thirteen-year-old boy wants to be told he's 'nice'!" Jonah protested.

"Okay, let's get through this, and I'll tell you when you're fourteen," Angela said, grinning.

They set the Elucidators to tell them how to open the doors and wake up kid Mom and kid Dad.

"Shouldn't we make ourselves visible again too, so we don't completely freak them out?" Angela asked.

"Oh, yeah . . . ," Jonah muttered.

He'd been so focused on getting information from the Elucidators that he'd stopped noticing that he, Angela, and JB were still mostly see-through from their time in 1932.

*And Mom and Dad probably wouldn't be able to see us at all, because they've never traveled through time,* Jonah reminded himself. He didn't think that their going into the time hollow would count. *But staying invisible wouldn't do me any good when I go back to talk to Lindbergh, because that would freak him out too. And anyhow, Gary and Hodge would be able to see me as translucent. . . .*

Angela turned everyone visible again, and then Jonah woke his parents and opened the cave door. He led his parents outside into the autumn sunshine. Both of them were blinking groggily.

"Where *are* we?" Mom asked. "What happened? What's going on?"

Dad let out a jaw-cracking yawn.

"Mom, Dad, I've got something to tell you," Jonah said. "This friend of mine, Angela"—he pointed, and she waved—"she's going to explain all the details. But I wanted to tell you . . . Katherine and I have been traveling through time constantly the past few months. Everything's kind of a mess, but I'm going to go off and try to fix everything and rescue Katherine. I just wanted to tell you that before I left. Because . . . I'm not sure I'm going to be able to come back."

They both stared at him blankly.

*I can't make them understand,* he thought despairingly. *This was a huge mistake.*

But then both his parents launched themselves at him, engulfing him in an enormous hug.

"We'll go with you!" Dad cried. "We'll get Katherine and have an adventure together. As a family!"

For a moment Jonah just let them hug him. He let himself hug them back and draw in the strength he'd gotten from thirteen years of them being his parents.

And then he pushed them away.

"I'm sorry," he said. "This is the way it has to be. I love you."

Quickly, because he was thoroughly embarrassed, he added, looking off to the side, "You too, Angela. Thanks for everything."

He glanced down to make sure that nobody was still touching him. Then he told the Elucidator in his hand, "Take me back to the plane at the airport!"

Jonah knew that once he said that, the entire scene in front of him would disappear. He closed his eyes. But he could have sworn he heard Mom calling after him, "Be careful! Make sure you remember to brush your teeth, wherever you're going!"

It seemed like no time at all before Jonah was landing again.

*Timesickness—not too bad,* he thought, blinking quickly. *Of course it shouldn't be, since I came through only thirteen years.*

It seemed that he was lying in the aisle of the airplane. His vision was already clear enough that he could see numbers above the seats—his head was positioned right below the seats in row 11, and his feet were stretched out toward the front of the plane.

*Okay,* he thought. *Stand up slowly, then go see if Lindbergh's sitting in the pilot's seat yet.*

He was just stretching his hand up to grab on to the side of the row 10 seats to pull himself up when he heard a voice near the door at the front.

"Let me get this baby into place, and then you can take off immediately," the voice said.

It was Hodge. Hodge was about to walk down the aisle, evidently to strap baby Katherine in. Of course. Of course Hodge would be sending her off to the future in this version of time too. Jonah knew that.

What Jonah didn't know was: Where could he hide to get out of Hodge's way?

# FORTY-EIGHT

Jonah's first thought was to scramble into the space between the rows of seats.

*This is a plane full of babies—it's not like they have long legs dangling down and taking up all the room between the seats,* Jonah told himself.

But there was barely any room between the seats to begin with. And with only two seats on the right side of the aisle and one seat on the other side, Jonah could tell at a glance that some part of his body was bound to stick out into the aisle.

*So . . . if not under the seats, then where?* Jonah thought, frantically peering around.

He saw a door at the back end of the aisle, just beyond row 12, and was already crawling toward it before his brain asked him, *Maybe the bathroom?*

Jonah opened the door the smallest amount possible, as silently as possible, and squeezed in. Then he inched the door mostly closed behind him.

*Hodge won't notice, will he?* Jonah thought. *Surely this will be one of those times when he's lazy and reckless and he won't look up and down the aisles to make sure nothing's changed since the last time he was on this plane?*

Jonah had to stand up, because there wasn't room to stay crouched down in the narrow airplane bathroom—and anyway, it wasn't as if he really wanted to crouch down with his face smashed against the side of the toilet. Even though Jonah knew that this wasn't exactly a regular airplane, the bathroom had a too-realistic smell to it. Jonah almost wished he hadn't gotten his sense of smell back so quickly.

*And maybe I should have been a bit more specific about exactly where and when I told the Elucidator to put me on this plane?* Jonah scolded himself.

He turned away from the toilet and peeked out the crack at the side of the door.

Hodge and Lindbergh were both on the plane now, directly in Jonah's line of vision. Hodge was bent over a seat in the second row. Lindbergh, in his blue pilot's uniform, was standing stiffly in the doorway that led to the cockpit.

Hodge straightened up, his arms empty.

"There," he said. "Now I'll be off."

*Wait—shouldn't he be carrying the baby version of me?* Jonah wondered. *Did I somehow end up on the wrong version of this plane?*

He was still timesick enough that it took him a moment to realize: The fact that Hodge wasn't carrying baby Jonah off the plane was actually proof that Jonah was on the *right* version of the plane. He needed to be on the plane that Gary and Hodge had sent off from its last stop—in 1932, probably—without any baby at all in seat 2C.

*It's just the other two versions of time where I was ever on this plane,* Jonah reminded himself.

Trying to figure out time and time splits and different versions of time made Jonah's head ache. And he needed to focus on a more immediate problem: Hodge was looking toward the back of the plane. Had he seen Jonah?

*No,* Jonah told himself, holding his breath and silently backing away from the door. *He's admiring all the rows of babies that are going to make him rich.*

Hodge turned back around toward Lindbergh.

"Remember," he said. "You must follow our instructions exactly, or you will never see your son again. See you in the future!"

Lindbergh nodded once, curtly, and turned toward the cockpit.

Hodge began walking toward the door back to the Jetway.

*He's leaving,* Jonah told himself. *He's leaving . . . he's left!*

Jonah heard the door click into place. Almost immediately, the plane pulled back from the Jetway.

Jonah shoved the bathroom door all the way open and took the first step back into the aisle. He had a clear view now of all the babies at the back of the plane—he couldn't have said who any of them were, because they all just looked like sleeping babies.

*I guess they aren't really anybody at all yet,* Jonah told himself.

They weren't the children they'd been in the past or in the twenty-first century. If Gary and Hodge had their way, these babies' entire identities lay in the future.

*Gary and Hodge aren't going to get their way,* Jonah told himself.

The airplane turned and zoomed suddenly forward, and Jonah realized he didn't have much time to stand around thinking about these babies. He took three quick steps—and stopped again beside row 2.

There was the only baby on the plane Jonah could recognize instantly: Katherine.

Like all the other babies, she was sleeping soundly. She had her thumb in her mouth, which made her look even more recognizable: Jonah could remember her sucking her thumb a lot when she was little. Sometimes, way back in their childhoods, she used to suck her thumb and hold on to Jonah when she saw something scary on TV.

Of course, that was back when her idea of scary was Cookie Monster on *Sesame Street*.

Before he quite thought it through, Jonah started unstrapping baby Katherine from her seat.

*Because if this doesn't work and I end up getting stranded somewhere—shouldn't we at least be together?* he told himself.

The plane lurched upward—taking off? Already?—and Jonah would have tumbled over backward, all the way down the aisle, if he hadn't quickly grabbed on to the back of Katherine's seat.

That made him think of the time that he and Katherine had sat on the backs of the train seats in 1903, when they were following Albert Einstein's wife across Eastern Europe. He and Katherine had been a great team then, no matter how much they squabbled.

*Stop thinking about the past,* Jonah told himself. *Just think about what you have to do now, all right?*

Steadying himself as the plane leveled out, Jonah lifted baby Katherine from her seat and clutched her tightly to his chest. Then he walked on toward the cockpit.

Charles Lindbergh evidently heard Jonah's footsteps,

since he turned around. But no surprise showed on his face.

"You *are* a Lindbergh, if you figured out how to escape from them and come with me," Lindbergh said calmly, even as he shoved one of the levels on the control panel forward.

Jonah had a sudden brainstorm.

"Uh, right," he agreed cautiously. "And if you really believe I'm your son, don't you think we should just go back to the 1930s together? Why bother doing what Gary and Hodge want you to do?"

"Because they've already proved that they can follow you anywhere you go," Lindbergh said, shrugging. The motion made it easier for Jonah to see the futuristic tranquilizer gun Lindbergh had strapped on his hip. Jonah remembered how he'd seen Lindbergh use that very gun in the simulation of what Gary and Hodge wanted Lindbergh to do.

*Don't do anything that makes Lindbergh decide he needs to use that gun on me,* Jonah reminded himself. *No sudden moves.*

"But—" Jonah began.

Lindbergh didn't wait to hear Jonah's argument.

"Mr. Gary and Mr. Hodge can still trap you; they could trap *me*—no, I want to finish this and get away, free and clear," he said.

That was what Jonah wanted too. But his "free and clear" wouldn't be the same as Lindbergh's "free and clear."

Jonah couldn't think of a good answer. The plane lurched slightly. To be on the safe side—and buy himself some time to think—Jonah dropped into the empty copilot's seat beside Lindbergh.

Lindbergh glanced Jonah's way.

"That baby will be safer strapped in place in the back," Lindbergh said. "This will be my first time landing this rig."

*If the plane landed on its own back at the airport, and if it's supposed to land on its own when Lindbergh's a baby again, I don't think it's going to take a lot of piloting skill for Lindbergh to land it once in the future,* Jonah thought.

He decided that wasn't the best thing to point out to Charles Lindbergh. Instead Jonah went straight for the main point.

"I'm not actually your son," he said, and was surprised that he managed to sound apologetic about it. "Gary and Hodge have been lying to you."

Lindbergh took his eyes off the instrument panel in front of him just long enough to glance toward Jonah.

"I already heard—well, *saw*—you say that back at the airport," Lindbergh said. "Mr. Gary and Mr. Hodge already explained to me that you would be confused about your parentage. It's understandable. You were kidnapped, after all."

"Yeah—by Gary and Hodge!" Jonah protested.

"Don't worry—you will lose your delusions once we get back to the 1930s and you're a small child once more," Lindbergh said soothingly, as if Jonah would automatically believe him just because Lindbergh said so.

Jonah remembered the proof that he and Angela had discussed.

"Look," he said, holding out the Elucidator in his hand. It still looked vaguely cell phone–like, which Jonah thought was good. It would look futuristic to Lindbergh. "This is a machine from the future that can do many things, and one of them is a DNA test. DNA is like—genetics. How people are related."

Jonah was pretty sure that that was a lousy explanation of DNA and genetics, but he kept going.

"I can take a hair from my head and a hair from your head and lay them across this Elucidator, and it can tell us whether you're my father or not," Jonah said.

As he spoke, Jonah demonstrated, making his gestures broad and dramatic so that Lindbergh saw his every move. Then Jonah laid both hairs across the surface of the Elucidator and said aloud, "Elucidator, please determine any genetic match between these two hairs. Reply verbally, so Mr. Lindbergh can hear."

"It's *Colonel,* not Mister," Lindbergh corrected.

"Sorry," Jonah muttered, feeling sorry only that he'd ruined the drama of the moment.

The Elucidator made various clicking sounds—Angela had thought to add that, because she said Lindbergh would be used to more mechanical devices.

"Here is your answer," the Elucidator finally said. "These two hairs belong to people who are eighth cousins, twice removed."

"See?" Jonah said. "I'm sorry, but—"

"Why should I believe you?" Lindbergh asked. "Mr. Gary and Mr. Hodge did the same test with the hairs, and *their* experiment showed that you are my son."

*They did?* Jonah thought.

He pulled his Elucidator back from where he'd been holding it out so Lindbergh could see.

"Why didn't you tell Angela and me?" Jonah demanded.

YOU DIDN'T ASK, the Elucidator flashed back.

Then, as if to prove its point, the Elucidator began showing video: Jonah with Gary, Hodge, Lindbergh, and baby Katherine in the airfield office. While Jonah was turned looking at Katherine, Gary very dramatically plucked a hair from Jonah's sweater, took a hair from Lindbergh's head, and pressed the two against his Elucidator watch. Gary's Elucidator lit up with the words FATHER-SON MATCH.

How had so much happened while Jonah was just turned around looking at Katherine?

He peered down again at baby Katherine, still asleep in his arms. Somehow that gave him the gumption to argue back against Lindbergh.

"Gary and Hodge told *me* that I'm not your son. They said I'm just an ordinary kid that got dropped off at an orphanage," Jonah said. "They're liars."

"How do you know they weren't lying to you and telling me the truth?" Lindbergh asked.

How had the conversation gotten so turned around?

"Because they've lied to me before," Jonah said. "And because I saw what they wanted to do, and part of that's just tricking you. If you do what they want, you'll be stuck in the future—as a baby. Turn this plane around!"

"I don't believe you," Lindbergh said quietly.

"Why should you believe them instead of me?" Jonah asked.

"Because they're the ones who say they'll give me my son back," Lindbergh said, staring out through the windshield into the darkness of Outer Time.

*How can I argue with that?* Jonah wondered.

He stared out the windshield too. Off in the distance he could see lights whizzing closer—always the first sign during time travel that it was almost time to land.

*What is there left for me to try?* Jonah wondered.

He could think of only one thing.

*Don't do it right away,* Jonah reminded himself, and it was almost like he had Angela and regular-age Katherine right there with him, telling him what to do. *Think about the consequences.*

Jonah spent about three seconds thinking about the consequences, and he was still convinced he had only one choice. The lights of the future were getting closer and closer.

"Here," Jonah said, holding out the Elucidator and the two hairs. "Take this. Make yourself invisible and travel anywhere you want to in time. If you go to my time period in the twenty-first century again, you can get a DNA test that you can pick out yourself. Test the hairs again. See for yourself who's telling the truth. Then meet me in the future, where we're supposed to land. You've got that tranquilizer gun—we can hold off Gary and Hodge together."

Jonah had handed an Elucidator to Mileva Einstein back in 1903, and everything had turned out fine then. Ultimately.

Wasn't it possible that everything would work the same way this time around?

Lindbergh at first made no move to take the Elucidator and the hairs. Did he think Jonah was just trying to trick him even more? Would Jonah have to grab the tranquilizer gun and use it himself on Lindbergh and Gary and Hodge?

Jonah was just starting to inch forward and shift baby Katherine off to the side, when Lindbergh muttered, "Fine."

He took the Elucidator and the hairs from Jonah's hand.

And then he pointed the Elucidator directly at Jonah and cried out, "Send this boy back to August 15, 1932! So I can meet him there!"

# FORTY-NINE

*I'm stupid,* Jonah told himself as he floated through time. *Stupid, stupid, stupid . . .*

He'd given away his Elucidator, and if Lindbergh did everything Gary and Hodge wanted, this would just mean that Jonah was stuck in the 1930s alone. Because Lindbergh would never get back, and neither would anyone else.

"Waaahhhh . . ."

For a moment Jonah was afraid that he'd become so pathetic that he was actually wailing. Then he realized where the wailing really came from: baby Katherine, still clutched in his arms.

"Sorry," Jonah whispered, which seemed to soothe her a little.

*So I won't be alone, exactly, but now I've doomed Katherine to being stuck in my original time period for the rest of her life. It would have been better for her in the future. Women still didn't get treated very well even in the 1930s, so Katherine will spend the rest of both of our lives telling me how I've ruined everything for her. . . .*

And JB would stay convinced that he was Tete Einstein, and he'd stay crazy and stuck in the twenty-first century. And Mom and Dad and Angela would stay kids—well, for as long as their branch of time lasted.

*I ruined everything, and I let Gary and Hodge win,* Jonah thought.

Why hadn't he thought before he handed Lindbergh the Elucidator?

*I did think,* Jonah defended himself.

Why hadn't he thought harder? Why hadn't he thought of this as one possible consequence?

*Even if I had, I still would have handed Lindbergh the Elucidator,* Jonah realized, a little startled at himself. *And there wasn't time to think any harder than I did. I really did do the best I possibly could.*

It was a surprise to be able to let himself off the hook like that.

*Sometimes you do your very best and you lose anyway,* Jonah thought, and it seemed that he was quoting somebody—last year's soccer coach maybe?

*So that's it?* Jonah thought despairingly as he floated through Outer Time. *Life's nothing more than a soccer game?*

*Sometimes you win, sometimes you lose—and then the game's just over?*

He didn't want to believe this. He still wanted there to be something bigger at work.

*Well, who says this is the end of the game?* Jonah told himself. *I'm still alive; Katherine's still alive—we'll invent time travel in the middle of the 1930s if we have to. Or maybe the 1940s. Or the 1950s. Or . . .*

Jonah couldn't really feel encouraged by these thoughts.

The lights of 1932 rushed at him, and he braced himself for the tearing forces of the last stage of time travel.

And then he was back in the dusty airfield office. Jonah realized that he was landing just a split second after he, JB, and Angela had left, because all the reporters were still streaming in through the door, pushing their way past the security guard and screaming out questions about Charles Lindbergh.

As soon as he figured that out, his brain started an annoying short-circuit.

*Um, isn't there something else you should be remembering?* It kept asking him. *That . . . that . . .*

Jonah blinked a couple times. With the hand that wasn't holding on to Katherine, he hit the side of his head, trying to get his hearing back.

And then he remembered the important detail he kept forgetting:

He wasn't invisible anymore.

# FIFTY

*Maybe they won't even notice me,* Jonah thought, blinking even harder to clear away the last blurriness of timesickness.

But the first thing he could see clearly was all the reporters staring at him.

And the first thing he could hear clearly was all of them screaming. "Who are you?" "Where did you come from?" "Who's that baby you're holding?"

*You've got to come up with a good lie,* Jonah told himself. *Think.*

Whatever he said could determine the rest of his life. He couldn't count on time travel anymore to whisk him away from dangerous situations.

Not that time travel had ever worked terribly well for him in the past.

"I—I'm a big fan of Mr. Lindbergh's," Jonah stammered.

"Colonel Lindbergh, I mean. I just wanted to see the man. So I snuck into this office with my little sister, and we've been waiting and waiting to see him."

"Out," the security guard in the doorway said, pointing emphatically toward the door.

At least the reporters stepped to the side to let Jonah go. Jonah had to lower his head as he walked past, so none of them saw the triumphant grin on his face.

*I convinced them!* he thought. *What kind of reporters are they, that they can't even tell that the person with the biggest story of their lifetime is just walking right past them?*

It was hot out in the sunshine, and the airfield was dusty and deserted. Jonah took his coat off—he certainly didn't need a winter coat right now, though he might later.

*What if I'm stuck here until winter?* he wondered.

Thinking so far out made his head ache. Jonah's throat was so dry that it hurt; the bullet wounds in his legs throbbed; and his stomach growled, reminding him that he hadn't had anything to eat since that one slice of toast back in the twenty-first century—decades ago, really.

As if on cue, baby Katherine screwed up her face and started to cry.

"I know, I know—I'll get us something to eat," he whispered to her. "I'll have to find us someplace to live, find us a way to survive . . ."

Would they have to go to an orphanage?

*When the last time around I starved to death in one of those?*

"Maybe in 1932 thirteen is old enough to just get a job," Jonah whispered. "Don't worry. I'll take care of us. We'll do all right."

Even though she was sobbing and throwing her arms about, Jonah held on to baby Katherine even tighter. Telling her that everything was going to be all right was the only way he could convince himself.

Maybe it was the only way he could convince himself not to just give up.

Behind him the security guard and the reporters were still shouting at each other. The security guard was yelling, "Out! Out!" at all the reporters, too. But the security guard was outnumbered.

At least that meant that the security guard wasn't going to come out and yell at Jonah again.

The screaming inside the airfield office got louder and louder. Now Jonah could actually make out some of the words over baby Katherine's wailing. Why were so many of the reporters screaming, "Airplane!" "I hear a plane!" and "Is Colonel Lindbergh coming back?"

Jonah looked up.

At first he saw nothing but a cloudless sky. But then there was a glint of silver overhead.

"Look, Katherine," he whispered in her ear.

Maybe it was the awe in his voice that got her to stop

crying; maybe she could even hear the hope. Maybe she could feel some hope herself.

*Just because it's an airplane, that doesn't mean it's Lindbergh coming back,* Jonah cautioned himself. *It's 1932. Maybe there are lots of airplanes, lots of pilots in 1932.*

Except Jonah was pretty sure there hadn't been lots of airplanes and lots of pilots in 1932.

The glint of silver drew closer, transforming itself into the shape of a plane. Jonah had the oddest feeling that he'd just watched an actual transformation—maybe even a time-travel compartment that had once held thirty-six babies putting on the appearance of an airplane that wouldn't be out of place in 1932.

The "plane" landed far down on the airfield and began taxiing closer and closer to the airfield office and Jonah. The reporters behind him stampeded past, crying out, "Colonel Lindbergh! Colonel Lindbergh!" "You're back!" "Can you just answer a few questions?"

Jonah stood frozen in place. Even baby Katherine seemed to be holding her breath, waiting.

The plane seemed much smaller than the one Jonah had been on with Lindbergh only moments earlier, decades into the future. The belly of the plane was much too bulbous, its silver skin too shiny, its wings and tail too blunted.

*That's just a disguise,* Jonah told himself hopefully. *Like an Elucidator always transforming itself to fit with a time period.*

The door of the plane opened, and Jonah couldn't help shouting, "Yes! Yes! Yes!"

It was Charles Lindbergh who stepped out.

This time Lindbergh was wearing the same brown suit and fedora Jonah had seen him wearing in Jonah's own living room back in the twenty-first century.

*What does that mean?* Jonah wondered.

He wasn't sure. But just seeing Lindbergh again meant that he had reason to hope.

The reporters stampeded past Jonah in an absolute frenzy, calling out, "Colonel Lindbergh! Colonel Lindbergh! Where were you?" "Whose plane are you flying?" "Where have you been?"

Lindbergh stood calmly in the doorway of the plane. His eyes seemed to take in the entire scene before him. His gaze passed quickly over Jonah and baby Katherine, as if Jonah really were nobody to him, just some poor starstruck kid who'd snuck into the airfield to get his autograph.

"I'll answer your questions," Lindbergh told the reporters, and Jonah's heart almost stopped. Exactly what did Lindbergh plan to tell them?

"But I have to take care of some other business first," Lindbergh continued. "Why don't you wait by the gate and I'll be over to talk to you in a half an hour or so?"

The security guard hustled the reporters back toward

the gate, and this time they went, even though they continued shouting out questions: "How's your wife doing?" "When's the new baby due?" "Are you worried about the new baby being kidnapped too?"

The guard saw Jonah still standing by the airfield office, and the man growled, "You too, kid. Out of here."

"No, not him," Lindbergh said. He jumped down to the ground. "I'll sign an autograph for the boy before sending him on his way. He reminds me of myself years ago."

Now, what did that mean?

One of the reporters swooped closer to Jonah and whispered in his ear, "Kid, come out and tell me your story before you go. Ask for Jimmy from the *News-Herald*."

*Sheesh. These guys never give up, do they?* Jonah thought.

But, herded by the security guard, they did eventually leave, calling out behind them, "At the gate in thirty minutes, Lindbergh! We'll see you then!"

Jonah realized he was holding his breath. Once the reporters were out of sight—and earshot—he stepped closer to the airplane, but off to the side a little, so if Lindbergh decided to dash over and grab him, Jonah would have a bit of warning and could run.

"What—what happened, sir?" Jonah called out to Lindbergh. "What did you do with the Elucidator after you sent me away?"

Lindbergh tilted his head, studying Jonah quietly. Jonah kept holding his breath.

"I'll tell you in a minute," Lindbergh said. "But first I have something to show you."

He reached awkwardly back into the plane and emerged with a bundled-up baby in each arm.

*So this* is *the same plane with all the babies!* Jonah thought, trying not to get too overjoyed. It didn't matter—his brain kept running ahead of him with happy conclusions. *And he still has all the babies! He must not have taken them to the future after all!*

Lindbergh jumped down to the ground, still clutching the two babies.

"Here," he said, holding them out to Jonah. "You can have them."

Jonah didn't recognize either baby, but that wasn't surprising. He hadn't recognized any of the babies on the plane before except Katherine. These babies were just red-faced and sound asleep, and that was all he could tell.

"Who are they?" he asked. "Why are you giving me these babies in particular?"

"Haven't you figured it out?" Lindbergh asked incredulously. He turned so Jonah could see the baby on the right up close.

"This one's Gary," he said. Then he turned so Jonah could see the one on the left. "And this one's Hodge."

# FIFTY-ONE

Jonah suddenly didn't care if the Lindberghs weren't a hugging type of family. He didn't care that he desperately needed Charles Lindbergh to understand that Jonah wasn't his son. Jonah threw his arms around Lindbergh, with baby Katherine, baby Gary, and baby Hodge smashed between them.

"You figured out a way to disobey them without them coming after you!" Jonah marveled. "You made them powerless little babies!"

"*You* made it possible for me to make them powerless," Lindbergh muttered. "I couldn't have defeated them without the Elucidator you gave me."

He said this grudgingly. Jonah guessed Lindbergh wasn't the type who liked to give other people credit.

"This isn't proof that I really am your son," Jonah said, pulling back away from Lindbergh.

Lindbergh nodded.

"I know that now," he said sadly. "Though I would have been proud to call you son."

"I already have perfectly good parents," Jonah said quickly. "Parents I want to go back to."

Lindbergh nodded again.

"I saw," he said. "I saw your life, I saw mine . . ."

Jonah glanced anxiously over his shoulder. Ever since the moment he'd seen Charles Lindbergh standing in the Skidmore living room back home, Jonah had been longing for JB or some other time agent to show up. But for the first time he was a little afraid of what they would say if they did.

No time agent was anywhere in sight.

Lindbergh put baby Gary and baby Hodge down on the ground.

"Um, they *are* just babies," Jonah said. "Maybe you shouldn't—"

"They'll be fine down there," Lindbergh said abruptly. "This is better than they deserve."

He pulled something out of his suit coat pocket—why was Lindbergh carrying around an electric razor?

*Oh—that's what the Elucidator's using as a disguise now,* Jonah realized as Lindbergh pressed the side of the razor and a tiny screen appeared on its surface.

"I *was* trying to figure out a way to outsmart Mr. Gary

and Mr. Hodge even before you showed up," Lindbergh said, as if he needed to defend his own reputation. "When they gave me that first, very limited Elucidator, I tried to disassemble and re-assemble it. See?"

On the screen Jonah saw a flight-suited Lindbergh floating through Older Time, peering intently at something in his hands.

"I did get it to do a few seemingly useless tricks—like providing a change of clothes, which I hid from Mr. Gary and Mr. Hodge, just in case," Lindbergh said. The scene on the screen shifted, showing Lindbergh alone at the bottom of the airport stairwell, where he was stuffing a 1930s suit into a modern-era pilot's rollerbag. "I wasn't sure what would come in handy. But I think I mostly just messed up that Elucidator's commands. Especially concerning the aging and un-aging."

Jonah gaped at Lindbergh.

"So you weren't trying to make my parents and JB and Angela teenagers again on purpose?" Jonah asked.

"What?" Lindbergh asked blankly.

Jonah decided to leave that issue for later.

"But after I gave you the really good Elucidator—and you zapped me away—what did you do then?" he asked.

"Well, first I changed clothes so I wouldn't stand out in that pilots' uniform," Lindbergh said, sounding proud he'd thought of that. "Since pilots are so rare and unusal . . ."

Jonah decided not to tell him that wasn't so much the case in the twenty-first century.

"And then I went to your century and found an independent DNA test as you suggested," Lindbergh said.

On the screen Lindbergh appeared in what seemed to be some sort of sterile white-tiled medical lab. Nobody else was around. Lindbergh swiped something out of a cabinet and instantly vanished.

"I remembered that I had seen one of your hairs on the chair in your family's home, so I went back and took that," Lindbergh continued explaining. "I wanted to make sure I was running the test with independent samples."

"That was smart," Jonah said grudgingly.

On the screen Lindbergh showed up in the Skidmores' living room in the same brown suit and fedora he was wearing right this minute. Jonah was hit with such an ache of homesickness that it took him a moment to put everything together.

"But—I saw you then!" he exclaimed. "That was just a moment before you kidnapped Katherine! I knew you were there!"

Jonah just hadn't realized that the first time he'd seen Lindbergh in the twenty-first century had occurred, for Lindbergh, *after* his disappearance with Katherine.

"Sometimes you do need to pay more attention to the little details around you," Lindbergh said, with a bit of sternness. He held the razor Elucidator up admiringly. "This little device saved me again and again from taking some subtle action that would end up having terrible repercussions."

"It didn't drive you crazy demanding that you ask it precise questions?" Jonah asked.

"Uh, no," Lindbergh said, looking slightly puzzled. "I always did ask it precise questions. Didn't you?"

Jonah decided not to answer that.

Lindbergh dropped the razor Elucidator in Jonah's hand.

"So that's everything, I guess," he said. "You can take it from here?"

Jonah gaped at Lindbergh.

"You're willing to just walk away from time travel?" Jonah asked, so stunned that he almost dropped the razor Elucidator down to the ground. "Or were you thinking that I get the Elucidator and you get that plane? That's not going to work. Because, see, even though they're not here now, there are time agents who enforce—"

"Of course not," Lindbergh interrupted. "Perhaps it *was* cheating a bit, but I saw the life that's ahead of me without time travel. My wife and I are going to have five more children. I'm going to travel the world, even more than I already have. I'm going to be a bestselling author and an ace pilot during—what is it that they'll end up calling it? World War Two? There will be things I say and do publicly and privately that others will judge me for, but since when have I concerned myself with the judgment of others?"

Jonah stared down at the Elucidator in his hand—and at baby Gary and baby Hodge on the ground.

"What am I supposed to do with a razor Elucidator, two babies who used to be my worst enemies, and an airplane that—well, I guess it really is sort of an Elucidator too?" he asked.

"You forgot about the other thirty-five babies I brought you," Lindbergh said. He pointed back toward the plane. "All the original babies are still on the plane."

*Except for me,* Jonah thought dazedly.

"But—" he began to protest.

Lindbergh clapped him on the shoulder.

"You seem like a smart fellow," he said. "I'm sure you'll figure it out. Now if you'll excuse me . . . I did see that my wife is due to go into labor with our second son, Jon, in just a matter of hours."

He turned to go.

"Are you going to talk to the reporters at the front

gate?" Jonah asked. "Are you going to tell them anything about—"

"Don't worry," Lindbergh said, chuckling as he looked back. "I've gotten very good at answering their questions without telling them anything at all. And it's not as if they'd believe me anyhow. They'd claim I lost my sanity in my grief."

And then he was truly walking away, leaving Jonah behind with the Elucidator and the plane and the babies.

"Wait," Jonah said.

Lindbergh turned around once more.

"I'm sorry about your son," Jonah said. "Your first one. I'm sorry you couldn't get him back."

For a moment even decisive Charles Lindbergh seemed lost.

"I have now learned," he began, "that even with time travel, some things just are. They can't be changed or undone or fixed. But people—people can heal. Even from events they believe are unendurable."

And then Lindbergh walked away, toward the reporters and the future he already knew lay ahead of him.

Jonah turned back around to face the plane and the babies. On the ground the baby versions of Gary and Hodge were starting to squirm and whine. Baby Katherine was doing the same thing in his arms.

Jonah looked around quickly to make sure no one was close enough to see him.

"Um, Elucidator, any chance you could fix me up with three baby bottles, with the right kind of milk for four-month-olds?" Jonah asked. He wasn't actually sure how old Gary and Hodge were now, but he cared more about getting the right food for Katherine. "Maybe bottles that could be propped up without someone having to hold them?"

He was willing to feed the baby versions of Gary and Hodge, but he wasn't going to cuddle them in his arms.

The bottles instantly appeared in the mouths of Gary, Hodge, and Katherine. All three babies started drinking greedily.

*Angela was right,* Jonah thought. *An Elucidator really does make getting food in a foreign time period much, much easier.*

He wondered if the babies on the plane also needed food, but when he peeked in through one of the windows, all those babies still seemed to be asleep.

"Elucidator, can you put me in contact with Angela now?" he asked. "Or JB, if he's sane again, or Hadley—or, really, just about anybody else in the time agency?"

NO, the Elucidator in his hand flashed back at him. NOT YET.

"When will I be able to talk to them?" Jonah asked.

IT DEPENDS, the Elucidator said.

"On what?" Jonah asked.

ON WHAT YOU DO NEXT.

*Oh, no pressure!* Jonah thought.

He looked down again at baby Katherine and baby Gary and baby Hodge, and at the airplane.

"You mean, it depends on what I do with the plane and the babies," Jonah said.

EXACTLY, the Elucidator agreed.

Jonah sank down to the ground, cradling baby Katherine on his lap. She clumsily slapped her hands against the bottle, but it wasn't like she could actually hold it well on her own.

Jonah tilted the bottle up so the milk flowed a little faster.

*Babies are so helpless,* he thought. *Dependent. Totally at the mercy of the people around them.*

He glanced over at baby Gary and baby Hodge. Babies were defenseless, too. Jonah could punch and kick and even torture his enemies now, and there was nothing they could do about it.

But that seemed so horribly wrong that Jonah was disgusted with himself for thinking of it. Gary and Hodge were *babies* now. They'd been awful as adults; they'd been downright gleeful trying to ruin Jonah's life. But as babies they were innocent. When they grew up again—if they grew up again—they might be terrible people once more or they might be good this time around.

*Or they might be totally disabled because of the strain of un-aging from adults back to babies again,* Jonah remembered.

Was that Lindbergh's fault? Or Jonah's? Or . . . nobody's? Jonah couldn't feel too guilty about what had already happened to Gary and Hodge. But what if Jonah did something with all the babies on the plane that also messed them up, just because he didn't know all the possible consequences?

*Andrea,* he thought with a pang. *Chip, Gavin, Daniella, Alex, Emily, Brendan, Antonio . . .*

He could picture each one of his friends. And he pictured each one of them with a crowd behind them of friends and relatives—everyone their lives had touched or could potentially touch, everyone whose lives could be ruined or repaired by Jonah's decisions.

What if what happened to the babies and the plane could ruin or fix time itself?

"I'm thirteen years old!" he said aloud. "I shouldn't have this much power! I don't know anything!"

In his arms baby Katherine startled. She stopped sucking on the bottle for a moment and stared up at him with large, worried eyes.

Then she giggled.

*She'd laugh at me if she were here as her right age too,* Jonah thought. *She'd say, "Haven't you learned something from time travel?"*

He had, actually. On his trips through time he'd seen again and again how often little, seemingly insignificant actions saved the day. He'd seen how tiny moments of helping one person had saved everyone.

*Whatever I decide to do with an entire planeload of babies is never going to be tiny,* he thought.

But he did know tiny bits and pieces about time and life and the other big topics he'd discussed so many times with JB: fate and God, philosophy and religion . . . and what was the purpose of life, anyway?

*God?* Jonah thought searchingly. *What should I do with this plane?*

It wasn't like he expected to hear a booming voice from above, giving him directions. But he felt a little less paralyzed. He could hear other voices in his head, especially JB saying again and again, *We have to fix history. We have to repair the mistakes that Gary and Hodge made, kidnapping those kids from time. . . .*

History had already been fixed for every single one of the thirty-five babies on the plane. Jonah didn't exactly know his own situation, but he'd seen how everyone else's past lives had worked out when he'd watched the monitors back in the time cave.

*So there'd be no reason for me to send any of them back to their original lives in history,* Jonah thought, and this was a huge relief.

He remembered Gary and Hodge sneering that Jonah's other time period, the twenty-first century, was history too, from their perspective. He remembered Gary saying, *It was never possible for time to survive with you or any of the other babies from that plane living in this time period.* He remembered Hodge saying, *Once that plane crash-landed in this time period, this time was doomed. It's always been doomed. You lived through thirteen years of it being doomed.*

What if that *wasn't* a lie?

"Were Gary and Hodge telling me the truth about my time period being doomed by the time crash?" Jonah asked the Elucidator.

MAYBE, MAYBE NOT, the Elucidator flashed back. THAT DEPENDS ON YOU TOO.

Jonah resisted the urge to throw the Elucidator down to the ground and jump up and down on it, smashing it into bits. The fact that baby Katherine was still in his lap was probably the only thing that stopped him.

He took a deep breath and tried again.

"What should I do to save everyone?" he asked.

EVERYONE WHO EVER LIVED, YOU MEAN? the Elucidator asked, the words scrolling across the screen. YOU DON'T HAVE THAT KIND OF POWER.

"You know what I mean," Jonah said. "How can I save all the people I care about? And save time?"

JONAH, I'M JUST A MACHINE, the Elucidator said. I COULD NEVER BE PROGRAMMED TO BE AWARE OF EVERY VARIABLE. I CAN'T TELL YOU WHAT TO DO.

*So I'm supposed to know more than an Elucidator?* Jonah thought despairingly. But there was an echo to that thought, an answer: *No. I'm just supposed to care more.*

He couldn't see a way clear to figuring out everything about the time streams Gary and Hodge had tangled together and split and reshaped and collapsed. But the Elucidator had said there was a possibility that the time crash hadn't—or wouldn't—ruin time. Without aging the babies on the plane forward—and maybe risking injuring them—he couldn't ask any of them what they wanted. But he knew what he would have wanted, if he'd still been one of them.

Was that maybe the best way for him to decide?

He took another deep breath—not rushing into anything, not being the impulsive, careless kid who'd annoyed Katherine and Angela.

He was still certain of his decision.

"Send this plane back to the scene of the time crash," he said aloud, and the words felt exactly right.

A second later the plane vanished.

And JB appeared in the space where it had been.

# FIFTY-TWO

This was adult JB, normal-age JB, conscious JB, and—as far as Jonah could tell—sane JB.

Still clutching baby Katherine and her bottle, Jonah sprang up from the ground and launched himself toward JB. It wasn't until Jonah and Katherine were engulfed in JB's arms that Jonah realized: JB was also holding a baby wrapped in a blanket.

"Why does everybody think they have to bring me a baby?" Jonah joked, because there weren't words to say everything else he wanted to. "I don't even like babies!"

"You did it," JB cried, reaching around both babies to pound Jonah on the back. "You saved time! And the other kids! And Katherine! And me!"

"And my parents?" Jonah began. "And Angela—"

"They're fine too," JB said.

"And they're the right age again?" Jonah asked anxiously.

"I'm sure they *will* be," JB said reassuringly. He shrugged. "The time agency took care of my problems first, because of my other issues. And then I left to come here as soon as I could—I couldn't wait to congratulate you for saving everyone."

"Well, really, Charles Lindbergh did a lot too," Jonah said modestly. "And Angela and Hadley and . . . and you, JB. You got me to the time cave, and you got the monitor to work just about as well as it could work, and . . . It really wasn't your fault that coming back here made you crazy."

He pulled back a little and gazed anxiously into JB's face. What if coming back to 1932 once more, even as an adult, created problems for JB all over again?

To cover, Jonah started to pull back the blanket hiding the baby in JB's arms.

"Who's this baby you're carrying around, anyhow?"

JB pulled the baby back away from Jonah, but not before Jonah got a good look.

This baby was painfully thin, and his eyes looked too old somehow, as if he had already seen too much in his short life.

Other than that, this baby looked like Jonah had as a . . . well, not a four-month-old. Maybe when he was a year and a half or so?

Jonah took a step back. Everything seemed frozen in the heavy August afternoon around him.

"How could you?" Jonah exploded. "Just when everything was fixed, you of all people are trying to split time again, putting two copies of me in the same time period, just like Gary and Hodge did—how is that even possible? How can I stand here looking at some replica of myself from another time stream?"

JB laid a calming hand on Jonah's shoulder.

"Jonah, this *is* the same baby Gary and Hodge showed you," JB said. "But it isn't you."

Jonah squinted hard at JB. He remembered how much, back at the airport, he'd wanted to believe that Gary and Hodge were lying to him. He remembered the other possibilities he'd thought of for the baby's identity, and how quickly he'd dismissed them.

"Then they did clone me," Jonah said.

JB shook his head.

"Why do you always go for the most outlandish, sci-fi explanation you can find?" he asked. "Isn't it easier to believe you have an identical twin?"

"A *twin*?" Jonah repeated. He peered down at the baby again, thinking, *Not me, not me, not me* . . . It was a huge relief, since this baby looked so pathetic and desperate, like a picture from a fund-raising appeal for starving children.

"But why didn't you tell me all this from the very beginning?"

"Time is very delicate," JB said. "And Gary and Hodge muddied so many things about this time period . . . what if we told you something that tipped the balance into letting them win? Or left a dangling paradox that made all of time collapse? There were a trillion ways all of this could have failed, and—we now see—only one possible sequence of events that could have worked. Only none of us could see the successful outcome until everything fell into place."

Jonah glanced anxiously toward the baby versions of Gary and Hodge still lying on the ground. It was almost like he had to reassure himself that they were still there, defenseless and defeated.

"But sending that plane back to the time crash—that healed the time split, right?" Jonah asked. "The fact that you're sane again and an adult again and could come back to rescue me—doesn't that mean that everything's going back to normal?"

"Um . . . ," JB began. He glanced down at a watch on his wrist. "Hold on a minute. I need to put your twin back in place."

JB disappeared for a split second, then reappeared. If Jonah had blinked, he would have missed the change. The only difference he would have noticed was that the baby JB had been holding had vanished.

Even knowing that he'd just witnessed JB sweeping in and out of time, Jonah still automatically reached out and swiped his hand through the space where the baby had been.

"Even in an overcrowded orphanage where children die of malnutrition, there was a danger that someone would have noticed that baby missing if I'd kept him much longer," JB said apologetically.

Jonah squinted at JB in dismay. He really only heard one word JB said: *Die.*

"Wait—you just took that baby back to die in an orphanage?" Jonah asked, horrified. "My identical twin? You'd show him to me and then just . . . let him die?"

Without even thinking about it, Jonah tightened his grip on baby Katherine. She bit down on the bottle nipple a little harder in protest, and a tiny stream of milk flowed down her cheek.

Jonah reached down and wiped it away.

*I should have at least asked the Elucidator to give that other baby a bottle too,* Jonah thought. *Or JB should have.*

JB put a steadying hand on Jonah's shoulder.

"Your twin brother would have died in original time, yes," JB said with a sigh. "But that changed, remember? He was only supposed to live a little longer than you did. In just a little bit, Gary and Hodge are going to steal him out of time to put him on the alternate version of the plane to the future. And then when they leave him at the scene of the time crash, you'll deliver him to your parents because you'll think he's you."

"Oh yeah," Jonah said. He wrinkled his nose, annoyed at having to remember that Gary and Hodge stealing the baby could be in Jonah's past but still in his twin's future. "But then, that stream of time with my twin in it? That's going to collapse. Gary and Hodge said so."

Just thinking about all that made Jonah feel strange. A moment ago he'd been outraged at the notion of JB condemning the twin to an untimely death. Of course the boy would end up just as dead if his branch of time collapsed. And yet the thought of some other kid—even his own identical twin—essentially living Jonah's life in an alternate dimension of time made him strangely jealous.

*It's all because of me that he'd have my same family,* Jonah thought. *Would he have the same friends, too? The same interests, the same experiences—would it be like he was just another version of me?*

Was it wrong for Jonah to be a little bit glad that that branch of time was supposed to collapse, so he didn't have to worry about any of it?

"Gary and Hodge originally *intended* that branch of time to collapse," JB corrected. "But you and Charles Lindbergh changed everything."

Jonah tried to keep the look of dismay off his face.

"Okay, so twin boy gets to keep his separate branch of time," he said, trying to sound casual and carefree. And glad. He wanted to sound happy that his twin got to survive.

"He's Jordan," JB said gently. "Your parents are going to name him Jordan."

Jonah made a face. He'd always thought Jordan was a stupid name. And there'd been a girl named Jordan Knowles in the same grade as him all through elementary school. Had kids in that other branch of time constantly said, "Jordan the girl or Jordan the boy?" just like kids said, "Taylor the boy or Taylor the girl?" about Jonah's classmates Taylor Wickerson and Taylor Donis?

"The two of you were Claude and Clyde in original time, so it could have been a lot worse," JB said.

*Claude and Clyde?*

Jonah decided not to ask which of them was Claude and which was Clyde. As far as he was concerned, the names were equally horrendous.

"I'm going to try to forget that you told me that," Jonah said. "Just tell me this is all over and I get to go home and I never have to worry about Gary and Hodge again, never even have to think about that other dimension that's out there. . . . It'll be like the other dimension that Second

Chance created back in the 1600s, right? It's not going to affect any of us in *real* time, is it?"

JB frowned.

"Jonah, the time agency is almost certain now about where Gary and Hodge went when we couldn't find them," he said grimly. "They were in Second Chance's alternate dimension, where they learned some of his secrets. So 'real' time, as you put it, was never as separate as we thought from that other dimension. And . . ."

JB let his voice trail off. He reached down and brushed baby Katherine's cheek, wiping away the last of the spilled milk.

"Tell me this," JB said. "Why did you send that plane-load of babies back to the scene of the time crash?"

"Because that's what I thought all the kids on the plane would want," Jonah said. "The Elucidator said it *might* work out. And that's what I would have wanted if I'd been on that plane."

JB's frown deepened.

"We thought you understood . . . ," he murmured.

"Understood what?" Jonah asked.

He wanted to hold on to his excitement over time being saved and JB being cured. But he couldn't get the memory of his twin's sad eyes out of his mind; he couldn't get rid of the nagging sense that JB really wanted him to keep worrying about alternate dimensions.

One of the babies on the ground—either Gary or Hodge—finished draining his bottle and let it fall out of his mouth. It hit the hard-packed dirt with such a bang that Jonah jumped.

"You *had* to send that plane back to the scene of the time crash," JB said. "Or it would have left a terrible hanging paradox that no one could have fixed. Time would have collapsed."

Jonah gaped at JB.

"Well, why didn't somebody tell me?" he asked grumpily. "Why didn't the Elucidator? I thought about that decision for a long time. You could have made it easy!"

"Some things are clear only with hindsight," JB said. "That's true even with time travel. The time agency was . . . well, I guess it's most accurate to say they were paralyzed with indecision. It's like you and Charles Lindbergh were teetering on the edge of a cliff, and they feared that just stepping forward to rescue you would knock you over."

"After Lindbergh left, I was standing in a grass field with nobody else around," Jonah grumbled. "Then I was sitting on the ground, holding a baby with a bottle. I wasn't on a cliff!"

"You were at the brink of Gary and Hodge's time split," JB corrected him. "Remember, they wanted their

'Unsettled Time' to start in 1932. Everything about time was at risk."

Jonah looked around. The airfield was silent and still; the wind sock by the office hung limp and motionless in the heat. Off in the distance he could hear a car engine—the old-timey kind that sputtered. But that was the only noise. It seemed as if even the reporters at the airfield's front gate had given up hounding Lindbergh and gone home.

"Nothing *looks* that different," Jonah said.

"Time was in flux," JB said. "Gary and Hodge intended a series of time splits, each one getting them closer and closer to their wealthy future. Instead there was one three-way branching, determined by who was in seat two-C of that plane when it arrived at the time crash."

Jonah thought he saw what JB meant.

"Me once, my twin once, and an empty seat once," Jonah said, ticking off the possibilities. Something struck him that hadn't occurred to him before. "Except . . . wasn't it really twice that that plane landed at the site of the time crash with an empty seat two-C? Once when I sent it forward, and once when Gary and Hodge did?"

JB's face twitched.

"No, it was only once with the empty seat," he said, and Jonah could hear the strain in his voice. "Gary and

Hodge were lazy and didn't think things through. After they tricked you into believing you were responsible for splitting time, they double-checked the twenty-first century only to see if you were still there in that version of time. When you weren't—not in that branch, anyway—they thought you'd died and time had gone on without you . . . and everything from that branch was already set up to lead directly to their glorious futures. So they didn't think they needed to send forward a plane with an empty seat."

Jonah pictured the drawing Angela had made on her Elucidator, and how the Elucidator changed it to show what Gary and Hodge wanted to happen. Jonah and Angela hadn't asked enough questions. They'd just assumed there *had* to be an empty-seated version of time. How else would Gary and Hodge get their glorious futures if the other two branches of time collapsed?

The thing was, if Jonah really had delivered his own infant self to his parents, the time period around that action really wouldn't have lasted long. But because the baby was Jordan instead, that branch of time had been fine.

*So I guess Gary and Hodge just wanted to torture me in that branch of time, making me think that everything was about to end,* Jonah realized. A new thought hit him. *Or . . . they thought I'd get so desperate that I'd make that branch of time end all by myself.*

He felt proud all over again that he'd escaped instead. With a little help from Angela and Hadley.

Only, did JB mean that Gary and Hodge had been helped when that branch of time stayed alive? Because it paved the way to their glorious futures without them having to work so hard?

Jonah thought of another problem.

"But . . . I stood on that empty-seated plane that you say wasn't supposed to be there!" Jonah protested. "I stood on it at the site of the time crash—and that was before I came back to 1932 and sent the plane forward for me to stand on it!"

"And . . . that's just one of the paradoxes you somehow navigated without ending time," JB said quietly.

Jonah realized he'd started breathing hard. Baby Katherine batted her now-empty bottle against Jonah's chest. Jonah took it from her and let his arm drop helplessly.

"I don't know how that's possible," Jonah whispered.

"Oh, there's more," JB said.

He bent down and picked up the bottle from beside the baby versions of Gary and Hodge. He gently eased the final bottle—also empty—from the slower baby's mouth. Both babies seemed to have dropped off to sleep.

"It turns out," JB said as he straightened up, "that it

really was the Elucidator that Angela had in her pocket, unbeknownst to you or me, that saved us when we were on Lindbergh's plane over the Atlantic and then when we were in Paris. I don't know how she showed such restraint, but she was convinced that she shouldn't even mention it until she was in 1932 again."

"But if I'd died over the Atlantic or in Paris in 1927, I wouldn't have even been able to go back to the site of the time crash to tell Angela to carry an Elucidator," Jonah said. "That Elucidator saved my life twice before I made sure that Angela had it to save my life. And yours."

"Exactly," JB said. "Also, you and Katherine saw Lindbergh at your house before you gave him the Elucidator that enabled him to get there that time around."

"Yeah . . . ," Jonah said, feeling a little proud that he had at least noticed that discrepancy. But why had his mind let him glaze over it so easily? What else had he half forgotten? "I know the time agency doesn't like paradoxes like that."

"*Like* them?" JB snorted. "They're illegal!"

"But time kind of protects itself, doesn't it?" Jonah asked. "Like how it worked out with the paradox of you being Tete Einstein. And . . . aren't there lots of things that people kind of forget or don't notice? Like the missing tracers?"

JB froze for a moment. Then he fixed Jonah with a level gaze.

"You figured it out," JB murmured. "You realized that you and the others should have been seeing tracers your entire childhood."

"And even Katherine should have seen tracers after we got back from the 1400s," Jonah said, glancing down quickly at the baby in his arms. Then he peered back at JB again. "The fact that we never saw tracers in the twenty-first century . . . that was a sign that time was really messed up, right? Gary and Hodge made it sound awful."

Grimly, JB nodded.

"It was," he muttered. He sounded like he could barely get the words out.

"But they said time couldn't be fixed!" Jonah protested. "And you still tried to fix it! You and the other time agents kept returning and rescuing the other missing kids from time—you took care of all of them. . . . Why didn't you tell me?"

"We were trying to protect you," JB said. "And protect time."

"But why did you even try if you didn't think it was possible to fix everything?" Jonah asked.

"We still had hope," JB said, spreading his hands wide apart in a gesture that could have looked like giving up—or appealing for help. "We kept thinking there could be some solution we couldn't see yet. And then . . . you found it."

Embarrassed, Jonah looked down at the ground. JB seemed to be giving him more credit than he deserved. It wasn't like Jonah had known what he was doing.

"Everything *did* work out fine in the end, didn't it?" Jonah asked, glancing back at JB. "You said everything's fixed now—Gary and Hodge were wrong, after all, about the twenty-first century being doomed. Weren't they?"

"They always started from the assumption that they would steal all of you missing children back after you turned thirteen and Damaged Time ended," JB said. "And yes, that *would* have doomed time. It would have been too much of a disruption."

"But we can rescue everyone from that time hollow where Charles Lindbergh *isn't* going to go and tranquilize them," Jonah said excitedly. "Right? So then the twenty-first century is safe again. And everything can go back to normal."

"The other missing kids from history are being rescued right now," JB said. He seemed to be speaking very carefully. "They're fine. But things going back to normal? Don't you remember that other dimension with your twin brother, Jordan?"

"Oh, right," Jonah said quickly, because he didn't want

to think or talk about his twin any more than he had to. "He can have normal in his branch of time; I can have normal in mine. Whatever."

JB seemed to be gazing off into the distance. Then he glanced down quickly at the sleeping babies on the ground.

"I told you Gary and Hodge always started from the wrong assumption," JB said gravely. "But so did the time agency."

"Right—because, you know all us missing kids? We are *fine* spending the rest of our lives in the twenty-first century," Jonah said. He sounded like he was trying to convince both JB and himself. "We can have what we wanted from the very start."

"Yes," JB said, surprising Jonah. Jonah looked at him sharply. Then JB added, "And no."

Jonah jerked his head forward and put on his most extreme *What are you talking about?* expression.

JB sighed.

"Barely avoiding tragedy with all those paradoxes—that created an incredibly powerful force," JB said. "A searing energy source greater than anything the time agency ever encountered before. We don't entirely understand it even now, but . . . it appears that that overwhelming force sucked all of Gary and Hodge's branches of split time back together again. Like an explosion in reverse. Time healed itself."

"Okay," Jonah said. He didn't really understand, but "healed" sounded like a good thing. "So my time branch is okay now, my twin brother's time branch is okay . . ."

JB winced.

"You're both okay, yes, and the time period around you both will be okay now, but . . . when you go back, both times will be the same," he said.

Jonah had no idea what JB was talking about. Then a bizarre thought struck him, and he hugged baby Katherine closer to his chest.

"Wait, you don't mean . . . you're not saying . . . When I get back to the twenty-first century, will I have a brother or a sister?" Jonah asked.

"You'll have an eleven-year-old sister named Katherine, just like before," JB said in a tone that Jonah was sure was supposed to be reassuring. There was something behind it, though, that kept Jonah from untensing his muscles.

"But?" Jonah prompted.

JB seemed to be gritting his teeth.

"Oh, pretty much everything else will be just like you remember," he continued. "Except . . . you'll also have a twin brother named Jordan."

Jonah stared at JB.

"But which of us will people remember being there before?" Jonah asked incredulously. "Me or him?"

JB cleared his throat and seemed to be choosing his words very carefully.

"Both," he said. "Everyone around you will remember both you and Jordan being there all along."

# EPILOGUE

Jonah floated through time, holding baby Katherine in his arms. JB had sent the two of them on ahead to the twenty-first century without him, because, JB said, he needed to figure out what to do with the baby versions of Gary and Hodge.

Dimly Jonah suspected that JB just didn't know what else to say.

*What was there left to say?* Jonah wondered. *"Thanks, Jonah, for saving all of time—sorry you ruined your own life"?*

Jonah remembered JB's original explanation: *There were a trillion ways all of this could have failed, and—we now see—only one possible sequence of events that could have worked.*

That made it impossible for Jonah to go back and beg, *Please! Let's undo this! Let's find some other solution!*

He must have been gripping baby Katherine a little

too tightly, because she started to struggle against him, pushing an elbow into his ribs, a foot up into his armpit.

Or was she just growing?

Jonah shifted her position from lying down to being held upright. Just in the moment it took him to make that one change, Katherine went from seeming like she could barely hold her head up by herself to being able to reach out and grab his face and turn it toward her. She blinked up at him, her eyes wide and innocent.

"Jo-Jo," she whispered. Then a moment later, "Jo-Jo 'tect Ka-Ka. Jo-Jo ba-ba."

Jonah remembered enough of Katherine's early toddler talk to be able to translate. Or maybe his time-travel translation help worked even on baby talk. Either way, he knew she was saying, *Jonah protects Katherine. Jonah's my big brother.*

"Yeah, and what do you call your other brother?" Jonah muttered, with more bitterness in his voice than anyone should have talking to a toddler.

Katherine didn't seem to hear the surliness. She tilted her head quizzically and answered as if it'd been a serious question.

"Ord'n," she said.

*Is that how she pronounces Jordan?* Jonah thought, horrified. *So . . . this proves JB was right? Even this version of Katherine remembers Jordan?*

Katherine—now probably about the size of a two-year-old—patted Jonah's face as if she knew he deserved her sympathy.

*This isn't just a "version" of Katherine,* Jonah reminded himself. *It's really her. Only younger.*

They floated on in silence for a moment; then Katherine evidently passed whatever developmental milestone had turned on her chatterbox tendencies.

"That bad guy," she said emphatically. "Bad guy made go bye-bye."

She kept talking. Most of it just sounded like gibberish to Jonah, but he had the feeling that she was trying to tell him the complete story of her kidnapping and un-aging.

"Well . . . , I don't really think Charles Lindbergh was such a bad guy," Jonah said. "Just desperate. And maybe too used to always being able to get what he wanted? Anyway, you should really blame Gary and Hodge, but—"

"Them *really* bad guys," Katherine said.

She had a thick headful of hair now, curling around her ears. Jonah had kind of forgotten that she'd ever had even slightly wavy hair.

"Right," Jonah told her. "But we don't have to worry about Gary and Hodge ever again. Because they're babies again."

"Babies go poo-poo," Katherine said, and giggled.

"They go *blech*, after they drink their bottles."

When Katherine was four, she'd been really good at making burping noises. Jonah had forgotten how funny that always sounded coming from the mouth of such a dainty little girl.

"Does Jordan laugh at your burping noises too?" he asked, and he couldn't keep the jealousy out of his voice.

"*Everybody* laughs at my burping noises!" Katherine said, chortling. She threw herself gleefully backward, tumbling out of Jonah's arms. He barely managed to catch her hand. But she curled her fingers trustingly around his thumb.

"When we get home, can I have ice cream?" Katherine asked. "Can we get Mommy and Daddy to let us stay up late and watch TV? Will you and Jordan play Clue Junior or Pretty Pretty Princess with me? Please? *Please?*"

*You and Jordan,* Jonah thought.

This was proof. Proof that what JB had told him was true.

Katherine kept blabbing on and on—now she was asking if he thought Mommy would draw a picture of a fancy dress for her to color. Jonah decided it was fine to interrupt. It wasn't like Katherine had ever been the type of kid who'd stop talking long enough to give somebody else a chance.

"Do Jordan and I play games with you a lot?" Jonah asked.

Katherine tilted her head sideways again, obviously thinking deeply.

"Not both of you at once, I guess," she said, sounding as solemn as a judge. She leaned in close and whispered conspiratorially. "Sometimes I think Mommy and Daddy make one of you play with me so I don't get my feelings hurt. They make you take turns."

*This actually makes sense,* Jonah thought. *Because she wouldn't have any memories of Jordan and me both playing with her at the same time.*

Jonah didn't think he spent too long pondering this. But the next time he glanced toward Katherine, she looked about eight—maybe nine. Her hair flowed halfway down her back. She leaned against Jonah's side, and the top of her head came almost up to Jonah's shoulder.

"You know you're the only one I travel through time with," she said. "You know Jordan always stays home. Don't you feel sorry that he doesn't get to have adventures like us?"

*No,* Jonah thought. But for Katherine's sake he only shrugged.

Bright lights appeared ahead of them, and Jonah braced himself for the zooming sensation that always came at the end of a time-travel trip right before he reached his destination. He tightened his grip on Katherine's hand.

"It's going to feel like time is tearing us apart," he warned her.

"I *know*," Katherine said sarcastically, and Jonah took that as a sign that she was her right age again. This was the almost-twelve-year-old obnoxious kid sister who'd been on practically every single one of his time-travel trips with him.

The sister he'd missed so intensely ever since Charles Lindbergh had stolen her away.

"Welcome back," Jonah whispered.

He wasn't sure Katherine heard him, because the zooming, tearing-apart sensation hit at that exact moment. For a while Jonah couldn't think at all. He felt like every atom of his being was yanked to bits and reassembled. Maybe he'd be the same person when it was all over; maybe he wouldn't.

He opened his eyes to find the world swimming in and out of focus. He was back in his family's living room, sitting in his father's favorite recliner. He turned his head and saw that Katherine was sprawled on the floor beside the chair—in the exact same spot where Charles Lindbergh had grabbed her and taken her away.

The slant of sunlight coming in through the window made him think that it was still morning. He squinted at the clock on the mantel, and the hands and numbers came into focus: It was eight fifteen. Probably the exact moment that Jonah had left the twenty-first century the last time, after he'd said good-bye to Angela and his parents and gone back to 1932. He'd just been standing by the time cave then, not sitting in his own living room.

Even in his timesick, blurry-eyed, confused state, Jonah remembered a warning JB had given him right before he'd left 1932: *As time fits itself back together, probably lots of things are going to seem jagged and off-kilter at first. To you and Jordan most of all, because you'll be the only ones who don't have memories from all the merged branches of the twenty-first century. Each of you will only remember your own branch, while everyone else will remember all three.*

"Ooooh," Katherine moaned beside him. "I feel awful. I hate timesickness. Hate it, hate it, hate it."

There was a clattering noise from overhead, as if someone had knocked over something in Jonah's room. And then there were footsteps—rushing through the upstairs hallway, maybe, then coming down the stairs.

"Katherine?" a voice called. "Did you get sick too? Did Mom have to pick you up at school and bring you home? Mom, I still get to watch whatever I want on TV, don't I? I get dibs on the big TV! I was sick first!"

It was Jonah's voice exactly, except different. Dimly Jonah remembered something his sixth-grade science teacher had said about how you never really heard your own voice as it truly was, because you always heard it conducted through the bones of your head.

A boy barreled into the living room and jerked to a stop. Jonah guessed that he was standing in the exact spot where Jonah had been when he'd first spotted Charles Lindbergh. This boy had Jonah's face. He was Jonah's exact same height, he had the same light-brown hair, and he had a deep dimple in his chin like Jonah's, just a little off center. But—Jonah reached up and fingered his own chin—his dimple and the other boy's were off center on opposite sides.

*Mirror image,* Jonah thought dazedly. *Sometimes identical twins are mirror images of each other.*

Also, Jonah was pretty sure that he'd never looked as disheveled and awkward as this boy. And childish. Somehow this boy looked exactly the same as Jonah, but so much younger.

"Who—who are you?" the boy stammered, gaping at Jonah.

Katherine snorted.

"Jordan, Jonah—the two of you have *got* to stop acting like the other one doesn't exist!" she said, sounding as bossy as ever. "You're exactly alike! You're practically the same person! *That's* why you're not getting along!"

*So that's how it's going to be,* Jonah thought. *That's how time—and Katherine—are going to work this out.*

Confusion swam in the other boy's eyes.

*Maybe this really is a total surprise for him?* Jonah thought, and he almost felt sorry for the other boy.

Almost.

Before any of them could say anything else, Jonah heard a car zooming into the driveway and braking abruptly. A second later the front door banged open, and Mom and Dad raced into the room with Angela close behind them.

All three of them still looked like thirteen-year-olds.

"I thought—I thought you were going to change back," Jonah stammered.

"We couldn't wait," kid Mom said. "We had to make sure all three of you were safe first. Oh, Jonah . . . , Jordan . . . , Katherine . . ."

"We were so afraid we'd lose all three of you forever," kid Dad wailed, right behind her.

"All three of you," flowed off both their tongues so easily, as if they really had had three kids ever since Katherine's birth.

Mom and Dad plowed into Jordan, standing in the doorway of the living room. They drew him forward and pulled Katherine up from the floor and Jonah up from the chair. And then all five members of the Skidmore family were engulfed in a huge group hug, with Mom and Dad sobbing with relief and Katherine chattering away about who-knew-what and Jordan still gazing around in bafflement. For his part, Jonah stretched his right arm out so he could clutch Mom and Dad and Katherine close. But Jordan was standing on Jonah's left, so Jonah kept his left arm pressed down to his side, carefully not touching the stranger.

Angela stood a few feet back from the whole reunited Skidmore clan. She raised an eyebrow at Jonah, and Jonah thought, *She knows. She was so involved with all the time travel that she remembers everything. She understands how weird this is for me.* But then Angela jerked her head up and narrowed her eyes a bit, and Jonah could tell she was trying to say, *You still need to hug your brother. It's even weirder for him. So you need to make the first move.*

Jonah thought about everything he'd had to cope with because of time travel. Confusion and hunger and fear and danger and near-death experiences. Way too much fish in the 1600s. Being kidnapped and being tricked. Needing to be rescued again and again, and needing to rescue others even as he was constantly terrified that he'd show up at the wrong time or do the wrong thing or follow the wrong plan.

And—oh, yeah—he still did have bullet-wound scars.

*But I survived all that,* he thought. *I can survive this, too. How could it be any worse?*

Jonah let out a deep sigh. And then he lifted his left arm and wrapped it around his twin brother, bringing his whole family together.

## AUTHOR'S NOTE

Much more is known about the kidnapping of Charles Lindbergh Jr. than the disappearances and/or deaths of any of the other missing children featured in this series. It is possible to line up certain facts to make it sound like an open-and-shut case:

Fact: On the night of March 1, 1932, the Lindberghs reported their twenty-month-old son missing. Charles Lindbergh showed police a ransom note found on the windowsill of his son's room. Police also found indentations below the child's second-story window that seemed to indicate that a ladder had been placed there. Soon after, they found a broken ladder a short distance from the house.

Fact: Over the course of the next several weeks, the Lindberghs received twelve more ransom notes that police considered authentic. Through an intermediary named John Condon, they ended up paying a ransom of fifty thousand dollars to the alleged kidnapper on April 2, 1932, in exchange for that thirteenth ransom note, which was supposed to reveal where the little boy was. Before the ransom was delivered, the Internal Revenue Service insisted on recording the serial numbers on all the bills given to the kidnapper.

Fact: Despite frantic searches by plane by Lindbergh himself and by boat by the Coast Guard, no one ever found a boat called *Nelly* where the alleged kidnapper said the boy was being kept.

Fact: On May 12, 1932, a man who was making a bathroom stop in a remote area less than five miles from the Lindberghs' house discovered the decomposed body of a young child. Some parts of the body were missing, presumably eaten by wild animals. But both Charles Lindbergh and the child's nanny, Betty Gow, examined the body and stated that they were certain it belonged to Charles Lindbergh Jr. Details that matched included the golden curls, the dimpled chin, and the bits of clothing that remained. An autopsy determined that the child had died because of a fractured skull "due to external violence." Based on the autopsy and the condition of the ladder, police theorized that the baby must have died the very night of the kidnapping after the ladder rung broke and the kidnapper dropped the baby.

Fact: In September 1934, a bank teller in the Bronx and the manager of a nearby gas station were able to provide authorities with information linking one of the bills from the ransom money to a man named Bruno Hauptmann. When police searched Hauptmann's home, they found more than a third of the ransom money hidden in his garage, with the serial numbers matching. The address and phone number for Condon, the Lindberghs' intermediary, were found written in pencil in one of Hauptmann's closets.

Fact: At Hauptmann's trial, eight experts testified that his writing and patterns of misspellings matched that of the ransom notes. A wood expert testified that the wood from the ladder matched wood in Hauptmann's attic. Though Hauptmann testified that the ransom money in his garage had actually belonged to a friend, Hauptmann was convicted of murder. He was executed on April 3, 1936.

What that listing of facts leaves out are the many questions that remain unanswered, which have led to an array of alternate theories ranging from the plausible to the thoroughly bizarre.

At a time when it seemed as though the entire nation was looking for the kidnapped child, how could his body have lain in the woods so close by for two and a half months without someone finding it?

How could that corpse found in the woods be the Lindbergh child when the little boy's height was listed as twenty-nine inches on all the WANTED posters—and the autopsy report says the corpse was thirty-three and a half inches long?

Why were Hauptmann's fingerprints never found at the crime scene or on the ladder?

How would Hauptmann have even known where the Lindberghs were that night? While their house in

Hopewell, New Jersey, was under construction, they'd gotten into the habit of staying there only on the weekends, and living with Anne Lindbergh's mother during the week. The only reason they were still in Hopewell on Tuesday, March 1, 1932, was because their son had a cold, and they didn't want to make it worse by moving him from place to place. Did Hauptmann perhaps have an accomplice who worked for either the Lindberghs or their relatives and tipped him off?

There was only one set of shutters in the Lindbergh child's room that couldn't be latched tightly. How would Hauptmann have known to place his ladder under that window?

Charles and Anne Lindbergh—and three servants—were all in the home at the approximate time of the kidnapping. How could Hauptmann have picked up the child from his crib, carried him out the window, and maneuvered down onto a ladder two feet below without anyone hearing the child crying or some other noise?

The Lindberghs had a dog. Why didn't it bark at the intruder?

Although the crime scene was compromised—especially by modern standards—there was evidence of what police concluded were both a man's and a woman's footprints near where the ladder had been leaned against the house.

Police assumed that the female footprint was from Anne Lindbergh walking around the house earlier in the day. But what if that smaller footprint was actually connected to the kidnapping as well?

From the very beginning, questions like those led some investigators and other officials—and then journalists, authors, and a wide variety of conspiracy theorists—to suggest that Bruno Hauptmann was either innocent or, at the very least, not the only one responsible for the kidnapping and death of the child.

One of the strangest theories that cropped up was that Charles and/or Anne Lindbergh themselves had killed the child—either accidentally or on purpose—and then concocted the whole kidnapping story to cover their own crime. Another theory blamed Anne's sister for the child's death; still another claimed that the child was kidnapped and killed by Japanese agents trying to divert worldwide attention from their invasion of China.

Other theories maintained that the Lindbergh child actually survived the kidnapping and was secretly raised under a different identity. In the years after 1932, many people claimed to be the "real" Charles Lindbergh Jr. In *Forward from Here,* a collection of essays published in 2008, Reeve Lindbergh, Charles and Anne's youngest daughter, said that more than fifty men had approached the family making such a claim at one time or another.

It appears that no one in the family ever took any of those claims seriously.

To this day the Lindbergh kidnapping consistently appears on lists of top "crimes of the century"—which is strange considering how many genocides and other horrific events occurred in the twentieth century. But the thought of the missing child tugged at the heartstrings of a country already battered by the Great Depression. And Lindbergh's New York-to-Paris flight had turned him into one of the first mass-media celebrities. In 1932 many viewed Charles and Anne Lindbergh as practically American royalty, and the loss of their child was seen as everyone's loss.

Also, some aspects of law enforcement and the justice system were changed forever because of the Lindbergh case. Kidnapping became a federal crime in June 1932, after questions over who had jurisdiction across state lines slowed the Lindbergh investigation. And news coverage of Bruno Hauptmann's trial became such a circus that, soon after, the federal government and all but two states banned cameras and broadcasting from their courtrooms. Although many courtrooms have since become more open, the issue continues to be debated to this day.

As a parent myself, I found it almost unbearably painful at times to read about the Lindberghs' ordeal related to the kidnapping. But I was fascinated by details of other portions of Charles Lindbergh's life.

He had an unusual childhood, and some of the stories about him even before his famous flight make him sound like nearly as much of an American folk hero as Paul Bunyan. Supposedly his father taught Charles to swim by throwing him into the Mississippi River. Charles learned how to drive a car when he was eleven; when he was fourteen and already nearly six feet tall, he drove his mother from their home in Minnesota to Los Angeles. In California, a policeman cited him for driving without a license—but that didn't stop his mother from letting him drive her all the way home afterward. The poor condition of American roads in 1916 meant that the return trip took forty days. Because Charles spent so much of his childhood traveling, it was almost a point of family pride that he never arrived anywhere in time for the start of a new school year.

Missing so much school meant that he didn't do particularly well. When he started college to study engineering at the University of Wisconsin (once again, proudly missing the first day of the term) the combination of his poor grades and his father's financial troubles led him to drop out. He switched to learning to fly instead, and got experience wing walking, parachuting, and barnstorming across the country; flying for the army; and then, when air mail began, flying mail between St. Louis and Chicago. Being a pilot was still a very dangerous endeavor in the 1920s—in just ten months of flying the mail, he twice had to jump out and let the plane crash without him.

When Lindbergh first heard about the twenty-five-thousand-dollar Orteig Prize being offered for the first nonstop flight between New York City and Paris, he was probably the only person who thought of himself as a potential winner. Outside of his fellow postal pilots, he was virtually unknown in the aviation world. Until he was able to convince city leaders in St. Louis to back his attempt, he had no way of buying or building a plane for the flight. And he had the seemingly crazy idea that one person in a single-engine plane would be able to fly more than thirty hours over the ocean, when just about everyone kept telling him that it would take a team of aviators in a multiengine plane.

When he got to the point of making arrangements for a plane custom-made for the flight, he and the engineer working on the plane had to double-check the distance from New York to Paris. They did this by going to the public library, putting a piece of string against the side of a globe, and calculating accordingly.

They came up with 3,600 miles, which meant that the plane would need space for four hundred gallons of gasoline. (When I used the twenty-first century method and checked online, the first answer that I got was 3,624 miles—amazingly close. Lindbergh ended up taking four hundred fifty gallons of fuel just to be safe.)

Leading up to his improbable flight, Lindbergh was so obsessed with keeping his plane as light as possible that he cut off unneeded portions of the maps he took with him. He had no way to see out of the front part of the plane, because he wanted that whole space used for storing gasoline. And, as Jonah guesses in this book, Lindbergh's plane was indeed made of cloth over a metal frame; the wings were made of cloth over wood.

Less than a month before Lindbergh planned to take off for Paris, two other pilots intending to make the same attempt were killed during a test flight. A French crew attempting the flight in the opposite direction—Paris to New York—disappeared over the ocean less than two weeks before Lindbergh took off.

But Lindbergh's flight was a success.

When Lindbergh landed in Paris, he'd been in the air for thirty-three and a half hours. Considering that he started the trip after a sleepless night, his main struggle over the ocean was just to stay awake. Many years later he admitted that, about twenty-three hours into the flight, he started seeing "phantoms" in the plane with him, who spoke to him with human voices. (Presumably they were just the hallucinations of a sleep-deprived brain, rather than time travelers from the future.)

The only food Lindbergh took with him was five sandwiches—his explanation to *Aero Digest* was, "If I get to Paris, I won't need any more, and if I don't get to Paris, I won't need any more either." Lindbergh didn't eat any of the sandwiches until he reached France.

An estimated 150,000 people were waiting for him at the airfield in Paris—he really did worry about some of them being injured by the propeller on his plane because they were so close to where he landed. He also soon had to worry about the danger to his plane, as the crowd swarmed the *Spirit of St. Louis* and tore off pieces of it as souvenirs. Lindbergh's first words, arriving in Paris, were, "Are there any mechanics here?"

Lindbergh's feat made him such an instant worldwide celebrity that a group of businessmen even offered him one million dollars to never fly again, because he was viewed as too great of a national treasure to risk his life again.

Lindbergh chose not to accept that money. Instead he became a leading spokesperson for commercial aviation, and continued to fly and explore in numerous locations, even as he also branched out into medical interests and worked on developing a mechanical heart. After he married, his wife, Anne Morrow Lindbergh, also got her pilot's license, and they took trips together all over the planet. Their flights to particularly remote areas served as a break from the media's relentless interest in their lives. Unlike many celebrities today, the Lindberghs mostly viewed their fame as a burden rather than something to be sought and nurtured.

With the kidnapping of their son, the Lindberghs' fame became a source of tragedy as well.

From the very beginning of the investigation, Lindbergh wanted to know every detail and control every step of the process. Anne Lindbergh wrote that she never once saw him cry over his missing son. But up until the moment that the body was discovered, Lindbergh desperately kept following leads that he had to have known were false.

After the child's body was discovered and identified and autopsied, the Lindberghs chose to have the remains cremated. This became one of the details cited by conspiracy theorists who claimed this "proved" the Lindberghs had something to hide.

An alternate explanation was that they simply did not want their child's grave to become the target for the same kind of media circus and public fixation that had followed every breathless detail of the kidnapping investigation.

Or—even worse—they didn't want anyone trying to dig up their child's remains to prove or disprove yet another crackpot theory.

As portrayed in this book, Anne Lindbergh was pregnant with their second child at the time of the kidnapping. She went into labor the night after Lindbergh spread their first son's ashes over the Atlantic Ocean. Jon Lindbergh was born early the next morning. Charles and Anne Lindbergh would go on to have four more children together: sons Land and Scott and daughters Anne and Reeve.

The family also continued living unconventional lives. Because of concerns about Jon Lindbergh possibly also being kidnapped, they moved away from the United States for a while during the 1930s, settling first in England, then on an isolated island off the coast of France. At the request of the US ambassador to Germany, Charles Lindbergh agreed to visit Berlin and inspect German aviation facilities. Lindbergh made positive comments about his German hosts and, on a subsequent trip to Germany, was given a special honor, the Service Cross of the German Eagle. Later, when Lindbergh spoke out against the United States getting involved in World War II, he was accused of being a Nazi sympathizer. His reputation was tarnished enough that once America did enter the war, his offers of help to the US military were largely rebuffed. Instead he worked for a time with the Ford Motor Company in connection with one of their factories that was building bombers. From there he became a test pilot, a test subject for extreme conditions for pilots, and a fighter-pilot instructor. Traveling with the status of a technician, he ended up in the war zone in the Pacific in 1944. Although that role should have kept him out of combat, he began flying bombing raids anyway.

After the war Lindbergh continued his travels, at one point even becoming one of the first people to meet a primitive tribe in the Philippines that had supposedly never encountered modern humans. However, his perspective changed toward the end of his life. Rather than constantly embracing scientific advances and improved aviation, he came to believe that scientific progress was often the source of greater problems. He began to speak out much more for environmental causes.

Both Charles Lindbergh and his wife, Anne, became acclaimed and bestselling authors as well as explorers. His account of his flight to Paris, *The Spirit of St. Louis,* won the Pulitzer Prize in 1954. Ultimately, their two daughters became authors as well, with Anne Spencer Lindbergh focusing on children's books. Ironically, one of her books, *Three Lives to Live,* became one of my favorite time-travel novels of the 1990s—long before I ever thought about writing a time-travel book with any connection to the Lindberghs.

The public's view of Charles Lindbergh changed many times over the years, from the simple hero of 1927 to the tragic figure of 1932 to the alleged Nazi sympathizer and antiwar activist of the later 1930s to the environmental activist of the 1960s and early 1970s. His writings include both noble, inspiring words and arguments that sound horribly racist and anti-Semitic to twenty-first-century readers. Even after his death in 1974, his image changed once again, when it was revealed in the early 2000s that he'd secretly had two other families in Germany.

By all accounts, Lindbergh never cared much about what the public thought of him. If the marvels of time travel truly had given him a way to see how his life was going to play out after 1932, he does seem like someone who would have had no regrets about anything he'd done, or was going to do.

But given how desperately he tried to get his son back in 1932, it's also easy to imagine that, if he'd had access to time travel, he would have wanted to use it to do everything he could to retrieve his son.

Wouldn't any parent who lost a child want exactly the same thing?

# ACKNOWLEDGMENTS

When I began writing The Missing series, it was a struggle to find much information at all about some of the early missing children of history. With the Lindbergh story, I almost had the opposite problem: So much has already been written by and about Charles and Anne Lindbergh and their family. Of course, some sources were more helpful than others. I began reading *The Spirit of Saint Louis,* Lindbergh's own account of his historic flight, because I felt I had to—but very soon I was drawn in and turning pages as if I were reading a suspense novel and I didn't know how it would end. I am in awe that Lindbergh could make the story of, essentially, sitting still for thirty-three and a half hours into such a riveting tale. And I would recommend the book to anyone who is curious about the flight or about the early days of aviation.

Two biographies of Lindbergh were particularly helpful: *Charles A. Lindbergh: Lone Eagle* by Walter L. Hixson, which is shorter and provided a quick overview; and the in-depth, more comprehensive *Lindbergh* by A. Scott Berg. Helpful websites included http://www.charleslindbergh.com/ and two sites full of details about the Lindbergh kidnapping: one maintained by the FBI and one by the New Jersey State Police Museum.

When I needed additional information about how three time-traveling thirteen-year-olds landing on Lindbergh's plane truly might affect his flight, I appreciated the help I got from my uncle, retired Air Force Command pilot Jim Greshel. Uncle Jim indulged my hypothetical questions, and even calculated how much fuel Lindbergh's plane would have had to burn by the time the kids arrived to prevent their added weight from turning into a serious problem.

The time-travel issues in this book became very complicated—paradoxes by their very nature are confusing, and I am grateful to editors at Simon & Schuster for asking questions and offering suggestions to make the book more understandable to readers: thanks to David Gale, vice president and editorial director; Navah Wolfe, associate editor; and Karen Sherman, copy editor.